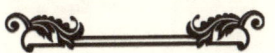

LIKE A SHIP ON THE SEA

THE HILTON LEGACY, BOOK 1

A NOVEL BY KELLYN ROTH

Published by Kellyn Roth, Author

Wild Blue Wonder Press

ISBN: 978-1-7341685-9-4

Scripture quotations are taken from the King James Version (KJV).

Cover design by Carpe Librum Book Design

Developmental Editor: Grace A. Johnson

Line Editor: Erika Mathews

Copy Editor: Andrea Renee Cox

admin@wildbluewonderpress.com
www.wildbluewonderpress.com

DEDICATION

This book is dedicated to my brother, James.
I feel bad for everyone else in this world. They don't know what they're missing! After all, I have the best brother.

TABLE OF CONTENTS

The Characters

The British

Lady Mary Cassidy "Cassie" O'Connell — a young woman in search of a home & a passion. Daughter of Lord and Lady O'Connell, the Earl and Countess of Auburn. Younger sister of Frederick "Freddy" and Catherine "Catie." Former schoolmate and dearest friend of Alice Knight.

The Knights of Pearlbelle Park — owners of an estate located in Kent, England. Mr. Philip and Mrs. Claire Knight and their children: Alice, Ivy, Ned, Caleb, Jack, and Rebecca.

Aubrey Montgomery — Cassie's suitor, who is sure to propose to her soon.

Gibson Ashfield — a most unsuitable man; dearest friend of Aubrey Montgomery.

The Americans

Patrick Hilton — a young man in search of peace in the storm. Patrick hails from the Hilton family of Boston, who own the Hilton Shipping Co.

Bellona "Bell" — a very good dog.

The Hiltons of Boston — Clarence and Dorothy-Lynn "Lynnie" Hilton and their children: Patrick "Trick," Lorelei "Lore," Gwendolyn "Winnie" Hilton. Clarence Hilton is Philip Knight's oldest friend.

Blanche Linden — daughter of the illustrious Linden family of Boston; promised to Patrick, practically since birth.

Herbert Jackson — son of the illustrious Jackson family of Boston; Patrick's dearest friend.

Peter Strauss — Alice Knight's fiancé.

The Strausses — Mr. Christopher "Chris" and Mrs. Lillian "Lilli" Strauss and their children: Peter, Andrew, Caroline, and Dahlia.

Mr. Riley and Mrs. Maddie Farjon — Peter's dearest friend and his wife. Parents of Polly and Susan "Susie."

Mr. Barnaby and Mrs. Caroline Webster — Peter's younger sister and her husband. Parents of Barnaby "Barnie."

The Baldwins of Philadelphia — owners of Baldwin & Sons, a rival shipping company. Mr. and Mrs. John Baldwin and their sons: John Jr. and Rupert.

Content Warning

Some readers are uncomfortable with certain types of content in the books they read. Though my novels are all closed-door romances with no gratuitous content, contain no swearing, and handle all topics discussed biblically, I have a brief list of content warnings for each of my books below. Some of these may contain minor spoilers. Read at your own risk! kellynrothauthor.com/content-warnings

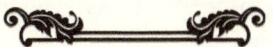

CHAPTER ONE

June 1881
Kent, England

PEARLBELLE PARK WAS BUSTLING with a frantic energy—that week-before-a-wedding rush that caused every resident to hurry their steps and hasten through their daily tasks with joyous aplomb. Even as Lady Mary Cassidy O'Connell entered the front hall, maids were laughing and chattering together as they dusted and swept the large foyer from top to bottom.

Upon her entry, a noticeable stiffening occurred, which she was used to, but she smiled and hoped for the best. She never meant to be a disruption, but she was arriving at an odd time, and she knew last-minute, finishing-touches cleaning must happen while the other guests were occupied.

The butler, a middle-aged man who was a bit too thick around the middle and a bit too thin on the top, approached her and bowed. "Lady Mary."

She nodded to him, ignoring the fact that after all these years, he still refused to call her Cassie. Which was to be expected when even her own almost-betrothed refused to call her by the affectionate nickname. "I am here before I should be, Marlin, aren't I? I caught an earlier train than I had anticipated." Her parents were coming soon enough. "Is Miss Knight ...?"

"She's upstairs, milady. Shall I ...?"

"If you could let her know that I've arrived, that would be appreciated. Will I be in my regular room, or have wedding guests left me scrambled?"

"I believe you are in the same room." He nodded his head toward the stairway. "I'll have one of our maids escort you there, if you'll—"

Before he could finish the sentence, Cassie held up her hand. "I hired a man to bring my things up from the village." An act of independence that had almost killed her, but she'd done it. She'd had to come early—she couldn't stay in that London townhouse, bearing her mother's scorn and her would-be fiancé's ownership, any longer. "I'll see myself to my room if you could take care of my luggage."

Then, before he could say anything further, she walked over to the grand stairs that coiled in confident status up from the foyer. High above her, paintings of cupids and clouds decorated the arched ceiling, and the cream-colored walls, though perhaps seeming overly sterile to some, were inviting to her—like sunshine after a dark night. Cassie loved nothing more than the feeling of being settled. Unfortunately, that so far hadn't proven a possibility anywhere but here at Pearlbelle Park, where she had spent so many happy holidays with her dearest friend.

Other than that, there was the London townhouse; the boarding school she'd attended from the time she was seven; and, of course, her father's land in Ireland, including a large castle rising from the sea on one side and the moors on the other, buffeted by harsh winds. A beautiful place but not a home.

The bright manor of Pearlbelle Park was so different than that dreary castle. Oh, the latter was lovely—in some ways. A castle can perhaps be a home—anywhere could be—but that one was not Cassie's. While her yearning for her own place might never be satisfied, at least she could stand close to the Knights and feel the bonds they'd formed here at their family estate.

It was almost as good as having a home. Almost.

"Cassie?"

She turned toward the sound of Alice's voice. "It didn't take you long to find me."

"They let me know as soon as you arrived." Alice stepped forward, in a rush as always, and embraced Cassie. Alice's carefully-piled dark hair and magenta dress were extravagant for a summer morning, but Cassie had rather suspected they would be. Alice had mentioned that her in-laws-to-be would be arriving on a morning train. "You said you wouldn't be here until the evening. I would've come and met you."

Cassie stepped back and tried to stop the wild twitching of her lips, but a grin emerged despite her best efforts. "I know how busy you are. I wasn't about to interrupt your day any more than necessary. Even so, I needed to come early. My mother has been ..." *Pressing me to marry before I'm ready. Discontent with everything I do. Angry about the facts of my life.* "Difficult."

"That's because she is a terrible person. But I suppose you already know that, better than I ever could." Alice paced to the other side of Cassie's room with a swish of her beribboned skirts and looked around like a general surveying her troops. "You know, you ought to stay in a larger room. You've been here longer than anyone, and you're not a visiting child. You're an adult."

"I wouldn't be comfortable in a larger room." Granted, this one was smaller than the chambers at her parents' residences, but that hardly mattered. Cassie was never one for grand and elegant when simple and comfortable would do. Besides, the larger the room, the draftier, and castles were always drafty. "Isn't calling me an adult rather a stretch?"

"You're as old as I was when I got engaged." Alice paused by the window briefly and drummed her fingers on the sill. The air around her buzzed with tension. Cassie could tell based on her posture that she was carrying the weight of the world on her shoulders—and that it wasn't proving easy, whether or not she admitted it. "I ought to get back to what I was doing."

"Which is ...?"

"Sorting through cards and gifts. Writing thank-you notes. I made some progress this morning, but Peter distracted me, and now I feel as if ..." She paused and straightened her shoulders. "It must be done."

Cassie sighed. If only Alice weren't so determined that she should push herself to the point of insanity. Which Cassie, of course, didn't mean literally, but sometimes it did seem that Alice lost a little of her Alice-ness every time she forced herself and those around her to attain unrealistic standards. Besides, it seemed unfair that she was missing these gentle days before the wedding.

Thankfully, from time to time over the years, Alice had been known to hear Cassie's voice. Perhaps Cassie was quiet, but with Alice, she also felt safe—and in safety, there was honesty. "Go on a walk with Peter this afternoon," she said. "Go spend time with his family—get to know them. You'll regret not doing that more than you'll regret missed thank-you notes to people who probably don't even remember sending you anything."

Alice scoffed. "As if I could just—"

"I'll take care of it. The notes may not be in your hand, but I know what you'll say, and I'll save anything that I know you'd want to respond to personally. But for business acquaintances of your father and schoolmates of your mother, you won't want anything but the basics, and I can do that." Cassie had been bred and raised to do these types of tasks. Might as well make use of the polite phrases that had been drilled into her from birth.

"I'm not sure—"

"*Alice*, please."

"You're here as a guest."

"I'm here as your bridesmaid—with the word 'maid' in the title, you can't expect me not to put a decent day's work in. If I really need help, I can ask Collins." Not that she would. Cassie was of the opinion that, once her maid got all her various belongings up to the room and unpacked, she deserved a break in the kitchen to catch up with the servants of the place she'd visited so often in the years since she was hired. "Now go!"

For the first time since Cassie had seen her today, laughter entered Alice's eyes—which filled Cassie with immediate and immense relief. "Very well, I'll go. I know it'll thrill Peter, and I suppose combined with the fact that I'll be getting out of writing those thank-you notes, it's worth it. But you don't have to."

Cassie waved her friend away. "I want to." It would give her some quiet time alone to sit and think, and even if it didn't, it would be worth it to bring a smile to Alice's face. "Go and spend time with your fiancé and his family and leave the annoying details to me. I want you to enjoy your wedding week."

Alice rolled her eyes. "As if I could." She paused by Cassie and squeezed her arm. "Don't work too long. Write a few letters, all right, but then come out with us. It's a beautiful day."

There was nothing like a beautiful day ... inside the Knights' library, breathing in the essence of old books and tea that always managed to hang in the air. "I'll join you in a while."

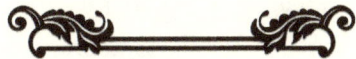

Steam swirled its way up from Cassie's cup of tea, and she watched it dance in the slanting light that seeped between the red curtains. The library was the safe haven within her safe haven. It was an extensive collection of books, all at least a few decades old, and though Cassie only read a moderate amount, she still appreciated the setting. It was a place of peace and academia, two things she admired immensely.

The door opened, and Cassie glanced up from the note she was writing to a Mrs. Rupert Angel. Mrs. Knight, Alice's mother, stood in the door. Quite the opposite of Alice in appearance, Mrs. Knight had golden-blonde hair and blue eyes. Granted, they were of a similar height—both of them several inches taller than Cassie—but they didn't otherwise appear much like mother and daughter. Alice definitely resembled her father more closely.

"Mrs. Knight." Cassie placed her quill pen in the inkwell and pushed back her chair. "I thought you were in the gardens with the rest of the family."

"I was." Mrs. Knight stepped forward and glanced about the library. "However, I felt you should be there, too."

Cassie gestured to the stack of notes before her. "As you can see, I have a vitally important duty. Or Alice felt so, and she is, after all, the bride. I want her to feel free to relax."

Mrs. Knight laughed, a soft sound that managed elegance. "I don't think there is a vitally important duty here, my dear, but at least I must help you. I don't think Alice was fair to ask this of you, but I know there'll be no stopping you from doing it."

"She didn't ask me, and if she had, it would still have been no imposition." Cassie loved Alice too much to mind a little bossing around, as long as it was relatively harmless. She saved her energy for larger conflicts, when reason and reality rebelled against her friend's ideas. "You don't have to stay here and work with me. After all, someone needs to see what type of family Alice is marrying into."

"I've seen enough." Mrs. Knight took a seat next to Cassie and held out her hand. Cassie obediently handed over a stack of papers—but not too many. "I know that they will love her and that she will adjust to them, and that's enough. So now you are my primary obligation."

Cassie never knew how to respond to such statements, as unused to them as she was in her own home, so she just pressed her lips together and nodded and wished she could say something kind that acknowledged Mrs. Knight's care for her.

A footman brought in a tray with more tea and Cassie's favorite biscuits, and though Mrs Knight said nothing further—engrossed, apparently, in the note she was writing—Cassie knew that the order had come from Alice's mother. Who else would've remembered her preference and seen that it was taken care of?

The silence was at first peaceful, but Cassie soon felt the familiar nudge to speak, and though she hadn't any idea that she was required to, she did want to know what was happening in the Knight household.

She asked about Alice's younger siblings, about all the visiting relatives, about what everyone thought about the wedding and the Strausses. She already knew what everyone thought of Peter. Cassie knew the entire family would probably have adopted him even if he hadn't been marrying their eldest daughter.

"What of you, Cassie?" Mrs. Knight said after most of the primary members of her family had been discussed. "Are you still courting Mr. Montgomery?"

Cassie looked down quickly, pretending to search for an ink blotter she knew very well had fallen between drifting sheets of paper to her left. "Oh, yes. Well ... I assume there'll be a proposal soon."

"You've taken your time with that." Thankfully, Mrs. Knight was focused on her current note, oblivious to Cassie's scrambling. "For some, that might be a warning, but for you, I believe it is a compliment. Besides, hurrying into marriage has never helped anyone."

Cassie nodded, though she didn't want to talk about it. There was so much in her life these days that she didn't know how to discuss, and she berated herself silently for it.

She was here, at Pearlbelle Park, and though it was true that the reason for her coming was meant to be entirely unselfish ...

She knew neither Mrs. Knight nor Alice would mind if she were to be vulnerable and honest. To admit her doubts about her relationship with the esteemed Mr. Aubrey Montgomery. To admit that her parents' pressure to marry him was about the only thing keeping her with him—with the exception of habit.

Cassie was a creature of habit, after all. Habits were the secure, small actions that made the mundane feel bearable—that allowed her to find peace and quiet in the hasty rush of life that so often was far beyond her control. As a child, she'd been passed about from place to place, person to person. She couldn't remember a time when summers and most holidays weren't spent with some distant relative or schoolmate's family. Her parents had not wanted a third child. They had had her brother, Frederick, the proper heir of the title and estate. They had had Catherine—dear Catie, with her big, blue eyes and her dark curls, a great beauty like their mother. Catie had always been wanted, and she had appealed to Mother's vanity. Cassie loved her sister, but she couldn't help but feel that it wasn't fair that Catie was Catie whereas Cassie was, well, Cassie.

Then, many years later, in an accident of nature, Cassie had come along. Her mother had never forgiven her for existing.

Not that her parents had truly spoken these thoughts. Even her blunt mother had never said, outright, that Cassie was unwanted. And perhaps she wasn't. It was more that Cassie felt that way than that, in truth, her parents resented her appearance into this world. After all, Cassie wasn't stupid. She knew that they had done at least one thing to make her appearance a possibility, and she wasn't to blame for that. She couldn't have stopped her own life, nor did she wish that she wasn't alive. Nothing as disturbing as that.

No, she was glad of life, glad that God had brought her into this world even despite her parents' lack of enthusiasm about that event. She was glad that God had created her, loved her, and put her in the place in the world that she currently was in. But that also didn't mean that she didn't wish for a better life.

A safe life. A life of her own making. A life where she could truly be useful and helpful. What use was she in a world where she was unwanted?

Which was another reason why the habit of Mr. Aubrey Montgomery was so difficult to shake. After all, without Mr. Aubrey Montgomery, Cassie would be forced to live with her parents forever rather than until they married. Granted, Catie had offered to take Cassie in, but Cassie didn't want to live as an awkward third wheel in her sister's life any more than she wanted to be the resented child of her parents. Catie was too busy for Cassie anyway, with her husband and her own home to take care of. She always had been, and she always would be.

There was Frederick, of course. Cassie adored him. But he, too, was busy, and his condescension was almost as bad as her mother's disdain.

Meanwhile, there was Alice, who had always loved her and seen her, in her Alice way. Of course, Alice wasn't the most emotional person in the world; truth be told, she bottled things up rather more than Cassie thought healthy. But Alice would fight for Cassie in the face of the greatest naysayers, who called her "Irish" like it was a synonym for sin and who taunted her for her freckles, though those were fading. Before, Cassie had hated them; now she hated to see them go. But she spent so much time inside these days that it wasn't at all surprising that she had lost the sun kisses.

A shame, for Cassie wanted to be unique if she could not be loved. She didn't believe that no matter how many things she changed about herself, her mother would really appreciate her for Cassie, the child she had brought into the world. Cassie was not a person Mother wanted in her life.

Lady Mary Cassidy O'Connell. *Hmm.* Maybe that was the person Mother wanted. But Lady Mary Cassidy O'Connell was hardly a person. Lady Mary was a figment of her mother's imagination. Cassie was the one who existed, and she needed to make herself a life elsewhere if her parents refused to allow her one in their household.

Hence Mr. Aubrey Montgomery. Hence how hard Cassie had fallen for him that first Season in London after her debut. Hence how great the love she had felt ... and now, how disappointing that she no longer felt the same way.

She ought to feel the same way. As she blotted the ink on her latest note, she scolded herself for the thousandth time for that error. How could she have felt that she loved him so greatly and yet been so wrong?

Screwing up her courage, Cassie forced words passed her dry lips. "Mrs. Knight, may I ask you a question?" It would've taken too much energy to simply ask the question, but this would force her to do so.

Or she could become a coward at the last minute. That would do, too. However, if Mrs. Knight was quick ... and she always was quick to speak when the need was greatest.

Again, without looking up, Mrs. Knight said, "Yes, dearest, say whatever you like."

It was truly the "dearest" that gave Cassie the courage to speak. Mrs. Knight used "dearest" so rarely—in reference to her second daughter, Ivy, most often.

"Mrs. Knight, have you ever ... That is, when you were courting Mr. Knight ..." Then she stopped in confusion, for she'd remembered that Mr. and Mrs. Knight's courtship had not been an average one. They'd eloped, after all, hadn't they? Was the information the same for couples who eloped? It must've been some wild, passionate thing. If they'd eloped, they'd probably not had many doubts. Not like Cassie, who was awash with them.

But Mrs. Knight set down her pen, and her piercing eyes met Cassie's over the table. Cassie had blue eyes, but she didn't think they were *piercing*—if they were, they certainly weren't unnerving. "Go on, Cassie. You're welcome, in this one instance, to ask me anything you like, if it would be helpful to you."

Cassie nodded and swallowed hard. It was one thing to be given permission and quite another thing to actually make use of said permission. "Did you ever ... Did you ever doubt?"

"Doubt that I should be with him, perhaps?" Mrs. Knight prompted, cocking her head. "Doubt that our relationship was the right choice?"

Cassie pressed her lips together.

"Yes?"

"Yes."

"I did. Though primarily after we were married." Her eyes did drop for a minute then, but if she had lost her composure, she regained it swiftly. "We had a rough start to our marriage, as you know. Our whole relationship was riddled with doubt. But it was the right choice to stay with him—and more than that, to not give up on him. You can be married and live together and have children together and not truly remain *in* your marriage. Not your heart or your spirit anyway, and those are the parts that matter. It is so vital, for that reason, to choose a husband with whom you are willing to spend the rest of your life ... and whether or not your circumstances change—when he inevitably changes through growth or through the opposite of growth, and when *you* yourself change—you must choose someone whom you will not give up on. Because that is what happens, Cassie. Couples give up, always too early. I wouldn't want you to do so."

Cassie shook her head. "Of course not. Though right now I'm not ..." *Not married.* Not even officially engaged, in fact. Not bound to him. She still had options, freedom. Well, some. Though she couldn't imagine herself leaving Aubrey Montgomery behind, giving up over a year of courtship, and starting afresh with someone new. But what if that was what she was supposed to do? What if that were her only option? What if the only way she could be with someone who she wouldn't "give up on" was to ... to ...?

Oh, but she didn't want to think about that. She *must* marry Aubrey. She must. What other choice did she have, with her parents and her situation?

"You're not married," Mrs. Knight finished for her. "So don't make the wrong decision, whatever that may be. But all women have doubts. You'll never find a perfect man, and you are not a perfect woman."

Cassie knew that, too. She was *far* from perfect. *God, don't let me ruin this.* She thought the prayer rather than uttered it; Cassie never knew how to speak prayers aloud. *If he is the right man for me, help me know it. I don't want to end up in a marriage that I'm not happy in—but what if this is my best chance?* Alice always claimed that Cassie would not fail to find suitors wherever she was, and perhaps that was true, but it would only be for her title, and though Aubrey might not show it well, he genuinely cared about her. In a way.

What fool would reject a man who genuinely cared for her? In exchange for what—half a chance that somewhere out there, a magical mystery man was alive who would make her happier? She wasn't marrying just for happiness, but to build a life, too. A life that she couldn't build when she remained under her parents' roof.

Besides, there would be other things. A home of her own. Children. The endless comfort of freedom to do nothing but what she wanted.

All she wanted was a life free of conflict and pain. Was that so much to ask?

"I'll think on that," she said, though she knew that Mrs. Knight would advise her further, if need be. At the moment, however, Cassie didn't feel she had the ability to hear more. Perhaps it was enough to have spoken some of those frightened thoughts aloud. "I can't imagine not being with Mr. Montgomery, though."

Mrs. Knight smiled softly. She believed that was a sentimental uttering, perhaps. "That's a good sign. I'm sure it'll be all right."

Cassie hoped so. It had to be.

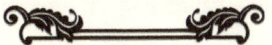

CHAPTER TWO

AFTER THE THIRD HOUR of sitting in her nightgown and wrap in Alice's bedroom, Cassie got the distinct impression that she would not be returning to her own bedroom. So much for having a quick chat to discuss the Strausses. By now, traversing the quiet, dark halls was pointless when it was practically morning.

She felt like a girl again, at Alice's dressing table redoing her hair for bed. A simple plait curled down her back now. She used to dislike her bright-red hair, but now it was a badge of honor, a testament to many bullies at school and many snide comments from her mother despite knowing Cassie got it from her Irish paternal grandmother. No, Cassie would not hate her hair, for so many seemed to, and someone ought to stand up for those fiery locks.

Cassie could feel Alice's tense shifting on the bed behind her and hear the constant crinkling of the crisp sheets. "We've only a week to go now! Frankly, I feel as if the date's rather rushed up on me. Wasn't it last week that Peter and I became engaged? That's what it feels like, and now we're up to last-minute preparations and families arriving ..."

"It's so exciting!" Cassie made sure to smile over her shoulder in what she hoped was a reassuring fashion. "I can't believe I'm going to be best friends with a married woman. You'll have to give me a lot of advice for when I'm married myself."

Alice's playful look made Cassie shudder. "When will that be?"

That question. And a week before the wedding, too! Cassie didn't know what to say, for she couldn't lie, but neither did she want to bring up the truth. Could she just avoid the subject? "My hair is always flying every which way these days," she murmured.

"Cassie? Is everything all right with you and Aubrey?" Of course ever-inquisitive Alice could never leave well enough alone.

Cassie sighed. "It's ... it's not all wrong, exactly. We're adjusting, I think, or I hope so. But I'm not so sure I want to adjust." Was "adjusting" even the right word? There had been such a difference in their relationship in the last six months, and the giant gorge between them had only deepened with every interaction. Aubrey didn't seem to feel it, but Cassie did, and it made her dreadfully uncomfortable.

The problem was, it wasn't just Aubrey. It was that *man*. That dreadful friend of his.

Apparently, Alice didn't think Cassie's explanation was ample, for her almost-black eyes narrowed. "Whatever do you mean?"

Cassie put down the hairbrush. "Let's not talk about this now."

"When will we talk about it, if not now?" Alice hopped off the bed, closed the distance between them, and placed a firm hand on Cassie's arm. No escape now. "What's made you unsure of him?"

Cassie schooled her face into even lines and composedly turn to face Alice. *Careful. Don't give away too much. And provide the simplest explanation so you don't have to talk about this until dawn breaks.* "Oh, it's nothing. Really, it's not. Only ... his friend Gibson Ashfield."

Alice wrinkled her nose, a look of utterly nauseous disgust coming across her face. Gibson Ashfield was far from her favorite person, a suitor from the earliest days of their first Season, who had treated Alice with no respect and, according to Alice at least, insulted her greatly. "I thought we weren't going to mention that name."

Cassie's hands clenched. She didn't want to broach the topic, but it was the best way to stem Alice's questions. How could she help it? "Oh, Alice, I wouldn't! Except that Aubrey is still friends with him and insists upon being so, even after I told him all that you told me. All about his character, his ... his *vile* actions toward you. He said I couldn't understand Mr. Ashfield, that I didn't know the whole story. All I heard was, 'I don't believe you.' Maybe that's not fair to him. We'll have to discuss it further. But what does it mean if he persists in keeping company with a man I wouldn't let my dog associate with?" Cassie released a soft huff, hoping it contained enough indignation to explain away all her worries. But if she had no other doubts about Aubrey Montgomery, she could've easily overlooked Gibson Ashfield.

Alice returned to the bed and sat down once more. "That's complicated, I'm sure. I don't know. I wouldn't ask you, on my behalf, to make any decisions, but if he disregards you here ... Well, I'm sure you've already done all the thinking. What was his manner like?"

There really was no escape. She'd have to pick a conversation and describe it, wouldn't she? She chose what she hoped was the best example of one of the politely restrained arguments on the subject of Mr. Gibson Ashfield and began describing it with her best Irish flair. Alice's eyes told her that the story was being accepted as "enough" details to sate her somewhat ironic lust for gossip.

Cassie-related gossip anyway. Was it gossip if it was Cassie simply telling stories about her life? She supposed not. And Cassie was usually grateful about Alice's constant picking at her. It made her feel wanted, and she liked having someone to rant to.

But now? On almost the eve of Alice's wedding? And when Cassie didn't want to arrive at the conclusion she was hurtling toward? That was a different matter entirely. This thing, this one thing, Cassie did not want to discuss. Not knowing how she felt was most disconcerting.

She rounded off the conversation by flopping back onto the bed with another sigh. "It'll be a hard decision, whatever I do. But let's leave that for now. I won't arrive at any decision this late, and I doubt I'll be quick. Let's talk about something lighter."

"What, then?"

"Wedding plans." That was what they were here for, after all, wasn't it?

Alice seemed more amused than Cassie had expected at this suggestion.

"Lighter? I find wedding plans quite mundane at this point. I'm sick of them and, further, of the stress they've caused my dear mother and all around her. I want to be married and have done."

"I know, but it's still fun, isn't it?" Cassie was praying earnestly that Alice would at least enjoy some of the process. It was so dreadfully romantic, after all, and Alice deserved some happiness.

Alice's lips quirked up at the edges. "It is indeed."

They talked about wedding details until Cassie at last felt obligated to point out that it was well past two in the morning, and they had best go to sleep, which they did.

But Cassie couldn't sleep. Not anymore. So she lay still, listening to Alice's steady breathing, and wondered what her future would look like. Alice's was practically written in stone at this point.

It was Cassie's that rested on shifting sand. And what would she do if the tide came in and wiped off every last, secure, safe, little habit she'd formed over the years?

"Patrick, Patrick!" From the seat beside him, his youngest sister bobbed up and down, pointing out the window of the carriage.

"Calm down, Winnie." Patrick Hilton refrained from rolling his eyes, but he did place a restraining hand on fourteen-year-old Gwendolyn's arm while he lowered his other hand to still his wiggling dog, Bellona. Winnie always acted like a child, and though Patrick didn't resent that—in fact, he would do all in his power to encourage it—he didn't appreciate the constant jostling that sitting beside her generally brought on.

On his other side, he heard the heavy sigh of his other sister, Lorelei. At sixteen, she was the epitome of maturity in her own opinion, and everything Winnie did now annoyed Lore.

"But do you see the mansion?" Winnie leaned back slightly and settled, but only somewhat, and a giggle of delight emerged from her lips. "It seems older than Grandpa's house in Virginia. Oh, and look at the columns!"

"Do control yourself, Winnie. You're being dreadfully common." Lore said this in a soft drawl, not an accent but rather an inflection caused by her extreme lack of caring about anything. Which apparently was a part of being sixteen.

"No fighting," Patrick said sternly, patting Bell's head. They were fortunate to have this brief reprieve from their parents as they rolled up the driveway to Pearlbelle Park. They would be staying as guests several days at this English manor, and Patrick wanted them to be on their best behavior. "Girls, please, let's be decent human beings for the Knights. They're busy enough without having to deal with unruly American friends."

"We're not their friends," Lore mumbled. Yet she was the one who would model polite behavior to Winnie, so Patrick focused his attention on her.

"They are Father's friends—or Philip Knight is—and I think that counts. Besides, I remember Mr. Knight from when I was quite young—if you were a few years older, you would, too, though I think he was gone before Winnie came along."

"I don't see why we had to come at all. I just want to go to Italy like Mother promised. We've been in England before." The constant traveling their parents tended to subject the girls to meant they were easily bored, a problem Patrick always ended up being the one taking care of.

"Yes, but we want to be kind to the Knights." Especially since sometimes his parents didn't prove polite guests. Though he supposed they'd be on their best behavior this time—a high-brow, socialite wedding was sure to arouse their protective instincts over the family name.

The large, black shepherd between his legs whimpered, and Patrick forced his posture to loosen. "That's all right, Bell," he murmured soothingly. "We're there now, and you can run around."

For the carriage had stopped, and in moments, the three Hilton siblings disembarked along with Bell, who immediately loped forward with a kind of enthusiasm Patrick no longer had the energy for. She was his Dutch beauty, his prize from a business trip with his father about a year ago, when he had first begun to take an active part in the Hilton shipping empire. Bell was the one constant in his life.

Mr. Philip Knight met them in the foyer of the manor house built in a classical architecture style. Not exactly to Patrick's taste but still beautiful in its own way.

"Clarence, it's been years." Mr. Knight shook hands with Patrick's father before turning to Mother with a somewhat fearful expression.

Fair, Patrick thought with a wry smile.

"And, Lynnie, you look lovely, as always." Mr. Knight's voice held the same tone as someone trying to avoid being kicked by a wild horse.

So he knows Mother well, does he?

Mother acknowledged him with a dip of her head and a few words spoken with an evident lack of respect. Apparently, old friendships mattered little to her—and Mother was never particularly kind to her friends anyway.

"I'll have a footman show you lot to your rooms. We're pleased you were able to stay for a few days! It will give us a chance to catch up. Oh, I'll go with you—let's walk."

Mr. Knight and Father started up the long stairway leading from the foyer, chatting about this and that, and Patrick, his sisters, and his mother followed.

"How is the business going, Clarence?" Mr. Knight asked. His voice held a light English accent, notwithstanding the fact that he'd been raised in Boston before returning to inherit his uncle's estate. "I know you travel constantly, though why you never come to see me, I don't know."

Father chuckled, clearly at ease with Mr. Knight. Patrick supposed his father *ought* to be at ease with a man he'd been through childhood, young adulthood, and a war with. Yet at the same time, Father was good at presenting a friendly front to anyone he might gain something from—one that never failed to turn cold at the first sight of trouble. "I ought to come more often. Perhaps I shall make a habit of it in future years. Especially since Patrick has been helping lately."

Patrick forced a smile as Mr. Knight glanced back at him. "I'm grateful for the opportunity to learn the running of the business."

Mr. Knight nodded. "Best to start them young. That's what I tell Claire, though she always insists the boys ought to be allowed to play. But they are much younger than your son, I suppose. I haven't seen you for a long time, Patrick."

"Yes, sir."

"The business has been going well," Father continued. "Baldwin & Sons continues to be a thorn in our side. But Patrick has some ideas to outclass them, don't you, boy?"

"Yes." Not the best of ideas, but Patrick did have two things to his advantage, and those were the head and breeding for business. Both assets allowed him to seamlessly slip into the running of his father's company—and though the work was tiresome and thankless, not to mention it didn't pay a cent, he would someday inherit the company. Not having his own disposable income was not a problem when everything was provided for him already—granted, with strings attached, but some strings were good. It was his responsibility to take the business and the family name seriously. What made a man was how he fulfilled whatever duties God assigned to him, and undoubtedly, the Hilton Shipping Company was one of those responsibilities.

Part of running the company was beating Baldwin & Sons to every new client and load of cargo.

As they continued up the stairs, Mother, an arm through Lore's, spoke to her in an undertone. Patrick tried to overhear, for who knew what his mother would see fit to say to his baby sister?

But Lore wasn't a baby anymore. She was able to correct whatever thoughts Mother put into her head herself. Patrick breathed deeply and forced himself to remember these simple facts.

A gaggle of happy, laughing children passed them as they reached a hallway winding above the foyer, and Patrick couldn't help but watch them run. They all careened around a central object—a young woman about his age with a lot of red hair and a contagious laugh of her own—cajoling her into something she seemed only mildly reluctant to do. They got her agreement as they disappeared behind the Hiltons, and Patrick grinned to himself.

It was good that this was a home full of laughter. He wondered who the lady was—another guest or a daughter of the house? He hadn't any real idea of who the Knight children were, only that there were three boys, the young woman who was getting married in less than a week, and two other girls. But by now, there were bound to be a variety of guests there from a variety of places. Surely if Patrick and his family had arrived all the way from Boston, it would be no surprise that others were staying at Pearlbelle Park, too.

He shook his head as they rounded the corner, and he caught his father's expression. The glare told him that his eyes had lingered overlong on the young woman in the hall, enough that he'd been caught. Yet he didn't flinch—he never flinched when, inevitably, he failed his father's idea of a faithful, steady man who was practically betrothed. But he wasn't betrothed, not officially. Though his parents expected that he would marry Blanche Linden, to the general public, he was not a chained man—yet.

The time was approaching quickly, and the fact that his father had been pressuring him to take the reins of the company in the last year meant that the time was even sooner than Patrick had expected.

He'd always known he'd be with Blanche, though. That was no surprise, and he had no right to act shocked by the simple fact of it. After all, he was perfectly content in his relationship with Blanche. *Perfectly*. It was functional, parent-approved, and would allow him to create a safe haven for his sisters away from the normal storm of his parents' tempestuous relationship.

After they were settled in their rooms, Patrick offered to take Lore and Winnie on a walk about the extensive Pearlbelle Park gardens. He enjoyed exploring anything and everything, and it was more fun if he could drag Lore and Winnie, and of course Bell, along.

He was informed that there were a number of guests and family members enjoying the outdoors, and this excited Winnie, who always liked to make new friends. Before they were even out the door, she dashed forward and managed to meet a few young ladies who stood at the end of the veranda. He recognized one as Dahlia Strauss, whom they'd met a time or two—though it also wouldn't be unlike Winnie to introduce herself to complete strangers and be best friends with them by supper—or teatime, or whatever was done here.

Meanwhile, Lore stuck close to his side. He offered her his arm, and she accepted it and walked stiffly beside him down a set of marble steps to the garden. There, on a cobblestone path, they wove around hedges and flower beds full of extravagant-looking blooms. They came upon a fountain and sat down on a bench to watch the water bubble.

Lore rambled, as she always did in moments of nervousness. She didn't know her place here, and she was at that odd stage between girlhood and womanhood where nothing was certain, including the way any given person would treat her.

"Patrick Hilton!" The moderately delighted exclamation came from his left, and he turned and then rose when he caught sight of Caroline Strauss—only it was Webster now, as she'd married. As with Dahlia, they'd met the Strauss family a number of times in Philadelphia while visiting family. Caroline, a few years older than Patrick but never beyond paying him a small amount of attention in her kind but not overfamiliar manner, had always delighted Patrick.

"Why, Mrs. Webster! I haven't seen you since before your marriage. This must be your husband."

The somewhat gangly man beside Caroline nodded, and Patrick and Lore were introduced to Barnaby Webster and Barnaby Webster Jr., whom Caroline cradled in her arms like the precious bundle of flailing limbs he was.

"I hadn't realized you'd be here, Trick," Caroline said, using the familiar nickname. Somehow Patrick knew that, despite her familiarity with him, he should not call her Caroline. She had an air about her that forbade it—she would be his friend, but he must be cautious with her. He respect-ed a woman who was able to lay a boundary without saying a word.

Yet he couldn't resist teasing her a bit. "Oh, Mrs. Webster, I couldn't stay away when I knew you would be present."

This amused her husband and frustrated Caroline, which had been Patrick's intention. He wouldn't have dared such a comment unless he knew the woman and the man in question fairly well. From what he re-membered of Barnaby Webster, he was not easily offended—and Caroline not easily swayed by idle flattery.

"Never mind that." But her posture had softened somewhat. "I suppose your father must know Mr. Knight."

"Yes, that's right."

She adjusted the child in her arms. "Would you like to hold him? I know how you are about babies."

Patrick assented eagerly—he never turned down an opportunity to hold a precious, warm, cuddly thing when offered—and Caroline made him sit on the bench he'd risen from. Barnaby Jr. was a pretty baby, with a brush of dark hair and big eyes already darkening to brown, and he insisted upon sitting up in Patrick's arms and kicking aside his wrappings, much to his mother's disdain and his father's delight.

"He's growing up far too fast." Caroline sighed and sat next to Patrick, reaching over to adjust her son's lacy dress. "Mama says he's not nearly as advanced as some babies his age, so I ought to be grateful, but I'd rather he stay a baby all his life. I suppose I'll just have to have another one, but I've been enjoying just Barnie, so I'm not overeager."

"How old is he?"

"Almost seven months."

"He's definitely getting big." He was all rolls and folds and double chins. "But I don't mind a fellow with a little weight on him. He'll be a strong one."

Barnaby Webster was beaming. "We think he's healthy, despite Caro's fussing. There's nothing wrong with him at all."

"I didn't say it was *wrong*—only that I don't like it." Caroline cast a smile her husband's way before returning her eyes to her child. "Isn't he fine, Trick? Have you ever seen a handsomer baby?"

"Oh, he's fine indeed." In truth, Patrick had never seen a funnier-looking baby, with large, round eyes, ears that stuck out, and a smile a mile wide, but he was charming in his own way, and Patrick always told mothers that their babies were the prettiest he'd ever seen as a matter of habit. Was it really a lie if it was true to the mother herself?

In the distance, he heard more laughter—including the laugh of a woman whom he remembered from not an hour before—and his eyes left the baby for a minute to view another group of merry guests. Amongst them was the redheaded lady.

He tracked her as she walked beside the young woman who, based on her resemblance to her father, was Alice Knight, with the same children dancing around them, tugging at the redhead's hands and receiving scolding responses from their older sister even as the lady herself seemed content to accept their rough advances.

Unfortunately, most women possessed a certain level of intuitive thought when it came to potential romance, no matter how slim the potential. This intuition, false or not, was usually accelerated by marriage. Caroline Strauss Webster appeared no different, and when his eyes returned to her, she looked both amused and pleased with herself.

"See something you like?" she asked, laughter tinging her voice.

He grinned. "Oh, Mrs. Webster, you should know I am an old, engaged man. I simply look to where the children are—you should know that."

"You're not engaged yet."

"You're not helpful, at all, ever, and you never have been."

She grinned and reached for her baby. "That's what my husband says."

Barnaby gave her a look that quickly turned into a smile, and Patrick remembered his impression when he had met the man during their courtship years not so very long ago—that they were a well-suited couple. It would take a very good-natured man to love Caroline with an utter lack of frustration, and Barnaby Webster was a patient, steady man who both needed her saucy strength and support and challenged her occasional bossiness.

Or that was Patrick's impression. He always made up these kinds of stories about people, and how often he was accurate was up for debate.

The last thing he needed to do was know a thing about the redheaded lady. Any information would be unhelpful and useless. For he had told Caroline the truth—he was practically engaged. He wouldn't risk his sisters' future for a story about a laughing woman, no matter how intriguing the laugh.

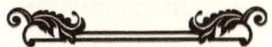

CHAPTER THREE

Patrick wasn't one of those men who felt ill at ease in a suit. In fact, if nothing else, it gave him a boost of confidence. He was dressed as well as he could be expected to, and though he didn't really know how to get to that point without Lore's guiding hand—his sister oversaw all things fashion in their household—he liked the result.

Still, that result usually came after a great deal of arguing over this and that between Lore, the expert, and Winnie, who could never keep her thoughts to herself. His necktie in particular had caused all manner of debate about its suitability, color, and the way each of them had knotted and re-knotted it.

It was blue, and he liked blue. That was enough for him, and when the fussing had ended, he was wearing the same one in a similar manner to the way he himself had tied it.

Now he stood in the foyer, waiting for a carriage that would take him to the church where the wedding ceremony would be performed. He believed that, with the exception of the Knights themselves, his family was amongst the last to leave thanks to his sisters' fussing. Thankfully, his parents had left earlier, so he'd been allowed to sort them out on his own. His mother definitely wouldn't have liked Lore's bossiness nor Winnie's impertinence, and his father might have become angry at the delay.

He heard a commotion from the stairway and turned his head to see the redheaded lady from the garden standing with one of the young Knight boys.

The boy, who wore a nightshirt and nothing else, was squirming and wriggling, but the lady's grip on his arm remained firm.

"I ... don't ... *want to* ..." And then his words were cut off by a scream.

"Caleb, you haven't any choice." Despite the apparent struggle, her voice was calm and even. "You can't go to your sister's wedding in a nightshirt. What would your mother say to you?"

"That maybe I can stay home?" He stilled then and turned his face up to her, dimples apparent as a sly grin took over his rosy face. "That maybe I won't have to sit still and be a gentleman, like Anna said?"

"That will most certainly not be happening, young man." A hint of a lilt appeared in her voice, the same lilt he'd heard in her laugh. What was it? Some form of English accent he hadn't heard yet? It sounded Irish to him, and she did look Irish, but he couldn't be right. He was aware of the prejudice toward that nation in Britain—and in America, too, for that matter.

Patrick ascended the stairs to the first landing, assessing the situation. The lady wore a beautiful dress, simple but elegant, white with a kind of pink-colored sash at her slim waist. She raised big, blue eyes to him, rimmed with light lashes, and arched similarly light eyebrows. Patrick and she had met, briefly, at dinners the last several days—but they'd yet to have a conversation, and he hadn't sought her out.

Somehow, he hadn't dared to.

Patrick wished he'd spoken to her earlier. Even if the wish was an ignoble one, he couldn't help it. Was it all right to notice that a woman was lovely, with no intention of anything but noticing? He supposed so, as long as the thought stopped there or shortly after it and was not accompanied by any desire of possession.

Patrick didn't want to own anyone. Not even Blanche, even though he must, he supposed.

"You're Lady Mary, aren't you? And this must be Mr. Caleb Knight." He was the second Knight son and judging by his appearance, around eight years old. His eyes were blue, too, though much lighter than Lady Mary's, or so Patrick judged now that he was closer. The boy had a scruff of dark-brown hair that stuck up in every which way, and his expression was belligerent, lips pouting in rebellion.

The lady, meanwhile, was calm. Her face was formed in a rounder shape than most, and her nose turned up slightly in a way that told Patrick she might be a mite stubborn. More stubborn than this little fellow, at least.

"Caleb." Patrick knelt down in front of the squirming lad. "Caleb, you look ridiculous."

The boy stilled and stared blankly at Patrick.

"You do! Utterly ridiculous, if I do say so myself. You need to be dressed like I am. You need to be dressed like a man." He patted his chest and, therefore, his suit jacket. "A wedding is a most important affair. And you like Peter, don't you? Want them to get married?" It was clear, if nothing else, that all the Knights adored Peter Strauss. Especially the children.

A small, bare foot was scuffed along the carpet on the stairway. "Ye-es."

"Good. That means you must help them get married."

Again, Caleb's eyes went to Patrick's face, this time with a tint of skepticism. "Help?"

"Yes, my boy. Help! Why, they need witnesses! You have to help them witness things. Besides, notwithstanding that, it's the right thing to do. Where is your nanny?" He believed her name was Anna, and the boy's earlier reference had somewhat confirmed that, but Patrick wasn't willing to say a name and be wrong. For some reason, he wanted to be accurate at the moment—perhaps to the point of suave, perhaps not. The lady stood above him, silent but seemingly relaxed, and he didn't want to appear a fool in front of a beautiful woman.

That sentiment was as manly as spitting.

"Upstairs ... I suppose I could let her dress me. *She* says I have to anyway ..." Caleb's eyes slipped up to the beauty above him. "Will you wait for me, Cassie?"

"I must." A smile graced her lips for the first time, stretching the joyful expression wide across her face. "But you will have to go in a separate carriage, as I'm Alice's attendant. Remember?"

He nodded. "I can do that. Do you think Ivy can go with me?"

She shook her head. "Leave Ivy alone. Ask your mother or Nettie, please."

Another nod, and he scampered up the stairs, legs flailing in his eagerness.

Then, and only then, did the lady turn to him. "Thank you, Mr. ... Mr. Hilton, isn't it?"

"That's right. Patrick Hilton. You're ... Forgive me, I never know how to use the titles correctly, but you're Lady Mary O'Connell? Or without the last name?"

A slight smile flickered over her face again. "Oh, just Lady Mary—the O'Connell is my family name. My friends call me—" Then she paused, perhaps considering whether a man ought to be calling her by an affectionate nickname when she barely knew him. She simply, after a moment, said, "Lady Mary is probably for the best."

He nodded. "I would offer to have you call me Patrick, but I doubt that'd be appropriate. You're ... you're Miss Knight's best friend, aren't you? Her bridesmaid?"

She nodded. "Along with her sister. Though her sister is really her maid of honor."

"Oh yes, Miss Ivy. There are six Knight siblings, aren't there?" Why was he standing here, asking inane questions? She probably had somewhere to go. She was clearly ready, but there must be last-minute duties of a bridesmaid to be fulfilled. Yet he couldn't seem to help himself.

"That's right. Miss Knight, Miss Ivy, the three boys, and our little Rebecca." She said this with such a tone of affection, the lilt in her voice even thickening as if the familiarity had caused a rush of emotion. She must be Irish—or at least have spent a great deal of time there.

"Everyone must be in a rush just now," he reflected, as if he knew anything about weddings other than being a guest. He hadn't any close cousins—his mother had been the spoiled youngest child of the Virginia McCulloughs, and all her brothers save one had died in the war, and

Patrick's father was an only child. Patrick was the oldest child of his family, himself almost too young to be married—though he was apparently expected to do so rather quickly.

That was a morose thought that he tried to put off, even though it was difficult. Being married was such a great thing. He'd been thinking about that a lot this week, as the wedding pressed closer and the talk of it grew thicker and more detailed. His parents had discussed it, too, and based on the light in their eyes, they expected Patrick to be next.

He hadn't known he was man enough to have his own household yet. But if his parents thought he was, perhaps it was true. Their relationship couldn't be called close, but it was certainly one of close observation. They had watched him with eyes like a hawk over the years, his every action recorded and measured. He would receive regular reports of how his activities had measured up. If he was really deserving of the title of eldest son of the Hiltons. If he was putting his parents to shame. If he was acting too Yankee or Southern, depending on the parent. All things he couldn't bear.

He was a Yankee. He knew that, and so his mother hated him. But sometimes he would become aware that his red hair and gray eyes belonged to the McCulloughs as much as his mother had. He bore the looks of the only daughter, the second surviving child, of the family now reduced to poverty and obscurity. And his father would never forgive him for the reminder.

Patrick wondered sometimes if his parents were conscious of the fact that they didn't much want the children they had. Oh, they liked having them. Patrick and his sisters were a sort of status symbol, in a way, but more than that, they gave their parents the security to move into the future with the understanding that they would always have something left behind.

But his mother hated that they were not *her* legacy. Hated that they were not McCulloughs but rather Yankee Hiltons. And his father hated that there was any bit of them that must come from the woman who he only seemed to bear for the purpose of raising his children.

Was it strange, then, that they didn't much want the three people who had stopped them from ending their farce of a marriage years ago? Was it surprising that no one in the family cared to maintain more than the thinnest pretense that they liked each other?

Yet Patrick tried. Oh, how hard he tried, to make a normal life for Lore and Winnie. Especially Winnie, so young for her age and so gentle despite her bravado. It was his mother who had first called him Trick. Had she meant it the way it seemed to Patrick? That he was a Trick played on her, for at the time she married—hastily and at only sixteen—she had believed that Clarence Hilton would stand with the Confederacy instead of immediately moving his family up to Boston.

But he hadn't. He had taken his money, his family, and his hereditary business and run far away from conflict.

His mother had had no choice but to follow.

Patrick always felt it was unfair that they should have to be children born based on a lie between his parents, for it wasn't something that faded over the years. It continued to haunt them at every turn, and it was exhausting. Patrick rose every morning with the weight of his family on his shoulders, and it seemed that no amount of prayers and supplications would make that go away.

Oh, Lord, is there any redeeming this mess? If I marry Blanche and move my sisters away and do things in my own way, will I still be chased by this, like a generational curse from the Old Testament? Is this forever how I will wake in the morning, staring at the sunrise and wondering why I have to feel this way, or is there a hope for escape?

He recalled himself to the moment in which Lady Mary had said a sentence or two about the Knights' general level of busyness, which was apparently high, and was now contemplating a route of escape from this strange man that stood before her, probably looking a little insane.

Maybe he was insane. He was a man born into privilege and unable to wrap his mind around the fact that the privilege was *a privilege*—and not a dread duty. He loved his sisters. He loved working at the Hilton Shipping Company. So why was it so difficult to rouse the energy to put on a smile and a laugh and get through day after day of doing just the type of thing he had always wanted to do? That should be simple.

He said something nice about how weddings were always busy and yet, he believed, joyous occasions, how he always enjoyed being a guest at one ... which was perhaps somewhat feminine. He chose not to analyze it, though. He had to say something or risk looking like a fool, and that seemed like the right sort of thing to say.

What was wrong with him? He was never at a loss for words, much less at a loss of what to do. He *always* knew what to do. He had been bred to know what to do. His raising demanded it.

Just then, he heard a footstep behind him and turned to face another man. He had blond hair and a somewhat annoyed frown resting on his face, and he was wearing a typical suit, much like Patrick's. The man seemed to be sizing Patrick up, which he wondered about.

Until Lady Mary spoke.

"Aubrey."

"Mary."

Oh. So they knew each other. Quite well. And probably, or at least as far as Patrick could figure out, the reason this Aubrey had been giving Patrick that look was because he was speaking rather closely with his girl. In Patrick's defense, he *hadn't* been that close, and he *hadn't* spoken about anything but the Knights, at whose house they were both staying. All the same, Patrick could not blame the man for being defensive. After all, Patrick would not let such a prize slip between his fingers easily, and a woman was much more than a prize.

A lot of men didn't realize the sheer favor women did by speaking with the opposite sex when they were probably more entertained by other women. But that was just his opinion. He knew most men would not agree. All he knew was that sometimes his sisters surprised him with their wit and insight, and Patrick preferred their company to any other in the world, even if they could be exasperating at times. And a woman one might desire as something more than a simple companion? That was something else entirely, the type of thing one gripped and didn't let go of.

Lady Mary would be the type of woman one didn't let go of. Like

Blanche, of course. He must remember that *Blanche* was his betrothed, or would be soon, and once that union was complete, he would have no cause to worry about issues of future companionship at all. For he would have her, and she was lovely and intelligent and surely, *surely* Patrick would find a happiness with her in his own household that he could not find with his parents.

Even though he would still technically be under his parents' thumbs. But it would be different. He would have a certain level of independence, right? They surely couldn't hold so fast on him once he was married, especially when that marriage was of their choosing, when they were the ones who, from the time Blanche and Patrick were small children, had orchestrated it to create a needed union between Hilton Shipping Co. and the Linden Railroad Lines, likely with an exchange of shares involved. Patrick would have to try to find out more of the details when he arrived home, for he was rather curious about exactly what the bride price for Blanche might be.

An outdated term? Yes. But everything his parents did was influenced by money, and when money was the key influencer, outdated ideas were easier to buy. New ideas were inexpensive to keep and led to the possessor of them being rather cheap. At least, in Patrick's opinion. Perhaps he wasn't exactly right, but he tried his best to keep up on the latest ideas floating about. Ideas had made the United States of America the nation it was.

He wondered sometimes if everything weren't going wrong, but he tried not to think that way. It was just his personal life, really, that felt that way, and he must think that there were happy things in this world or he would lose his mind. And then he must find those bits of happiness and bring them to his sisters so they would never be unhappy.

Lady Mary passed him on the stairway, running to her man as Patrick supposed she ought to do. She stopped in front of him, and her white hands fluttered like nervous butterflies at her side. "Aubrey, I'm glad you were able to come." Her tone was formal now, regimented and strict, marching its way in proper English submission to his eardrums.

"Of course I came." The tone of the man's voice indicated some small amount of affection. Not enough, but he was ever a skeptic about such things. "And this is ...?"

"Oh, Mr. Patrick Hilton." She turned to Patrick. "Mr. Hilton, this is Mr. Aubrey Montgomery, my ... A dear family friend."

At those words, which Patrick himself felt the sting of, Mr. Montgomery's arm went to Lady Mary's waist in a protective gesture. Even if there was no proper way of referring to him, like betrothed, it was clear that Mr. Montgomery considered himself to be more than just "a family friend" to Lady Mary.

A message Patrick received loud and clear. And he wanted to clarify to Mr. Montgomery, further, that he would by no means interfere with such a thing. He allowed his posture to loosen and stepped back on the landing, effectively giving any possession of the area around Lady Mary over to the man she loved. Or Patrick hoped she loved him, at least. She probably did. Otherwise, why would she allow him the familiarity of the arm around her waist?

They chit-chatted about this and that for a minute until Lady Mary exited the scene, and Patrick and Mr. Montgomery were left to stand alone in the hall, waiting for the promised carriage. An awkward moment ensued as both men hurried to extricate themselves from the foyer with all haste.

Patrick resolved to apologize to Lady Mary. He hoped his actions hadn't been misconstrued, and he would hate if it led to a conversation between Mr. Montgomery and her later. Patrick so disliked causing trouble for others.

Yes, he'd apologize—but after the wedding was over and everyone was more settled. Hopefully he'd be able to catch a moment with her to do so.

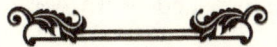

Chapter Four

A LICE'S WEDDING WAS BEAUTIFUL, though Cassie wasn't sure if that was because it was actually beautiful or because she saw the whole thing through tear-misted eyes. She was happy for Alice, in the way she had been since the first letter after her engagement, when her thrilled best friend had announced her somewhat unexpected betrothal.

Now, Alice stood—now Alice Strauss, not Alice Knight—with glowing eyes and her hand clinging to her husband's arm, quite apparently unaware of anyone's presence. For there was no one but Peter in that room right now, not to his wife. Cassie could tell that from the look in Alice's eyes, the way every word was said with a glance at him for approval, the whispers and the smiles that accompanied them, and Alice's laughter at things that weren't funny or joyous but just because that was how she felt.

If only my life was that way. But the small, selfish thought disappeared from Cassie's mind as soon as it could be removed, and she put her head down and focused on keeping in line the variety of children and young men and women who were present as guests and as members of the household.

The wedding breakfast was a success, and Cassie was determined nothing about it should cause any member of Alice's family or the happy couple themselves a moment of stress.

Aubrey lingered near her always, and she felt a kind of austerity between them that there never had been before. She wasn't sure why. After all, she should be able to control herself and treat him normally.

But something in her, when faced with Alice's joy and her own lack of interest in the man she was going to marry, *must* marry, had caused a stiffening in her spine, a tightening in her throat, and an agony in her chest that could not seem to be dispelled. With Aubrey at the center of it, how could she not feel coldly toward him?

Yet these feelings should be controlled. They must. *God, what is wrong with me?*

"Mary, can we talk?"

Of course. Her actions must lead to inevitable consequences, and one of them must be Aubrey's noticing the way she was behaving, even if she was determined for him not to.

She followed him away from the dining room, where the main celebrations were happening, into the front hall. He stood there, looking unsure, half reaching for her but not yet willing to touch her.

He never was. He could never bridge that gap. Oh, he had held her hand, embraced her, kissed her, but those moments were so few and far between. Cassie appreciated his restraint, especially given that they had delayed their inevitable union so long, but at the same time, the fact that he so rarely reached for her except when upset was concerning. Shouldn't he desire her, and shouldn't that desire lead to more of a struggle?

Yes, he was of a restrained personality. She had appreciated that in the shy first year, uncomfortable in her own skin, but she was older now. A year might not be long, and she was sure anyone she communicated these thoughts to would laugh at her, but it felt like a lifetime. She had been forced to debut by her mother, but it had grown her into a woman. Had God used it for good, or was her mother finally right about something?

"Mary, are you all right? You don't seem well."

She shook her head. "I'm fine. Let's go back to the party."

"No, I ..." He paused and shook his head. "I don't know what's wrong, but you're definitely not yourself. You've hardly looked at me all this morning. My mother asked me about it during the ceremony. You wouldn't look our way."

"Can we talk about this later?" Despite her resolutions to remain calm and not let on to her feelings, her frustration was rising. "For now, I need to focus on Alice."

He pressed his lips together and nodded. "That's reasonable. We'll discuss it later." His hand trembled. A better woman would've taken that hand, reassured him.

But she was so tired, and she feared her own reaction if she remained by his side much longer.

She turned to leave, expecting no resistance from her usually passive fellow, but he called her back with another soft repetition of her given name.

"Mary."

She paused without turning. "Yes?"

"Who is Patrick Hilton?"

She stiffened. The man from the stairwell? Granted, he had been a guest at Pearlbelle Park for the past several days, but she'd barely paid him any heed, even when they'd been introduced at dinner his first night there. He was American, maybe a year or two older than her, and had two younger siblings there who were both in high spirits, especially the younger of the two, who went by Winnie.

That was all she knew of him. Except that his smile was winning, his manner with Caleb at once relaxed and playful, and his ears stuck out too much in a way she couldn't help but find charming.

Why should she find a man's faults charming? It would make sense if he were particularly attractive, but he was not, and Aubrey *was*. She hastened to the denial. "The first time I spoke with him was on the stairs, and you saw that."

The approval this announcement sparked in Aubrey's eyes bothered Cassie. It shouldn't. He had a right to be possessive. After all, it wasn't jealousy when one belonged to someone.

And she *belonged* to Aubrey. Or she would very soon, which was all the same. She expected a proposal any time now. He had told her a month ago that he was delaying on purpose to take things slow and to make sure all his assets were in place before he added the "complication" of a wife, but that couldn't take him much longer.

And Cassie, with her aimless life and lack of other offers, had nothing better to do than to wait until Aubrey claimed her, whenever that might be.

"I don't want you to think I don't trust you," Aubrey said. "I just didn't like the way he looked at you. I suppose he was just admiring your beauty. You cannot be blamed for that."

Yet she had lingered, even when Patrick's long pauses and staring should have unnerved her. She had lingered when she *could* have and *should* have left. And though she couldn't blame Mr. Patrick Hilton for looking, she could blame *herself* for not leaving.

A prisoner as always to her thoughts, upon returning to the dining room, she forced herself to serve. She didn't know any other way to calm the sometimes-obsessive wanderings of her mind than to give herself wholly to others, so she did so.

As it turned out, between Alice's cousin Posy, Peter's younger sister Dahlia, and Patrick's younger sister Winnie, there was much room for the kind of boisterousness and giggling and games that a group of young women could get into. Add onto that a variety of young children, mostly boys, and there was plenty of opportunity for Cassie to serve as a sort of nanny. Not that the Knight boys' nanny, Anna, wasn't present, but Anna was ever over-worked, and she had already taken the youngest child, Rebecca, away, kicking and screaming, to calm down after a tantrum.

Which was strange, because Rebecca was usually so calm.

Of course, it wasn't every day one's older sister got married. Cassie had been much older than Rebecca when Catie got married, but it had felt a little like her whole world collapsed. Though Catie was very different from Cassie and not exactly the motherly type, and though they had generally been raised in different places, at least Catie was pleasant to Cassie. At least she offered advice and aid when she could. At least she *loved* Cassie.

Cassie's mother did not.

Of course, avoiding her mother was also a part of this equation. Directly after the wedding, Lady Auburn had tried to corner Cassie and ask her questions, but she had avoided her, saying she had duties as a bridesmaid.

They weren't assigned duties, granted, but she could make up duties as needed, and that was her current occupation. There were always things to do. Mrs. Knight stopped her at one point and murmured, "Thank you," as she took Caleb by the shoulder and guided him away. At another point, Ivy briefly broke away from the bridal party to offer Cassie some aid, but she looked relieved to be allowed to return to her sister.

At last, it was time to see the couple off on their honeymoon. Alice paused to embrace Cassie and whisper a few soft words of friendship, and then Peter and Alice were in the carriage and gone.

The other guests lingered, though a few eventually made their way off. Aubrey himself intended to take the afternoon train back to London with his mother and sisters, as he had much to do the following week and wanted to prepare himself.

Cassie wished she could be a little disappointed, at least a little, that he must leave. Instead, she felt relief that she would be allowed this respite with the Knights. Her parents would leave for London on the same train, but Cassie had asked to stay a few extra days. She wanted to help the Knights with the transition and perhaps see what Peter's family and friends were like, as it would be a bit before they all began making their way back to America.

Cassie ignored the fact that, after the honeymoon, Alice, too, would be journeying to America with her husband. Cassie didn't want to cry about that yet. She'd best save those tears for the quiet of the night after Alice was already gone.

No member of Alice's family had been quite so restrained. Mrs. Knight's eyes had been clouded, and her husband had wept openly at several points. Certainly Alice's governess and dear friend, Nettie, had been crying, and Ivy was a mess.

Further, as Cassie had suspected, it was Alice's wedding causing Rebecca to act out, and she'd burst into tears at the inevitable realization that Alice was leaving for a honeymoon and would not be back that night. She was inconsolable; nothing could be done to convince her that Alice would come back in a few weeks and that the visit would suffice to raise her spirits. Mrs. Knight held her for a long time, but Cassie eventually took Rebecca so Mrs. Knight could return to her guests.

Three-year-olds were far too heavy to pace the floor of a nursery with, but Cassie was determined to do so until her arms gave out. She had too much sympathy for the endless plight of a youngest sister to do otherwise.

"I just want Alice," Rebecca said over and over. "I want Alice to come hold me."

Cassie crooned and hushed and made promises that Alice, a married woman with her own life and an upcoming move to a new country, could never keep.

It was honestly strange that Rebecca had clung so strongly to the idea that Alice would come and comfort her. Alice was never really the comforting type. She was a bit stiff around children, with the exception of her brother Caleb. However, it was possible there were a great deal of daily interactions that meant nothing to Alice, and everything to this cherub.

At last, Anna arrived to relieve Cassie. She handed the child over, whispering promises to come in the morning and play with her that Rebecca perhaps appreciated and perhaps did not, and left the room.

As she walked down the long, dark corridor in the upper floor where the nursery was, she rubbed her sore arms and wondered how long it would be before they bore the weight of her own child.

That would be nice. She wanted to be a mother, at least of a few well-behaved children. Then she winced, for that was not a guarantee. Was she really ready to be married if she was having such thoughts? After all, why marry and therefore allow herself to become a mother if she was already resenting her imaginary future children for their ill behavior?

All children misbehaved. Cassie didn't mind handling other peoples' misbehaving children. But it was a different matter entirely to imagine having to be a mother day in and day out, with no sort of relief.

And she couldn't be the type of woman who handed her children off to a nanny with only an hour or so in their presence every day. She knew it was considered borderline common, but she wanted to nurse her babies and play with them and make them feel free to run to her at any time of the night or day.

She wanted her children to have everything she hadn't had. There had never been a lack of money, of possessions, of material things. But a lack of love? Oh, Cassie would never bring children into the world who might lack that. Was that so much to ask?

The walls of Pearlbelle Park seemed to close in on her then, the dim hallways of the evening a prison rather than her usual haven. Sighing, she knew she must either go to the library or out of doors.

It had been a warm day, and perspiration still clung to every inch of her weary form. A breath of fresh air would do her wonders, she decided, so she slipped down a back staircase and found an exterior door Alice and she had often escaped through in the wee hours of the morning, off to ride horses or go to the nearby lake or simply run through the garden.

How was Alice an adult with a husband? It was Alice's wedding night, and though Cassie was disinclined to give that much thought, it did pass through her mind.

I'll have to do that, too. She swallowed. Surely she shouldn't be filled with revulsion. What was wrong with her? *I need to pray.*

But she didn't pray. Her mind buzzed, and there was no one to distract herself with. Altruism offered no salvation when one was alone. Maybe that was what God wanted.

The cool air of the garden greeted her in a welcome rush, and she sighed, traversing the familiar paths with haste. She at last came upon her favorite fountain and sat down on the stone bench opposite. Her eyes fluttered shut, and her fingers found the cool marble and gripped the edge of her seat.

"Pray, Cassie," she mumbled to herself. "Pray, even if you don't want to. You know better than this. It's going to be all right, but you know you've got to—"

"Pray. Right. Seems reasonable enough."

She couldn't help it; she jumped, in spite of her illusions of control, and her eyes flew open. Standing before her, in front of the fountain, was Mr. Patrick Hilton. Next to him stood a large, black shepherd dog, who was wagging his or her tail cheerfully.

He grinned somewhat sheepishly and reached up to rub the back of his neck. "I'm sorry to interrupt, and to have startled you, and I hope you will pray after a moment, but I saw you, and it felt like fate. I've wanted to catch you all day today, and I hadn't managed to yet."

She straightened her shoulders. "Oh. Why did you ... why did you want to speak to me?" She was nervous, sitting here in this rapidly darkening garden with a man she barely knew, but if he spoke his piece quickly, she could allow it. The lights from the mansion shed a glow over them, as they weren't far from the building. She was at once relieved by the possibility that anyone could be watching them—and frightened.

He reached down to rub his dog's ears as he spoke. "I only wanted to apologize. I hadn't realized you were engaged, and even if you weren't, I would need to act more gentlemanly than I did, keeping you there on the stairwell asking inane questions. What would my girl say to me if she were here?" He smiled and shoved his hands deeply into his pockets. There was a duality to this man: his posture, tone, and expression all spoke of a cheerful confidence despite clearly being ill at ease. "Of course, Blanche is patient with me, for she knows me, and she knows further that I have a tendency to ask questions and bother people and in general make myself an absolute nuisance. I've long been on a mission to understand the world and the people in it, and though I doubt I'll ever arrive ... Here I am rambling and hindering your prayers." He tipped his head upwards, and she noted that his face managed a boyishness at times despite being lined in a way a man of perhaps nineteen oughtn't to be. "Look at the stars tonight, Lady Mary! I only came out to enjoy them, and for a moment of silence, so I'll walk on and leave you to your chat with God." He looked back at her, tipped his hat, and turned to leave.

"I'm not engaged." The words flew from her mouth before she knew she was going to speak them, and she barely refrained from clapping her hand over those offending lips. How dare they tell him what he didn't need to know?

His eyes returned to her, scanned her face as if analyzing the situation. Which Cassie wished she could do, but she didn't know what to do or say to make what she'd said more appropriate. "I see. I just assumed given Mr. Montgomery's obvious—Well. I'm not precisely engaged either, I'll admit. Could it be a similar situation? We ought to be engaged, and we fully intend to be married, but some lazy fellow hasn't managed to get down on one knee …" He shrugged in an exaggerated manner before pressing his hand dramatically to his heart. "Of course, in this case, that's my fault. You've no blame in your situation. I'm writing my own doom, while you watch your pages unfold and probably stack up reasons Mr. Montgomery will be made to suffer for the next fifty years."

She didn't know what to say to that. All she knew was, he talked too much, and the time it took her to process what he was saying meant her responses were unnecessarily delayed.

At last, she managed to assemble a reply. "We've talked about it, and I believe he will propose soon. I just … We're not like Alice and Peter." Once the words bubbled forth, they couldn't be stopped. "This isn't romantic and wild and a little unorthodox like their relationship was and is. Mr. Montgomery and I are expected to be together, and it makes sense for us to take time with the transition. To be a little careful. He's waiting until the time is right."

"Oh, I'm sure. I didn't mean to insult him." He frowned, and beside him, his dog sympathetically thumped its tail against the ground, a steady tattoo. "I'm full of helpful thoughts and actions today, aren't I? I noticed he took you into the hall. I hope you weren't scolded for talking to me. Feel free to rebuke me in future."

"No … not scolded." Cautioned, but not scolded. And here she was, not exercising caution once again. But she thought she liked Mr. Hilton. He was a little like her brother, Freddy, which she supposed all came from being an older brother with two wildly different and equally annoying younger sisters. At least, she thought that was Freddy's situation, and it was certainly Mr. Hilton's. "He trusts me."

"I'm sure he ought to. I'll leave you." Again, he turned.

Again, like the fool she was, she stopped him. "You didn't do anything wrong, speaking to me as you did. And thank you for helping with Caleb. He can be trouble, but we love him. Could I ... could I walk with you? If we stay in sight of the house? I don't want to be alone with my thoughts just now."

He hesitated, and Cassie was the one scolding herself then. Would he be offended? She should not have let on that there was anything in her mind at the moment but nice, neat, organized thoughts that would cause no one trouble, least of all herself.

Yet he simply looked at her for a long time and then nodded. "Yes. Walk with me. Let's go on this path that runs below the veranda. I know there are a few people standing there. They'll become our unwilling chaperones."

She stood and fell into step alongside him. His dog bounded ahead, taking wide strides before stopping to chase a scent off into the darkness. They walked in silence for a time, listening to the muffled conversations around them of other guests and the chirping of the crickets. The air held that mix of warm and cool of a summer evening, and Cassie relished it. But more than that, she relished having someone to walk beside, to feel as if she were sharing the weight within her even if she were not. Not really.

"You said there was a lot on your mind." His feet shuffled as he walked, scuffing at this and that in a restless manner. "Would you be offended if I offered you a penny for your thoughts, or is it too cheap an offer?"

She laughed, though the sound didn't come out just right, at least to her ears. "They're not even worth that. Save your pennies, and I'll tell you for free."

"Nonsense." Again, he shoved his hands into his pockets and then withdrew them with a few coins upon his palms. "I have a dime and two pennies. Payment for candies—sweets, if you like—purchased in London for my sisters. I'll have you know that my sisters are hopeless; I begged them to exchange their pin money when we got here."

She shook her head. "I'm not going to take your money."

"Are you not going to give me your thoughts?"

"I can."

Swiftly, before she had time to react, he took her hand, opened her fingers, and placed the coins there. "There. Capitalism in action. If only it were so easy to teach my sisters. Now, go on. What's on your mind?"

She rolled her eyes but kept the coins nonetheless. "Oh, it's nothing. The normal fretting of a young woman with cold feet. You wouldn't be interested."

"I have two sisters. I hear about things I'm not interested in all the time."

"Mr. Montgomery and I have been courting over a year now, and I suppose I'm feeling ... That we ought to be somewhere we aren't yet."

He nodded, his jaw working slightly as if he had to digest those words. "I see. I can understand that. There's room for adjustment in every relationship. Is waiting for that proposal a strain?"

It had been at first, when Alice got engaged and began planning her wedding. But Cassie had soon learned that whatever spark she'd felt for Aubrey in the early days of their relationship had deteriorated into a sort of friendship, which had further deteriorated into two people who moved in the same circles, the same rooms, even in the same embrace but failed to truly see each other.

But who broke an understanding with a man over a missing spark? Sparks came and went. No one ever promised they would last forever.

She'd only hoped it would last her through the honeymoon. That hadn't even been planned, and here she was, resenting him for being the man her parents wanted her to marry. Which wasn't fair at all. In fact, it should make her want him more.

It just didn't.

"It's not so much the proposal. I'm restless. I know he's the man my parents want me to marry, and they are not the most ... They don't care for me particularly."

He shuddered next to her, and she paused, looking up at him in confusion. But he gestured for her to continue.

She wrapped her arms around herself. "I'm struggling with the questions we all ask ourselves from time to time. Am I living within God's plan for me, or am I off on a path entirely separate from Him? How do I know if I'm doing what He wants?"

He looked down, but she could see his smile still. "And here I am, stopping you from praying, when that is your most vital tool."

She sighed. "I've had such a hard time praying about it lately." They approached the end of the path, coming out of sight of most of the windows, and paused there, facing each other. His dog returned and sat at his feet, placid and well-behaved. "Do you ever wonder about ... about your ... your girl? Blanche?"

He nodded. "Sometimes. But I know she's the right choice for me. We've been expected to marry since we were infants, and that decision was not made lightly. It was as much the decision of ... of people with much more life experience than I have ... as mine."

Her eyes flew to his face, searching. Did he mean that his parents had chosen his fiancée for him, same as her? "Oh. Did ... did ...?" What could she ask this man, and what couldn't she?

He shrugged. "My parents and hers made the match. I suppose that happens a lot in your circles, but I've learned the expectation of Americans is that they are beyond such old-fashioned arrangements. We're not. The decision was made because our fathers both own companies that would do well working together. The fact that we're going to be married has already eased their connections over the last fifteen years. We both have always expected to marry each other. But I know it is God's will, too."

How could he know? That was what Cassie wanted to know, for she didn't have any idea of what God was saying to her about Aubrey. Perhaps she hadn't listened much ... She'd been complaining more than praying lately. That thought made her lower her head in shame.

"But it takes a while to get there. I had some rather obvious indicators that Blanche was the woman I was to marry. Maybe it is not so obvious for you. Which is why I say that I should not have interrupted those prayers."

She forced herself to raise her eyes to his face and smile once more. "Oh, never mind. I can pray later. I *will* pray later."

"Good. I'm sure I can keep you in my prayers, too. I think if I were not so sure that I was to marry Blanche, I would be wondering if I ought to break our understanding, too. My parents are not particularly easy to get along with either, and if I had not so much reason to please them, I would prefer to spite them." He chuckled. "But that was never an option for me. I have a great deal of responsibility in my family."

"Of course." Not helpful to her, but at least things made sense for him. "And I'm sure God will give me clarity."

"He will." He tipped his head to her. "Perhaps I'll see you tomorrow. I'd like my sisters to meet you. They're loving little demons, and I'm sure they'd like you."

She smiled. "I'd like that. I'll be out with the children."

He laughed. "You have a servant's heart. Good for you. I've tried to have the same, but I admit, there's a hint of exasperation in me as I watch my sisters. Never mind that. Tomorrow, then?"

"Tomorrow."

He walked away, and Cassie wandered in the opposite direction, determined to pray sincerely—even if some of the time, her mind returned to her conversation with Mr. Hilton, tempting her to allow her thoughts to focus on him overlong.

Yet she trusted God to give her all the restraint she needed to not become confused by a handsome, charming man. After all, she belonged to Aubrey Montgomery.

Didn't she?

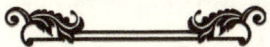

CHAPTER FIVE

FROM A SAFE DISTANCE, Patrick caught sight of the intriguing Lady Mary on a garden bench the next morning. A small girl sat on her lap, and Lady Mary spoke softly to her, head ducked so their noses almost touched. Her soft laugh filled the air, and Patrick tried not to reflect on the obvious.

Blanche hated children.

Why had that thought popped into his mind? It didn't matter. He'd asked her last year, actually, if she would want a child, at least one that Patrick could love and care for and raise in a way entirely different from the way his parents had.

She had agreed, albeit reluctantly. Patrick assumed that once their baby came, Blanche would become more agreeable to the idea of motherhood. After all, faced with a tiny thing, soft and sweet and all yours, how could any sane human resist? Babies were meant to be loved.

Yet his own mother had managed a certain degree of coldness toward her children. Patrick believed she loved them, at least more than Mr. Hilton did. It was just that her selfishness overwhelmed even her best intentions.

But Blanche would be different, and if nothing else, Patrick believed he would love his child abundantly enough to make up for it.

It'd be all right. Everything was going to be all right. No need to panic.

Beside him, Lorelei slipped her arm around his, and he relaxed. "Patrick's fussing about something again, Win. What will we do with him?"

He glanced down at her. "I'm just thinking about having to spend two more days taking care of you two before you're contained in a train compartment again."

"Whatever you say." Yet, much like Caroline Webster, Lorelei had followed his eyes over to Lady Mary. "Is that the earl's daughter you wanted us to meet for unknown and unspecified reasons?"

"She's pretty! And a redhead. Oh, Trick, you could have ginger babies!"

"Winnie! That's entirely inappropriate." Yet his tone was milder than it should've been. This wasn't the first time on their travels that his sisters had suggested someone other than Blanche as a potential wife for him. He reached out and tugged at one of her auburn braids. "I know better."

"He might have a redhead with Blanche, for all we know."

"That'd be better than a baby who looks like *her*." Winnie grinned, and Patrick already followed her train of thought. "After all, the world plainly needs fewer brunettes."

Lorelei frowned. "Keep it up. I'll shove one of those braids down your throat."

"Both of you stop it. Act like ladies."

Lady Mary put the child down, and the girl ran off toward her brothers, who were playing in the distance. Lady Mary's eyes caught Patrick's, and she smiled and waved.

"Friendly, too," Lorelei muttered under her breath to Winnie, but Patrick ignored their antics and led them toward Lady Mary.

Introductions were made, and both the girls were polite, if a little giggly.

"I heard you're going to Italy soon?" Lady Mary smiled. "I loved Italy when I visited."

Winnie's eyes widened. "You've been there?"

"Oh yes. My mother insisted I tour the more fashionable parts of Europe just a few years ago."

"What was it like? Of course, we'll find out, but did you enjoy it?" Winnie's palpable joy made Patrick beam. Lorelei was also excited, he thought, though she worked hard to pretend to be bored by the conversation. She'd grow out of that, he thought. She was already beginning to.

Lady Mary obligingly answered all of Winnie's and Lorelei's questions while Patrick stood to the side. He offered a thought or two, but Lady Mary clearly knew more about Europe than he did, and he wasn't about to interrupt her with his own half-formed opinions. He'd traveled but never really spent time getting to know the countries he'd visited. He intended this trip to educate himself as much as the girls, though of course, Lore and Winnie would be his first priorities.

"That's only a fraction of what there is to see! I loved wandering about whenever I could escape my mother and governess. Honestly, it can be so interesting to stand in the middle of a street and watch people from a completely different country simply being people." Lady Mary's blue eyes deepened like the trough of a wave as her excitement grew. She must have a love for traveling. His first impression of her would not have indicated that. She seemed shy, timid, quiet. Unlikely to adventure across the Continent.

Yet now she was describing her time in the Swiss Alps. Granted, it seemed her exploits were often solitary, but she'd clearly enjoyed them. Much of her interest was cultural or artistic, but the joy of doing something—*anything*—was clearly as present in her spirit as it was in Patrick's.

"I wish you could write to us while we're there," Lorelei said, speaking for the first time in a while. "It's clear you have so much to offer us. Patrick never remembers the interesting details, just the practical ones, much as we adore him—"

"And much as he is truly a very, very good brother," Winnie insisted, a devious twinkle in her eyes.

Patrick watched as Lady Mary paused and glanced between them, her lips forming a firm line. Unfortunately, her eyes then went to Patrick's face, and he instinctively looked away despite the fact that she obviously knew he had been staring now. Her next words were measured. "Oh, I don't have much real information that you couldn't get out of any guidebook."

"Yet the personal touch would mean so much!" Lorelei insisted. "If you're too busy to write us, that's one thing. However, I would love to hear from you."

Of course Lorelei had decided to be assertive with a stranger in the most embarrassing way. Even Lady Mary, who didn't know the girls, couldn't fail to see what they were up to.

"Then maybe Trick could write to you, too!" Winnie inserted.

Lorelei must have pinched her arm, a signal that that was a step too far, as Winnie jerked away from her sister, but the words were said.

Yet Lady Mary just laughed, as if the idea itself were too ridiculous to consider. Which, truly, it was. "Oh, I don't know about that."

"Girls, you mustn't bother Lady Mary." Patrick sent a look to both of them. "She has a life of her own to live, and she can't be dedicating all her time to humoring you."

Winnie pouted, but Lorelei smirked.

If she thinks she's touched a nerve, she's wrong. Everything is splendid. I don't wish for circumstances to be different. I don't.

"Winnie." Lorelei deliberately turned to her younger sister, her back to Patrick. "I just realized you must see the stables! Let's go at once. Perhaps we'll meet Posy Parker there—didn't she say she was going riding?"

"Oh! Yes, I believe she did." Winnie beamed a little too brightly. "Let's go."

Patrick frowned. He wasn't about to be abandoned with matchmaking intentions again. "I'll come with you."

"Oh, Trick, you'd be in the way!" Already, Lorelei had started backing down the path, pulling Winnie along with her. "We'll see you both in a while! Don't bother following us. Why don't you wait here and chat?"

"Oh yes, wait here and chat!" Winnie echoed.

Then they were gone, as suddenly as two mischievous sprites might disappear into an enchanted forest.

Much like a Shakespeare character, Patrick felt like a fool.

"Well." Despite his fears, Lady Mary's voice was full of laughter. "They certainly know what they're about."

Patrick turned to her, actively working to wipe his frown away. It wasn't hard when he faced her, as weak as that might make him. "Hmm. Yes. You mustn't take them seriously. They're high-spirited, and there is a bit of a rivalry between Lorelei and Blanche that makes it difficult for either of my sisters to accept her. I'm sure that will change in time."

"Oh, undoubtedly. I hated my sister's husband—and I don't use that term lightly—until I got used to him. He seemed so foreign, interfering in my tidy family life and dragging my sister away from me to his own estate and his own life. How awful, I thought. Now I have a sweet niece and have come to realize that my brother-in-law isn't so bad." She smiled and inclined her head. "You may be many things to your sisters, Mr. Hilton, but you will never understand being a younger sister."

He couldn't help but laugh at that—her playful tone, her posture. He'd never been so charmed by a woman's utter adorableness. He had never let himself. That should scare him, but he wouldn't think about that. *God, help me. I'm a selfish man.*

"You're right, of course. I'll be similarly defensive, whenever my sisters find their husbands, so *that* I do understand. When my mother talks about their futures, it frustrates me. Granted, my mother would have them marry far younger than I would prefer, but, I admit, there is still a certain degree of irrationality to my stance."

"Oh, absolutely. Every older sibling has a certain degree of irrationality. You should've heard my brother!" Here, she shook her head, her nose wrinkling even as her eyes twinkled. "He'd have me believe that all men are evil—he himself being, of course, excused from such harshness. Older brothers are obligated to share such thoughts with their younger sisters."

Patrick couldn't help but agree with that, but it occurred to him that it would probably be for the best if he distanced himself from Lady Mary. He'd been stepping ever-so-slightly closer without realizing it, and he managed to gain the necessary distance from the lady with a concerted effort.

"How did your prayers go last night?" Hopefully God would be a decent, proper distraction. "If it's not too private. Don't feel that you must tell me."

She raised her eyebrows, as if surprised he remembered. "They went well, I think. A bit scattered—such nights often create a feeling of desperation within me, and it is hard to shake. Yet God is surely greater than my own flaws."

"Perhaps it's not a flaw so much as a trial to be overcome." He hoped so, for his prayers were not always as effective as he would like. There was seldom peace found in his requests. "I was not raised in a Christian family, precisely, so perhaps that is a part of it. My greatest source of inspiration has always come from the pastor at my local church, but he's not here anymore."

"I'm sorry to hear that."

"Yes, it was difficult. I didn't see him as much as I could have in that last year before he died. Sometimes I think that my responsibilities at the company have the wrong precedence in my life." He shook his head. "That's neither here nor there. You wouldn't want to hear about it."

She eased closer. Of course she did; nothing could ever be easy. "I would care to hear. You heard enough of my troubles last night, surely, for me to return the favor."

He shrugged. "Oh, it's simply this dedication my father has to the Hilton legacy, and the expectations placed on me by both my mother and him sometimes feel contrary to what I ought to be doing. If I had any choice, I might not work for them forever, but it's a moot point. My question becomes, why must we live life in such a harried way? Why is the rest Jesus Christ offers so easily discarded? Oh, but I shouldn't worry you with my quandaries." They were all unsolvable anyway. To save his sisters, he must work for his father's company. To work for his father's company, he must push himself to the limit—and then a little farther.

"I don't mind being worried. In truth, I've few worries of my own." She cocked her head slightly. "I always think otherwise, but I am incorrect, of course. I have a lovely life. My question would be this: why must you be so dedicated to your family's legacy, as you call it? I've heard America called the Land of Opportunity. Why can't you make a life for yourself separate from them? You're a man. There's no reason why you couldn't do something different, or at least operate within your father's company with certain boundaries."

The perspective of someone outside the situation, no matter how clever and insightful she seemed, must ever fail to grasp the whole picture. "Oh, there are any number of reasons why I can't just leave. My sisters are the primary ones. After all, if I were ever, say, disinherited, Father would swiftly marry them off to whomever he thought might best run the company in my stead. I would not have that happen to them. I want them to have better husbands than the ones my father would undoubtedly choose."

She pressed her lips together, seemingly disagreeing with this statement, but after a moment of indecision, she nodded. "That makes sense. I see your point, certainly. It is honorable of you to wish to guard your sisters."

One of the Knight boys ran up, calling, "Cassie, Cassie!" and Lady Mary turned to his voice and knelt to greet him. He was younger than Caleb, but she treated him with the same gentle seriousness.

Patrick excused himself, determined to go on a long walk and shake off this entire conversation. Somehow, everything about Lady Mary rattled him to the bone. That couldn't be a good thing, even if he weren't already promised to another.

Cassie thought about Patrick far too much over the course of the night and then into the morning, too, as she packed her trunk with the help of a maid.

She was alone on the carriage ride to the train station, and her thoughts continued, taunting her with their very presence.

His honesty at certain points intrigued her more regarding the things he didn't tell her. She had a feeling that something was wrong there, that he shouldn't be as dedicated to his parents as he was, but to be fair, she was obeying her parents exclusively. What reason had Patrick not to obey, technically?

The carriage pulled up to the station at the village of Creling, and Cassie stepped down—only to find herself face to face with the man himself.

Of course they'd be taking the same train. She'd known that. Hopefully her surprised expression wasn't clear.

Mr. Hilton inclined his head to her. "Lady Mary. I—"

Before he could get another word out, his sisters pounced on her. Not literally, but that was the impression it gave, and the younger Hilton girl did give her a rather enthusiastic hug.

"Lady Mary!" Gwendolyn exclaimed. "Oh, you're traveling to London, too, at the same time? It's fate!"

"It's the train schedules, Win." Mr. Hilton cast his sister a somewhat irritated look, though there was still a degree of affection there.

Cassie guessed he was starting to resent his sisters' matchmaking. She had best extricate herself from this situation as soon as possible.

"It's lovely to see you again, Lady Mary. Perhaps you could sit with us?" Lorelei suggested. "I'd love to talk with you more. I feel that our conversation yesterday was cut short, and we never got a chance to renew it."

That was hardly true.

"Stop bothering Lady Mary. I'm sure she'd appreciate a quiet ride to London."

Ignoring her brother, Lorelei continued, "Mother and Father are in a separate, private carriage, so we have plenty of space. Come sit with us! It'd be lovely to have you there."

In truth, it would be better to sit with someone than alone all the way to London, with nothing to entertain her but her thoughts and a book she'd already reread twice, but she sensed that Patrick would not be pleased.

Yet his expression softened as he looked at his sisters; he was certainly an easily influenced older brother. "I don't object to Lady Mary's presence personally, but I'd rather her be comfortable wherever she is."

His face was inscrutable; of course it was. He shrugged. What was she supposed to take from that?

"I'll travel with you, as long as it's really not an inconvenience." Why not please his sisters if she could not decipher how to please him?

In no time, they were all settled in the carriage, and the train was chugging on toward London. Gwendolyn chattered about the trip to Pearlbelle Park, the upcoming trip to Italy and other parts of Europe, and her hoped-for experiences at every stop. Lorelei was largely silent, but her eyes were on Cassie, analyzing her in a nearly unnerving way.

Mr. Hilton spoke little, except to occasionally attempt to calm Gwendolyn's exuberance or make sure Cassie was comfortable—which she appreciated, despite its being largely unnecessary.

As she listened to Gwendolyn and watched Lorelei, she couldn't help but feel a pang of sympathy toward both of them.

Lord, it'll be hard to never see these girls again. Gwendolyn plainly needs more female guidance in her life, and it's not up to her sister to provide that. Lorelei could probably do with a gentler touch of her own. It's clear that the Hiltons hold their children in low regard, and a brother cannot take the place of parents ... Sometimes he can't even be a mentor. He's too close to the situation, and they're all so alone. Oh, Lord, show me what to do!

Gwendolyn ended one of her rambles with a contented sigh, leaning back on the seat for a fraction of a second, but she soon straightened once more. "Oh, Lady Mary, I wish we could keep talking!" Where before the suggestion had rung with the peals of matchmaking, it now spoke of sincerity—and Gwendolyn was clearly not capable of guise. "There's so much I would say to you."

Before Mr. Hilton could say a word about that, Cassie knew what she herself ought to say. "I wish I could, too. There's so much in this world to be discussed, Gwendolyn, and I would consider it an honor to be your confidante. In truth, I need one of my own, with as many things as I've to consider." That small admission of vulnerability cost her, but she pushed through. "I would love to deepen my acquaintance with all of you, for our mutual benefits."

This said, she couldn't help that her eyes wandered over to Mr. Patrick Hilton's face. He had removed all expression in an instant. She knew Lorelei and Gwendolyn had turned their eyes to him, too.

At last, his gray gaze shifted to her. "I know we discussed your need for prayers about certain situations. Am I free to refer to those situations in my sisters' company?"

Apprehension tightened in Cassie's gut, but she nodded.

"You're a Christian, as am I. So we are brother and sister in Christ. That said, we cannot correspond *privately*. You know this. We are both bound to another, and even if we weren't, given that we have no expectations of each other, it would be inappropriate for us to continue a private conversation. I'm sure Lorelei and Gwendolyn know this, despite some hinting to the contrary that has happened recently. However, that impropriety only exists if the letters were between the two of us. So my question is, would you write to all three of us? To my sisters in particular, but with the understanding that I would read your letters, write responses with them, and perhaps offer a few ... words of encouragement? And advice, if I can." He paused, then continued, with a playful smirk, "I am, after all, a seasoned professional in the art of honoring my parents while also following God. I have come to peace with it."

Cassie wasn't sure about that, but she was attracted to the idea that such a situation might prevail.

"There is no risk for me. I know myself. I know how things are between Blanche and me. I'm sure you know yourself, too. It's only about having someone to talk to. Further, I'd like it if a woman like you rubbed off on my sisters a little. You seem so ... so beyond your years. And"—he cast a glance between his sisters—"they are not beyond their years."

Despite his detracting with the teasing of his sisters, the compliment to herself warmed her as none had in years. No one ever called her mature. They rarely commented on such things. But he had, and she rather liked it.

"I see your point," Cassie murmured. "Perhaps ... perhaps ... yes. Let's ... If your sisters agree, I would like to do that."

Addresses were exchanged. Promises were made. Further conversation was had. But Cassie's mind spun throughout the remainder of the trip to London.

Her prayers that night were full of a dangerous *what-if*. For he was sure in his relationship, but she wasn't, and she had to be honest with herself. Though he said there was no danger, what if there was? What if the danger came not from him, but from her?

Cassie already knew that her heart was a shallow, fickle thing. She had thought she was attracted to Aubrey, and that had not proven to be anything but a shallow inclination. Already, before they had even become engaged, she had lost interest in him, resenting him for the simple claims of a man who loved her and wanted to marry her.

What if every relationship she entered into was doomed to end that way? What if she were not capable of restraining her emotions, keeping every thought captive as the Lord commanded?

No, she could never truly trust herself again. She must instead place her heart in the Lord's hands ... especially in regards to the danger of Patrick Hilton.

"Lord, just keep me. Keep me safe. Keep me safe from myself and my heart and ... everything that may betray You. Oh, Lord, help me—help me."

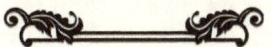

CHAPTER SIX

P ATRICK'S FEET MADE SOFT scuffing sounds along the ancient stones
under his feet, while Bell's paws clacked noisily. Around him, tourists
milled and natives shouted, and he strolled on, enjoying the atmosphere of
one of his favorite cities in the world.

He had grown up a sailor and therefore a traveler. His father's company
fetched and delivered all over the world, as it had for generations, and now,
with modern innovations and communication, it was expanding at a rapid
rate.

Patrick went with his father when he could. He'd done most of his
schooling in a ship's cabin, the gentle rocking of the boat carrying him
through as advanced an education as multiple tutors from multiple countries could give a lad.

He remembered with a smile his last tutor, who had been so continually
seasick. Patrick had had so little sympathy at the time, but now he felt bad
for the poor man.

Pigeons scurried off as Bell dashed forward, barking. He whistled, and
she returned to his side obediently, but her anxious, dark eyes and occa-

sional whines told him this was not a choice she would've made if not for her loyalty to him.

"Easy, girl. You can't go on scaring the locals. We're guests here, remember?"

Bell paid him little heed. As always when fixated on something, it took all her energy to follow one command. She couldn't hear anything but the basics of "heel" and "sit" and "stay" when surrounded by milling birds.

They walked on, through archways and ruins, his feet taking him farther toward the outskirts of the city. After some time, he glanced at his pocket watch. It was nearing noon, and he really ought to be with his sisters for lunch.

Would they eat on the patio again? He hoped so. It was a hot August day, but he loved sitting under the curling grapevines and sipping a cool drink, watching his sisters argue about what they would do in the afternoon.

His mother never joined them. She had wanted to go on this trip to Europe, and she had wanted to bring the girls and "introduce them to culture," but she largely left all three of her children to their own devices. Meanwhile, she sat in her hotel room on her chaise lounge and fanned herself and made her maid miserable.

His father was out on business day and night, even on the days when he was not supposed to be working. Patrick had only gotten the last few days off to explore the city when he'd pleaded to be allowed to spend some time with his sisters, making sure they saw the sights and, therefore, completed their feminine educations, before he dug into endless mounds of paperwork.

A crinkle in his pocket reminded him of the reason he'd originally gone on a walk in the first place. The first letter from Lady Mary had arrived today, and he'd wanted to screen it before handing it to his sisters.

As he'd anticipated, Lore and Winnie had jumped at the idea of talking to an English lady—*a real English lady*—via letter for the next few months. Furthermore, he'd become convinced during those last hours before they'd left Pearlbelle Park that Lady Mary was a pleasant woman who would be good to his sisters in her letters. She'd given him both a

London address and directions to send a letter to some distant spot in the Irish countryside, and he'd been curious.

But he hadn't asked. He didn't need to know anything about Lady Mary or her life. He already knew far, far more than he should.

It had been insane to offer to write her, even with his sisters reading every word. But he couldn't help himself. Not when she had looked so lost. Not when her light eyelashes had fluttered over her deep-blue eyes and her lips had trembled, and he could tell someone needed to step in.

He wasn't sure what the situation exactly was that made her feel so bound to Mr. Montgomery, but if she was bound, at least he could ease her way as she prepared for a relationship she didn't want.

If that was even God's will. But he brushed off the idea that it might not be as if it were the most improbable thing in the world, when really he knew next to nothing about her life.

No, she would marry Mr. Aubrey Montgomery. Patrick felt that was important for some reason. And he could perhaps help. His plan was to let his sisters ramble at her, hopefully raising her spirits—for at least he thought they were amusing—and then he would include short notes based as closely on Scripture as possible that might be encouraging.

And she would have someone to ramble to, which was perhaps the most helpful thing.

But despite the fact that, for some unknown reason, he trusted her somewhat, he would read her letter before letting his sisters see it.

Was he overprotective? Oh yes. But someone had to be protective of Lore and Winnie. His parents weren't. Not really.

His parents were so discouraging to their daughters. He wondered if they knew that. Last night, they had gotten into another fight. They didn't even have the pretense of a shared room anymore, and still, they had found each other with the express purpose, Patrick thought, of making themselves, and all around them, miserable.

The fight had been about Lore and Winnie. Father thought Mother was spoiling them, leading them into unserious and silly ways and encouraging all the wrong parts of their education. Father saw very little room in life for art, beauty, enjoyment, or childhood.

But Mother wasn't any better. Mother thought Father was trying to turn them into Yankee girls who "thought too much and would be of little worth to anyone." She was right that Father was too serious. She was wrong that the cure was to skip education entirely.

The girls needed both a practical education and an education in the arts, but more than that, they needed proper attention paid to their spirits, for those seemed to fade more every day. Lore became more serious, and Winnie became sillier.

If God was lost to them ... Patrick would rather die than let that happen.

When they had been young, Lore and he would convene in Winnie's room, which was the one farthest from their parents'. They would talk to Winnie loud enough that she couldn't hear their parents fighting. They would joke and laugh and sneak midnight snacks from the kitchen, and no one had cared what they did, and it had been a kind of beautiful freedom.

Now Lore was too serious, too intent on pursuing studies to please her father and then a man to please her mother, and Winnie knew as well as the older two that their parents hated each other and had little regard for their children. What Winnie would do with her life was a mystery. She rarely discussed anything grounded in reality.

Patrick didn't know what to do for either of them.

The letter crinkled in his jacket again, reminding him that he must pay attention to its contents sooner or later. Arriving outside the tall and elegant hotel they were staying in, he reached into his pocket and withdrew it. The pages in his hands were so small yet suddenly seeming to hold such import.

Would the influence of a decent woman like Lady Mary be helpful?

That was what Patrick wanted from Blanche, of course, but she couldn't be expected to care about his sisters until after she was his bride. All the more reason to marry her when he got back to America.

He would use these two, long years touring Europe to work out his father's new connections here, to help his sisters see that there was beauty and purpose in this world, and to adjust himself to the idea that he would soon be a husband.

And then possibly a father.

He was too young for this nonsense, but he'd shoulder through nonetheless.

He sat down on a delicate-looking metal chair outside the hotel and broke the seal.

Dear Lorelei, Gwendolyn, and Mr. Patrick Hilton,

Thank you again for letting me write you. I am honored to make the acquaintance and now the friendship of such a kind Christian family as yourselves. I am further excited to hear more adventures from your Grand Tour. When I was sixteen, my mother spent the whole summer taking me from place to place. I saw so many lovely sights. I'll never forget wandering the streets of Florence in the mid-afternoon, alone but feeling so a part of the noisy, lovely crowd of people. I learned enough Italian to get by, and I horrified my maid when she found out I'd slipped out on my own. Please tell me how you are enjoying Florence, as I believe that is the spot where my first letter will reach you.

Unlike you, I did not have such a long tour. Two years in Europe must be quite an experience for you! I hardly know what I would do with all that time away, as I enjoy the quiet privacy of home. However, I often find myself a wanderer by circumstance if not by nature, and I'm sure I should adjust, as you all have.

If you could, Lorelei and Gwendolyn, please tell your older brother that I am in London with Mr. Montgomery. He has been all that is kind. I don't know if I mentioned this to Mr. Hilton or not, but Mr. Montgomery has acquaintances I find myself caring little for. I think you ladies both would forgive me for admitting that I am not sure of him for this reason, but you surely know that marriage is a great undertaking. I would not want to rush hastily into it and find myself bearing the consequences of my mistake for a lifetime. Yet I'm sure if I were to be quite fair to Mr. Montgomery, I would be as taken with him as everyone else I know seems to be.

Speaking of acquaintances in common, Mr. and Mrs. Peter Strauss will be on their way to Philadelphia by the time this reaches you. I will see them off in London. I'll miss our lovely Mrs. Strauss, of course, but we all know that this idea that friendships must end with distance is a lie. Besides, they will come and visit family in England from time to time, and I will be here, as always.

The letter went on, comparing experiences she had had in Europe with what his sisters might encounter. She wrote formally but with an edge to her tone. He could easily read through the lines to her thoughts, no matter how politely she phrased them, and that gave him some level of comfort. She didn't have a great deal of artifice, but she had the breeding to hold herself back somewhat.

Patrick wasn't sure if that was a flaw or a strength. Whatever the trait was, it was certainly one they shared.

He found himself wondering about Mr. Montgomery's acquaintances. If he had friends who were not, to her at least, appropriate—which, granted, could have a myriad of meanings—perhaps that tied in strongly to her reluctance to commit herself to the man himself.

Of course, if she simply meant he associated with men below his social sphere or something like that, that was a different matter entirely than if they were evil companions, those literally proverbial sorts that were sure to lead a man to discovering his own vices.

Yet Patrick could be sympathetic to her desiring her husband's connections be of a certain class, too. Her entire future, both social and financial, could be determined by whom he associated with. It was no different in America, and anyone who didn't think so had never had any money.

It was understandable, but was it right? Patrick wasn't sure about that one.

She concluded the letter by beseeching his sisters to feel free not to reply to her if they were too busy. Which would not happen. Patrick would make sure of it, even if he had to work it into their schooling.

Penmanship was a skill, wasn't it? And letter-writing? That was the sort of thing their mother wanted them to learn, and even their father couldn't protest the fact that writing an excellent letter was a necessary skill for life on this earth.

Just as he was finishing the letter, he heard "Trick!" called in two girlish voices and turned on his chair to see his sisters running out to greet him. Lore wore her brown hair tied back neatly with a blue ribbon, while Winnie had forgone pulling her auburn hair back at all.

He'd have to talk to her about that, though not now. Later, in private. He didn't like addressing things in public both because of their inevitable embarrassment and because that called attention to the issue.

"Good morning!" he exclaimed. "I have a letter for you from your Lady Mary."

"Oh, she's not ours," Lore protested.

"I thought she was yours!" Winnie added, grinning.

"No, I'm Blanche's, remember?"

Both girls rolled their eyes, but they accepted the pages from him without further comment.

As they began reading, Patrick felt obligated to give at least a few instructions. "Lady Mary mentions her somewhat unsure relationship with Mr. Montgomery. I wonder if you two couldn't think about what you would do in her circumstances. Does his association with men she doesn't approve of, for whatever reason, really disqualify him from the office of husband? What sort of men would it have to be for you yourself to discontinue the association?"

Lore turned tired, gray eyes to him. "Trick, please don't turn this into another learning experience."

"Yes, Trick." Winnie scowled at him before going back to struggling with Lore to see the same page at the same time.

"I want you two to know that this world is meant to be learned about and explored."

"Which is what we are doing! Now stop interrupting."

So he sat in silence while his sisters read the letter, occasionally arguing over where they were on the page or making soft comments to each other.

Patrick waited, unable to resist smiling at them despite the fact that he felt a little silly. But they made him smile, with their bickering and their innocence and their love of a good letter.

Never had such good girls been raised by such unobservant, unloving parents. There was no one but God to thank for that—only the Lord could've given Lore and Winnie the joy and courage they possessed. Patrick prayed that God would allow them to maintain these attitudes throughout their life, even in the face of adulthood and the various trials and temptations it would bring.

"What do you think?" Patrick asked when they at last put the letter down. "Was it the right decision to write to this woman?"

"Yes." Lore spoke with the assurance of someone who knew what she believed and, further, was sure that she was right about it. "She seems lovely. We'll write back to her. Will you write, too, Trick?"

"I may put a brief note in with your letters, yes, but you'll remember that both of us are bound to other ... other people." He wasn't sure how to word it. It would be easier, surely, when they were both engaged, but that obviously wasn't the current situation. "I need you both to maintain a realistic understanding of what Lady Mary is to us. She's a friend to you. I'm going to send her a few, short letters because we are talking about things concerning the Bible and ... and those sorts of things. And I hope she will have a bit of an influence on you, too, because you could both calm down and grow up a little."

Lore frowned. "That's true of Winnie but not of me."

"It's true of both of you."

"And what about you?" Winnie protested. "You're not perfect."

"I didn't say I was!" He'd rather implied he was better than them, but that was beside the point. He was the older brother. Of course he would make that implication whenever he could. "All right, forget I said that. But just know that I think she is the type of woman who could make an excellent mentor."

"Unlike Blanche?" Lore suggested.

"Oh yes!" Winnie giggled. "Blanche Linden, daughter of privilege and owner of a thousand dresses that she never wears more than once. Do you remember that time Potato hopped up on her skirt, and she squealed like a banshee? Oh, Trick, it was so funny!"

Patrick frowned. Though he did sometimes find Blanche a little ... *feminine* ... she was a woman, and he figured all men had to deal with that aspect of marriage. Women weren't men. Lore and Winnie were always so judgmental of people, expecting them to be far more than they were.

Frankly, he was, too, but he generally chose to ignore that fact in favor of more pressing ones. He had enough flaws to think about without becoming obsessed with every one that passed through his mind.

"Potato is a particularly naughty creature, so I might squeal if confronted by him with no warning, too." Potato was Winnie's badly-behaved spaniel who generally had the run of the house due to having been an adorable puppy whom Patrick's mother had allowed on the sofas. "Blanche is a lady, and it's important that we treat her like one."

"Oh, come off it, Trick!" A rare giggle bubbled up from somewhere within Lore where childhood still held the reins. "Blanche is a stick in the mud, and we all know it. She's only two years older than me—and there she is, parading herself around like the Queen of Sheba."

Patrick wasn't sure of that, but what he did know was that Blanche was deserving of all the respect he could muster for her. After all, he was going to marry her, and he'd best treat her with at least some small degree of consideration for that reason.

"We'll have lunch and discuss it further. How's that?"

Winnie moaned. "This *is* a learning experience."

"Everything is a learning experience!" He rose. "Come on, let's go."

CHAPTER SEVEN

November 1881
London, England

C ASSIE REARRANGED FOR THE dozenth time the hothouse flowers Aubrey had sent her. Roses shouldn't have required much arranging, but she couldn't get the ferns surrounding them to lay the way she wanted them to.

Patrick had encouraged her to enjoy the small gestures Aubrey did for her, and she did like flowers. Even roses, which were rather a dull choice and certainly not her favorite, delighted her. Further, Aubrey had selected them himself—or if he'd sent his man, which was another option, at least the card was in his own hand.

He'd written, "For my fair English rose, with all my love," which felt like it didn't exactly describe her, but she dismissed that thought. He was doing his best; he had put legitimate effort into making her happy lately. What more could a woman ask for?

The letters to the Hiltons had helped. She pushed herself toward optimism and often found that her lot wasn't as bad as she'd previously thought.

"Mary?" Aubrey's voice called her from her reverie as he approached her in the conservatory at her parents' townhouse.

Cassie looked up with a smile she didn't have to force. Yes, she could definitely make this work, even if it felt unlikely at the present moment. She wanted to have a marriage, children, a home of her own, and a husband was a necessary part of that. Surely she could manage that, even if from time to time, she had doubts or wished he were different. That was the case with every relationship—or at least that was what Patrick felt. He thought that every relationship did and must have at least some degree of conflict.

We are all sinful beings, after all, Patrick had written. *We are all living in a fallen world, facing obstacles of greatness that can only be defeated by our all-powerful God. We are not obligated or expected to fall madly in love and see no flaws in our husband or wife. And that's the way it should be. We should expect at least some degree of sadness in our earthly lives, and a great deal of that sadness must come from relationships.*

It sounded sensible when laid down in writing, but surely he wasn't thinking of the *facts* that Cassie was. The facts brought to her mind by the most personal type of relationship.

There were events and situations she would have to endure with Aubrey Montgomery that she wouldn't have to face with anyone else in this world, and that was overwhelming. She would have to look him in the eye every morning and night for the rest of her life and accept her choices.

And could she? She thought so. She wanted to believe so. But sometimes, when she lay alone on her bed at night, no longer able to be distracted by a good book or the exhaustion that always seemed to inundate her after a day full of interactions with Aubrey and other people she wasn't close to, she would wonder. Her thoughts would be everywhere, tempting her to a greater anger and frustration than she was willing to admit.

And sometimes she wondered if Patrick were really in love with Blanche Linden. If he weren't, for he spoke little of feelings and so much of duty that Cassie was almost sure he wasn't, would he really go through with the marriage even in the face of his lack of affection for her?

On the other hand, Cassie also felt sympathy for Blanche. Did the girl know his indifference? Did she care?

Perhaps not. Perhaps no one cared but Cassie, who had seen too much of love beyond her fingertips and too much of indifference in her own home to want anything less than an affectionate relationship.

But Aubrey was affectionate in his own stoic way. He simply seemed to struggle to speak his feelings into existence, always exerting his efforts to remain calm when she could have done with a little wildness. Yes, yes, she'd make it work. She didn't have to return the feelings—or perhaps what she had felt when she first began to court him would return in time.

She hoped so.

Aubrey was smiling and seemed even more pleased upon seeing what she was doing. He stood next to the table that held the vase she had been rearranging and reached up to finger a petal on one of the roses. "I'm glad you liked them enough to give them your attention."

"They are lovely. Thank you."

"Of course." He rolled his shoulders. "I thought we could go for a walk today. Your mother granted us permission to go. I said we'd stroll through Hyde Park."

She nodded. Her mother would probably have given Aubrey permission to kidnap Cassie and escape to Scotland if that was what he wanted. Mother would never do anything that might displease Aubrey, for she so badly wanted to get rid of Cassie—and already it had taken a great deal longer than she'd planned. "I'll go get ready." She would need to bundle up. Though snow had yet to fall, it was still a cold day in London. November was swiftly giving way to winter, and it wouldn't be long until the first snow fell.

Soon she was bundled up and walking down the streets of London with Aubrey. He talked about this and that, all light things—about his sisters and his mother, about their plans for the Christmas holiday, and about how soon he hoped to propose. Which he was still putting off. Apparently, he even had a ring now.

Cassie couldn't turn him down. She couldn't.

Perhaps she would like him more if she were to just give him more access to her life. If she were to just tell him more and allow him into her innermost circles. For at the present moment, she certainly wasn't, much as she wanted to. There was a part of her that increasingly became distant from Aubrey, that could not be his, that would *not* be his. And she didn't know how to change that, how to share it with him. Yet she must try, for if they were wed, there could be no secrets between them.

Perhaps if she playacted, if she pretended to be all she was supposed to be, she would feel as if they had a real relationship instead of an empty charade. Perhaps the fault lay with Cassie, not with Aubrey. He was doing his best, after all, and she had done nothing but dismiss him even in the face of this.

"You'll stay in London for Christmas, then?" she reiterated—or at least she thought it was a reiteration. Paying attention to what Aubrey was saying to her was difficult sometimes, too. He did have a very monotone voice, and his subjects rarely varied, but she was simply being rude. Even if she didn't particularly like the idea of marrying him—and she would soon, she was sure—she could resign herself to the fact that they must be friends. She shouldn't even treat a stranger with the disdain she'd been treating Aubrey with lately.

What had gotten into her?

He confirmed that his family was indeed staying in London for Christmas, as much to be near to her as anything. Cassie nodded and tucked this information away. It was fair to assume, then, that he intended to propose some time before Christmas. There was nothing stopping him, after all. He had certainly spoken to her father at several points. Not that she had the type of relationship with her father in which he would tell her such a thing, but at least she believed that was what had happened.

And anyone, anyone in the world, would be a better housemate for her than her parents. She had to learn to love Aubrey. It was her duty, same as it was Patrick's duty to love Blanche Linden. It was time to accept that.

"Aubrey, do you ever feel a need to reach out to someone ... someone who is not related to the situations you are currently going through and ... and use them to process a thought or two?"

He gave her a sideways glance that let her know that the question was a strange one, but he answered all the same. "Not particularly. I like talking to people who understand the situation, as their perspective must then be clearer."

"Who do you talk to?"

"Gibson, of course, though you don't like hearing about that."

No, she didn't, but she'd have to adjust herself to the fact of his friendship with Mr. Gibson Ashfield if she was going to be in a relationship with Mr. Aubrey Montgomery. He'd made it more than clear that he didn't intend to end that friendship no matter what Cassie said.

"Who do you talk to? These mysterious people who aren't involved in your life?" He paused in the pathway, smiling but looking more bemused than supportive.

She swallowed. "I have been discussing some small details of our relationship with the Hiltons via letters since they are touring Europe, and some of our conversations have been amusing to me. You met the family at my friend Alice's wedding. We talk about this and that, including how I feel about … about us."

Then his face changed. It became dark and brooding, and his next words were the harshest she had ever heard him speak. "I'd like you to discontinue that correspondence."

Her eyes widened. "But—"

"Mary, I can't believe you'd do that! Have you any idea how inappropriate that is?"

"It's hardly inappropriate, Aubrey! I'm talking to the Hilton girls. They're so young, and they can use so much guidance as they tour Europe. Their mother does not provide the prerequisite information, and—"

"But you're not just talking with them, are you? Mary, you don't think I didn't see your eyes slide to that Hilton man again and again during the wedding, do you? I saw. I know that you were … I don't know what you were doing." He threw up his arms and then paced away from her, then back again. "I assume you communicate with him directly. There's guilt in your eyes that says so."

Cassie's heart squeezed. Oh, she did write directly to Patrick, but he claimed, at least, that all her responses were read by his sisters. Surely, if it were just his words that were kept private, that wasn't so bad. But a part of her heart knew that what she was doing, no matter how encouraging it was, was not appropriate.

For they were both promised. Understandings existed that Patrick would marry Blanche Linden and Cassie would marry Aubrey Montgomery. And nothing, *nothing* on earth, could stop that, for she must marry Aubrey. She must escape her current life and live one that was safer, that allowed her to have her own home.

She must escape the pain of rejection, the fear of being alone. She must make her own place.

"If you ask me to stop writing to them, I will," she whispered. "And if you would like to see their letters, you are welcome to." She kept her tone quiet, appeasing. She didn't want to fight with him.

His eyes softened. "I don't need to see their letters, but I would like it if you ended the correspondence."

"What if I were to write only to his sisters? I would hate to disappoint them. As I said, you could read those letters—they are all innocent."

He hesitated. "I would not need to read them, but if you were to clarify that you need only write letters to the Miss Hiltons ..."

"I have not written to him. Sometimes he has included a note to me, but I have not written directly to him."

"Very well." He sighed. "Keep doing it. But know that I want to keep you for myself, Mary. I've no interest in sharing you with another man."

"I know." It was a reasonable request. Spouses should be able to claim such things.

So why did it feel so restraining?

December 24, 1881

Christmas should be a time for celebration, but Cassie found herself dreading it. Aubrey was going to propose. She knew it.

Perhaps not today but soon.

They sat around the dining table at the Montgomery household, everyone merry and laughing, and he was seated next to her.

His hand found hers under the table, and she squirmed.

She couldn't push him away, and yet she wasn't sure she wanted him to propose tonight. In fact, she was moderately sure that ... that ...

Oh, Lord, how can I go through this? I can't marry him. I can't. I can't spend the rest of my life with him. I can't bear his children.

It might be better than being with her parents for the rest of her life.

Lord, what if Patrick doesn't marry Blanche Linden? What if ... what if this isn't just passing attraction? What if ...?

The thoughts swirled as the dinner progressed. She forced food into her mouth, forced herself to chew and swallow, nodded when it was appropriate, and in general, sat in silence.

Her eyes met Gibson Ashfield's across the table. She wished he weren't at the Montgomery's house. Wished anyone had the decency to hate him as she did.

But when she'd spoken to Aubrey about it last night, he had ignored her. Rejected her thoughts once again with the shallow excuse that they were lifelong friends, that he would not leave Gibson to his own devices.

That the man needed him.

The only thing Mr. Ashfield needed was a sharp kick in the trousers, but Aubrey didn't believe her. Didn't listen to her. Didn't care about her opinions.

Anger brewed, but she tamped it down, as she always did when it burned hot and bright in her soul. She couldn't let herself be angry—at Aubrey, at Gibson, or at her life.

Yet the fury still rose, and she scarcely knew when dinner ended. She passed into the parlor with the ladies like a ghost, unfeeling and unthinking.

Sometime later, the men appeared, and there was to be music, but Aubrey stood in the middle of the floor and called everyone's attention.

No wonder her parents liked him. While being uniformly boring, he also managed to be the perfect host. He would continue to grow his societal influence while also being a safe and predictable choice.

Plus, his financial connections would support the O'Connells, and Cassie's children would have the joint benefits of wealth and a background of nobility.

This had all been chosen and laid out by her parents.

Aubrey continued speaking, saying something about how he was delighted to have every guest here, how they were honored to host Christmas Eve celebrations in their home, how he valued every member of their little party—"little" meaning about two dozen lords and ladies and gentlemen.

There was no escape from it. When she married Aubrey, her life would stay the same.

You don't belong here.

The thought pressed in on her. Oh, she was born in this world, but something told her to run from it—not from her status but from her parents. From the influence they held over her.

And that influence would not end if she married Aubrey Montgomery. It would deepen.

Marriage was too serious a commitment to be entered into lightly. She must consider carefully her next step.

But what, Lord?

"Of course ..." Aubrey angled his body toward her. "The guest who has most captured my attention, as always, is Lady Mary. For the last year and a half, she has charmed me upon every meeting. In every way, I have considered her the perfect woman. She is the essence of loveliness and nobility, and I have come to care for her ... very much."

Oh, Aubrey, must it be here? For there was only one way this line of talk could go. She gripped the rough arm of the chair she sat on, the small one in the corner of the parlor that was embroidered with crimson leaves, and the blood rushed to her ears, but she forced her eyes to remain glued to his face.

He approached her, a smile on his lips and his eyes full of panicky embarrassment, and she knew what this cost him. To raise the courage, to do this here—because he felt it was the best way to do so. Because he had decided, somehow, that this was how one proposed to a woman. And he was doing it. He always did what was right.

God, what do I do?

"Lady Mary, you have known for some time my intentions."

God, tell me what to do. I don't know what to do.

"Make me the happiest man in the world."

I'm cornered, trapped, and You are the only One Who can give me a light, a path out. Show me the way. Show me the way, and I will walk in it.

He knelt then, reached for her hand, and held out a band of silver with three rubies intricately curved amongst the tendrils of metal. She trembled but extended her own hand, not knowing what else to do.

Help me. Help me. I'm too weak on my own. Please help me.

"Do me the immense honor of becoming my wife."

Then everything stilled. The blood rushing through her ears. The pounding of her heart. The spasming of her throat. Even Aubrey seemed to freeze on the floor there, and the guests, all in various stages of shock and delight and amusement, were still.

But her thoughts rose, and though it might not have been God, perhaps He was the Voice that filled her, that brought sensation back and forced her to speak.

"I'm sorry, Mr. Montgomery. I will not marry you."

Then pandemonium broke out.

Oh, not from Aubrey. Of course not from Aubrey. He stiffened and then rose swiftly to his feet, his eyes tracing over her face, his expression one of brokenness and disbelief.

But there were shocked gasps and hushed whispers among the other guests and what sounded like a cry of pure shock from Mrs. Montgomery.

And her parents rushed forward.

"Mary, what are you thinking? You must be mad." Her mother's hand came out and gripped Cassie's arm until it hurt, until she knew the marks of her fingernails would be visible on her arm below the velvet sleeve of her dress for days to come. "You don't realize what you've said. Of course you will marry Mr. Montgomery."

"I will not." She whispered the words, but her voice was strong. She whispered the words, but there was not a shred of hesitancy. She knew, somehow, without knowing anything else, including the exact "why," that she would not be marrying Mr. Aubrey Montgomery.

And after that, a great many words were said by her parents. Aubrey looked hurt, but he said little, and Cassie said nothing. Eventually, she was taken to a private room with her parents, Aubrey's mother, and the man himself, and there was a great deal more discussion.

But Aubrey and Cassie said nothing.

And at last, Cassie was taken home.

Then the true berating started, and usually Cassie would've melted under her parents' anger and disdain. They called her all sorts of words then, but those slid off Cassie like water off a duck's back.

Why was she suddenly impenetrable when she never had been before? *God, is that You?*

She heard some of what they said, of course. She had disgraced the family. No man would take her now. She was, in practicality, a loose woman now; there would be no redeeming her.

They would be sending her to Ireland, to Auburn Hall. She would be required to stay there. They would not put effort toward her future anymore, not if she was not going to marry Aubrey Montgomery, whom she had so sinfully, so immorally led on.

She was not a lady. She was not a woman of good character. She was hardly their daughter.

Yet she heard a whisper again, soft but strong: "I will never leave thee, nor forsake thee." What was there to fear with a promise like that?

She turned her face toward a future open with possibilities that night.

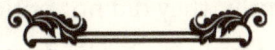

Chapter Eight

January 1882
Rome, Italy

I T HAD BEEN SOME time since he received a letter from Lady Mary, but Patrick didn't consider that to be unusual. Her letters had been more restrained of late, especially in reference to him.

He guessed that Mr. Aubrey Montgomery had truly won her heart now. She was likely engaged, and with that, his influence on her would need to end. Which was a good thing. Patrick had a little over a year now to refocus his thoughts before they would be returning to Boston, to day-to-day life, and to Blanche.

Then there would be a wedding.

He would only be twenty-one, but his parents considered that to be old enough. Patrick believed it was for most people, but a part of him was inclined to doubt that for himself. Nonetheless, he did his best to resign himself to the fact. Better to get it over with, to adjust himself to the idea of marriage early on in his life when it must necessarily be a vital part of his life until the day he died.

But he was surprised when a waiter approached him as he sat in the café below the hotel. His silver tray contained a slim letter from England. This one was addressed not to his sisters, as the others had been, but directly to him.

How strange.

He had thirty seconds in which to slide it into his pocket before his sisters arrived, and thankfully, they did not notice and, therefore, did not ask anything. Which was fortunate, for he never lied to them. He would bend the truth, but if they saw a letter and asked about it, he would tell them what it was.

And they would want to read it. But something told him that, more so than normal, it was important that he read this letter before his sisters did.

He munched down on a *cornetto*, sipped at a *latte e cacao*, and avoided speaking for the majority of their breakfast. His sisters babbled about their wish to travel to the Alps, and Patrick shut the idea down, insisting they stay in the south until spring came.

"It's just around the corner, and there is much to see toward the south. We'll go to the beach."

"But it's a time for snow, Trick," Winnie said disapprovingly. "You simply cannot deny us snow in January."

"I can, and I will. We'll see snow in March or April when it's a bit tamer but not all gone. Until then, it's cold enough here for my taste. Let's enjoy milder winters—we'll be in Boston soon enough."

They both acted disgusted but accepted his decision without further question. Really, Patrick had business deals to conclude with his father, and with more and more of his time being eaten up by those activities, he wanted every spare moment in the evenings and early mornings to be spent with his sisters.

At last, he knew he must rise, and he did so, leaving his sisters in the capable hands of the Italian tutor hired for music and language practice.

Winnie was learning the violin.

It was hideous.

Meanwhile, Lore plodded along in her studies with confidence but never quite perfection. Though he might tease, he loved watching both of his sisters learn new things, for it was so reflective of their personalities.

But he could not watch today. Whistling for Bell, he jogged out of the café and through the gray, bustling streets. It was chilly but not quite cold, and the jog soon had him working up a sweat.

He came closer to the edge of the city and hailed a cab to take him to Focene. He was already later than he wanted to be, but thankfully, his father had chosen a hotel to the west this time, making it easier for Patrick to navigate there within a reasonable hour to hour and a half, depending on how many people were also driving there on any given day.

He could have gone with his father much earlier that morning, but he never wanted to miss breakfast with his sisters. If his father must, Patrick would not. That was the way he made almost every decision in his life these days.

On the drive, shivering in the back of the rattling conveyance and questioning his decision to pay the fee to drive ten or fifteen miles when he could've gone with his father in his hired carriage, Patrick withdrew the letter from Lady Mary and broke the seal.

Dear Mr. Hilton,

You may find it strange that I would write to you, but I could not communicate this to your sisters. However, I did not feel this was something that could be shared in any other way, and I was sure you would care to hear it.

I have broken my relationship with Mr. Aubrey Montgomery for good.

He proposed Christmas Eve, and I could not accept. Sense, logic, and morality forbade me from doing so. More than that, God forbade me.

My parents were understandably furious. Their tempers have yet to cool, but I am adjusting to that. In a fit of pique, my mother dismissed my maid and completely removed my access to pocket money. This bothers me little. I am far better clothed, fed, and supported than most women in this world, even of my status, and I do not mind doing things for myself. Plus, the other maids have taken great pity on me and my occasional bouts of incompetence. I say this because I don't want you to believe I am anything but what I am—and that is rather spoiled, even when I am a victim of my parents' wrath.

By the time you receive this letter, I will be in Ireland. My father's castle, Auburn Hall, is to be my home for the foreseeable future. My parents have made it clear that if I do not marry Mr. Aubrey Montgomery, I will spend the rest of my life in exile.

But it is better to be in exile, to be alone, to be unsupported and even friendless, than to marry a man who God tells you not to marry. I will follow Him, and He will sustain me. Don't misread this letter as a cry for pity; I am quite content with my decision and, further, have been feeling so blessed by every little thing I experience.

The castle may be drafty, but I will have extensive apartments and beautiful furnishings and all I wish. My pin money may be gone, but I have more gowns than I could ever know what to do with, and I can alter them to last for years. Plus, I've no idea that my mother will be able to resist sending me money for gowns for long—she does so care about such things. And I have no maid ... Oh, horror of horrors! Don't tell my mother how little that bothers me. I would sometimes rather do without, though I have sent her off with a good reference.

I'm rambling, however, and you have already heard the primary reason for my writing. Mr. Hilton, I am free. I am free as the birds in the sky and the waves against the cliffs.

I don't know if I will hear from you again, but I think you ought to know.

Sincerely,
Lady Mary Cassidy O'Connell

P.S. I have since the time I was a child of two or three years old used the name Cassie to refer to myself. This became my name at boarding school, and it is the only thing my friends call me, though many of my relatives cannot be persuaded. I am well-adjusted to Lady Mary; however, should you find Cassie easier, you are welcome to use it. I know myself better when I am called that name. —C.

Patrick sat in shock and tried to adjust himself to what she was saying. It was mad. She had broken her understanding with Aubrey Montgomery. Why had she done it? All common sense rebelled against the thought. She was supposed to marry him. *Supposed to.* It was the right choice from every angle.

Why had she ended the relationship?

Yet the decision was made. It was there before him in black and white ink, in her utterly feminine script, speaking both of her breeding and education as well as her slightly whimsical nature, which came through so clearly in her letters.

"Lord God, she is free."

Why had he whispered that prayer? He folded the letter and tucked it back into his coat pocket, but his fingers returned to the pages, brushing against them wonderingly, as if he couldn't believe it wasn't a dream.

He pressed his lips tightly together. He was a fool. An utter fool. That was why.

He sat stiffly in the carriage until it arrived, then stepped out and paid the man. He stood above a sandy beach that stretched toward the north; below him, a group of men stood, plainly arguing about this and that.

This was a tourist beach, though it was more frequented by locals from what he understood. His father had an opportunity to buy a stretch of it and perhaps turn it into a dock that would enable him to work more directly with sellers and buyers in Rome.

But Patrick already knew as he walked down toward his father and a group of men who were sliding about in the damp sand and cursing the now steadily falling rain that it was not suitable.

No, they needed rockier ground. Perhaps they could build to the south, but that was not available. He ignored the sand getting into his shoes and the wind whipping at his coat and jogged the last few hundred yards to his father.

"There you are, Patrick."

Introductions were made that he scarcely heard, and he was caught up on what had been discussed, both with their business partners and with the sellers of this strip of land.

His father had already made the decision to buy the land with hopes of selling it at a higher price later. Mr. Hilton was trying to devalue the land and drive it down in the sellers' eyes so that they could get it as cheap as possible.

So with a mighty effort, he forced himself to focus on the matter at hand.

When the evening of that seemingly endless day finally arrived, he dragged himself—exhausted, cold, and hungry—to his room.

It was then that the thoughts began to plague him.

He wanted to write back and reassure Cassie that she was not alone. That if she had no other friends, at least he could be one to her. That he would help her, advise her ... rescue her.

He wanted to rescue her. Just like he'd been rescuing his little sisters all his life.

That was a dangerous feeling for a man who would be getting engaged to be married in a little over a year.

So, with his heart pounding and his hands shaking, he took out his pen and wrote.

> *Dear Lady Mary,*
>
> *Thank you for updating me on how things are going for you. I see you were able to arrive at a conclusion. Perhaps it is not the one we wanted or the simplest, but I pray that at least it was the right one for you.*
>
> *I return to Boston next year, and I will then become engaged to Blanche. My story is very different from yours, you see. How interesting to see your tale unravel so differently from mine! The world is full of so many people and so many things.*
>
> *I want to thank you for the care and attention you have given my sisters. They adore you, as well they ought. Now they are becoming more and more consumed with their studies, and I don't believe they will be able to continue writing to you, which is a shame because they have so enjoyed these letters. I shall make sure they send you a note from time to time, but you know how girls of this age are. They are so occupied with Italy and will soon be with Switzerland, Germany, France, and Spain. You understand*

my meaning, I'm sure; they will write when they can, perhaps when we return to our homeland, but I believe it is best if they avoid distractions for the time being.

I wish you all the best in the world,
Patrick C. Hilton

The ink was blotted and soon dried. The letter was sealed. Tomorrow he would place it in the hands of a postman.

And that was the end of the distraction that was "Cassie."

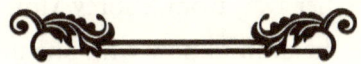

March 1882
County Kerry, Ireland

Dear Mary,

In answer to the question posed in your last letter, yes, your brother is well and has been receiving your letters, but I have asked him not to reply to you for a time. Perhaps in a few more months. At present, I feel that it is not important for you to receive a letter from any member of our family, and I will attempt to limit my correspondence to simple facts—however tempted I may be to remind you, once more, that you have thrown away your life.

As for the reason behind my letter, I realized that my one error in sending you to the estate for the time being is that you are unattended. Though I still hold to my decision to let your maid go, I believe you ought to have someone to make sure you are acting as a lady, not a wild heathen, while you run about Ireland.

With this in mind, I will make sure the housekeeper expects you to hire a maid. You may interview a few girls from the village and train them to your purposes. It's not ideal, but then nothing about your situation is.

I hope you are spending your time in deep reflection. I am unsure what your future may look like, and I hope that that lack of assurance will allow you to reconsider the actions you have taken.

Sincerely,
Catherine O'Connell, Countess of Auburn

The brief letter fell onto Cassie's lap, and she sat still, staring off into the distance and contemplating, like her mother had suggested, her actions. But unlike her mother, she found little to be disappointed in.

The Lord had guided her away from Aubrey Montgomery, and it wasn't even a situation where she didn't know why. She understood clearly that she was not supposed to be married to Aubrey Montgomery. Other than that, her future was hazy; however, that didn't matter. What mattered was that she had, to the best of her ability, followed God's will.

A month and a half ago, a letter had come from Patrick, and though she'd been disappointed, she had accepted it. It had seemed unlike him—panicky, tired. Yet she didn't blame him for not wanting to talk about her problems anymore. There were dark nights when she wasn't even sure *she* wanted to talk about her problems anymore.

She folded the letter and sighed. There was nothing to be done but to keep living. And more than that, to pray earnestly.

She rose from her seat at her dressing table and paced to the window. Outside, a heavy mist blanketed the ground, but it was starting to clear slightly as the sun peeked above the horizon. She rubbed her hands over her face and began the ritual of dressing in her multiple layers, tying her hair back in a simple plait, and straightening her own rooms.

There were maids at Auburn Hall—of course there were. But Cassie wanted to either have one close maid who did everything for her or be entirely independent. She could not have an intermediate option wherein she was forced to be on intimate terms with a relative stranger. Of course, she had been trying to get to know the maids at Auburn Hall. They were just resistant to her presence—and Cassie knew why. They were all Irish, and though Cassie technically had a great deal of Irish blood, she was an English lady. An oppressor. And no matter how sympathetic she was to their cause, it would take time for her to win their trust, if she ever did.

She could hope. She did hope, every day. But it seemed unlikely that anything less than six months to a year of consistent effort would actually win over the servants at Auburn Hall.

And now she would have to hire a maid from the village. She was surprised her mother hadn't asked her to offer a promotion to one of the live-in maids, but her mother wanted Cassie to go through the painful evaluation and interview process. Not that Cassie would make it nearly as painful as her mother often did. No, Cassie was of a different kind than her mother. She wouldn't be ridiculously needy, nor would she find fault with every maid she was brought. She had loved the maid she had before this, and been content with her, and now she was determined to be similarly content with the next one.

She *could* dress herself. It was just that most of her clothes required an extra hand, and again, she refused to accept one from the staff. The process of buttoning dresses up the back, for instance, was particularly painful, but she got it done through sheer stubbornness.

Though everyone always said Cassie had learned her stubbornness from elsewhere, Cassie knew that she'd inherited it from her mother. That was exactly how the Countess of Auburn was, just about different things. Like making sure she got all she felt was her due as a lady.

At last, Cassie finished her dressing and slipped out of her bedroom. She ran through the halls of the castle, her skirts caught up in her hands, and in no time, she was outside on the green grass, the sea salt hitting her face with the harsh springtime wind.

"Lord, what am I supposed to be doing here?" She paused and stared up at the sky, but no answer was provided for her. "What good can I possibly do?"

She kept walking, her feet scuffing through wet moss and scattered gray rocks, until she came to the cliff face. Daunting, it jutted out over the tossing sea. There wasn't a storm, but the breeze was more like a gale, and Cassie squinted into it, occasionally pausing to wipe her face from the sea spray.

"It's beautiful here, at least," she admitted. Her few happy childhood days before she'd met Alice and the Knights had taken place at Auburn Hall. Here, she had run barefoot and wild, her hair in kinks and knots trailing down her back and her nanny chasing her in utter horror at her behavior. And she had been friends with the servants then. She had loved the people in the village then. She had rejoiced in being Irish then.

Now what was different? Oh, she still rejoiced in her heritage and loved every facet of her country even if her parents refused to believe it was *their country*. Yet she wasn't welcome in the same way. No longer a child or even what one might call a girl, but a woman with a brain and reasonable ability. She must be associated with the cruelty of the English lords ... whether she liked it or not.

And what she could do to change that reputation was beyond her knowing, for what could one lonely lady do?

She spun on the top of the cliff, laughing at her own daring, then made her way to the rocky path that wove its way down to a small pebble beach below that would allow her access to the churning waves that spoke so deeply to her own soul.

"Lord, why is everything about my life so complicated?"

She couldn't help but ask the question, though it was not exactly accurate. After all, she had a safe place to sleep and plenty of food to eat. She had clothes on her back and friends, even if they were not near her or currently in much contact with her. Alice had somehow dropped off the face of the earth since October—Cassie assumed she was simply busy with the many occupations of married life. A few scattered letters from Mrs. Knight, upon Cassie's request, noted that Alice was hinting that she was expecting a child, so Cassie believed that was what was occupying her.

"May her life be happy, Lord," she whispered. "Happier than mine. May she enjoy her husband and her child, if she's going to have one. And may she write me a long letter describing her dear baby's dimples and laughs when she is well rested from that."

How soon would it be? Alice had already been hinting at a possible pregnancy in September or so, in her last letter to Cassie, but it couldn't be that she was that far along or Mrs. Knight would've surely known more.

But it was best not to think about these things that she could not in any way verify. She would know soon enough, whether from Alice herself or Mrs. Knight. Perhaps Cassie ought to write to Peter. He was a champion letter writer.

Cassie would be lucky to find a man like Peter. Oh, he wasn't really the type she admired herself. On the other hand, Cassie wasn't sure she knew herself anymore. She had certainly been attracted to Patrick Hilton, but at one point, she'd been attracted to Aubrey Montgomery, too.

That seemed different somehow, but her memories of those early days with Aubrey might be colored by her current situation. After all, she had liked him a great deal when she courted him. When Alice began communicating again, Cassie would have to ask her how she had seemed—and compare that to how she currently felt about Mr. Hilton.

It wasn't that she loved Mr. Hilton. Oh no. She would never again put the name of "love" on a feeling that referred to someone she'd just met. Not unless it was the universal brotherly and sisterly love that a Christian ought to feel toward all people. And of course, there was a different thing—infatuation. She could call that love if she wanted, but she knew now that it would not last.

No, she did not love Mr. Patrick Hilton; however, she wanted to pursue him.

What a sad world a woman's was.

"But You designed it that way." Catching herself before she risked tumbling down the remainder of the rough-hewn steps, she gripped a sharp, wet rock and glanced up at the sky again, as if God were there instead of everywhere. But it gave her something physical to point herself toward, so she did so, even though she knew it was largely ritualistic. "You designed women to be pursued and men to be the pursuers. I wonder why that is. Would my impetuous behavior get me in trouble again? But I now have no chance with him whatsoever simply because he doesn't believe he can leave Blanche Linden."

She'd come to believe that perhaps the other alternative was that she had misread the situation. Yet whenever her fingers traced over the words of that last note, curious more than longing, she came away with that same impression: "He is scared."

She couldn't seem to find a way to tame that thought, even though she had determined that she would avoid writing to him.

How had he explained that to his siblings, though? She often wondered that. His sisters were sharp as shattered glass—they surely knew their brother far better than Cassie did, too. Did they think his behavior strange? Did they wonder about whether or not he was in his right mind? Did they sometimes think about Cassie—why he had cut off communication when they had written such sweet letters back and forth, why he probably refused to speak of her?

But these were empty fantasies. She reached the bottom of the path and scrambled over rocks to reach the brief stretch of sand that was primarily comprised of small pebbles. There, she stood, watching the water and feeling the mist that buffeted her from either side, dashing itself against the rocks around her, while here this little haven remained a simple, washy expanse of foam, and she sat, and she waited for herself to feel something from God.

For she always did these days. The first time she had come down since arriving at Auburn Hall, she had felt peace—and that had been marvelous. Another time, fear had confronted her as she faced the perilous waves—and she had fought through it with God, finding her courage in the small shoal until she had emerged, up the steps triumphant, a changed woman.

God kept changing her, over and over again. It was particularly marvelous how, every time she was sure her changing days were over, another small part of her was found to be bothered with. Then she would scratch at it, like a child picking a scab, until God found a way to heal her at last.

"Lord, give me a future. Any type of future. I'd be happy with whatever

You bring me—but please let me do something here. Please let me make an impact; let me matter."

Even if that was just the maids learning to accept her presence, Cassie could be happy with that. If she could be encouraging to them, if she could provide any kind of aid or show them anything about God through her witness, that would be worth it. But there was nothing—no one to talk to, precious few to write to, and she began to go slowly mad with nothing to do but walk and read and sometimes play the piano in that haunted library that she didn't even like reading in.

The servants ignored her. There were several horses kept there, but none for riding—not that Cassie liked riding horses much, but she might have learned again if there were a real reason for doing so.

"I believe I can be of use wherever You put me, but just show me how!" she cried at the waves. "I don't know what to do, and though I want to serve You, there's not enough for me to do here."

But Cassie knew that everyone had a purpose unto the Lord, and that must be true of her, too. It would be equally true of a bedridden invalid living by herself, unattended and slowly wasting away. If that were to be her situation, she would find something to do.

"I need a next step. Help me find that next step," she whispered.

Then she knew, as surely as she had known on Christmas Eve of last year that she was to reject the proposal of Mr. Aubrey Montgomery.

She was to hire a maid from the village.

Cassie sighed. "That's not much." But neither was she one to turn down a direct order. "Of course I'll do it, but I wish it were ... more." She always did. Perhaps she ought to be thankful that it wasn't a more difficult task, and perhaps once she completed the first step of trusting the Lord, more steps would appear.

All she could do for now was hope.

Lord, please, let that be enough. Fill me with a passion for You and allow it to eclipse my need for more. Only in You can I find contentment.

She turned and began the long and treacherous climb up the slippery rocks.

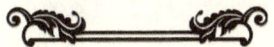

CHAPTER NINE

C ASSIE DECIDED, TO AVOID a great deal of undue disappointment amongst the people of the nearby village, to ask the housekeeper to recommend a girl who she believed would amply fulfill the duties of a lady's maid. The housekeeper had not thought twice before giving Cassie the name of Una Doyle, and now, a few days later, Cassie was waiting in her sitting room for the girl.

She appeared right on time, ushered in by the housekeeper, and stood there clutching her cap nervously. She had curly, dark hair and large eyes that might've been gray or hazel; Cassie wasn't sure due to the constant blinking and winking.

"Why don't you take a seat? Would you like tea?"

The girl bobbed a curtsy. "Oh no, milady, I won't be ... I won't be wanting that. Thank you for asking me to come here. I'm needing of the work."

Cassie nodded. "You can relax, then. I'm needing of a worker. Your name is Una Doyle?"

"Aye, milady." Her nervous shifting continued.

"Have you ever been in service?"

"No, milady. I've been at a shop in the village until it closed last year, and since, I've been workin' my dad's land. I ... I don't have much experience, but I'm a quick learner."

"That's what I'm looking for." Her mother would've sent out of the county for someone with more experience, but Cassie was not her mother. She refused to be anything like her. Besides, what did she have to do other than train a girl to be a lady's maid? With that knowledge, Una could get a job elsewhere whenever Cassie moved on, assuming she did. "You live with your parents. Are they nearby? Have they other children?"

"Aye, milady, they're near the village. It's a small farm, but it's a good place for us. I am the oldest of ten children."

Cassie's eyebrows rose, and she looked Una up and down over her teacup. "You can't be any more than eighteen years old."

Her shoulders straightened. "I am nineteen, milady."

"Excuse me. I didn't mean that as an offense." She set her cup down and folded her hands on her lap. "You simply look young to me, but we are the same age. I was surprised by such a large family with you being the eldest, but then I also believe children are a great blessing."

Her posture seemed to loosen then. "Indeed, they are, milady."

"What are their names?"

Una blinked. Cassie wasn't sure why she'd asked in the first place, beside the fact that she liked names, as it wasn't information one needed in an interview.

However, Una responded a moment later. "Ciaran and Rian are the older boys—then Maura, then Tadhg, and Kathleen, Aislinn, and Brighid—and last, Diarmaid and Flann."

Cassie nodded. "I won't remember them, though I'll try, but thank you for telling me. Five boys, then, and five girls? That's a good family."

"Aye, milady."

Cassie collected herself and asked a few more questions, then outlined what Una's duties as her lady's maid would be. Una grew confident while discussing these simple tasks, and Cassie knew she could do it. With a little training, yes, but she could do it.

Lord, what do I do? Cassie wanted to choose someone who needed help, as she wanted everything in her life to be helpful right now. After all, she had so little to do—what she did do needed to count.

She knew Una's parents must be poor—was it even possible to be at least comfortable in this world if one wasn't titled or a possessor of ancestral land? Cassie wasn't sure. A few vague but pertinent questions led her to learn that Ciaran and Rian were both working at neighboring farms to make ends meet. However, things were still bad enough that they wanted to immigrate to America.

Una and the two older boys did not expect that they would be able to go along.

"Do you want to go with them—if you could, I mean?" Cassie asked.

"I don't know." Una dropped her eyes to examine her shoes; they were not in the best of shape but they were passable. Her dress and coat must be several years old, but the family had plainly put her into something reasonable to allow her to interview for the position of lady's maid to an earl's daughter. "I suppose I want to be with my family, but I don't know how I'm going to be able to do that. You know how things are in Ireland, milady, surely." She raised her eyes to Cassie's face. "I have heard rumors that you were sympathetic. That you would not treat us as others had, though there is nothing you can do about ... about Lord and Lady Auburn. But, milady, you know that there is little for us in Ireland. Not for so many of us. My parents stayed when every one of their siblings have already left or died, and their parents before them stayed when every last family member of theirs had left or died. It is better, aye, than it was then, but I can't believe there's anythin' left here anymore. What sort of future will we have? Even if we were to go to Dublin or some other town, it would still not be what we are promised if we go to America. That is, if anyone's telling anyone the truth about anythin'." She flushed and looked about ready to melt into the floor at that, but she didn't begin apologizing excessively, which Cassie appreciated.

Cassie deserved apologies from no one, and yet she never had the courage to gently say, "Please do not apologize to me, for I am just another person."

She wasn't even sure how she knew she was just another person. She oughtn't to. She ought to believe she were special like some of her peers did. However, a combination of Alice's strong opinions and the constant prejudice against Cassie in England—due largely to her parents' lack of support and the fact that she was often judged before she could introduce herself—had led to the conclusion that she was just another girl.

With her parents' withdrawn support, she was now simply a well-taken-care-of prisoner. She was provided for, but she knew there would no longer be any type of support. She was rather uncertain at present if she would even have a dowry should she ever decide to marry. Based on the way her mother was behaving, it seemed unlikely. The money would probably be spent on something else, and it was no small sum at that.

"You're right, Una. Of course you're right." And she was even more right about a small village like this one being more impoverished than most. "Perhaps some of them might do well in Dublin or another town, but going to America may be the right choice. Though, of course, they will have to know that it won't be easy there. I've heard there is prejudice. The opportunities spoken of are hard to come by. You will be poor, and you will have no land, and you will all have to work."

"Yes." Una wrapped her arms around herself. "But, milady, my children may not have to. Not in the same way."

Cassie shuddered. Something about that quiet confession caused tingles to race up and down her spine. "When are your parents hoping to leave, then?"

"They need to save up more money," Una replied. "I think they will have enough in a few more years. It's best to wait a bit, I suppose. Flann is only a wee boy, and they'd like to see him stronger."

"Is he weak now?"

"Aye, and he has a dreadful cough for a babe. The rest of us are strong and sturdy, but Flann isn't quite like us. He was born too early."

Right. Cassie had learned that people could survive in situations that shocked her, but the children who might have thrived in a rich household could not in a poor one. Good food, plenty of rest, and a life of leisure made all the difference. It couldn't be helped, but it was easier to die when one's world wasn't perfect.

"I see." Cassie fidgeted with her hands on her lap for a moment but soon arrived at a decision. "Una, I will hire you. Perhaps your wages will help your family go to America sooner rather than later. I want you to be able to go with them, and your brothers, but I'm not sure how I can help with that yet. We'll have to see what happens."

"Thank you, milady." Una seemed almost afraid to commit to a further reaction, but her eyes glowed, and Cassie knew she had made the right decision.

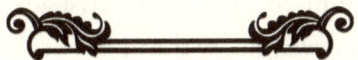

April 1882
Adelboden, Switzerland

"You know you're doing the wrong thing." Lore's arched eyebrows and pinched lips would have betrayed her thoughts on the situation even if her words hadn't dripped with her skepticism of her older brother's choices.

Patrick didn't blame her. He'd not shared the contents of his letter to Lady Mary, and he'd only summarized her last letter to them, and both his sisters were furious. Still, he said nothing. He simply took a sip of his piping hot chocolate, rich as it only was in this area, and allowed his eyes to look out the windowpanes to the snow-capped peaks. Hotel *Hari im Schlegeli* was still somewhat undiscovered and privately-run, and Patrick had chosen it as their destination for their two-week foray into Switzerland for those reasons.

It wouldn't be long until this haven was more popular, though, of course. Everything was always ruined by people.

Winnie gave him a similarly furious glare. "Think how abandoned Lady Mary must feel! She's alone, Trick, for all we know. What if something happens? What if her parents lock her up in their castle and she meets with a terrible fate?"

Patrick rolled his eyes. "That sort of thing only happens in those dime novels you read. In real life, things are much more complicated. She'll be fine."

"You don't know that! If you were really her ... her *friend*, you wouldn't have told her not to write to us." Winnie had caught herself, which was an improvement. Usually they associated Cassie more intimately with him, which only confirmed to Patrick that he was making the right decision in cutting her off.

He had to distance himself from the lovely Lady Mary, especially in his thoughts, or he would never follow through with his duty.

His duty was vital to him. For his sisters' sake, he needed to marry Blanche Linden. The thought filled him with dread, but he had to push through. *For his sisters' sake.* Because he loved them more than he needed to chase his own happiness.

Happiness was a lie sold by the world to distract him from what he truly needed to do.

"*Engstligen* Falls." He swallowed the last gulp of his hot chocolate; it burned on the way down, but he coughed his way through it. "We're going to *Engstligen* Falls today. It's a bit of a trek—almost twelve miles—but you said you wanted an adventure."

Lore raised her eyebrows over her toast. She was ever typical in her eating habits, regardless of where they visited. "Oh, is *Engstligen* Falls a good place to go to forget that you have human feelings?"

"I've heard it is!" Winnie exclaimed. "You can go there and toss your genuine, solid-gold heart into the waters, and it drifts all the way down to the Mediterranean."

"I'm not quite sure *Engstligen* Falls runs into the Mediterranean," Patrick mumbled by way of response. He wasn't going to address their comments. Not this time. He was the adult here. He didn't have to explain his actions to them, despite the fact that he'd tried. Multiple times.

Their fury had not cooled with every conversation on the subject. If anything, his lackluster excuses had angered them further.

"Trick has a point," Lore continued. "Would solid gold drift? I don't think so."

Winnie tapped her chin in fake consideration. "No, but I'm fairly certain Trick has a flesh-and-blood heart in him somewhere. It just happens to be gilded over with fool's gold at the moment. Does flesh and blood float, Lore? Could it float all the way to Ireland?"

"Hmm." Lore pursed her lips. "I've heard human bodies float, so I imagine—"

"That's quite enough." Patrick stood. "I'll wait for you outside."

He hastily quitted their little parlor. The sarcastic comments followed him all the way to his private bedroom. There, he added layers to his outfit and swiftly made his way out of their chambers and out the front door.

The chalet was a new build, with snow still dripping off its eaves, and Patrick stood in front of it, breathing slightly heavily and trying to ignore the inevitable truth.

He could tame his heart. He could. He'd spend the next year until their return to America taming his heart, and by the time he returned to Blanche, he'd be at least resigned to the fact of her. He hoped for more, of course. He hoped that he could establish a caring partnership with Blanche, where they could work together to build their place in society.

He knew his sisters would be a while, and there was water nearby. Granted, it was a peaceful river, but he was determined to reach it. The fact that it meant cutting straight down a hill on damp, green grass and through small trees bothered him little.

So he hurried—almost stumbling once or twice but grateful for the concentration of keeping on his feet—down the hillside. At last, he reached the edge of the rocky stream that flowed so calmly here. Farther up in the mountains, it must cascade and churn, but here it rested.

Patrick sat down on a large rock and attempted to pray.

He used to pray daily by routine, and hourly, by habit. He used to feel close to God, to seek His guidance in his day-to-day life. Why did God feel so distant? Why were all the experiences he had come to expect suddenly gone? That peace, that feeling of comfort?

He placed his mittened hands on the hard, rough surface of the rock and bent his head, but he didn't know what to say to God. Because even if it were simply his heart betraying him in the worst possible way, he didn't like that he'd had to make the decisions he had made.

He regretted them deeply.

But even the act of apologizing and allowing himself that small comfort which generally led to moving on wasn't a possibility. He couldn't write to her again. He feared what would happen if he did.

Further, it wasn't fair to Cassie—Lady Mary, he meant.

She deserved so much more than a brief conversation with a man who was soon to be betrothed to another. It would go beyond the bounds of honor and common sense to subject her to his words again, even if they kept everything aboveboard.

At this point, feeling as he did, there was no keeping things "aboveboard." Every action he made in regard to her would lead to dishonor.

So his decision must remain final.

"Lord, why does it hurt so much?" he whispered. "Why does everything have to hurt so much? I thought I was a simple man, more than content with my overly generous lot. I am blessed with a steady job that I enjoy, unlimited resources, and two sisters whom I have the joyful duty of protecting. That should be enough. The other details shouldn't matter so much."

He believed in joy rather than happiness, truly. However, joy was always such an impossible concept to grasp. It flitted between his fingers in a way that joy wasn't supposed to.

Wasn't joy supposed to be the thing that lingered? The thing that transcended human reason and found its way into the hearts of Christian men and women?

"There must be something wrong with me," he concluded. Though that was the condition of all humanity, wasn't it?

He knew there was a point at which head knowledge was supposed to fail and the Holy Spirit to step in. However, did the average person reach those breaking points so easily? For Patrick was certain, despite words spoken amongst his few friends who professed an open Christian faith, that only broken souls truly needed to experience an emotional connection to such things.

After all, wasn't God a Creator Who valued logic and order?

Wasn't that all Patrick was trying to grasp? The logical next step in his life?

"It's all about Winnie and Lore," he reminded God, feeling somewhat defensive now. But he shouldn't have to defend such statements. God should know that it was all about his sisters. "It's about protecting them. Giving them a better future than my own. And again, my own future is charmed. I have no reason to reject the blessings I have been given."

Yet the weight of his parents' expectations, the way they treated his sisters and him, and even the spiritual influence they wielded frightened him.

Was he wrong to feel this unease? As if he needed to do something, anything?

"It is only restlessness and discontent." He jerked to his feet and started the climb back to the hotel with these words.

Perhaps the hike today would clear his mind. If nothing else, it might make him too tired to think, which was to be desired these days.

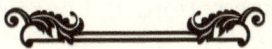

CHAPTER TEN

May 1882
County Kerry, Ireland

CASSIE CLOSED HER BIBLE and met Una's eyes in the mirror. "You don't mind me reading aloud and mumbling my thoughts under my breath, do you? It helps me think it through, and I sometimes do struggle to think it through."

"No, I don't mind, milady." Una laid Cassie's hairbrush on the vanity next to her and smiled into her reflection. "Though I hope you don't think you're going to convert me using the same Book we both read on the daily."

Cassie couldn't help but chuckle. "No, I don't. I've known Irishmen and -women far too well to hope to do that, though I sometimes believe that that would be best for them, in my own prejudice. But then, I don't know much about Catholicism."

"Would you like that I should teach you?"

"Would you like that I should teach you what we believe in the Church of England?"

"No."

"That's my answer as well. I don't have any real need to learn it as I will not personally do anything against it—you know this, don't you?"

Una nodded. "Do you believe I will go to hell for being a Catholic?"

Cassie frowned. "Did someone tell you that was the case?"

"Oh, aye, many a time. Some of the servants here are Protestant, you know. They don't believe that Catholics are really Christians. There's all sorts of talk about our superstitions and our being worshippers of idols. You know it's as much because we're Irish as anything, though."

Cassie nodded. Her experience with Catholicism came largely from her Irish nanny when she'd been tiny, and she'd learned that, though she would never give up being Church of England, she could not hate Catholics, nor could she dismiss their claims to salvation uniformly. She found their beliefs confusing and counterintuitive to what she believed, to the point where many elements of the religion seemed unbiblical or at least extra-biblical. However, she was sure that was true of other denominations, too. She just wasn't aware of it as much since she hadn't known anything except Catholics and Anglicans all her life.

Peter, of course, had told her he was "something like a Baptist but not really," and she supposed she had met other Americans, too, and people in her travels through Europe. But she'd never really asked them a lot about their denomination.

She wondered if Patrick was a part of any particular sect, and how it compared to what she personally believed, and if she ought to be as skeptical of him as he probably would be of her Anglican upbringing. He was American, after all, and though there were people in America with similar views, they all disliked the English, didn't they? Or was that old information, dating back many years? Cassie wasn't sure.

"Will that be all for today, milady?" Una stepped back and admired her finished work, which truly wasn't that impressive, but Cassie was willing to give her any amount of credit. Cassie had been painstakingly teaching Una to do her hair, and though it was slow learning—for both of them—they were finally at a place where a simple twist at the back of Cassie's neck didn't make Una's hands shake.

That was something to be celebrated if anything was. Further, it meant she was able to take the next step she'd been longing to since she started working with Una.

Meeting her maid's eyes in the mirror, she asked, "How would you feel about taking me to meet your family today?"

She blinked. "What do you mean, milady?"

"I'd like to meet them, of course." What else could she possibly mean? "You talk about them so much, and they sound lovely." Also, they sounded like people who desperately needed help and who, because Cassie desperately needed people in her life, might be able to be friends.

But she didn't say any of that to Una. She didn't admit her own desire for friendship, for more people in her life, and for, of course, some way to serve God. She didn't believe it would convince Una to let her go, and at any rate, these last several months, Cassie had run into problem after problem while trying to make herself useful.

A lot of it was due to prayer. God kept telling her no in response to all her best ideas, and she could not ignore God. Even if God were silent and Cassie moved forward, there usually ended up being something that stopped her from being of any earthly use to anyone.

What was God waiting for? She was here. She was willing. She was bored out of her mind. Why didn't He use her?

Yet she would not stop looking for opportunities. There must be some fashion in which God could work through someone like Cassie. It just had to be discovered. She would not fall into passivity; she would not allow this time of isolation to drive her mad. She would find a use right where she was, come what may.

"I suppose so, milady. But you know ... we are not grand. And we have nothing to give a guest."

"Do you think your parents could understand that I simply want to meet them, without receiving anything? Or would it only worry them to have me come?" That was the sort of concern Cassie often dealt with. She wanted to help, but there were so many expectations about her class, and more than that, a kind of dislike or at least awkwardness around her existence. She didn't want to make anyone's life worse if the only thing she had to do was distance herself from them.

Sad as that was.

"No, I could make them understand." Una cocked her head. "Only, milady, why would you want to go? Forgive my impertinence, but we are just normal people, and we live on a normal farm, in a normal cottage. It's nothing compared to what you have here."

Cassie met Una's eyes in the mirror. "That is exactly why I want to go."

An hour later, they were walking along a country lane, nearing a run-down cottage surrounded by a scattering of children and chickens, in about the same quantity. In the distance, she heard voices raised in singing, and she glanced at Una.

"My family," she explained in a low voice, "working in the fields. Likely preparing them for another planting."

Cassie and Una soon were noticed by the children, four of them with ruddy cheeks and wind-tossed hair and bare feet. They ran to meet Una, shouting her name, but stopped, immediately becoming subdued and unsure, when they saw Cassie.

"It's all right," Una called. "This is the lady I work for, but she's kind."

The children then ran up. There were two girls, a boy, and a baby that must be little Flann. The oldest girl, looking to be about eight, had the baby of a year or younger on her hip, and the younger girl and boy were perhaps six and four.

"This is Aislinn." Una pointed to the older girl. "An' Brighid, Diarmaid, and of course, Flann." She reached over to tap the smaller boy's head, complete with a small section of dark curls, like all his siblings.

"It's nice to meet you lot." That was all Cassie could manage, for, once more, she was overwhelmed by a feeling that something was impending.

Impending purpose? Impending rejection? She wasn't sure—only that she was trying her best to pray about it.

"The older three who are still at home work in the field with Mam and Dad, and Aislinn tends Flann while Mam can't—he shouldn't be out in the cold all day long." Una squinted at her younger sister. "So what are you all doin' out in the cold, then? You should be inside."

"It's a lovely day." Aislinn adjusted the baby in her arms defensively. "It won't hurt him. Mam says a bit of sunshine can be good for a babe."

"Perhaps." Yet Una looked skeptical. "Let me have him and run to the fields. Fetch Mam in, but tell her that it's all right—that I have brought a lady to meet her, but she shouldn't fuss or the lady will be disappointed. She doesn't want to cause any fussing."

"Exactly." Cassie forced a smile past her trembling lips. "I don't want to be any trouble at all."

"You're not trouble. Not yet." Una took Flann from Aislinn's arms, and the girl took off, her skinny legs flying as she circled around the cottage.

Five minutes later, a woman, a man, a girl in her early womanhood, and a boy of perhaps twelve arrived. The family resemblance was obvious, and Cassie hurried forward to greet them.

There was a hint of reluctance in their reception of her, but they were friendlier than some in the village had been, giving Cassie hope.

After a few stilted pleasantries, Cassie blurted out the only words that came to mind, as she had suddenly begun to do in these last few months, like the fool she was these days. "Can I … can I help you with whatever you're doing today? Would you teach me?"

Immediately, she scolded herself. Of course she couldn't help. She was a weak woman with delicate hands and a dress worth a year's rent to this family. She would only get in the way doing manual labor. What earthly good could she do other than to cause problems and make the family uneasy in the process?

She was nothing but a disgrace.

Yet as these thoughts arose, she snuffed them out with all the vehemence she could manage and allowed the Doyles the simple courtesy that they were due—to respond to her query.

"Oh, milady, you wouldn't want to be doing that!" Mrs. Doyle was the first to speak. Mr. Doyle still seemed shocked by her presence—all he did was rub his dirty hands against his dirty trousers and grip them into fists as if he didn't know what to do with them. "We're planting, and it's hard work. Nothing like you're used to. Oh, we're happy to have you here, and happy for the work you've given our Una, but you ... you shouldn't work in the fields. You're a lady."

"But I'm a lady sent home in disgrace by her parents. If I'm too good for honest work, what am I supposed to do? I've just been sitting in a castle since Christmastime, almost alone, and though I have a good life, a charmed life, it's a very empty and lonely one." She glanced around at the circle of faces and saw a mix of surprise and sympathy, but the words kept pouring out of her. "I could use friendship, really. That's why I hired Una—not that she's not wonderful and capable, but I don't precisely need a maid so much as a companion. And when she told me about her big, lovely family, I knew I had to meet you. Now I am here, and I see you all, and I think, as anyone ought to, 'What a fine family! If only I could count myself amongst them.' I have all I need in this world—but people."

"But a church, milady." Mrs. Doyle stepped forward. She now had Flann on her hip, his head against the safety of her shoulder and her hand steadily patting his back. "Christian friends. You lack that."

"She's not Catholic, Mam," Maura, the next girl younger than Una, protested. "Una told us that."

"Hush, Maura. I won't turn her away for that." Mrs. Doyle smiled. "Not these days. After all, I knew her grandmother."

"You did?" Cassie had known that her Irish grandmother, her father's mother, had lived not far from this village and had maintained some friendships with the people who lived there. However, she'd died when Cassie was a baby, and the only stories she'd heard had been colored by her mother's dislike and her father's grief.

"Aye." Mrs. Doyle switched Flann to her other side and pressed a kiss to his chubby neck. "She was a lovely woman, and no mistakin' it. We all liked her. I was a girl, but I remember her kindness. She was an Irishwoman amongst the English aristocracy. Aye, your grandfather had an Irish surname and Irish land, but he wasn't Irish—not like your grandmother. And they both knew it, both knew the cost of their love. A price your father didn't pay. A price your mother never made her pretty, brunette daughter or her heir of a son pay. But we all know in the village, milady, that you have been punished for that love. There is always a sacrifice, isn't there? Like Christ's on the cross, a cost of love. We all know that, Catholic and Protestant, don't we?"

Cassie swiped a hand over her tear-filled eyes. "Yes. We all know that."

"Never you mind it. For now, you may come up to the field—and we will see what you can do." She turned to her husband. "If that's all right, though I feel there's no reason she shouldn't come along if she wants to."

He glanced at his wife, then turned his eyes to Cassie with a soft smile. "Oh, aye, that's all right. Have her come."

The baby was passed back to Aislinn, and the rest of the party began their way behind the house to a desolate field plowed into rows. Cassie was set the task of seeding, the only difficulty being that she needed a great deal of instruction that she knew was taking away from their workday. But Mrs. Doyle was kind, and once Cassie got the hang of dropping seeds at correct increments, the mother stayed to watch Cassie for a bit and chattered about her two oldest sons, who were working in the village, and how her children were getting on and even, dreamily, their wish to travel to America.

Cassie listened, hands dirty and heart feeling lighter than it had in months.

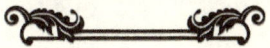

CHAPTER ELEVEN

Six Months Later

October 1882

I vy Knight was marrying a man from Scotland, and from Mrs. Knight's letter, the Knights were shocked and delighted. Cassie was pleased for Ivy but, more than that, thrilled by the excuse that even her parents could not deny.

Cassie would be returning to Pearlbelle Park.

There was more to it than that. She'd read and reread the letter from Mrs. Knight, and every time, a little more of her heart broke.

For Alice and Peter had lost their first child, and though they would be traveling to Pearlbelle Park for Ivy's wedding, it was clear from the lack of correspondence, a similar trait across all Alice's relationships, that Alice had not handled it well.

Those were the gentle words Mrs. Knight had used: "Alice has not handled it well." She followed those by, "Peter sounds devastated, too."

Crushed hopes and dreams could not be easy on either of them. The long months of waiting for a child, only to lose him—for it had been a darling, little boy—at birth was devastating.

Cassie still grew tearful whenever she read the letter. Mrs. Knight sounded a little broken, too. Cassie had an idea they all were.

She found herself whispering, "God, why?"

Una said it was simply one of those things. That it happened to everyone. Cassie knew that, but she had not believed it would happen to Alice.

With only a few days before she was due to leave for the wedding, she received an urgent note that the date had been canceled.

A few days later, a letter arrived, again from Mrs. Knight.

> *Dear Cassie,*
>
> *You doubtless received notification that Ivy's wedding has been postponed. We are not yet sure when it will happen. Due to the nature of the cancellation, of which I will inform you, it is impossible to set a date.*
>
> *Alice tried to take her own life. From what we understand, she has been facing deep melancholia after the loss of her son. A few days ago, she reached a breaking point. I cannot explain all the details, as such may break her trust. However, since this event, she has not been herself, as is to be expected. We wait for her to come back to us to set a date for Ivy's wedding.*
>
> *Cassie, our hearts are broken for her, but we trust that God is greater than this. Please pray for Alice, and for Peter, and for all of us as we try to discover how to best love and support her.*
>
> *We know God can and will reach her, but there is certainly a lot of uncertainty. We want to believe she will recover completely. I hope God will reach her and assure her of His never-ending love and strength. If that doesn't happen—if we never get our Alice back, if we cannot convince her of how valued she is by us—I'm not sure what the next step is.*
>
> *More than anything, I cannot believe I did not see this coming. Most of us can't. Please add Nettie to your prayers, as well, for her guilt is great.*
>
> *We hope you will come whenever we are able to have the wedding, and we hope that Alice will be glad to see you whenever that time comes.*
>
> *Sincerely,*
> *Claire Knight*

The letter was set on the bed next to Cassie, and wordless prayers were uttered.

December 1882
Pearlbelle Park
Kent, England

It was a very different Pearlbelle Park that Cassie entered in December of 1882 than the one she had visited in June of 1881. Oh, it still felt like Pearlbelle Park—and most of the same people were present within its halls. But the atmosphere was entirely different.

Perhaps others didn't feel it, people who weren't as connected to the family as Cassie was. They didn't see the reasoning behind Ivy's delayed wedding.

Cassie might have been forced to live in a world without Alice.

Worse yet, she had not been allowed to come see Alice until now. Her parents had told her to travel for the wedding and only for the wedding, and hearing of Cassie's eagerness to leave immediately had only strengthened her mother's resolve.

She wanted Cassie to make a good appearance, but she didn't much care if she had the friendship of the Knights. Only that she was at the wedding, where she could be seen. The simple act of being near a suffering friend was not something her mother could or would prioritize.

So Cassie spoke briefly with the butler in the front hall, his eyes darkening, bushy eyebrows furrowing as she mentioned Alice's name. She learned that Alice was with Nettie, which was not something Cassie was going to interrupt, and Ivy and the rest of the family were in the midst of more wedding preparations.

But Peter was in the library.

Cassie asked the butler to send tea in and made her way to her favorite room in the house.

Peter had a book and coffee and looked comfortable on his own. Which made it a shame that Cassie had to interrupt him, but if she had any opportunity to learn what the situation currently was with Alice and how to help her now, she would take it.

"Peter?" Embarrassed, she stood in the doorway, shifting from foot to foot. "May I speak with you for a time? I'm sorry to interrupt."

He looked up, and a smile spread across his face. He gestured to the chair opposite from him and set his book down. "Of course. Alice is just at Nettie's cottage but should be back soon. She'll be disappointed she wasn't here to greet you."

"Oh, I know. I keep my own timeline these days." More so than she had last year. Independence was good for her but also led to her doing things strangely, which in some ways was a good thing and in others, frightening.

"That's perfectly all right. Do you want to ring for something to drink or eat? I know you must've traveled all day."

She crossed the room and took the seat he had gestured to. "Oh, I already spoke to someone about it." As she said these words, a footman entered with a tray, and she poured her own tea while Peter sipped his coffee and stared at the glowing coals in the grate.

"I suppose you want to know what happened." He took a rather over-large gulp of his coffee and was silent while he swallowed it. She could feel how nervous he was.

"Yes, I do. But only if you want to tell me. Frankly, I'm only sorry I couldn't be here sooner. I ought to have been, but I was not allowed to leave except for the wedding, which of course was postponed. My parents will be here, too." Much as she dreaded their arrival. "But I managed to slip away from London early. I wanted to speak with you, and Alice, and understand fully how I might best help." She knew all she could offer was a listening ear and a few words of encouragement, but she prayed that that would be enough.

Though in such a situation, how could anything truly be enough?

Alice and Peter had touched a depth of grief that Cassie was unfamiliar with. Oh, every life had struggles and moments of sadness, but save for a few difficulties here and there, Cassie had little to complain about. Granted, her life in the last year had been difficult, but not impossible.

"Your support and your prayers are appreciated." His fingers tapped the edge of his coffee cup restlessly, and at last he set it down with a *clink* on the table beside his chair. "There was little I could do myself, so I never know quite what to do when we're offered aid. There's nothing that can be done. So many things have already happened. Now we simply wait on the Lord for healing in His own time."

"Of course." Cassie knew this was true, and she further understood the feeling of helplessness. Oh, not helplessness this great, but certainly she'd felt helpless in some of the darkest nights of the last year, and now ... now she didn't know how to help Alice at all. "Do you need to talk about it? I can listen, if nothing else."

"Perhaps not with you. Not that I don't trust your ability to listen, but it's raw, and I seem to lose a little more of myself every time I speak about it." He offered a tight smile this time, one that she didn't really associate with Peter. His words were unusual for him, too. "I hope you don't mind. I just need to be careful about who I talk to and what I say, and for now, that involves avoiding any weakening. It won't last, of course—and I know it's not healthy. But I have cause to believe that it would behoove me to get through the next week before letting myself be melancholy again. I can avoid the thought if I need to."

Understandable. Yet, again, unlike Peter. "And Alice?"

He nodded. "She'll talk. She's finally found her tongue, and it's good for her to have someone to speak to. Honestly, I want her to keep talking, even if it's a struggle for me."

"Right."

"Not to say I haven't discussed said events with Alice, but ..."

"Of course. Of course. Peter, you don't have to explain anything to me. I'm sorry, and I won't ask you to be anything but what you are. How is

Alice handling … She must have a great deal to think through, and now she has to be present at Ivy's wedding, too."

"Of course. I'm not entirely sure how tomorrow will go, but she has seemed to be happy for Ivy. I don't know what I wrote you, or what Claire wrote you, but you might've heard she was … somewhat unpleasant to Ivy. She seems sorry for that, though she also has acted as if the memories are hazy."

"Perhaps they are."

"Perhaps. Perhaps they are not worth addressing yet, even if they aren't." Again, his lips attempted to lift in a smile, but they failed, pressing in a grim line instead. "I don't really know what to do, honestly. We've made some progress, and I feel as if we have a future. But … there's so much that we need to sort through. I'm not sure how we'll … We must." He sighed and glanced toward the fire again; she saw his hand shake as he moved it from his lap to the arm of the chair.

This was so hard. Even from the outside, Cassie could see the struggle in Peter, and she could only imagine what Alice was going through.

"I only wish I could …" She stopped herself, for the helplessness was something that must affect Peter, too. And to a greater degree, for Alice was not a woman who shared her inner thoughts easily, and more than that, she was not a woman who desired aid.

Yet she needed help somehow. And how ill-equipped were the people in her life to give that to her? What did one do? Every novel featuring such misfortunes was too easily resolved to allow a real understanding of how one reached healing—or it was a tragedy. Cassie wasn't willing for Alice's life story to be a tragedy. Filled with tragedies, yes. But not in and of itself Shakespearean.

"Should I speak with Alice? Do you … do you think I should give her space or …?"

"No. Don't do that. Keep trying." Here, a bit of a smile did manage to break through, though he didn't turn to her. "We should always, always keep trying. Anyway, something has changed in her—she listens to reason. She's apologized to … to people she's hurt. I see the change in her—I do.

But it's so hard sometimes when I'm still reeling a bit from ... everything. *Everything.*"

Cassie nodded sympathetically. It must feel like there was no part of their life or world that remained untouched by tragedy and fear. Peter couldn't be blamed for needing time to think that through, for needing to only share that empty, broken space within him with certain people. And Cassie didn't mind that one bit.

But she would talk to Alice. Even if she could never quite understand, she would talk—for Cassie could never see herself abandoning her friend, even if the road to being her friend was a long and rocky one.

CHAPTER TWELVE

Alice went straight to her room when she came back, and after giving her what Cassie considered to be sufficient time to settle, she made her way to the family quarters and stood, body stiff and fearful, waiting to grow the courage to make this first vital move.

But she must. For Alice. Perhaps for herself, too, for she could not abandon Alice, even if she did not know what she could do. She would stand by her friend even if there was nothing she could do but stand there and feel awkward and wonder why someone like Alice must suffer.

At last, she raised her hand and knocked.

A long pause.

"Who is it?" Alice's voice was softer than Cassie remembered, and tired, but it wasn't as heartbroken as she had been anticipating.

Though perhaps it was ridiculous for Cassie to expect Alice to be heartbroken all the time. She supposed she wasn't sure what she had expected. All she knew of deep grief came from novels, and in novels, heroines pouted and lounged on sofas and wept uncontrollably.

That didn't feel like Alice. What would she be like?

"It's me. Cassie. I ... Did anyone tell you I was here?"

Before she could get more words out, the door flew open and Alice embraced her.

Cassie dropped her head onto Alice's shoulder and shuddered, relief pouring through her. She had been received, and affectionately, and perhaps that was enough. It ought to be enough for anyone.

"Oh, Alice, I'm ... I don't know what to say. Does anyone know what to say? Did they write it down? Can I read it before I speak to you?"

Alice drew back, and though her eyes were glistening, she smiled and shook her head. "No one knows what to say, and if they did, they wouldn't write it down, but I don't begrudge anyone any reaction. Not anymore. It's enough that you're here."

"I'm glad to hear that."

They stepped into the room, and Alice gestured toward a chair. "Sit. We'll talk."

"Only as much as you want to. You don't have to ... If it's painful, I mean, you don't have to talk. I'll understand."

Alice sat on the edge of the bed and folded her hands on her lap. "I can talk. I don't know why, but I can. I shouldn't be able to, I don't think, but it seems as if the words are suddenly pouring out of me. All my fears, all my insecurities. At least, with the people I'm closest to."

Cassie nodded. She could understand that—once the dam broke, it was hard to tame the flood of woods.

"You know what happened, I presume?"

"Some of it."

"We lost two children."

"Oh. I only had heard ..."

"Of one, I know. The first was a miscarriage, and it was early on." She swallowed, and her eyes went down to her hands. "The second was our son, which you have doubtless heard about. It was ..." Her voice caught. "It was too late. He wouldn't breathe. He wasn't going to ever, I suppose. Peter keeps telling me, over and over again, that there was nothing we could've done, but I so badly wanted him to live that sometimes it's easy to blame myself. To say I wasn't strong enough."

"But you know that's not true."

Alice's lips were pressed in a grim line. "I know a lot of things are not true. My head seems to have accepted them, but a lot of the lies are ingrained. I know the miscarriage wasn't my fault either. Yet sometimes, when it's dark and quiet, I don't know how to push the lies away."

Cassie nodded. "Of course, in my cool and collected way, distanced from the whole thing save through empathy and love for you, I can say that the way to challenge that is with Scripture—with God's Word—and with prayer. However, it's never easy in the moment."

"No, it's not." Alice sighed, and her eyes, distant but not as soul-tortured as Cassie had feared, fixed on a point over Cassie's shoulder. "Peter has been marvelous through all this. He was the one who dragged me back into life—the one who forced me to live when I didn't want to. That was two months ago now. Nettie has also helped—oh, and everyone has been so kind. Ivy is a dear. She has every right to be frustrated with me for forcing her to cancel her wedding, days before, and reschedule it to now."

"When it's a life-or-death situation ..."

Alice inclined her head. "True. Yet I can't help but still feel grateful that she had the sweet kindness to think of no one but me when I hardly deserved it. When I don't believe I would've given her the same regard."

Cassie smiled. "Ivy is a good woman."

"Yes, she is." Alice unclasped her hands and placed them on either side of her, regarding Cassie with the ghost of a smile. "Where have you been?"

"Ireland," Cassie supplied. "I think I mentioned in a letter or two that once I refused to marry Mr. Aubrey Montgomery, my parents banished me. You might not remember the letter clearly, though. It would've reached you in January, and I understand ...?"

Alice pressed her lips together. "I was not well then, but I thought I was. I remember the letter vaguely, now that you mention it. But I don't remember all your letters. I think you said you had hired an Irish maid and gotten to know her family and ... and that you were rather bored."

"Yes. I was."

"Have your parents released you from exile, then?"

"No." It was unlikely that they ever would, though perhaps Cassie's mother would eventually forget why she was angry. "I'll return to Ireland after the wedding. There's no escaping, I'm afraid. But it's such a small thing compared to ... Compared to anything," she finished. "My lot is a blessed one. I know that now."

Alice sat in silence for a moment, seeming to mull this over in a very un-Alice-like way, then she spoke. "I wish I could rescue you, per se, and take you to America with me. I could use the help. All I can think of, whenever my mind wanders back to Cincinnati and our home there, is 'How will I face that empty nursery?' I could use someone to steady me, and Peter needs as much steadying as I do. I could use a friend. Someone like you. I love Peter's family, but we are not near them, and that is also very difficult. You would be even better—don't tell my mother-in-law I said that. Oh, but that's nonsense."

Of course it was, for Cassie could never abandon everything in England and Ireland and follow Alice to America, much as she wanted to help her friend in every way possible.

Yet as Alice and she talked—about Alice's lost babies mostly, for Cassie found that with a bit of prodding, Alice could talk for hours about the boys she'd never met, as if she knew them intimately despite having never held them alive—Cassie began to think.

And a prayer began to whisper through her soul: *Lord, what if?*

Alice's words got her crying, and then Cassie cried out of sympathy and moved to embrace her friend, and even as all her attention was taken with Alice, an undercurrent crept in, pulling at her.

Lord, where do You want me? Is this what I was waiting for? Where do You want me?

In time, she left Alice to rest and went to her own room. She washed her face and sat in front of the vanity with her Bible open, but she didn't read it. She just prayed.

The next morning was the day before Ivy's wedding, and if there had been a hustle yesterday, there was even more of one today.

Because Alice and Peter both naturally gave the festivities a bit of distance, while still offering their general observation and blessing, Cassie felt obligated to do the same.

Late in the afternoon, she let Alice be again, as her friend was suddenly the type to take frequent naps when before, she'd despised any kind of afternoon rest. As always, when left to her own devices at Pearlbelle Park, Cassie wandered down to the library.

Peter found her there not an hour later and took the same seat he had earlier, across from her. Only this time, instead of exhausted and careworn, he looked thoughtful.

"Alice said something today that made me think, and I'm not sure how you truly feel about it, so feel free to say no. But she mentioned to me a desire to have you come home with us, to Cincinnati, when we go. She wants you near her, and after discussing it … After discussing it, I felt that it seemed like a logical solution to one of my main problems. Which is that I cannot leave Alice alone, but I also have to start working again if I hope to feed and clothe her. And … I wanted to ask, how do you feel about that?"

A slow smile had begun to spread across Cassie's lips as Peter spoke, and when he finished, she tried to tame it but was moderately unsuccessful. "I've been praying about that idea. I … I want to help, Peter. Yet what help could I really be?"

"She needs a friend more than anything, but I know it's more than a simple inconvenience for a friend. It's … it's life-changing. It would be a long-term trip. You would have to leave everything you know, cross an ocean, and live in an unfamiliar land as a foreigner for at least several months. We could get you there and back, likely, especially if Alice's parents would be willing to help. However, you won't be living in a situation comparable to what you're used to. More than that, Alice mentioned your parents may not be in favor of it."

Cassie bit her lip. "That is a consideration. As for the inconvenience, don't mention it. I have nothing here."

Peter nodded. "You could stay with my cousin while you're in Cincinnati. He and his wife have an extra room and enjoy hosting people. They have two little girls, so it may not be a quiet household."

"But I am so tired of the quiet!" Cassie exclaimed. "Sick and tired of it."

The first real smile she'd seen since she arrived broke across Peter's face. "You make it sound almost too easy."

"It would be easy for me! Oh, I'd need to seek God further, but, Peter, I've been waiting for something to do. For an opportunity. For a way to be useful." Her soul bubbled up in joy then, and though she felt that was not an appropriate emotion to bring before Peter just then, it was also the type of feeling that ought to be appropriate anywhere.

"But it won't be easy work," Peter protested. "I should warn you of that. You've seen, probably, how broken Alice is. How broken we both are. Any time spent with either of us, especially in somewhat-close quarters, will be exhausting. You will need to make sure you take days off, for it is almost a job, and some types of jobs require moments alone. The emotional ones anyway. I think pastors are the most in need of a sabbatical, and though you would not be a pastor, that is the same sort of heart-related work that makes one need respite."

"I will take it when I need it." Yet surely God would give her the strength for whatever He wanted her to undertake. "But don't worry, Peter. I won't go into this foolishly. I will pray, and I will thoroughly consider what you've said."

"But you are amiable to the idea?" he asked.

"More than amiable. I am willing. I am ready! I have done nothing but sit alone with God and my thoughts for the last year. I want something to do, something useful and good that will exhaust me a little, and in the meantime, fill my soul with contentment, for every creature on this earth needs a job or else they risk boredom."

Peter cocked his head. "I think we all do, in our own way. I'll tell Alice what you've said, and we shall move forward slowly. I suppose we ought to concentrate on Ivy's wedding first, but once that is over, we'll make plans, if God seems to be willing."

After that, he left her, and Cassie once again found that the time she'd set aside for reading was consumed by prayers.

She was beginning to mind that less and less as time went on.

A few days later, plans were all but finalized for Cassie's trip to America. She had felt nothing but confirmation in her soul, and Peter and Alice felt much the same.

The only problem that occurred to her was that of the Doyles. She didn't want to abandon Una in Ireland again, nor could she realistically rip her away from her family. Further, Cassie wasn't sure if her mother would agree to continue paying the girl's wages.

It seemed awful for Cassie to travel to America while the Doyles, who so much wanted to be there, were forced to remain back in Ireland, stuck in a cycle they couldn't break loose from.

When her mother had arrived for Ivy's wedding, staying only a few hours after, Cassie had described the situation to her. To her surprise, her mother had breezily accepted the explanation, saying it wouldn't hurt for her to spend a few months in "abject poverty." Perhaps it would teach her the path she was on if she continued choosing such "ruinous ways."

Cassie's father offered her a large sum to pay for traveling expenses to and from England, to buy clothes, and in case she might need anything else.

Her parents were never anything but extravagant.

As soon as the money was in Cassie's hands, she had only one thought: the Doyles. She had plenty of clothes, and she would not need most of the ones she had anyway. A few simple items would suffice for the time that she was in America. Traveling expenses were a moot point, given that the Knights had instantly offered to cover all of their passages.

Which meant that if she gave this money as a gift to the Doyles, she could easily provide the remainder of the funds they would need to set up for America.

It was more wonderful than words could express.

And when Cassie told Una and she immediately burst into tears, Cassie knew she had made the right decision.

She was going to America.

CHAPTER THIRTEEN

January 1883
Atlantic Ocean

T HE SEA AIR ALWAYS called to Patrick like a siren, and therefore, before the sun rose over the whipping waves below him, he'd find himself standing on the deck, watching the sailors work and taking deep breaths of the wondrous stuff.

Even when he was small and had yet to do much sailing, Patrick had never gotten seasick. There was probably more salt running through his veins than blood; his father had made sure of it. He'd been out on his father's sailboat before he was out of skirts.

Of course, on land or at sea, his sisters slept in. Patrick never could. There was always so much energy coursing through him; he found it impossible to lie in bed when the world was awake.

They were journeying across the sea to America at last. His mother had gotten bored and headed home a few months ago; his father had stayed in Spain, concluding business. But Patrick had taken his sisters to Madrid by himself and then back to London, and now they had boarded the steamer taking them home.

Home! He must admit he missed it. Every ship must have a home port, and Patrick was no exception. The sea was fine, was home to the ship, but it wasn't safe.

He must return home now, marry, and settle, like every man.

Behind him, Bell barked, and Patrick whistled. She came clattering over to him, her nails clicking on the deck.

"Easy, girl. What'd you see?"

Bell whined and wiggled, leaning against his leg but ever glancing over her shoulder, her big, black body twitching as if she wanted to run back whence she came. He hoped she'd not been bothering one of the workmen. That could only lead to trouble, and he needed to get his dog home safely without any kind of claim that she was ill luck. There could still be superstition amongst the crewmen, even on these sorts of passenger steamers that were usually home to the more refined types.

He saw nothing but a woman standing near the railing. She wore a blue dress under a woolen coat, and a few escaping tendrils of red hair danced about her shoulders under her brown hat.

It couldn't be.

He ought to turn and walk back to his cabin. Start his day. Make believe that it had been a ghost haunting him on the deck. With his hand knotted in Bell's thick coat, he considered that option for a long moment.

Then he sighed. He couldn't do that. He had no idea why she was on this ship, but she must be a first-class passenger, which meant they would dine together, and he couldn't ignore her.

Probably.

So he'd best begin now. Despite the fact that, looking back, his last letter to her had been rather embarrassing. More than that, he'd been rude, and he probably would have never heard the end of it if he were to reveal to his sisters the real reason he'd stopped writing to Lady Mary Cassidy O'Connell.

Who wanted him to call her Cassie. Who was presumably still single. Who even now, with her face turned toward the sea and the wind lashing against her small frame, looked a picture.

So he released his grip on Bell, who sprinted down the deck to Lady

Mary, clearly recognizing her.

She turned from the ocean, and her eyes met his. Her mouth became a perfect *O* of shock—she had not realized he was there.

"Lady Mary!" he called. As he grew closer, he pasted on a smile. "You don't remember me, I suppose. Patrick Hilton, from Mrs. Strauss's wedding. And this is Bell, my faithful girl."

She glanced down at Bell, who had trotted up to her and sat primly at her feet with far more composure than Bell usually possessed. A small, gloved hand reached out to tentatively pat Bell's head, and yet the lady said nothing.

They stood there for a time, in silence, and Patrick's guilt grew. Why had he behaved as he had? Surely he could've found a less silly way to break off contact. Or perhaps he could've naturally distanced himself while allowing his sisters continued access to her.

Whatever he should've done, it was not what he had done. And a gentleman never let such a thing pass by without apology.

"I'm sorry," he said in an undertone. "I was wrong to cut you off like that. I was so busy in Italy, and I didn't think. I'm sorry."

Then her eyes, so bright blue they almost took his breath away, did rise to his, and Patrick was reminded of why he couldn't let himself have contact with this woman.

He would soon be promised to another. No, he *was* promised—he just wasn't engaged.

"It's all right. I understand. You had more honor than I did in that." She removed her hand from Bell's head and placed it back on the railing. "I should've cut you off before I did. But I so enjoyed writing to ... *to your sisters.*"

She rushed the last few words, and Patrick's pride swelled at the idea that perhaps, really, she enjoyed writing to him. Yet that hardly mattered, for she was not a part of his life. She was not and never would be.

"You're going to America?" An obvious question, for they were both trapped on a ship heading that way.

Trapped perhaps was a bit of a strong word. Presumably, she wasn't kidnapped and forced onto the steamer.

"Yes. I am. With Peter and Alice Strauss. I'll ... I'll be staying with them for a bit. To help Alice out." She lowered her voice. "Alice had a rough year, and I want to support her."

Of course. Not only were they traveling the same way, but Cassie had a selfless reason for doing so.

"I'm ... I'm going home. With my sisters. Mother went earlier, and Father is staying behind for business, so it's ... it's just us."

She inclined her head in acknowledgement. That was probably all information she could've guessed.

For now, there was nothing else he knew how to say. He tried, once or twice, to make small talk, but he could tell she was unwilling.

Yet he couldn't help himself. In spite of all sense and logic, he wanted to be near her. As soon as he realized what he was doing, he excused himself, after making an offer to see her back to wherever she needed to go.

She turned him down, releasing Patrick, Bell at his heels, to hurry away from her, wildly frustrated with himself.

He found an empty spot on the deck, where few people were milling, and took to pacing up and down, up and down, his coat flapping behind him with his speed.

"What am I doing?" he mumbled.

Bell whimpered, trying to keep pace, and though she was faster and stronger than Patrick, she eventually gave up on his sharp turns and sat down to watch him.

"Lord God, what am I doing? I'm being so unfair to her. Why do I keep trying to talk to her? I need to just let her be."

I want to be near her. I want her in my life.

It couldn't be. So why did he keep feeling so drawn to her?

Allow me to focus, Lord, he begged. *Allow me to focus.*

"Of all the coincidences in the world, though!" For the first time since they'd begun this journey, Alice's eyes were laughing again, and though Cassie rather begrudged that the cause was her own discomfort, she couldn't help but smile at her friend's frank joy. "That he would be on this boat at the same time we are!"

"Before I know it, you'll be proclaiming 'This is fate!' or something along those lines." Cassie pulled her knees up to her chest and stared out the small porthole. She herself wasn't sure how she felt about the realization that Patrick and his sisters were on the same boat as she.

Perhaps it shouldn't bother her. Of course, she wasn't exactly bothered so much as surprised and a bit concerned as to how their interactions might go. She didn't begrudge Patrick his rejection of her, but that didn't mean she particularly wanted to see a lot of him. Further, she wasn't sure what a potential interaction with his sisters might look like. What did they think of her? How had Patrick explained her not writing after a certain date, when before their correspondence had been so warm?

Surely there was no logical way to explain it.

"I don't believe in fate, but I do believe in God's hand."

Peter lowered his book. "Now, Alice, don't go getting her hopes up." But his lips were twitching. Much like Cassie, he was clearly bemused by Alice's enthusiasm. "Patrick Hilton seems like a decent enough man, but we can't forget that Cassie may not want anything to do with him after that letter."

Cassie had told Peter everything at Pearlbelle Park while they were preparing to leave, and he'd expressed disgust at Patrick's actions and then immediately admitted that he himself had made certain mistakes in his relationship with Alice that had left him without the true ability to judge. That said, Cassie couldn't imagine a man as faithful as Peter would cause

Alice the worries that Patrick Hilton had already caused her.

"Yet he's here now." Alice folded her arms across her chest. "I know how one can become blinded. Especially when you're raised in a certain class with certain expectations."

Peter chuckled. "Ah yes, the high pressures of having an exorbitant amount of money."

"You laugh, but you know how I felt during my Season, and Cassie felt much the same." Alice pressed her lips together. "Men must be the same. Why, even Aubrey Montgomery—I'm going to keep talking about him, Cassie—certainly must have felt like he had to marry, despite not caring very much to do so. The cad."

Cassie raised her eyebrows. "That's comforting. To know that the man I courted for several years probably only wanted anything to do with me because he was pressured into doing so."

"It's nice how Alice puts things into sharp perspective, isn't it?" Peter stood and shuffled through his trunk. "She makes you wonder if there's any worth whatsoever in yourself."

"I am just trying to—Peter, what are you looking for?"

"My ... brown-colored ... jacket."

"It's ... No. Here." Alice stood and batted Peter's hands away. "I told you that there is a system to packing the trunk."

"Alice, come sit down," Cassie protested. "You're supposed to be comforting me."

Alice handed Peter the previously hidden item of clothing. "My goal is not to comfort; it is to encourage. There's a difference."

"I'm happy to hear that, for I doubt I need comfort." Actually, Alice was the one who did, though usually it was best not to tell Alice she needed comfort ... but to just offer it. "Nonetheless, I think you should sit down and talk to me."

"I think we should go for a walk on the deck and look pretty and make him come out of hiding."

Peter glanced at the ceiling with a sigh and put on his jacket. "I'll take you, I suppose. I was going to pray, though, so you'll have to be quiet."

"We can be quiet," Alice said.

Cassie pressed her lips together and nodded a little more emphatically than was needed, deliberately widening her eyes. "Quiet as mice."

Alice mimicked Cassie's expression. "Quieter."

Peter, too, caught on to their lightheartedness and smiled. "All right. Let's go."

As they left Alice and Peter's small compartment behind and began the ascent to the upper decks, Alice's cheerful attitude was half veneer and half a childlike response to spending so much time with Cassie. At least, that was how Cassie interpreted it. She wasn't entirely sure how she really felt, but it seemed like Alice was determined to get through their travels in a cheerful manner, and Cassie was not about to stop her, even if it seemed like hiding was not the best way to work through one's grief.

But what did Cassie know about such things? Very little, it appeared.

In no time, they were walking along the deck. They left Peter alone to pray and leaned against the railing and watched the gray water below them and chatted about this and that.

They had not been on the dock more than ten minutes before Cassie heard a somewhat familiar voice calling, "Lady Mary! Lady Mary!"

She paused and glanced over her shoulder and then Alice and she were both obligated to turn to see Gwendolyn Hilton dashing up the deck, her straw hat hanging on perilously by a blue ribbon tied to her auburn curls.

Behind her, more sedate but still making good time with long strides, Lorelei walked, her gray eyes sparking with disgust. She had her brown locks, also curly like Gwendolyn's, tied up like a lady now. Cassie almost shuddered to see how much she'd grown. She was a woman now.

Cassie didn't envy her for whatever pressure her mother would be putting on her within the next few years to marry.

Perhaps it wouldn't be so bad. Perhaps Mrs. Hilton would be gracious and allow Lorelei whatever time she needed to find someone nice to marry who would take good care of her and love her plenty.

But that wasn't the world Patrick lived in. If he would not fight for the privilege of choosing his bride, his sisters would need to fight for choosing their own husbands, if they even chose to fight.

Did he understand what power he wielded as the eldest son? Cassie thought not.

Because he was afraid. And Cassie didn't need anything to do with a man who was afraid.

Yet that did not extend to his sisters. So she returned Gwendolyn's embrace warmly and introduced both Gwendolyn and Lorelei to Alice, who greeted them, though with a noticeable stiffening that reminded Cassie that she must now be careful of expecting Alice to be outgoing.

"I can't believe we're on the same boat! Trick told us, and we were both so thrilled." Gwendolyn cast a look at her older sister. "Weren't we, Lore?"

Lorelei nodded, and though her face remained stoic, there was a spark in her eyes. Cassie was sure of it.

"How was the rest of your tour?"

"We're not home yet," Gwendolyn said, "but I liked it, I think. My favorite place was France, but Lore liked Italy best. Didn't you, Lore?"

"I did. Especially Florence. But that feels like a long time ago now." A small smile quirked about Lorelei's lips. "I suppose that sounds silly. It's only been about a year."

"No, I know what you mean." A lot could happen in a year. A lot could happen in a *month* with the right circumstances. "I was partial to Florence myself, as you know. Oh, but I fell in love with Vienna. Did I tell you the story about that?"

The girls shook their heads, and Cassie drew them both away from Alice, entertaining them with the tale of a young Austrian lord or baron or whatever he'd been and an evening of playacting to be a lady when she'd really been nothing more than a child.

She let her voice lilt with the joy of a good tale, and Lorelei and Gwendolyn clearly liked it. A quick look confirmed that Peter had found Alice, who seemed deflated as if the simple act of greeting the girls had exhausted her.

Interesting.

But Cassie would worry about that later. Peter would take care of Alice, and hopefully Alice would take care of Peter, and Cassie could chat with Patrick's sisters about Europe and the delights of spending ridiculous amounts of money to see countries in a way even the locals couldn't.

Which made her laugh, because it had seemed to be such a part of her life before, and now it didn't seem like her at all. Why was that? Was it the Doyles or the loneliness or the fact that she was growing up that made her teenage years feel distant and romantic, like a blur of bright colors and flashing lights she could never hope to visit again?

Lord, don't let me be too dramatic, when I so need to be Your child, with all the joy that entails.

However, sometimes being dramatic seemed to help, a little, as long as it wasn't all the time.

She got the idea that Patrick had sent his sisters to her. Perhaps he was tired; he had seemed tired. He'd lost an inch of height from the slouch of his shoulders, and there had been dark circles under his eyes.

He looked like a harried man, and she wondered how even someone deep in denial could fail to realize that that was not how a godly man acted. If he were really abiding in God's will, he would not act like that. He would *not*.

Yes, it was for the best that her attraction to him had come to nothing. Though his motives might not have been pure, it was good that he had separated himself from her.

She drew herself into the present, determined to love his sisters and show them a little of what it was to live a joyous life.

Perhaps she could even introduce them to what she herself had been doing. "I've been in Ireland, as you know. It's been interesting. My maid, Una, comes from a family of ten children! They are going to America on this same boat. We could perhaps try to discover them. They would be belowdecks."

Crowded but not in a hull of some freight ship. She had assured that with her contribution. As it turned out, the Doyles had been mere pennies away from being able to afford the trip to America.

Peter had offered to help, bless his heart, but Cassie was the one with disposable income and quite a lot of it. The Knights had paid her fair, so she'd been free to give the Doyles all the money her mother had given her for gowns, other expenses, and her own ticket.

There had even been extra after the Doyles had purchased their fare, which shocked Cassie as she had been rather frightened of sending the Doyles to America, even given their relatives in Boston, with no extra funds.

The fact surprised her, but of course, the Doyles were all rather cramped in a tiny space, so it was certainly not a glamorous trip. At least it was short. That much she was grateful for.

Upon meeting the Doyles, Gwendolyn was delighted and fell in love with the children, whereas Lorelei was stiff and a little awkward. But they both were dear girls, and they tried to be pleasant.

"You'll have to look after them for me," Cassie said as they walked back toward Lorelei and Gwendolyn's berth. "They'll be in Boston, where I cannot visit them. Though if you do yourself, you should go with your brother." Wherever the Doyles ended up couldn't be a particularly pleasant area. "Promise me that?"

"Of course," Lorelei said at the same time that Gwendolyn made a face.

Cassie hoped she hadn't put any ideas into Gwendolyn's head, but it was clear Gwendolyn would do what she wanted when she wanted to do it, with or without permission or encouragement from those around her.

In the hall outside their rooms, they met Patrick.

"Where've you been?" he asked as Gwendolyn threw her arms around his neck in a tempestuous hug. "I thought you were going walking on the deck, but now I've found you've been exploring?" There it was. The trace of fear in his voice. The "I would die if anything happened to you" of a man who couldn't bear to have any small thing go wrong when it came to his sisters.

But part of growing up, and of life, was having things go a little wrong.

"We went to meet the Doyles," Lorelei said. "They're a poor family, and I think they need us, Trick."

His eyes went briefly upward in an expression of despair. "Girls, we've talked about this. Our personal incomes are somewhat limited, and there is the matter of keeping you both clothed, and also, throwing money at a problem is not always the solution. You remember that couple in Berlin?"

Lorelei smiled somewhat sheepishly, while Gwendolyn scuffed her foot across the floor, her shoe making a squeaking sound against the polished deck.

"But thank Lady Mary for entertaining you—I really am grateful to you for it." He turned his eyes toward Cassie. "They rightfully adore you, and I'm glad you could spend time together. I hope they'll see you again, if you care to. They always love adventures, and I know you will take care of them."

Cassie nodded and murmured something polite and helpful, but her heart wasn't in it. She knew he expected her to spend the remaining few days of the trip with the girls, but to distance himself, and that wasn't what she wanted.

Yet she would see the Hilton girls, and she would love them in spite of herself.

And perhaps she'd love the Hilton boy in spite of herself, too. But that wasn't worth thinking about, for it was clear that he would never love her.

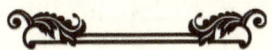

CHAPTER FOURTEEN

PATRICK STOOD A RESPECTFUL distance down the deck, his hand resting on Bell's head, and watched Cassie talk to his sisters.

They were seated directly on the deck, adorably out of place but seeming not to mind much. The three of them had their heads bent together and were engaged in a deep discussion. There was a Bible open on Cassie's lap as they had come upon her in the midst of study, and apparently she had allowed his sisters to join her. Even now, the Bible was passed to Lore, and Patrick tried not to be pleased with the seamless way Lady Mary Cassidy O'Connell pulled his sisters into her faith.

They could be difficult to rope into concentrating on anything outside their specific interests, and Patrick felt he had neglected them spiritually in recent months. He hadn't known what to say. His own soul felt so badgered and empty. Surely it wasn't neglected, but his prayers had grown less frequent.

If he were honest, he would admit that his prayers were hindered by his lack of obedience. God was trying to lead him *somewhere*, and Patrick was unwilling to stumble his way to *somewhere*.

Especially if that accidentally led him to Cassie. That was where his thoughts wandered more often than not, and he wasn't sure why. After all, she was just a temptation to be avoided. His feelings toward her must be deceptive. The very idea of allying himself with her was rooted in a long stream of poor choices. Ones he must not repeat.

"Patrick!" Winnie waved wildly in his direction. "Come on over here."

He barely restrained himself from glaring at her. She knew very well he intended to keep his distance, but neither of his sisters were particularly supportive of that plan. Nonetheless, he didn't feel like he could avoid them once he was directly ordered to approach. He reluctantly crossed the deck and knelt with Winnie between him and Cassie. "What is it?"

"Tell Cassie how you've always explained the timeline of the Exodus and all about those Egyptian pharaohs you researched."

He frowned. "Winnie, I haven't studied that in well over a year. I don't think—"

"Oh, Trick, you remember!" Winnie took his hand and gave it what appeared to be a squeeze but was more like a pinch. "Sit with us and talk."

"Better yet." Lorelei rose to her feet. "We'll take Bell for a little walk, and you explain it to Cassie. That way, we don't have to hear all the boring nonsense all over again, and Cassie can be informed."

"Oh, good idea!" Winnie stumbled to a standing position and dashed off before anyone could say anything more, Bell at her heels.

Lorelei grinned and followed her.

Cassie straightened slightly. "They're never subtle, are they?"

"Hardly ever." He scowled. "Obviously you realize—"

"That you want nothing to do with me and vice versa? It's painfully obvious, Mr. Hilton, and it's perfectly all right. At least you have the sense to realize we can't just go on as we were."

He stiffened and cleared his throat. "I ... I meant no offense. You understand that I ... I must do ..." He hesitated, trying to find a way to properly word his thoughts. After all, they were muddled within his own mind. Vocalizing them seemed impossible. "I must obey my parents, Lady Mary. That's the simple truth. They have requirements of me that I must fulfill. It is an extension of God's command to honor your father and mother. Further, by doing so, I can secure my sisters' futures."

She rose. "I understand that you believe that."

His forehead furrowed. He *believed* that? As in, it wasn't really true?

Scrambling to his feet, he faced her. Perhaps he ought to loosen his posture, to pretend he didn't understand her meaning. Perhaps he ought to walk away. *Perhaps.*

However, something came to a boiling point inside him, and his next words definitely had an undertone of frustration that he hadn't expected.

"I believe it because it's true. Just because you are free to avoid responsibility and do whatever you like does not mean that is true of me. I am in a position I cannot easily abandon. I know a woman might not understand—"

"This has nothing to do with me being a woman and everything to do with me following God's will in my life."

That was entirely unfair. "What do you mean by that?" He was following God's will in his life. Why wouldn't it be God's will for him to protect the innocents in his life? To love his sisters? To follow the command to listen to the wisdom of his parents?

"I mean, Mr. Hilton, that you do not do as you ought. You don't act like a man who is following God. You act like a man who is confused, bogged down by his own sin and pride, to the point where you are unable to see what is obvious to everyone but you."

"Which is?"

"That by following your parents off the face of the nearest cliff, you are doing a disservice to yourself, to Miss Linden, to your sisters, and to God Himself. In the name of not rebelling against them, you rebel against your Lord and Savior." Her blue eyes flashed then, full of a hardly restrained ire, though her words remained quiet and steady. "You're not at all the man I'd hoped you were, which doesn't matter to me. I, too, am an imperfect Christian. However, if I were to advise you at all, I'd say you need to look within yourself, see if there's a hint of the Holy Spirit, and listen to what He's saying to you."

Patrick stepped back, distancing himself from her as much as he could without actually removing himself from the situation. He forced a smile on his lips, as if this was some light conversation about the weather or what their plans were for their next holiday, and he kept his response light despite the overwhelming desire to defend himself more stringently. "I can't believe you're making assumptions about my spiritual state."

She cocked her head and raised her eyebrows. "I can't believe you're ignoring a vital Bible verse. Matthew 7 ... oh, is it 7:16? At any rate, you know the words: 'Ye shall know them by their fruits.' I don't have to look into your heart to see that your behavior does not align with God's commands. However, since that is truly none of my business, I do apologize for speaking to you so rudely. Now, if you'll excuse me, I'd best find the rest of my party."

She walked away, and Patrick was left to find his sisters and attempt to act as if nothing was happening. As if he wasn't secretly seething.

As if he didn't believe everything she'd said had at least a thread of truth to it.

Patrick was watching her, and Cassie didn't know how to feel about it.

She wanted to pretend he was angry still, but he had clearly calmed down, and though all his conversation was aimed at his sisters, his attention was on her.

And Cassie didn't know what to do about that fact.

She had been sincere in wanting to distance herself from him. She did wish him well, but it was clear he wasn't about to take the steps she felt would be necessary to his growth as a person.

Hopefully, that wasn't simply her pride speaking. She believed her perspective was grounded in Biblical thought, but she didn't want to judge him. However, when his actions were clear for her to see, and when he insisted on telling her what his plans were, it was hard not to involve herself.

Even Peter, who always tried not to make comments about the private lives of others, had told Cassie he didn't approve of Patrick's actions. When Peter felt the need to make a critical comment about a near-stranger's life, Cassie felt there must be something to it.

After dinner, Cassie followed Alice and Peter out of the dining room, intending to join them for their usual prayer time. However, she stopped when her name was said in a quiet tone.

She turned to meet Patrick's eyes.

"Will you walk with my sisters and me? I want to speak with you. I'll be quick."

She glanced back at Alice and Peter to confirm that they had heard. Alice nodded, and Cassie returned her attention to Patrick. "Yes, of course. I can't stay long, but I'm happy to hear what you have to say."

They walked out on the deck. The stars were bright over their heads, and Lorelei and Winnie chatted at first about this and that, but then they bolted ahead, not out of sight but certainly out of hearing, given the brisk breeze that whipped about them.

"I'm sorry," he said. "I am determined to keep to my plans, but that was no reason to use a harsh tone with you or to ignore what was truly well-meaning advice. Further, I know that there are many ways in which my relationship with God could improve. I will think on that more; thank you for reminding me how vital it is to never let that aspect of my life fall by the wayside."

She nodded, her lips pressed tightly together, but didn't trust herself to speak.

"We dock in a few days, and that will truly be good-bye. I'm sure there will be no more chance meetings." Even in the dim light, she could make out his smile. He always smiled, or almost always, even when his subject was not particularly a cheerful one. "I am grateful that God brought you into my life for a short time, and even more grateful that He brought you into my sisters' lives. I hope you can continue to correspond with them, though of course I do not expect you to. They are darlings, and I love them, but you needn't feel the need to bother."

She shook her head. "It is no bother." It would always remind her of him, for his sisters were adoring toward their older brother, despite his flaws, and their letters had always been full of him. However, she would bear up. Though she wasn't sure even Patrick knew it, there was something lost in both of his sisters. They seemed as determined as Patrick was to march on, but Cassie knew as well as anyone how hard it was to grow up without your parents' love.

"I'm sure they appreciate it. Honestly, there is a lack of ... feminine guidance. In both their lives, but especially in Lore's." He sighed. "I hope that once I marry Blanche, that will change."

She couldn't help raising her eyebrows, though she looked away to disguise her skepticism. "Is that so?"

"Yes. Blanche could perhaps offer some guidance on ... oh, I don't know. Things they won't talk about with me. Boys." She could hear the smirk in his voice. "I've kept both of them from fussing about that too much before their time, but I also think there are things they don't tell me."

"Oh, perhaps. But they're good girls." They had occasional bouts of high energy that even Cassie found exhausting, despite being only a few years older than Lorelei, but they were perfectly healthy adolescents in all regards. She didn't think either of them was overly prone to unhealthy infatuations.

"I agree, but I still want them to be safe and well-guided, and there are some things even the best brother cannot provide." He stopped walking and turned to look out over the railing. "I can provide them with a more peaceful life by working hard. Father has spared them both any involvement in the company, more because I have taken the full burden than because they are girls. I think, were I not here, he would have them both in the offices. You know the company will someday be split between the three of us, financially, but I don't want them to have to worry too much about the details even then."

She came to stand next to him and looked down at the dark and churning waves. "I didn't know that was possible."

"Oh, it is. Though I think the laws are different in England than America. That's why you hear of American heiresses marrying earls and dukes and princes." He cast a wink her way. "Mother would like for Lore and Winnie to do the same, but we'll see. I think that once I am married, Mother will be content for a time, and we can finally have some peace." As he said those last few words, he released a sigh.

She turned to him, sympathy welling as it always did at the most inconvenient moments, and suddenly, they were close. Too close.

And her eyes darted to his lips, and she wondered if he'd ever kissed Blanche Linden, if he knew that she had kissed Aubrey Montgomery, and if he knew how easy it would be ...

"Trick! I think I saw a whale!" Winnie's voice proved Cassie's salvation, and she turned back to the sea below as Patrick's sisters' footsteps approached them at a rapid pace, Bell's nails clicking on the deck behind them.

"It was just a shadow," Lore protested.

Cassie felt Patrick turn to them; he replied something or other and then turned back to her as if nothing had passed between them.

"Should I walk you back to your cabin?"

"Oh, no! Go investigate any potential ocean life. I'll find my own way." She could use a quiet walk back to reorganize her thoughts.

So Patrick Hilton left, and Cassie prayed.

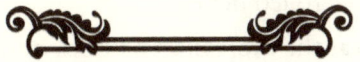

The ship would be docking in Philadelphia in the morning. Peter and Alice had suggested one last evening stroll on the deck, and Cassie had agreed.

Still, she couldn't help but think of that walk, that brief conversation, that stolen moment with Patrick. He'd been avoiding her fastidiously since that night last week, though his sisters had never been far from her side during the day.

Yet Cassie worked hard to stay present in the moment, for she was needed here with her friend.

Alice was moody now. The more Cassie watched her, the more she realized that. And granted, if anyone had a right to be moody just now, it was Alice.

Cassie and Peter paused, let Alice walk a few steps ahead of them, and chatted about this. His observations matched Cassie's.

"She's doing better than she was," Peter said. "I must believe she's doing better than she was. Sometimes I'm skeptical of her truly being better, but I know she is. It's just sometimes difficult to embrace when I ... when I have seen her lie to others about how she is feeling."

Cassie nodded sympathetically. From what she understood, Alice had stopped talking to Peter sometime after the loss of their son. However, she had presented a cheerful front to her family—crumbling at the first hint of pressure but almost indiscernible to all but Peter. "Yet I think she's being honest with us."

"You know I can hear you both." Alice hesitated on the deck, and she looked to Peter first, then to Cassie with a hint of a smile. "What's the use of scheming about me if you're in my hearing?"

"We are not scheming," Cassie protested.

"Even if we were, I think both of us want you to know what we're scheming about." Peter inclined his head. "The rules, remember?"

"Oh, the rules." Alice rolled her eyes.

Cassie had to laugh at the expression on both of their faces. Apparently, there had been some mistrust in Alice toward Peter—*Peter*, of all the men in the world—when it came to his relationship with his cousin's wife. Though Cassie didn't know the whole story, she did wonder if Alice's fears were grounded in any kind of reality.

But Peter insisted there was some truth to what Alice said, and he was nothing but honest. Cassie had an idea there had been more misunderstanding than actual betrayal, but Alice had felt it deeply.

There was now a set of "rules." Cassie didn't know the exact limits of them, only that apparently they meant Peter was not allowed private conversation with her. They were Peter's rules, though, not Alice's, and as such, Cassie had let Peter decide what counted as "private" and what didn't. They could sort out that on their own; she wouldn't interfere.

Alice tilted her head up to look at the stars. They were so bright out at sea. "It will be hard to be in Philadelphia."

"Yes, but I will be with you, as will Cassie." Peter circled his arm around Alice's waist. "My family adores you. They will do nothing but love you, as you know. Don't doubt them."

Alice's smile was tight, but she didn't pull away from his touch. "I doubt everything now. But I suppose I must take one moment at a time. At this moment, it's us and the stars. Cassie, look at them all! What a glorious lot they are. I never fail to notice them as I cross the Atlantic, and they remind me of God's infinite greatness. I desperately need the reminder. There is so much that distracts from it, and I don't want to be distracted anymore."

"As long as we continue seeking God, we have nothing to fear." Peter drew away from Alice but took her hand. "Let's go to the bow."

They walked on, talking softly, and Cassie kept looking up at the stars.

Help me continue seeking You, Lord.

Chapter Fifteen

February 1883
Philadelphia, Pennsylvania

A S THE STEAMSHIP PULLED up to the docks in Delaware Bay, Cassie stood slightly to the left of Peter and Alice. Both of them had turned sober faces toward the west, and Peter's arm was firm around Alice's waist. Without speaking, they had both communicated apprehension and also a level of strength that Cassie knew she was not invited to partake in.

But that only made it easier to turn to the Hiltons, when they came, to the laughing girls and the somewhat stoic man whose expression just about matched Peter's.

Yet Peter and Alice had lost a child. Patrick lost nothing but what he allowed himself to lose.

Lorelei had told Cassie on the second or third night of their journey that the reason Patrick was "acting strangely" was that he was reluctant to marry Blanche.

Of course, Cassie tucked this information away but chose not to immediately address it. She had an idea that Lorelei and Gwendolyn both wanted her to marry their brother.

She'd gotten this idea because Gwendolyn had been comparing her to Blanche all week, and in the comparisons, Blanche always fell short. *"Blanche wouldn't do what you are doing,"* was a common refrain, but also, accounts of what Blanche would do were shared.

It appeared that neither of the girls really liked Blanche. However, Cassie wasn't sure of how many of the "facts" she was presented about Patrick's intended were accurate and how many were fantasies or, even worse, straight lies concocted by his sisters.

And though it was flattering to be liked, it was better that the girls adjusted to the idea of Blanche Linden being a part of their life. She would be their sister, and the girls would be better off with her than with their parents, no matter what she was really like.

Having never seen another side of Patrick, Cassie hadn't been aware that, to his sisters' eyes, Patrick was "acting strangely." To her, it seemed like all his words, all his actions, were centered around a consistently confusing personality.

Perhaps the mixed signals he never failed to send her were more due to his own confusion than any lack of understanding on Cassie's side. Especially if his own sisters didn't know what he was doing or why half the time.

The ship was docked. They would be leaving soon. Gwendolyn clung to Cassie's arm and begged her to write; Cassie met Patrick's eyes over his sister's auburn head.

He nodded.

"I will," she promised immediately. "If you'll give me your address, I'll give you mine as soon as I can. I'll write to you both."

Ever practical, and somehow also ever conniving, Lorelei reached into her pocket. "Here. I've got it for you."

Cassie accepted the slip of paper and looked between the pair of sisters. They were so different, yet the looks on their faces were identical. They were both very pleased with themselves.

Meanwhile, Patrick was fastidiously ignoring all three of them.

Lovely.

There was nothing quite like a man who lived in another world, one of his own making, a gray sort of world.

Yet Patrick was not a "gray sort of world" man. She would've known that even from just his sisters, but she knew better simply from their conversations. He was a bright and shining man, when he let himself be.

But his courage always failed him right before he stepped out of the shadows completely, and there Cassie and he were again, refusing to meet each other's eyes while his sisters made sure they would never be far away from each other.

Apparently, Gwendolyn couldn't bear this type of behavior from her older brother, so she turned from Cassie to Patrick and looped her arm around his. "Trick, what are you looking at? Don't you know we're all bidding Cassie good-bye?" It hadn't taken more than a few days' walking the deck and visiting with the Doyles and talking to Peter and Alice for both girls to pick up "Cassie."

"A lot of this belongs to Baldwin & Sons," Patrick replied without turning to Cassie, hardly acknowledging his sister either. "Not this dock, but the ones on either side. We need more of a foothold in Philadelphia. I'm trying to think how to do that."

"Oh. Boring business." Gwendolyn sighed heavily. "Trick, do you ever think of anything else anymore? You've been poring over financial papers and all those dreadful dock designs the whole voyage. Can't you just enjoy something?"

"Yes, Trick, you're a dreadful bore," Lorelei added.

Patrick did turn from the industrial view then, his eyes flicking from one sister to another and to Cassie. His look to her was almost pleading. "It's my duty to do it."

"And so?" Lorelei scoffed. "You said I was too young for duty, but who determines that? Mother certainly disagrees. So you set rules for yourself that you don't ask either of us to live under. What does that say about how gold standard these duties are?"

Patrick simply sighed and turned back to the docks.

"Tortured souls are fine in books but not in real life," Lorelei said, primarily aimed at Cassie, but Patrick's stiffening shoulders confirmed that he had heard the jab.

"Anyway, I won't let Trick make me any less happy to be home, to get to see my friends, and to get to write to Cassie."

Patrick pushed back from the railing. "Let's go make sure we didn't miss anything in our cabin, girls."

"But, Trick!"

"Now."

The three of them walked away, and Cassie grabbed the railing in her hands and glanced to make sure Alice and Peter were still entertained with each other. Seeing that they had no need of her, she did what Patrick had done and looked out to the docks and calmed her breathing. She was angry, and she always tried not to show anger outwardly, even if it must bleed into her heart and make it pound unnecessarily, her chest catching with the indignity of it all.

He was denying her even the basic politeness of a distant acquaintance, and he was using her to mentor his sisters, and he knew it.

He had apologized that first day when they had met on the deck, but to apologize and continue on the path he was on was nothing. It was an empty gesture; it helped no one.

Just as Cassie's rage had risen to a barely containable level, a hand grasped the railing next to her. She looked up into Patrick's eyes as she stepped back. He was breathing heavily, and his face was too pale for normalcy.

"Cassie." His eyes were sharp and clear; he leaned toward her with a trembling intensity. "Cassie, let me write to you."

"What?" she whispered, glancing over her shoulder, but Peter and Alice could not hear them at this distance, with the crowd pressing in on all sides. Ducking her head toward him, she filled the space that he would not. "How can you even suggest it?"

"Because I need your help." She was standing close enough to feel the trembling of his body. "I need you to talk me through this in a reasonable way. Please. Just put in a note for me when you write to my sisters."

She stepped back. "Are you marrying Blanche Linden?"

His face twitched. "Yes. I have to."

"Then why do you think we ought to write to each other?" She reached for the railing once more as the boat lurched, but he stood still somehow, and she hated him for it. "If you intend to marry her, you should have nothing more to do with me or any other woman. You should be faithful to her. You *must* be faithful to her."

"I intend to be, fully. That's why I need to write to you. I want to ... I just want to have something that is mine."

"Like your fiancée?" Exasperated, she turned away from him. "Patrick, you should know better than that."

"I will make sure my sisters read all you write me, as before. It's no different than it was when we were in Italy." His eyes pled with her, and she wanted to give in. She wanted to do this thing that would bring him happiness.

But his reasons were different now. His motives seemed less pure.

"I will write to your sisters," she said. "I will not mind if you read them. But surely you understand that what you are asking of me is unreasonable."

He stilled then, and his eyes went over her shoulder at some distant point. He stood still for a long moment, then nodded. "You're right. It is unreasonable. Forgive me. Please don't allow this request to come between yourself and my sisters." He sighed, his eyes now glued to the deck below him like a chastened child. "I'm sorry, and I wish you all the best."

He disappeared into the crowd, and she found her way back to Alice and Peter.

In Philadelphia, they went first to Peter's parents' home, where they would stay for a few days while they waited for the train to Cincinnati.

Peter had warned Cassie that his family could be excessive and, further, that he was unsure how any of them would react to meeting Alice again for the first time since she had attempted to take her own life.

"I know they will mean well," Peter said softly, his eyes on Alice's face and his hand in hers on the drive through Philadelphia. "However, I cannot guarantee my mother's subtlety or my father's empathy. Their letters have been kind and sad."

"Everyone has been kind and sad," Alice said. Her eyes were a murky gray, full of a weight they hadn't had since they began their trip.

At last, they arrived at the Strausses' home, which was a pretty little place. Its garden lay still and dead, but as they walked up the path to the front porch, Cassie caught sight of a few struggling, pale-green sprouts popping out of the soil.

Spring was on its way.

The door was flung open, and Peter and Alice were both embraced, and Cassie hung back and allowed them the joy of a greeting after a long parting.

She could sense the stiffness in Alice, when before she had spoken of nothing but her affection for the Strausses. Cassie hoped that feeling would leave soon. It was clear Peter's family adored Alice.

It took a moment or two, even after they had entered the house, for Alice to recall herself and introduce Cassie. The Strausses and she had met, yes, but that seemed like such a long time ago now, a distant and faded memory of wedding plans and new relations and great joy. It must seem even longer to Alice and Peter.

So Cassie was reintroduced to Mr. and Mrs. Strauss; their youngest child, Dahlia; and their older daughter, Caroline Webster, who had a husband, a son, and a new baby on the way.

Mrs. Strauss placed a hand on Alice's arm. "Alice, let me see you to your room. Everyone else can see you later. All right?" Her words were soft but firm, and Cassie stepped back, her eyes going to Alice's face.

She hoped Alice wasn't about to receive a scolding. Despite appearances to the contrary, that was the last thing she needed right now.

"Mama." Peter's voice held a hint of his own type of sternness, almost reproach.

Mrs. Strauss glanced at him, but her eyes immediately went back to Alice. "Please?"

"Of course." Alice's words held that breezy tone that indicated nothing mattered at all. She used it when things mattered very much.

Peter looked lost when she walked away from him, even though she was only going upstairs, even though she was just with his mother. After a few attempts to engage him, his family let him be, and then their focus was on Cassie.

Caroline Webster was the first to speak. She had taken a seat in the parlor and had her son sitting next to her; his glazed eyes and somewhat-mussed hair told Cassie little Barnie had recently risen from a nap.

"We were so glad to hear that you were coming home with them." As Caroline spoke, she rubbed her son's back, occasionally reaching up to stroke his thick, brown curls. The boy must be about two, and he was at that delightfully chubby stage. "I didn't see her before she left. I felt sick to think ... Well. I am certainly glad that you are here and that you will be with them in Cincinnati. I've always felt ... I think Alice needs someone to talk to." Her halting sentences were accompanied by a glance at Peter. Cassie supposed the Strausses believed a part of Alice's mental collapse could be owed to the move to a different town in a different state, something that Peter had apparently initiated without consulting Alice as he ought to have.

"I'm glad to be here, too," was all Cassie could allow. She was glad to be here with Alice; she was glad she would be present when the traveling was over and Peter was at work and Alice must be at her own home, in the quiet, where her own thoughts must come back to her.

Cassie prayed she would be able to make some difference in Alice's life, even if it were a small one. And Peter, too, with his sad eyes and his serious demeanor, could certainly use some support.

"How is she?" Mr. Strauss asked, his German accent thick as he spoke. His gaze flickered from Peter to Cassie.

"She is ... grieving." Cassie pressed her lips together. "Grieving, but that doesn't mean she doesn't need your love."

"Are there certain subjects that ought to be avoided?" A smile twitched about Caroline's lips, but there was a hint of irony to it. "I feel like a walking advertisement for motherhood right now. It's hardly fair to her. I wouldn't blame her if she doesn't want to speak to me just now."

Peter shifted toward them then, his eyes coming into focus. "Please don't avoid her, darling. That'll hurt her more. We ... That is, I hope she'll be all right. I want her to be, but, Caro, even if she isn't, would you distance yourself from her?"

"Of course not." She seemed indignant at the suggestion. "I just don't want to force myself on her. But you know I love her, Peter—we all love her. And we love you, and we want you to feel safe with us, too."

"Which I absolutely do." Peter shifted in the chair. "I think I'll go see what's keeping Mama and Alice."

"Oh, I'm sure they're—" Caroline began, but before she could finish, Alice and Mrs. Strauss entered the room.

Alice went straight to Peter. Cassie caught a glance of her face—she'd been crying, though perhaps not much—and then she reached Peter, placed a hand on his arm, and asked him to come away with her.

He agreed, of course, and they walked out of the room.

There was certainly not much privacy to be had in the Strauss home.

"What did you say to her, Mama?" Dahlia sent her mother a glare. "I can't bear to think you made her cry."

Mrs. Strauss sighed. "I just said that we loved her and valued her and that she ought to feel free to rest for the next few days and not spend time with us, if that were what benefited her most. You know how I am about this whole affair, from the start to the finish. I'm hoping some of my prayers have at last been answered, but I certainly fear that they have not been."

Mr. Strauss straightened on his chair. "She'll be all right, Lilli. They both will be. We know they've turned to God in this; that will be enough."

"I know. It's just not something you can look at logically or emotionally. There can only be God; otherwise, it seems like such an unfair and random set of tragedies."

"It does at that." Mr. Strauss's eyes went to Cassie then. "What shall we call you? You are a lady, aren't you?"

Cassie nodded. "I am, but just Cassie is fine for me. Really, I don't want to go about parading my title—I understand that could be awkward here."

"Not awkward, but I'm delighted to call you Cassie, if allowed the privilege," Mrs. Strauss said. "Perhaps you could call me Aunt Lilli. It's a step away from offering me no honorific, and it's stopped many a young thing from stumbling over what I really want to be called, which is just my name. Will that do?"

Cassie nodded. "Yes, of course." There was little that would please her more.

There was much to be done during her time at the Strausses'. That comforted her, for she knew well that if she spent too much time thinking, her mind would wander back to Patrick.

It always did, but she knew that with God's help, she could take control of her thoughts.

The Doyle family would be settling in Boston, as they had family there, and Cassie did not expect to see them afterward, though she had made Una promise to write. They would bid good-bye to each other in a few days, but the Doyles had had to stay in Philadelphia to sort out their papers.

However, when she had spoken to them the day before, every single one of them had been excited to begin their new life. Now Cassie must focus on moving forward with whatever God's intention was for her future—the first step being, of course, helping Alice.

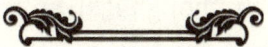

Chapter Sixteen

Miss Blanche Linden wore an extravagant cream-colored dress that was surely made of silks and satins. Around her neck was a triple strand of pearls, and her earbobs matched, while tendrils of dark hair curled down from that sort of pile the rest of it created at the top of her head.

Patrick examined her closely as he sat across from her in the Linden family's parlor, a cup of coffee in his hand and Lorelei at his side, looking just as pretty as Blanche did, with her hair up in a similar fashion, her dress the same length and style, and one of his grandmother's jewelry sets adorning her.

Maybe it was a problem if he thought his sister was just as pretty, if not prettier, than his would-be fiancée. Maybe it was a problem that he found neither of them particularly attractive except in a passing way associated more with affection than the love a man ought to feel for the woman he was going to marry.

Yet he did find Blanche lovely enough, like any of the girls he'd grown up with who had become great beauties. Or so he was told. Patrick had been complimented on Blanche's beauty more than once. That was how 'decent' men did it; they complimented a woman in her man's presence in a polite way, then privately, amongst other men, added congratulations as if she were a horse he'd bred or a ship he'd built.

Patrick didn't care much, though if the men had been talking about his sisters instead of Blanche, he might've gotten defensive. Perhaps he was too protective, but he found that in general, he did not much care if he was. Lore and Winnie were everything to him. Without them, his life would have no meaning, no purpose. What good was the Hilton name and business, his poor excuse for a life, without them?

Blanche was speaking again, something about her friends having re-turned to Boston from New York, where they'd gone shopping. She was lamenting having not joined them, but she'd apparently waited for him to arrive, not wanting to miss him.

Which was sweet. He needed to start thinking of it as sweet. Even if she'd done it with obvious reluctance and was currently rubbing his nose in it, that didn't mean he shouldn't be grateful.

Lore sent him a look that indicated she felt Blanche's jabs at their lateness arriving back in Boston were a bit underhand, too, but Patrick ignored her. There were many more things to think about than Blanche's one-time complaint. He'd failed her in so many ways, and she was to be his wife.

So he sent Lore a look in return that he hoped indicated that she was to be quiet, and Lore sighed and slouched back on the chair.

Chaperoning was not her favorite duty, but Patrick and Blanche had the purest of pure relationships.

Maybe if they didn't—maybe if the temptation existed to be alone together, to embrace and kiss like a normal couple might—Patrick might like her more. He wasn't about to find out, though. He'd figure out how to touch her after they were married. No reason to rush into it.

"Patrick." The whine in Blanche's tone indicated that he had already been called once or twice and not answered her.

"Sorry, what did you say?" He smiled at her, doing his best to put on a charming façade and convince her, at least, that his whole heart was in this moment with her. That he lived for these stiff visits and their public appearances. That this was what he wanted, and she should want it, too.

Lord God, what am I doing?

He had no answer for that question. Could even God rightly answer it?

"I asked if you knew if Herbert Jackson is back in town."

"Herbert?" Patrick hadn't spoken to his schoolmate since before he left for Europe, save a passing letter or two. Patrick wasn't much of a letter-writer, unless he had a very good reason, and Herbert could be positively brusque about everything and anything. "No, I hadn't heard. He ought to be." Like Patrick, Herbert was heir to a different kind of empire. His fortune rested in factories, primarily for clothing. As such, he was required to attend board meetings that Patrick believed were still held in Boston.

Poor Herbert. Supposedly, he was better at obeying his parents than Patrick was. Patrick had always liked the Jacksons; they were a quiet couple who adored their only son, and yet Herbert wasn't quite as spoiled as some sons of privilege Patrick knew.

"American royalty," Patrick mumbled under his breath and laughed sardonically.

"What's that, Trick?" Lore's smirk said she'd heard him and just wanted to put him on the spot with Blanche, who wouldn't appreciate the expression.

"Nothing, my dear." He subtly kicked her.

She glared and folded her arms across her chest.

Blanche cleared her throat and poured herself a fresh cup of coffee. "Do you think he'll be at the dance next week?"

"At the Harveys'?"

"Yes."

"Perhaps." He frankly didn't have any idea of what Herbert's socialization plans were, though he would like to catch up with him. "I can send him a note and ask, if you want."

"Oh, no. That's all right." She sighed and sipped her coffee. She took it like Patrick did—black and strong. Patrick should be grateful for the simplicity of that, but instead, he found himself comparing her to a woman he knew who swirled thick cream and at least two spoonfuls of sugar into her tea.

What did it matter that he knew that?

Cassie took her tea like Winnie, actually, though Winnie put even more sugar than she did. The idea, it appeared, was to disguise the fact that they were drinking tea at all.

Patrick had a different method. He took it plain and forcibly removed his brain from his taste buds with every sip.

However, everyone was different. Like Blanche, he preferred the taste of plain black coffee.

He wondered vaguely what Cassie's reaction to coffee would be. Surely she'd had some at some point in her life, but it seemed less available in England.

He pinched his leg through his trousers to recall himself to the present. He was in trouble if all he could think about was Cassie, even when he was supposed to be getting to know Blanche.

The visit continued for another half an hour, agonizingly slow and boring. And then Lorelei and he left and began the walk back to their parents' house.

"You know she doesn't like you," Lore murmured as soon as the door was shut behind them by the Lindens' butler. "She barely tolerates your presence. How are you going to marry this woman?"

"You shouldn't call her 'this woman,'" he said absently, shoving his hands into his coat pockets and scuffing his feet along the cobblestones. "She's going to be your sister."

"Is she, Trick? Is she really?" He could feel her eyes on him without looking. "I love you, and so does Winnie. We were talking about it last night, actually, after that awful party Saturday."

Patrick did glance at her then. "What about Saturday?"

"Everyone in the room knew you were barely tolerating her, and you mentioned meeting Cassie on the boat several times to the Pents. They asked me about it. Word is going to get back to Mother and Father about that, and if it does—"

"I will tell them that I met a friend, and I mentioned it to the Pents because they know the Strausses. Or they knew the Strattons, anyway, and they would likely care to know what Peter Stratton's namesake is up to these days."

Lore rolled her eyes and heaved a sigh heavier than her years. "You were talking about Cassie O'Connell, not Peter Strauss, and you know it."

He scoffed. "She was with the Strausses."

"What does it matter who she was with? You only ever had eyes for her. Besides, even if Mother and Father don't find out, it's hardly fair to Blanche."

"Blanche has had her own wandering eyes. I consider us even." In fact, if he were a wise man, he'd be a little more careful of Herbert Jackson, but he trusted them both. More than that, he knew they both had no choice.

Just like Patrick. He had to marry Blanche, had to keep the union of the Hiltons and Lindens pure. He hadn't spoken to Herbert lately, but it was entirely likely that, nice or not, his parents had a plan for him, too. Or would at least influence him toward a specific future.

Jackson cared even more about his parents' opinion than Patrick did. Surely, he would do anything to please them.

It would not please any of the first families in Boston to have their son steal the betrothed of another son of one of the first families in Boston. It was an unforgivable sin to interrupt an understanding, no matter how vague.

"Doesn't that concern you?" Lore tugged at his arm, and he turned to catch tears in her eyes.

He stopped in the street, heedless of the mulling humanity—the clopping of horseshoes and rattling of carriages, the shouting of other people from this street to others as they strolled down the street on this warm spring morning. "You're crying?"

"No." She dashed her hand across her eyes. "Never. But I am angry."

"I think you're crying."

"I am *not* crying."

She was, but perhaps it didn't matter. Perhaps Patrick had to stop caring. Perhaps he had to make decisions that were best for his sisters, even if they didn't think they were the right ones.

"Lore, I am doing the best I can for you and Winnie." He placed his hands on her arms. "Please understand that I must be allowed to make my own decisions."

She blew a quick puff of air between her lips. "But if they are for us—"

"We'll talk about this later." He turned and continued down the street. Hopefully she would forget by then.

Cincinnati, Ohio

They stepped into the small house in Cincinnati, and both Alice and Peter, who had chatted with Cassie for most of the train ride there, went silent.

It was a pretty little place. She could see the marks of Alice's decorating, subtle and traditional but somewhat classic. Still, it was clear she had not cared to tend to her home in the months before she left. Stack of books sat by an armchair by the fireplace, a sofa had a blanket tossed over the end in a haphazard manner, a pillow was oddly askew on the other chair, and a pair of spectacles, plainly Peter's extra pair (for he wore them when he read), rested on the side table. This seemed more in line with what Peter would want than what Alice would allow.

Cassie supposed the last time Alice had been there, she had not been in much of a mood to clean. She wondered if Peter felt that, too. Had he felt Alice's absence in the maintenance of this household.

Peter's posture relaxed when, before doing anything else, Alice crossed the room, picked up the blanket, and tucked it under her arm. "This was in the office space, Peter."

"It was cold the night before we left; I read late."

A look passed between them that Cassie couldn't guess the meaning of. She just knew that there was a kind of intimacy there that she didn't dare intrude upon. "I went to bed early."

"Right."

Then Alice straightened her spine and turned in a small circle. "This is it, Cassie. There are two ... two bedrooms upstairs." Her voice caught, but she forced a cheery smile immediately after. "The kitchen is at the back, and there's a little yard with a garden—and, of course, the necessary."

"Riley and his wife live on the other side of the garden. We fixed up a gate between the yards." Peter pressed his lips together. "That can stay, can't it, darling?"

"I'm not going to be that unreasonable." Yet Alice's shoulders had stiffened at the mention of Riley and, in particular, his wife. "We had a cat, Ophelia, too, but ... I admit, I lost track of her."

"She's with Maddie," Peter prompted, his eyes softening. "I didn't take the best care of her in ... in the last few months before we left. Essie took pity on her a number of times."

"Essie?" Cassie glanced between them. "You'll have to remind me of who everyone is."

"Essie is Riley's younger sister, my other cousin. She lives with a married couple who are dear friends of ours—Felicity and Terrence Tappet. Felicity I may have mentioned by the name 'Flick,' which is what she commonly uses." Peter picked up his case again. "I'll get our things to our room and then we can sort out Cassie's place with Riley. He told me he'd put her in the back bedroom. It sounds like they plan on putting Susie in with Polly as soon as she's old enough."

"All right." Alice's response was distant as she crossed the room and examined the stack of books, then picked up Peter's spectacles. "I'm sure that's fine."

Peter walked up the staircase opposite them, and Cassie came to Alice's side. Alice's hands were shaking.

"Here." Cassie removed the spectacles and took the blanket. "He has an office?"

Alice nodded. "Yes. Behind the kitchen. He likes it because the wood-stove is on the other side, and it keeps him warm in the winter. Let's ... let's put the spectacles there, too. And he has shelves for these books. Or he did."

Cassie tucked the spectacles into the pocket of her dress and picked up the stack of books, the blanket tucked neatly under her arm. "I can take care of this. Sit."

"I'm not going to—"

"Alice, sit."

Alice sat on Peter's armchair, but her face held a strained expression. Cassie took care of her armload of paraphernalia and came back to find Peter kneeling next to the chair, speaking softly. Alice's eyes were fastened on his, and she seemed more relaxed.

Cassie hated to do it, but she cleared her throat, and he was on his feet at once.

"I suppose I'll walk over and let Riley know we got in. Shall I take Cassie or just see that her things get over there?"

Alice spoke before Cassie could. "She can stay with me. I want to un-pack." She stood. "Cassie, would you mind terribly?"

Cassie shook her head. "That's what I'm here for."

Peter left, and the women walked up the stairs. The door to the left, closed tightly, was ignored; they proceeded into a small bedroom that still bore the marks of illness somehow after all these months. Pitchers and bowls, cloths draped over odd places, a stack of towels on a chair in the corner, a few mysterious-looking medicine bottles resting on the vanity.

Peter had opened one of the two trunks that sat in the middle of the room, along with Alice's smaller bag, which rested on the bed with its cheery, blue quilt.

Alice looked around her and sighed. "This is where it all happened, I suppose. It seems so light in here. I remember it all in shades of gray."

"Is your memory still faded about the details?" Cassie ventured.

"No. Keener than ever. Sharp but gray." She shook her head. "Never mind that now. I don't really need help unpacking, I don't think. I'm not an invalid; it's only my spirit that doesn't seem so strong anymore, but that doesn't stop my body from moving, at least not once I have begun. It seems like whatever state I am in is the state I stay in, unless moved by some exterior force. Getting out of bed is the hardest. But when I am on my feet ... Oh, it's better to work, Cassie."

"So it's my company that is wanted, not my aid?" Despite these words, she reached into Alice's trunk and withdrew a dress. These days, Cassie would rather work, too. It was a new feeling, but she couldn't help it. There was nothing so frustrating as standing still.

Alice nodded. "That, and I wanted Peter to have a few moments alone with Riley. I never will be able to understand their friendship, but it seems that Peter gleans more real comfort from Riley Farjon than any other man I know. He's such a wild, insensitive, flippant man. I don't know how Peter bears him. But he does, and they both rely on each other." A smile appeared then, somewhat sarcastic in nature. "I want Riley to be that stable influence for him. Peter is trying so hard to be strong. Oh, he's cried, and his prayers are full of agony, but then in the daytime, he makes himself function for me. Perhaps with Riley he can ... Well, maybe he can be weak around Riley."

Cassie doubted it. That didn't sound like any male friendship she'd ever heard of. However, she didn't know Riley at all and her knowledge of Peter was largely secondhand. "I'm glad he has a close friend. I know what you mean. He's been unlike himself. I hope he finds the courage to grieve."

"He can't do any worse than I have." Alice pressed her lips together and reached into her small carpetbag, then withdrew her Bible and placed it on the bedside table. "I feel as if I must learn him all over again, now that this grief has so changed him. Oh, he hopes for me—he prays for me—he strives for me. But I can't bear to think that he is so changed, so much more serious than he ever was before. His demeanor toward me is the same in some ways, but in others, it couldn't be more different."

"How so?" Cassie deliberately said the words with her head in a wardrobe; she knew Alice spoke more when not closely watched, at least when speaking with Cassie.

"Oh. Little things. He speaks of a future with just me. I know it's too soon to truly talk about children, but I have learned it is never too soon to hope. I'm not willing to change my dreams yet; Peter is already there. He talks about how he is grateful for my life. I'm grateful, too, but I want more than to exist. I want to live, Cassie." Alice paused. "I would go back into that river if I weren't going to really live."

Cassie whirled from the wardrobe. "Don't you say that!"

Alice shrugged casually as if she'd just been commenting on the weather or today's fashions. "I will live, so it doesn't matter. I never have had such a desire to live in my life, Cassie. Oh, not always. There are the dark nights and the rainy days, where God feels so distant and nothing seems worthwhile. But then He comes alongside me and says, 'I created you, didn't I? What are you going to do about it?' I can never back down from a challenge, Cass. It's one of my few good qualities."

"One of many," Cassie corrected. They were hard to discern, but Alice did have strengths. They simply needed to conform to God's will, much like how Cassie's stubborn will and independence could be powerful when operated by God's hand.

"Perhaps, perhaps not. Regardless, I feel as if I'm waking up all of a sudden after a long slumber. I have done nothing but pray and listen, and I'm not hearing words, but I'm feeling things. Is that what all you quiet folks mean when you say you're listening to God?"

Cassie laughed. "I think that's what some of us mean. I feel as if God largely gives me ideas, and I act upon them when they align with what I know of Him and of His plans. I always find it vital to work out my own salvation with fear and trembling. Too many people steadily plod along or dash forward outside of God's will; I refuse to be one of those people."

"I think I shall refuse, too." Alice picked up a shawl and shook it out before tossing it on the bed. "Let's put gowns away now, and underthings, and anything extra can go on the bed. Oh, gloves, too. I can't remember where I kept the things."

Cassie nodded and placed two pairs of gloves on the comforter. For a time, they worked in silence, then Alice spoke again.

"He won't touch me either." Her words were a hallowed whisper.

"What do you mean?" Cassie had seen Peter touch Alice. Actually, they were seemingly attached at the hip these days. He always had his arm around her, her hand in his, his lips pressing against her hair, her cheek, her neck. Overall, it was sweet and an unusual change of pace given their previous stiffness around each other. There were also times when it was a little more than Cassie wanted to see.

"I mean, he touches me. Obviously. It's just ... Oh, never mind."

Cassie cast her eyes toward the ceiling and prayed for patience. Alice was such an innocent, despite being the married one of the two of them. She stumbled over even the simplest of admissions. But Alice had been with child twice, and Cassie had an older brother and an older sister who had filled her in on every detail of that process at probably a too-young age. Now, she wasn't so young, and she was able to hold herself at a reasonable distance, in general, from the privacy of marital intimacy while still being in possession of the facts.

It wouldn't scar her young mind. She was too certain of her relationship with Christ to be dirtied by simple knowledge, and her purity wasn't going to be scarred by an admission from her dearest friend that all was not right in her marriage.

After letting a moment or two go by, Cassie cleared her throat. "You mean he does not wish to, or has not tried to, resume marital relations."

Alice's glare was full of all the offense and indignation that she'd always possessed throughout their childhood. "You know I can't talk about that."

"So don't talk. Let me." Cassie sat on the edge of the bed. "It's too soon, Alice. All right? Give yourself permission for it to be too soon."

Alice's lips twitched, more from frustration than amusement. "Since what event? Seven months since our son died. Five months since I tried to take my own life. Four months since I began to heal my spirit. When has it been enough, Cassie?"

"That's not my decision to make. It's yours and Peter's."

Alice made a show of being busy for a moment, then gave up, with a heave of her shoulders, and took a seat next to Cassie. For a long time, Alice sat in silence, then her voice was a barely discernible whisper. "I don't think he wants me anymore."

"Not true. Do you see how he looks at you? You're his world."

Alice's noise wrinkled. "It's not a full marriage, though."

Cassie held out her hand. "Bible, please."

Alice gave her another look but took the Book off her bedside table and handed it to Cassie.

She flipped through it for a few moments and then found the chapter she wanted. "There." She handed the Book back to Alice and tapped the verse. "I don't care what you say. This is a time of fasting and prayer, Alice. Of course, as I said, you must speak with him about when that time ends."

Alice's eyes scanned the verse, then the ones around it, and she quietly closed the Book and put it on the bedside table. "All right. I suppose that's something off my conscience, at least." There was a tightness about her voice that Cassie instantly recognized as the edge of tears.

Cassie cocked her head. "Is it really so bad to wait a little? If he feels it's best, I mean, even after you've talked it through. I suppose I ought to be glad to hear that it is not a burden—that you miss ... everything." She shrugged and stood. "I wondered." Freddy and Catie had offered her very different perspectives. Freddy, unmarried and intent on putting it off as long as possible, had said all men were awful and she should plan on turning her face to the wall and thinking of her duty to County Kerry to get through the dread duty of marriage. Catie, married and in love, had spoken in only romantic terms. Less helpful but more hopeful.

"It's actually ..." Then Alice stopped herself, and Cassie turned, for Alice was going to cry if she didn't manage to weasel her way out of the conversation.

Cassie wasn't going to let her. "Not so good?"

Alice hesitated. "Yes. No. I ... I don't know." Tears tracked their way down her face. "I know we can't not. It's in the Bible and everything. Peter said he won't ... He says we can't unless ... I don't know quite what he wants of me, but it's something different than what I was giving him. You know I've always been a little ... broken."

"No. I don't know that." Cassie lowered herself down next to Alice and wrapped her hands around the bedpost, feeling suddenly in over her head without anything to cling to. "Did Peter say that?"

"No! No, of course not." Alice paused and opened the drawer of her bedside table. Her hands were trembling too much to grasp anything more, and Cassie rose, withdrew the handkerchief she was seeking, and pressed it into Alice's hand. Doing something felt good, stabilizing.

"What did he say? If you can tell me."

Alice's hands were fisted, one around the handkerchief and one in the skirt of her dress. "He said that he realized I didn't want him in the way I ought to, and he felt we ought to wait until I could. He said that what we'd been doing was wrong. He called it perverted, Cassie! I didn't tell him how much that hurt me. Maybe I should've ..."

"You should have. You can now! It's never too late to explain something to Peter. Promise me you will?"

Alice released a shaky sob but nodded.

"Perhaps he was a little harsh. He can be strict in his moral stances. We both know that about him. Yet I'm sure he could give a clearer accounting for what he meant. In the meantime, if you will tell me, Alice, what about intimacy makes you feel the way you clearly feel?" Summoning all her knowledge of Alice, Cassie poured it into her next words. "You're dreading it; that's why you're so upset he won't get it over with. Like any chore, you don't want to delay. But you know in your heart that that is not how it's supposed to be. What made it a chore?"

Alice went silent, and for a time, Cassie sat still and waited. She wasn't sure Alice would be able to discuss it, but the words came at last. "It wasn't always like that. Not ... not at first. But after we ... After the miscarriage ... It really is my fault." Her voice caught again, and she dropped her face in her hands, and another sob ripped through her.

Cassie remained kneeling beside the bed, her arms on Alice's, holding her steady. "It doesn't matter whose fault it was. Maybe it wasn't anyone's fault. But what about that hope, Alice? How can you move forward differently?"

"I'm not sure."

"But will you commit to doing so?"

"If it's possible."

Cassie sighed and leaned back, regarding Alice pensively. "Hmm."

Alice dropped her hands and took a few deep breaths before she spoke again. "What does that mean?"

Cassie might as well be honest. "I was only thinking that if God said something is possible, and if all things are possible with God anyway, that's a rather silly thing to say."

A shaky laugh, and Alice nodded.

"All right. So first step is to talk to Peter about it, right? Tonight, if you can. Remind him that he used the word 'perverted,' tell him that was a jab you didn't need just now. Make him explain in detail what he meant."

Alice nodded again.

"Then, the second step, I imagine, would be to establish a timeline for when you will come together again. That's more or less what the Bible says, isn't it? Tell him you need to work to figure out what was wrong and how to fix it before then. Hopefully, from then on, the steps will fall into place easily. But it's just that first step, Alice. If you can take one step, you're practically there."

Alice straightened and dabbed at her face with the handkerchief. For a long time, she said nothing, only breathed sharply, like the burden was almost too much for her.

Cassie rose then and shuffled her way through drawers to put away the things they'd piled on the bed. It took her about ten minutes, which was sufficient for Alice to gather the strength to rise, brush her hair, and straighten herself somewhat in the mirror.

"I'm sorry you heard that, but maybe if it's worth fighting for, it's worth a brief conversation." Her voice was level again; she was back to herself. "I'm afraid this is one thing you may not get an update on, though."

Cassie shrugged. "I'll know when I meet my first godchild."

Alice laughed. "Oh yes, it'll be that simple, I suppose. Thank you, though. You're right. The essence of everything is to hope, take the first step, and have faith that that will be enough for God to do the rest."

Cassie nodded. "I'm going to go find your husband."

"Oh, is that your job, too?" Alice smirked into the mirror as she brushed her fingers lightly under her eyes, where a slight puffiness and a great deal of redness betrayed her. "We should've written up a list of duties; you're already doing far more than we planned on."

"We're all a little out of our element, aren't we?" Cassie mused. "Anyway, I will find your husband, hopefully by way of a place to sleep tonight."

She set out and soon found Peter crossing the garden with a man at his side. He was taller than Peter by several inches, had blond hair and crystal-blue eyes, and carried himself with confidence. At his side was a medium-sized, brownish dog who stuck close enough to his legs to be attached to him.

"Mr. Farjon." She inclined her head to him.

"Lady Mary! Thank you for coming. We're all grateful. Do you ride?"

Cassie raised her eyebrows. "Do I ...?"

"Ride horses. I bought our Mrs. Strauss one." He gestured over his shoulder with his thumb. "Keeping it in our stables with mine, feeding it, and paying for everything about it, as I have explained to my dear Penn multiple times, but it is hers."

Peter sighed. "And I just spent the last twenty minutes explaining to Riley that—"

"That he is being a bad husband, and that we, all of us, want to make Alice happy except Peter, apparently." Riley's glare was half teasing, but Cassie caught the frustration, too. "Penn, it's a small thing to me, and it could be such a big thing to her."

"You do realize that the way ... the way it happened ...?" Peter's voice trailed off. He couldn't finish the sentence, but all present knew how it ought to be finished.

Alice had ridden her horse, Athena, to the river, where she'd attempted to drown herself. Independence had become a dangerous thing suddenly, at least in Peter's opinion. Truly, Cassie felt Alice deserved some monitoring, but surely they could be cautious of where she rode and when, especially given that the horse was housed by Riley.

Yet Cassie understood Peter's caution, too, in addition to the fact that it was an overgenerous present.

"We'll talk about it later." Riley rolled his shoulders. "Lady Mary, my wife is waiting to introduce you to your bedroom. I'll first introduce you to her and then collect your luggage. Sound about right, milady?"

"Please, call me Cassie." She had an idea that she'd better give permission for him to use the nickname or submit to being "milady" for however long she was staying with him. "You have two daughters, don't you?"

This was the right thing to say, for Riley launched into a speech about how his daughters, Polly and Susan, were the most precious things in the world who she could not fail to be absolutely in love with by "suppertime."

Miss Susan Rose Farjon—or Susie or Rosey, depending on who was talking about her—was a little shy of a year old, whereas Miss Polly Grace Farjon, who Riley called Dolly Girl and Baby Doll interchangeably, was newly three. Cassie expressed her utter eagerness to meet them, grabbed Peter's arm and urged him to go to Alice, and allowed Riley Farjon to lead her back through the gate between the two gardens and into a considerably better-kept, greener, fuller, neater garden with colorful flower beds and rows of vegetable sprouts.

A child with blonde curls and her daddy's blue eyes stood under an oak tree to their left, next to a freshly made swing, and watched them, a thumb tucked in her mouth.

So Cassie was introduced to Polly first, then ushered through the back door to be welcomed by Mrs. Riley Farjon.

Cassie could see at once how Alice's resentment was roused by the petite, pretty woman with an apron around her waist and her ruddy baby on her hip, but Cassie could not share the jealousy. Perhaps she would if she felt her place were being usurped by the woman—unbidden, Cassie's mind flew to Patrick, though she brushed the thought hastily away—but as it was, she would get along well enough living with the Farjons until such a time when Peter and Alice could stand on their own.

The only question was how long that path would be.

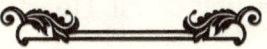

CHAPTER SEVENTEEN

T HE LAST TWO WEEKS had been full of unexpressed thoughts, and now they overwhelmed her, insisting some sort of utterance must take place.

Cassie didn't want to discuss Patrick Hilton with Alice or even record thoughts on him to the pages of her journal. She just wanted to forget. But writing letters to his sisters provided a less-than-perfect distraction, and at last, she put pen to paper to write a letter she could never send.

Dear Mr. Hilton,

It seemed wrong to call him "Mr. Hilton." To leave her heart out of the equation, to inform the disobedient thing that he was not "her Patrick," even if Alice stubbornly insisted on calling him that. Yet what choice did she have? He had forced her to distance herself, and that was indeed what she was doing.

She stared at the dark ink on the white sheet of paper and waited for "Mr. Hilton" to feel right. It didn't feel right, and it didn't feel right, and at last, she continued the letter, giving up hope that it would ever truly describe how she thought of him.

Maybe in time. Maybe when she heard from his sisters that he had a new bride and a home of his own and a baby on the way. She could put together a pretty picture of his life and adjust herself to the thought.

But not now.

"Lord, what am I doing?" she whispered. She waited for guilt, for the anguish of a saved sinner fighting against God's will, but felt none. "You need to convict me," she mumbled absently as she put the pen to the paper again. She'd write and then pray over it. Hopefully conviction would slam her in the face as she prayed.

She needed it to, at least.

Dear Mr. Hilton,

As I said I would not and could not, I am putting a brief note in for you along with the longer letter I have addressed to your sisters. By now, you must be settled in Boston. I am in Cincinnati, and I currently write to you from a small desk which doubles as a vanity in Mr. Riley Farjon's house. He has a lovely home, and I am getting on well with his wife and daughters. I think I may bring his younger, Susan, back to England with me. Do you think they would notice? She has about my shade of hair but curly and soft as silk. But she could almost be my daughter. What a fanciful notion!

She paused and frowned at the sheet of paper. Why was she talking about Susan? That hardly felt appropriate, yet she supposed it was hardly *inappropriate*. Just odd.

Yet as soon as she'd mentioned the Farjons, Susan's small face had popped into her mind.

However, since Cassie could not put this "note" in with the letter, since she had said she would not, its ramblings should be of no concern to her.

She dipped the pen in the inkwell and continued.

I spend most of my days with Alice, while Peter works either at home or somewhere else in the city. He has picked up some extra work at Mr. Farjon's offices. As you may know, Mr. Farjon is a lawyer, and Peter has been able to help him with drafting various papers. He puts in several days a week of this and then writes in the evenings on those days. On most days, honestly. He works very hard. I am encouraging Alice to see what a hard worker Peter is, despite his relaxed appearance, when he knows that he must support her. That's to be respected greatly, and Alice so needs to respect Peter so that he can begin to feel a little normal again. Or just right, for the first time. I don't know how he felt at all before recently, but he certainly is in pain these days.

She paused again as she thought about Peter. She felt so much sympathy for him. Oh, she felt a great deal of sympathy for Alice, too, but that had always been the case. Her sisterly love for Peter was new, rising more and more as she watched him treat Alice with so much love and patience.

As she knew how much the last year and a half had weighed on him, how much he had gone through to be alive and whole. Mostly whole, anyway.

She continued the letter.

Peter's sister Caroline is going to have a baby this summer, in June. It was hard to tell, at least most of the time, when we visited in February, that such was the case. Oh, if you knew, of course it was obvious; but at first glance, it was not.

Babies start out so small. Of course, we all have seen a newborn and known this, but think how tiny they must be at the very beginning! I think I remember hearing that after only a few months, they have all their little fingers and toes. At that age, they cannot hope to live outside of their mother, but to think that God could make such a tiny thing in such a perfect way is almost impossible to believe.

Until you see the grief of parents who have lost their children to miscarriage or stillbirth. Alice and Peter speak of the son they held in their arms, but there was a miscarriage, too, very early on. That child receives as much attention, nearly, though perhaps the impact is not as universally felt.

It makes me want to weep for the beautiful pain of it all. How could something so tiny have left such an indent? Have you heard about how the entrance spot of a bullet can be quite small and the exit wound enormous? Is that how it is? Someone wiser than me will have to say.

Again, she paused and looked over the words she had written. She ought to tear up the missive, to discontinue this fantasy of writing to him, but something stopped her, stilled her.

She kept writing.

I'll attempt to write more that may interest you. I hope you have spent many long days with Miss Blanche Linden. I hope she appears as pleasing to you as I know she always has before; I hope you have made plans. Please tell me when the wedding date is to be, and I will pray for you!

I wish for you a marriage free of pain. I wish you a household of children, if that is God's will, but more than that, a household of laughter and joy and love. I wish that your wife may be a comfort to you. I wish that you may know, always, what a blessing she is, and that she may return the favor.

Perhaps she oughtn't to send this. Her frankness might displease him, and perhaps a harsh response on his behalf would stem her errant feelings.

He could be as displeased as he wanted with her. She was not his, and he was not hers. She had no obligation to please him any more than any other human.

She had only the obligation to be kind to him, as a Christian to a human being on this world, and to encourage him, as a sister to a brother.

She hoped he believed the same as she. If he betrayed them both, it would be a messy affair. If he broke his trust with Blanche Linden, especially if he still wanted to marry her, it would be messier still.

Yet Cassie still didn't fear for herself. She had loved and loved and received nothing in return often enough. This, too, she could bear. She was sure of it.

But more than that, Mr. Hilton, I hope that you will turn to God. I know I have urged this before. I know that that was the changing point in my life the December before last. I prayed, in one desperate moment, and God stepped to my side as surely as any friend could have. I felt the Holy Spirit's comfort and encouragement, and I knew at once what I was to do.

May the Holy Spirit so fill you and yours, so that you may all do mighty things for the Lord. I do not yet feel I have done anything truly mighty, but I wait. Not with false courage nor with pride, but with confidence in the Lord.

When you stand before Him, Mr. Hilton, with an open heart and ready hands, something will happen. If you continue standing still, eventually that uneasy feeling comes over you, and you know you must do something.

You know you must work for God's Kingdom.

What matters is discovering what our work is to be. Mine has seemed so small, for I am small and of little significance. Yet I look at what God has done through me, and my soul fills with the realization that no matter how small I am, no matter how miniscule my actions are, and no matter how frightened I am, I serve the same God Who led Moses across the Red Sea, Who caused the walls of Jericho to crumble.

Who made the whole earth, Mr. Hilton. The whole earth, that we now stand on.

I serve that God. That God, the one and only true God, Who causes the sun to shine and the grass to sprout and little babies to grow in dark places until at last they come out into the light, screaming and wrinkled and utterly perfect.

Mr. Hilton, if you serve that God, there is nothing to fear but a separation from Him. Do not be separated! I beg of you, if nothing else, to not be separated.

She bit her lips. Had she gone too far? She did not have to send this letter. She should stop, rip up the sheets, and seal the letter to the Hilton sisters without any included note to their brother.

She didn't.

Perhaps you are in shock now. You have shocked me a great many times. I feel as if I must bring as much of the Lord between us as possible. You can understand that, surely.

However, I will acknowledge this. I am a woman. There is something out of place when a woman goes about preaching to a man, specifically a man who is older than her. It would be one thing if you were my son or nephew or a young student of mine in some manner. However, you must take what I say here with a grain of salt given our respective positions. I will send this letter, but I hope that you will read it and not refuse the truth of my words only because I have no right to tell them to you.

The only woman who has the right to speak to you this way, I suppose, is your mother, and I've an idea she won't. But you know who the people to turn to are in your life, if you really think about it. So turn to those people, if you will. I only want your happiness.

For my sake, be happy. I am of the opinion that only a close relationship with the Lord Jesus Christ can bring joy into our lives. So you understand, then, why I wrote what I wrote. I want you to feel that joy.

I know we cannot write still, and I am resigned to that fact. We were never meant to correspond in the first place; however, I feel some of my words were left unsaid in a rather unhealthy way, so I will leave this "note" in. I anticipate your sisters' response to my letter.

Sincerely,
Cassie

She'd instinctively signed her name as Cassie, and perhaps that was the wrong choice, but she thought it unlikely that his sisters would write to and talk about Cassie and he would somehow remain a correspondent of the distant and forbidding "Lady Mary."

She certainly wasn't writing to "Mr. Hilton," no matter what she pretended. No, her pen couldn't form words to "Mr. Hilton," the son of Hilton Shipping Co. She couldn't write to the man so tangled up in his "duty" that he was losing sight of God's will in his life. She couldn't write to the man who bent to his parents' wishes in the most underhand way she'd ever seen, not truly obeying, as their slight relationship was surely not something his parents would approve of, but never doing enough to earn their wrath.

No, she was writing to Patrick. Patrick, the man God had created, who must be somewhere within Mr. Hilton. He had to be there, hiding behind those soft, gray eyes and that ready grin and his easy charm with near strangers.

That was the man she wanted, after all. Why shouldn't she write to him?

The letter was sealed. It would go out in the mail in the morning.

And she prayed and prayed until she didn't know what more to say except, "What do I do, Lord?"

CHAPTER EIGHTEEN

April 1883
Boston, Massachusetts

Dear Lady Mary,
Dear Cassie,
Dear Lady Mary,
Dear Cassie,

PATRICK PAUSED BEFORE CRUMPLING that fourth sheet of paper, but he did it. He had to do it. He didn't have a choice.

My dearest Cassie,
My darling Cassie,
My love, my good angel, my heart,
I am an idiot. I am an idiot. I am an idiot.

He stared at the four words, repeated over and over again, on the sheet. Beside him sat several sheets of paper with his sisters' responses. They had been swift to write pages of cheerful words to Lady Mary Cassidy O'Connell.

Patrick had not a word to offer.

She had been fierce in her "note" to him. Granted, it had almost been a whole sermon.

At first, he had hated her for it.

He still did a little.

She was right. He hadn't been able to take it from her.

He supposed this was the reason she insisted they must not write to each other. There could be no comfort in her words to him, and she knew it. Patrick was the one having a hard time accepting that. What had he expected? She was a woman of faith. Her faith must be brought up somehow. And she had done so.

He looked at the four words repeated on his most recent sheet of paper and sighed.

This wasn't going anywhere. He crumpled the paper, tossed it across the room to join the others in the now-overflowing bin, and stood. He rolled his shoulders and ran his hands over his eyes.

It had been a long day. He'd read her note in the morning, when it came in the mail, and spent every minute up until about noon fussing over it. Then he had brought the letter to his sisters over luncheon, and they'd chatted about it as they always had, and Patrick had calmed considerably.

But her personal letter to him, he had not shown to his sisters. He did not quite believe she intended him to do so either. Not those words, so full of her fire and spark and yet also her kindness and heart.

She must have quite the heart, this Lady Mary Cassidy O'Connell. She had a rare spirit but also an unexpected gentleness. Or perhaps it was the spirit that was expected and the gentleness he didn't know what to do with. However he approached it, he found her puzzling but not in a way that frustrated him.

Which was perhaps the fact that was actually infuriating. She was behaving herself so well, expressing herself so well, and he couldn't even decide how to categorize her in his mind.

Perhaps he never would.

He needed to get out of his room, away from his small desk that his father had set up when Patrick was in his early teenage years in hope that he would start "being serious."

It had worked. In a way. Patrick had certainly started doing anything necessary to please his father. Whether or not that was a sincere change in his person or an empty gesture was what was up for discussion.

He hurried through his family's townhouse and out the door. Then he stood on the cobblestone street that had probably been there for at least a hundred years or so and looked up and down the long row of elegant houses.

At last, he started his walk, striding between houses until he reached a tall, black, metal fence, its hundreds of posts standing like dark, shadowy sentries in the evening, dim between their stone generals. A fountain spilled water in the middle of a patch of grass, but a park wasn't what he was looking for.

He needed something wilder tonight.

As he made his way toward the harbor, the wind began to pick up, catching at his jacket and causing him to grasp for his hat, but he was bareheaded. How had he forgotten a hat?

He jogged then, face against the wind, and he began to laugh without at all knowing why. At last, he reached the docks and wandered through the stillness of the industrial area. He wasn't being particularly wise, out here all alone. It wasn't dangerous, but there were small risks for anyone at night in an area where all types roamed, especially sailors and the unemployed.

Yet what did he care? What did it matter? What did any of it matter?

He finally found the mooring of a big steamship, the name *Hazel Leanne* painted on her bow. He'd never quite figured out who that ship was dedicated to, and his father never told him such things. He supposed it could've been a mistress or an animal or a long-lost sister. He would never know.

Because Patrick wasn't friends with his father. He wasn't even his father's son. He was an employee. An important employee, but still an employee, kept for room and board and an allowance that had him tied to his parents and their bank account.

He was not allowed independence. He didn't necessarily use all of his allowance every month, and he could use less, but it mostly ended up going to Lore and Winnie anyway.

He wasn't sure why. They didn't need the money. And it had never occurred to Patrick until that moment that he ought to be trying to save something of his own, whether in cash or in his own bank account.

An interesting thought but unnecessary if he married Blanche and continued working for his parents. His understanding was that his "allowance" would stretch to accommodate his bride and any children that came along.

Yet as he stood there, looking up at the mighty vessel, he questioned whether it had been the right choice to not prioritize some sort of independence. Even now, he had a scattering of bills and coins in his pocket. There was more than that left over from earlier this month in his room, saved as a gift for Lore given that her birthday was coming up.

But he'd already bought her a book he knew she'd like. Maybe instead of searching for something in addition to what he'd already gotten her, he should reinvest that sum, even if it was just in his mattress.

His father wouldn't stop him from opening a bank account of his own, would he? After all, Patrick had limited access to his father's accounts, for the purposes of running the business and in case of emergency. He was twenty-one. He ought to have his own bank account.

Why didn't he? What had he even been thinking?

Then he stopped himself and furrowed his brow. Why was he thinking about this in the first place? He never had before.

"God?" He whispered the Name, faintly, unsure why he'd done it. "I know we speak when I can, but perhaps I've been remiss in not doing so more often. I do want to serve You. I ... I thought I was. Perhaps I am not, however. Was that Your idea? About the money, I mean? Why do You care?"

Of course, it was a stupid question. He knew it at once. God's entire reputation was based on caring very much about even the sparrows of the field. How much more did He care about Patrick and apparently Patrick's nonexistent bank account?

He also remembered a few Proverbs vaguely. A lot of them were about not loving money too much, and Patrick certainly didn't lay too much of his own up. However, there were a few others that felt moderately convicting.

It was not wise to spend all of one's money. That wasn't being a good steward of one's resources. God ever called for caution, and Patrick was not being cautious.

"It's not my money, though," he argued.

Yet he worked hard every day and sometimes late into the night. Although he was working for his father, that did not change the fact that he was doing honest work, and though his allowance could not especially be called a fair compensation, on top of room and board, it was generous enough.

"Lore and Winnie get the same amount or more," he protested further.

As he sat there, he began sorting through what he received every month. He didn't need to buy more clothes; the ones he had would do for some time, no matter what Lore said. He didn't really need much of anything. An occasional expenditure would come up, but in general, he could live simply in his parents' household and put away most of his money.

It was a poor laborer's wage, he thought—a factory laborer, perhaps. But if he were wise with what he received, he could lay up enough to support a small family in a simple way for some time, if he needed to.

What did that matter, though?

Yet the press to be cautious wouldn't leave his soul. He couldn't deny it, no matter how he tried.

He widened his stance and looked upward at the ship before him, a symbol of his family's strength, another guardian of his prison cell. "Lord, what am I supposed to do?" he whispered, the words faint at first and then growing. "How can I serve You best? Don't You want my sisters to be safe? Don't You want ... don't You want *me* to be safe?" The last words died back into a whisper, and guilt swarmed.

He shouldn't care about his own safety. He should be brave. It was his sisters that mattered, that mattered so much that he couldn't imagine doing anything but devoting his life to them.

Yet when he assured his sisters' safety, he assured his own, too.

And what if safety wasn't the most vital piece of the puzzle? What if life was about something more than that?

Cassie believed so. She had left the assurance of a marriage, a husband, a household, and children, in favor of following God's will in her life.

"But it could just as easily be Your will to marry Blanche, couldn't it? To fulfill my duty?"

His duty to God ought to be greater. He knew that. Just, in the last two years, as the noose around his neck tightened, leading him toward Blanche Linden and the Hilton Shipping Co. and all his other obligations if he were to obey his parents word for word, he had drifted away.

Shame flooded him, and his head bowed with the weight of it.

Yet before he could stay too long with the guilt of his own lack of faith resting on his shoulders, a verse came to mind: "If we confess our sins, He is faithful and just to forgive us our sins, and to cleanse us from all unrighteousness."

"1 John 1:9," he repeated, memories of days spent with a strictly religious tutor coming to mind. He hadn't much cared for the man at the time, but he was glad now that so many verses had been hammered into his head.

When was the last time he'd actually thought about one?

"Forgive me." The words went up to the clear night sky over Boston Harbor; the wind whipped him, but he stood still and watched the stars. "Forgive me, Lord, and give me the strength to do better. I will listen, if You care to say anything. Help me."

There was no immediate answer, but Patrick stood for a long time, watching the stars and remembering everything he'd already known.

Late April 1883
Cincinnati, Ohio

Dear Cassie,

Thank you for that last "note." I was not to send a reply, but I had to, because I wanted to thank you. You were right that it expanded in both length and strength to something more than that, but I was nonetheless grateful for it.

You made me think. I went on a walk last night and did nothing but wrestle with God. I'm grateful no part of me was put out of joint, but I did come back listening and waiting, not angry and frustrated.

Though you are right that it is not entirely appropriate for us to speak in such a way, I appreciate that you did. I needed your words when I read them. I suppose God must have sent you to me for a reason.

I don't want to go on too long. I feel as if my mind is too full of thoughts to properly express any of them. They are crowded in there suddenly, where formerly there had been nothing but empty space. I will have to remove them slowly or risk them crumbling in my hands, like something delicate.

In the meantime, I could not delay sending you my sisters' letters, selfish as that would be. Therefore, here they are. Both Lorelei and Winnie were thrilled to hear from you, and their letters reflect that. I don't know if you understand how much of a light you have been to the whole Hilton family.

For now, I'll let you go. I hope the Strausses are well. I'm trying to pray more. I apologize once again for my behavior. You can be assured that this will be my only letter to you.

Sincerely,
Patrick Hilton

Cassie set the note down and glanced at the two much longer missives from his sisters. She'd have to read them later. She'd snuck these letters up after breakfast, but it was time to go over to Alice's house. Peter would have already finished his meal and gone; she wasn't supposed to leave Alice alone.

Even though Alice had become more and more independent and would probably start the process of kicking Cassie out of her house sooner or later.

Which Cassie didn't mind in the slightest. It just brought to mind the question of "What next?"

She took a look in the small mirror that hung above her vanity-desk. She'd lost a little weight in the last year, but otherwise, she was as young and pretty, or pretty enough, as she'd been when she'd first attracted Aubrey Montgomery.

Perhaps when she returned to England, she could open herself up to the possibility of a relationship with another man. Even if she never precisely fell in love, she was sure she could love a man devotedly, if God willed that she should do so.

Perhaps that was the next step. To admit that there was nothing else in America after Alice was settled. To move on and find a life for herself.

Yet she felt no true indication that she was supposed to be doing anything.

Maybe Patrick would finally figure out what he was supposed to do. Maybe that would give her some kind of answer. Or maybe it wouldn't.

She rose with a sigh and made her way through Maddie's kitchen and through the garden and into Alice's backyard, which was slowly starting to take form.

But Alice wasn't out in the garden today, despite the fact that Cassie was fairly certain that had been her original plan.

She walked through the back door. "Alice?"

"I'm upstairs."

Cassie followed Alice's voice up the staircase. The door to the nursery was open now.

That was an interesting development. More than interesting, it was shocking. Alice had sworn she wouldn't be able to enter that room for months to come.

Cassie walked through the doorway. It was a surprisingly light room, with the curtains pulled back; she had somehow thought it would be cloaked in shadows and dust. Instead, it was moderately clean and neat.

Alice knelt next to a chest of drawers, several piles of small clothes around her. "Come help me." Her voice was steady and even but not all right. There was a subtle difference to its timbre; she was shaking inside, though her hands remained steady.

Cassie crossed the room and knelt next to Alice. "What are you doing?"

"Putting everything away." Alice gestured over her shoulder to a table. "I'd laid out most of the necessary clothes there, where I thought they would be easy to catch up as I needed them. But we hadn't much, of course, so there's plenty of room for it to be neatly packed away until ... It can be packed away."

Cassie nodded and picked up a tiny cloth that she wasn't even sure of the purpose for. She folded it, set it to the side, and picked up another one.

For a long time, they worked in silence.

"Tell me something, Cassie." There was that catch in Alice's voice, but she kept her words low and soft.

"What sort of thing?"

"Anything."

Cassie's mind scrambled, and she spoke of the thing most recently on her mind. "I received a letter from Patrick and his sisters."

"Oh? Really? What has he to say for himself?" A pause, which Cassie wasn't sure how to fill. "Did he mention his thoughts on your letter?" Alice knew everything about that now. Wise or not, Cassie hadn't been able to resist telling her in detail what she'd said to him, despite her fears surrounding those words.

"He did. He said he is going to try praying more, and of course he assured me that he would not write again."

"Hmm."

"He also said that he had a lot to think about. He appreciated what I wrote him. He was thankful. I'll let you read what he said if you want, and what his sisters say; I haven't read their letters yet."

"I would like to, but only if it's not bothersome." Alice smiled then, her hands at rest on a bundle of lace and ribbons resting on her lap. "You know I care deeply about this entire situation, as much because it's a good distraction. But this ..." She gestured around herself. "This is good. I'm trying not to think about it. When Peter comes home tonight, I'm going to ask him to sit with me here and pray."

"That's a good idea. I'll make sure to leave you alone." Though she was doing that more and more in the evenings. Though Peter still wasn't himself, he was getting better, and Cassie knew time alone with Alice was one of the contributing factors. For Alice was trying so hard, and God was helping. Cassie knew He was.

For a time, they worked in silence, then Alice cleared her throat. "We fought last night, after you left."

"Really?" The exclamation was impossible to control. When she'd left them, they'd been acting perfectly normal. "What happened?"

"Oh, I don't know." Alice leaned back and stared at the ceiling, a slight smile ghosting her lips. "I hardly know how we began. All I know is, I was furious at him, and he at me, and yet we didn't go to bed angry. We calmed down, we talked, and I slept in his arms and was happy. I didn't know it could be like that."

With Alice? Cassie hadn't known either. "So it was a good thing?"

"I don't think arguments are ever really a good thing, but it's good that he knows I'm not fragile. Not that I think he expected to fight with me, I don't think. Oh, I suppose I am fragile, but I can stand up to him, and he to me, and we're not going to make it if both of us can't do that, Cass. Further, I'm glad that, at least in this case, we were able to arrive at a resolution."

"And how did that make you think to come up here?" Cassie could pretend she believed the two events were unrelated, but Alice's actions always immediately followed a realization, and this was the action Alice had taken.

"I realized that this was the boil I was refusing to lance. I'm going to straighten up this room, and yes, the door will close again when I leave, but if I want to come back, I should. It's a significant room, but I am not afraid of it. I am not afraid of anything that happened, or will happen, at least in this moment. I refuse to buckle to fear now, at my bravest, and I am preparing myself for my weakest moments, when I certainly will fear. I'm praying that God will carry me through even then, when all I can do is 'be still,' but until then ... Cassie, I'm going to act when I can in what small ways I can. I refuse to let this place haunt me whenever I am hurt. I am going to sit here and tell myself that this is one more thing I can handle."

Cassie took Alice's hand and squeezed it. "Good. That's exactly what I want to hear."

They worked for perhaps another hour, then they left, and the door did close. The rest of the afternoon was spent in the kitchen.

When Peter arrived home, Cassie made herself scarce. There were some areas where she could interfere, but this was certainly not one of them. Furthermore, she had letters to read and reread and attempt to write coherent responses to.

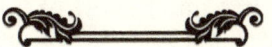

Chapter Nineteen

Late May 1883
Providence, Rhode Island

T HE LAST MONTH MONTH had been busy ones both for Hilton Shipping Co. and in Patrick's personal life. He'd been praying. He'd been saving money in his newly opened bank account, which his father had surprisingly not so much as mentioned yet. Patrick had been trying to find a solution other than marrying Blanche.

He hadn't come up with one yet. He wasn't sure if there was a solution. But if there was, he wasn't about to ignore it.

Lorelei had turned eighteen recently, and ever since, his mother had been mentioning more and more that in time, Lorelei would have to find a husband. Winnie was just two years behind her.

Patrick was beginning to realize that even if he married the woman his parents wanted, he would not be able to rescue his sisters from their own arranged marriages.

The thought would occur to him on lonely nights when he watched the flames flicker in the fireplace and twirled his pen through his fingers and dreamed of writing all the things he didn't dare to, that perhaps the best way to secure their future was to establish a precedent not of obedience but of rebellion. Yet that couldn't be right.

Lorelei was with him more and more these days. Even now, she sat at his right side, looking adorable with a funny little white hat pinned to her head, the blue ribbons flopping about in the sea breeze.

She sent him a glare. "How much more of this?"

He laughed. "You ought to be ashamed of yourself. You were practically raised on the water, and Blanche is doing better than you."

"Not much better." Blanche sat across from them in the Jacksons' sailboat, looking as put out as Lorelei.

Patrick had met with Herbert Jackson earlier in the spring, and they'd set up this sailing date. The Jacksons' sloop was drifting on the calm waters off the "summer cottage" they owned outside Providence.

Toward the bow of the sloop, Herbert Jackson and James Pent were chatting about their boats. Patrick wanted to join the discussion, but he couldn't leave his sister and almost-betrothed alone. James had brought his fiancée along, too, but Miss Myra Elliot was sitting by James, and he had his arm curled around her shoulders, so it wasn't like she would offer much buffer between Lorelei and Blanche.

Patrick presumed his parents had insisted Lorelei come along with him today in hopes that, out of necessity, Herbert and she would be tossed together. That would make another good connection for the Hiltons. However, since Patrick and Blanche never acted much like a couple, no one else was obligated to.

Not that Myra and James could seem to help it. Patrick had known them both since they were children, and he'd never seen anyone so smitten.

James was from Philadelphia, and the Hiltons—or at least the Hilton children—had spent many summers with them. Actually, Winnie had recently developed an infatuation with him. Not that it was serious. Winnie decided upon someone new to marry about every week.

How dangerous that could be in the hands of his mother or even his father. She was so easily influenced. He couldn't bear the idea of Winnie locked in a marriage that would crush her spirit or hurt her spiritually just because her parents were looking for a profitable match and Winnie was too romantically minded to resist.

"Patrick, you're looking a little green." Blanche's voice cut through his thoughts, and he focused his attention on her face.

Next to him, Lorelei giggled, the sound the most girlish, delighted noise she would ever make. "Trick, you were just scolding us, and now—"

"Oh, I'm all right." He shook his head to clear his thoughts. He needed to think about other things. "Pent!" he called. "Is your little boat very like this one?"

James half turned; he had been murmuring something into Myra's ear and looked rather frustrated. "Ask Jackson. He's been in it, and he claims to be the expert. Jackson, why don't you peddle your lies to Hilton and see if he doesn't correct you? He knows more about sailing than either of us combined."

Herbert left the two lovebirds alone at the bow to continue their ducked heads and whispers—friendship was a great creator of private situations for couples caught in the constant expectations of their parents—and made his way back to sit on the narrow bench next to Blanche.

Fixing his eyes on Patrick with a serious smile, Herbert gave all his attention to a speech about the comparative merits of his sailing vessel versus James Pent's.

Usually Patrick would have given his entire mind to Herbert Jackson's words. Usually Patrick would have become lost in the conversation and given no heed to anything else.

Usually Herbert Jackson's hand was not resting on Patrick's be-trothed-to-be's arm.

Usually Blanche Linden did not pay anyone in her general surroundings much more heed than what was polite. Certainly Patrick had never seen her eyes so focused on anyone's face, clearly attentive to their every word. She certainly didn't ever lean in, as if every word he was saying was of the utmost fascination to her.

Yet that was what was happening. Lorelei noticed it, too, though she said nothing. She simply glanced at him with slightly raised eyebrows.

He chose not to acknowledge her.

The rest of the day, which would have so delighted and interested Patrick, was a blur. He could think of nothing but the fact that Herbert Jackson was attracted to Blanche Linden. He had to be. There was no other accounting for the unconscious touches, the attention he gave her when she asked a question, the way he took care to say things that might interest her.

Objectively, Blanche Linden was well-suited to Herbert Jackson. However, that didn't give Patrick a great deal of comfort. He was objectively well-suited for Cassie. At least, he believed so. Did that lessen his duty?

He heard a still, small Voice urging him to wait and see.

He tried. He really did. He waited while the boat was docked. He waited throughout the rest of the evening, while they ate with the Jackson family—toward whom Blanche was decidedly more polite and considerate than she had to be—and then bedded down for the night.

The next morning, he waited as they began the trip back to Boston. He watched Herbert Jackson continue to show genuine favor to Blanche while he remained his polite but somewhat distant self with the other members of the party.

Patrick waited patiently for Blanche to mention the favor. Explain it. Say something that might indicate that she knew what was happening, or at least that she knew Patrick knew.

Nothing.

It wasn't until they were back in Boston, with Patrick ready to walk Blanche home to her parents after stopping by the Hilton house, that he felt that he could speak about it.

"Want to meet Bell's puppies before you go? They don't look like little rats anymore." That had always been Blanche's excuse before when he brought up his pride and joy—six adorable puppies created by the planned breeding of Bell with a German-imported sire named Apollo. Now they were adorable, wiggly things who would be going to their new homes in a short month. Patrick still hadn't decided who would be receiving the pups, but he was determined that they would go to good families. He fully intended to keep at least two, though.

Blanche hesitated and tried to come up with an excuse, but when Patrick begged, she agreed.

He so often resorted to begging with her these days, and perhaps he should have realized that before. However, in that moment, he found himself tracing over the last several months with Blanche.

She didn't even want to be around him, did she?

They walked to the back of the house to the kitchens, greeted the cook, and stepped into the small corner of the pantry given over to puppy-raising. They all came rushing out to greet them, and Blanche stiffened. Patrick knelt and picked up a small, black one that Patrick thought was the twin of Bell.

"I call this one Juno." He held Juno out, but Blanche stepped back and refused to take her; she did, however, pat the puppy's head—rather awkwardly, but at least she was making some sort of an effort.

"He is rather adorable, I suppose," she admitted. "I'd just rather keep this coat clean."

"She. Juno is a Roman goddess." Why didn't she know that? He thought it was common knowledge. Hadn't he talked to her about his childhood fascination with those mythological gods at any point? It had been fleeting, but it had left a mark on him. Generally just in the way he named his pets, but still. Lore and Winnie certainly knew that. He stroked the top of Juno's head; the puppy arched her back to eagerly lap at his hand.

The appearance of Juno's tongue made Blanche cringe. Granted, she could have a preference if she needed to, but it seemed silly to Patrick, a lover of dogs and of dog tongues, that he should remain with a woman who had such a preference.

Herbert Jackson wouldn't mind, though. The type of woman he was looking for would be one like Blanche Linden. She was raised to never touch anything so unsanitary as a puppy tongue. Why hadn't Patrick seen that before?

Blanche talked about Herbert Jackson constantly, and Herbert mentioned her in an off-handed way from time to time, too. In the process of being around Patrick, Blanche had been with Herbert a great deal. Further,

Patrick had never considered it unusual before that the two would discuss each other—he'd assumed their association had been through him, not *around* him.

Now, suddenly, as if his eyes had been opened for the first time, he wondered if that was the case.

"Blanche, are you and Herbert Jackson ... Are you talking to each other?"

The color drained from her face, and she raised her dark eyes to his face slowly, a slight pout on her lips. "Why do you ask?"

That was as good as an admission of guilt. "I saw the way you looked at each other all this last weekend. Then I thought, 'My, they do mention each other a lot.' Herbert is not a talkative man, yet you are the only woman he speaks of. I assumed it was because I am promised to you. Now I wonder if it's not because he has an interest in you."

She bit her lips and reached out to pat the puppy's head briefly, narrowly escaping Juno's tongue, as if placating him with the action. "Would it matter to you?" The words were cautious, measured.

"Depends on the level of the association." He did not blame her for her hesitance in speaking thankfully; after all, Patrick had become the soul of caution in the last several years. Oh, he'd been practicing caution all his life to please his parents, to save his sisters. His relationship with Blanche was a natural extension of that. But never more than now did he want to be careful what he said. "I have my own confessions if we are being entirely honest. However, if we are to continue as we are ..."

She nodded quickly. "Of course. Of course. We ... He comes to see me. Sometimes once or twice a week, when my parents are not at home. He has for a few years now. We ... we didn't mean ..." She stopped herself again, and her eyes went downward, focused on the tile at their feet as if it were the most interesting thing in the world. "We didn't mean it to continue."

"But it has?" He lightened his voice and accompanied the words with a smile. "How much has happened, Blanche?"

"Not much." She shifted from foot to foot, her voice small, like a naughty child being called to account for her flaws. "We talk, mostly. Lately, though ..." Then her eyes rose to his face again, and a flash of defiance appeared in them. "Patrick, if I am to live my whole life bound to you to allow my parents the additional security of a merger they could've made through simple business contracts, if I am to bind myself to you forever, what difference do a few kisses make? If you will have fifty of my remaining years, can he not have fifteen minutes here and there before you and I are bound? You know you don't want this either, and I have kept myself pure. Pure enough, anyway. Isn't that all that matters? You'll have the pieces of me that matter. Let Herbert have what my parents don't care about, and what you don't care about either, if you admit it." She was angry now, her eyes alight and her face contorted. "Let him have my heart for now, and I will do what I must when the time comes for me to do so. But I know you are writing to some ... some *woman* in Cincinnati. Gwendolyn told me. I don't care how far it's gone; I don't want to hear about her. But I doubt you have the resolution to give her up once we are wed. I will be honorable, though. I promise. Just ... just give me this." She deflated slightly at those words. "Don't tell my parents."

While she spoke, Patrick stood still, his ears ringing and his mind swirling with a thousand feelings and thoughts, but when she completed her rant with that sigh, those words of utter defeat, he couldn't help his reaction.

He laughed.

He laughed so hard he was forced to put the wriggling puppy back in the whelping box with her siblings and catch the wall to hold himself upright.

"It's not funny, Patrick," Blanche said, but her tone held more confusion than anger or despair now.

"It is funny!" he exclaimed, straightening slightly but still shaking with mirth. "You're betraying me, and all you care about is that your parents don't hear!"

She scowled at him. "It's not really betrayal."

"We can debate that later, but I'm not sure it matters. You haven't the slightest interest in marrying me?"

Her scowl deepened. "As if I had any choice, Patrick. My parents—"

"Never mind your parents or mine or anyone but you and me. And maybe Herbert. I've my own interests, as you surmised. But you want out, Blanche?" He took her hands in his and forced her to look at him. "If you had your own soul back and could do what you want, it would be Herbert who you married, wouldn't it? Be honest."

"Of course." The words burst from her as if they were the most important in the world; however, she could not stop herself from following them with, "But it hardly—"

"Look. If that's what you want, I'll figure it out. Though I can't pretend it's a grand gesture on my part. I haven't the slightest interest in marrying you either."

She was a woman, so she had to look offended, but that didn't faze Patrick in the slightest. Never had anything been clearer.

He had to find a way to separate himself from Blanche. God's will couldn't be more obvious in this situation. To marry a woman who took the commitment to him so lightly before they were even engaged was suicidal. He had to separate himself from her. What he did next would be up to God, but this first step was clear.

"I need time, Blanche." That was the main issue; moving forward in a hasty manner could hurt them both. He wasn't sure what his parents' reaction would be, much less her parents', but he was sure it would not be positive. "I'm not sure how I'll arrange it, but I'll at least make sure you can be with Herbert."

Blanche herself was standing still and quiet; it took her a long while of staring at the wall to rouse speech within herself. But at last she did, training her eyes on him. "Patrick, if you can do it in a way that doesn't get me disinherited and that allows me a future with Herbert, I am more than willing to do whatever you want. Can I ... can I tell Herbert?"

"You should tell him as soon as you can," Patrick confirmed. "I also have plans of my own to make. But be cautious. If either of our parents catch a whiff of this before we are ready, we will be in deep trouble."

Blanche nodded. "I ... I know. I will be careful."

"Good."

They left the puppies, and he walked her home. He was polite to her parents. He acted as if nothing had changed, and they seemed to notice nothing different about him.

But his head was full of plans and dreams.

Lord, please let this be the right decision.

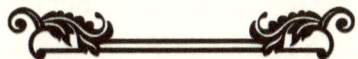

Mr. Hilton sat behind his elaborate oak desk, papers stacked about him and one particular set of contracts resting before him. He looked up briefly when Patrick entered the room but otherwise had no reaction to his son's presence.

"Father, may I speak with you?" It was time to be honest, at least about his relationship with Blanche, if nothing else.

Mr. Hilton grunted and moved one page under another. "Is it about business?"

"Rather. I wanted to discuss the future of—"

"Will you go to Cincinnati next week?" His father did drop the papers he was holding then. "I want you to complete our deal with the Ohio-Wabash group. I had intended to do it myself, but I'm needed here in the next month. Baldwin & Sons is trying to establish their footing on the Erie, and I refuse to let that happen."

Patrick raised his eyebrows. That was unusual for two reasons. First, because his father never sent him on solo trips unless it was something small; the Ohio-Wabash deal certainly was not. Second, because his mind was seldom anywhere but in Cincinnati these days. "But—"

"Patrick." His father's brown eyes narrowed slightly, turning steely as they so often did. "You can do this without disappointing me, surely."

"I ..." Patrick was tempted to turn it down. It would not be a good thing for him to be in Cincinnati, and further, he had much to do in Boston if he wished to break his understanding with Blanche while establishing a place for both of them to land in case everything went south more rapidly than they'd anticipated.

However, the words stuck in this throat, and his father talked on, briefly summarizing what Patrick would be doing in Cincinnati.

It would only be a brief trip. There was no real reason for Patrick to see Cassie. He wouldn't have to bother her; he could focus on completing his business and then return to Boston.

After his relationship with Blanche Linden was ended, and if he was able to settle the situation with his parents amply, he would consider contacting Cassie. Not before. Even then, he wasn't sure it was a good idea. He knew Cassie was disgusted with him; surely contacting her wasn't a good idea.

Yet he agreed to take the trip. It might be the last endeavor he ever undertook on his father's behalf. He might as well end on a positive note.

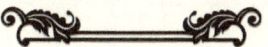

Chapter Twenty

Early June 1883
Cincinnati, Ohio

T HE STREETS OF CINCINNATI, which had been so busy hours before, were clear and quiet. Patrick shifted his briefcase from hand to
hand and rolled his shoulders. It had been a long day. His sore shoulders
and cramped left hand were a testament to the unique challenges presented
by the company heads he had spoken to.

Details of the Ohio-Wabash deal had proven unnecessarily complicated,
and what should've been a few hours had stretched on to twelve. He was
thankful now that he'd sent a message ahead last week to reserve a first-class
hotel rather than attempting to catch a late train back east.

He yawned, grateful when he caught sight of his hotel at last. Now he
just had to catch a few hours of sleep before returning mid-morning to sign
a few remaining papers, then he could head for home.

It was also good that he had already determined not to see Cassie despite the fact that they almost coincidentally were in the same city. His
stay would be brief, and to bother her now, when she had already made
her opinions so painfully obvious, seemed almost cruel. This late night,
incompatible with any type of visiting, surely was a sign from God that

Patrick had made the right decision.

That hadn't stopped him from walking by the church she attended with the Strausses. During a mid-afternoon break, Patrick had navigated to the address given in a recent letter to his sisters. Cassie had discussed her thoughts about a sermon preached there, which she had partially disagreed with.

It hadn't helped Patrick to realize even more sharply than he had during their brief correspondence last year that their thoughts were almost identical. That afternoon, he had stood in the empty Baptist church, wondering at his own strange impulses and praying as best he could.

The building was small and so different from the Episcopal church he attended with Lore and Winnie in Boston. He wondered what Cassie would think of it. He honestly wasn't sure what he'd do once he returned. Though he appreciated the philosophy of the head pastor, there was a lack of life in the congregation, at least in Patrick's opinion. He wondered if, like Cassie, he might be able to reconcile himself to differing beliefs to be a part of a more active church.

He entered the lobby of the hotel and approached the desk. An exhausted-looking clerk thankfully still sat at the desk. "No vacancies," he muttered without looking up.

"I actually have a reservation under the name Patrick Hilton. It could've also been recorded under the name Hilton Shipping Co."

Yet the clerk had no record of that nor of any outstanding reservations for the evening.

Patrick's brow pinched in a mix of exhaustion and frustration. "It would've been made last week." A reminder had been sent yesterday to confirm the reservation, but he didn't add that detail in the name of not confusing the poor clerk further. Patrick did, however, produce the message he'd received from the hotel confirming the receipt of the booking.

The clerk grew more frazzled by the moment as the evidence stacked up in Patrick's favor, but what could he do? There was no room at the inn. A manager was summoned, and a complimentary stay offered at the expense of the hotel in the future, but that did not help with Patrick's present difficulty.

He was alone at night in a strange city without the benefit of a roof over his head.

He chose not to argue with the employees; they could not change what was. He simply left the hotel and proceeded to another one.

He was met with a similar answer.

Three hotels and an hour later, Patrick was far too exhausted to continue. He would have to settle on a bench at the train station and attempt not to sleep. Falling asleep in public with important documents in his briefcase was simply not an option.

As he approached the train station, his eyelids drooped, but his mind seemed to sharpen in that odd way it did from time to time when an unnecessarily clarifying thought seemed to appear out of nowhere.

The people you do *know in Cincinnati are the Strausses.*

Patrick brushed the thought off. The idea of appearing at the Strausses' home at a little past midnight was inconceivable. He hardly knew them, and it would be a horrible inconvenience. Further, Cassie slept in the next house over, and the Strausses would, of course, tell her all about his late-night appearance.

You're going to risk losing important documents that could cause serious issues for two companies in the name of avoiding embarrassment?

Yet the risk was small.

Wasn't it?

He yawned again as he stood in the street, alone, his senses already deadening with exhaustion.

Peter Strauss will never turn you away. Sometimes it is a requirement of you, and every other sane person in this world, to rely on others for help. Go to another Christian and ask for the same common decency you would hope to offer yourself.

Grumbling, Patrick knelt and opened his briefcase. Cassie's note was tucked into a small side pocket, and the return address was clearly marked on the outside in her feminine script.

What could it hurt? Other than his pride, what could it honestly hurt?

He hated inconveniencing people, but sleeping at the train station was not an option, and he was not sure he could stay alert all night. Further, he desperately needed a place where he could shave, change his clothing, and look presentable for the final details of the business deal tomorrow morning.

With a heavy sigh, he turned his feet in the direction of the Strausses' home. He knew where it was; even as unfamiliar with this city as he was, he had the address, and it was not far from the church he had walked into that afternoon.

At last, he found the street and then the Strausses' home. It was a cheery, little place, unassuming but neat with white shutters covering the windows.

Of course, the Strausses would be asleep ...

Yet a glow of lamplight under the edge of the left shutter hinted that he might be incorrect in that assumption.

Screwing up his courage, he lifted his fist and knocked at the door as gently as he could while still hoping to be heard.

A moment later, the door swung open to reveal Peter Strauss standing, fully dressed but in his shirtsleeves, his hair standing up at a few odd angles. His spectacles rested on top of his head, and his eyes blinked as if he had been half asleep.

"Patrick Hilton?"

Patrick inclined his head. "Peter Strauss."

"Oh." Peter glanced over his shoulder. "It is, in fact, after midnight. And this is Cincinnati."

"I am aware. I ... had business in town, and it's a long story, but I wasn't able to find a hotel. I had a reservation, but it seems to have been lost." Patrick shrugged. "I thought about sleeping at the train station, but I feared I would have some rather important documents stolen from me, and I don't know if I'd be able to stay awake." Even now, he was struggling to smother a yawn. "I know this is a terrible imposition, but if I could simply sit on a chair in your house overnight, I would feel so much better."

This seemed to recall Peter to himself, for he stepped back from the door.

"Of course. Come in. You can take the sofa, if you like."

Patrick nodded gratefully and entered the house. Peter must have been reading, for a book lay across the seat of a nearby chair, and a lamp flickered on the table next to it.

"I was just about to head upstairs for the night. I couldn't sleep when Alice wanted to, and now I know why." Peter smiled. "I had to let you in the house. Here. I'll fetch a blanket from my office."

He disappeared and then returned a moment later with a blanket. "If you like, there's a pump in the backyard, along with the necessary, and you can find a basin in the kitchen. You'll stay for breakfast? I think Alice would be happy to see you."

A bold claim for any man to make on his wife's behalf, but Patrick didn't know how to politely turn down hospitality. He was unused to offers of hospitality in the first place. "I would appreciate that."

"Good. Does your train leave tomorrow?"

"In the afternoon. I have a few business matters to conclude here in the late morning, or else I would have left sooner. I am terribly sorry for the imposition."

"Not at all. It's no imposition." Peter seemed more energized by his appearance than anything, and Patrick felt obligated to accept these polite words. "I had better leave you now, though. Alice has doubtless heard our voices, and I'd rather not force her to run out and demand an explanation. I'll see you in the morning."

Peter disappeared up the stairway and into what Patrick presumed was his bedroom, and Patrick settled down on the sofa and fell asleep almost instantly.

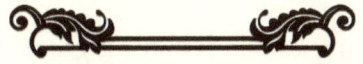

Patrick was up before the sunrise and dressed and shaved before Peter and Alice Strauss emerged from their room. Coffee was brewed, and Mrs. Strauss treated Patrick with a kind of cold indifference that indicated *exactly* where he must stand with her friend.

"I think I'll go over to Maddie's and ask her a question," she said, before breakfast was finished cooking. "You can watch the eggs, Peter."

Peter nodded, but the slight squint of his deep-set eyes indicated that it was an unusual decision.

It wasn't confusing to Patrick, however. She was going to warn her friend of Patrick's presence. That was fair enough.

The lady disappeared, and Peter turned to him. "What time is your meeting?"

"Ten. They had to meet with their lawyer and finalize some paperwork first; he was unavailable yesterday." An oversight that had bothered Patrick to no end and almost made him convinced that he ought to abandon the deal entirely. However, it seemed that there had been a few unforeseen circumstances in the lives of the owners lately, and he could understand that. It was a wonder Patrick's job performance hadn't suffered. He certainly had enough on his mind. However, the ability to remain professional regardless of his personal feelings was ingrained in his very being—it would not be easily dropped.

"Do you have time for a walk before then?"

Patrick stilled. Was he going to get a talking to? He'd learned to anticipate them, stiffening his resolve and forcing the words to slide off him like water off a duck's back.

Yet perhaps it wouldn't be the worst thing to hear some honest words from a man like Peter. Not that Patrick believed he was perfect; he simply trusted the man to listen to God. Patrick felt like an utter failure in that area.

"I do," he said, forcing a smile despite his gritted teeth. If he was going to get a scolding, and actually listen to that scolding, he would put on a cheerful façade for the duration. "Any time you like, actually."

Strauss shoved to his feet. "Let's go now."

"But ..." Yet it was the man's house and the man's breakfast.

"I'll write Alice a note. I've an idea she'll be longer than she thinks. There's some chatter going on over there"—he gestured toward the back door—"that will take a considerable amount of time."

"Very well."

Strauss jotted down a few words on a slip of paper, which he set on the table, removed the eggs from the burner, and they made their way out the front door.

At first, they walked in silence in the cool morning. The sun danced and sparkled off dewdrops on the colorful flowers spilling through the white picket fences that lined the street. He absently noted Lorelei's favorite shade of geraniums—bright orange.

Strauss cleared his throat. "I know you spoke with ... Lady Mary ... for some time. I don't think you intended to contact her again, or at least that's what I've gathered from the snippets of conversation that seem to happen around me these days. Yet now you are here."

"Not intentionally. Obviously I came to Cincinnati with a purpose, and it didn't include her." Patrick sighed. "I'll be honest, Mr. Strauss; I had intended to leave her alone. I still do. It's probably better if we don't see each other. I've done a lot of things I'm not proud of, and though it was not what I wanted, she has suffered for them. I was unfair to her, and even if she doesn't care for me, she must see that I was not cautious of her feelings or of my own. I trust God to forgive me and help me find a way back to Him, but I would not entangle her in this mess. Not unless I were sure it would be safe to invite her into it, which I do not think it is."

Strauss paused, and Patrick was forced to stop walking and face him. "Love isn't safe. That's the idea of it."

Patrick clenched his fists. He didn't like the implication that Cassie's feelings for him might be loving. Of course, he wanted that, but it wasn't right. The right thing to do was to take care of his business, which was greatly in need of tending, and allow her to escape unhindered from the whole affair. "This is not an established relationship. She is free to go."

"I suppose you're right."

They kept walking, yet there was not the slightest possibility that Peter was done talking. Indeed, he spoke again.

"What if God brought you to Cincinnati and kept you from getting a hotel and prompted you to come to us so you *could* see her again?"

Patrick's shoulders hunched. That was the thought he'd been trying to avoid since he first arrived at the Strausses' house. "That is possible." All too possible, and he didn't know what to do with that information.

"Have you prayed about it?"

"Somewhat." He'd been praying, but it had been remarkably similar to arguing. Patrick knew it was foolishness to argue with God, to present human arguments to the Creator of the universe. There was no such thing as "talking some sense" into the Lord. Yet Patrick had been trying.

"Would you like to pray about it now?"

Patrick scowled. He had been right; Peter was an impossible man. Yet Patrick knew he had no choice but to pray about it—to refuse would be a sin at this point—and so he agreed.

And he tried not to be too disappointed over the amount of peace he felt about seeing her afterward.

"Are you sure about this?" Alice's eyes were dark and worried. "You don't have to see him."

"You act as if anything actually happened. As far as he's concerned, we're distant friends. *Acquaintances* is a better word." Cassie drummed her fingers against the kitchen table at Alice and Peter's house and played with her eggs. She'd decided to come over for breakfast, but Patrick and Peter had both disappeared, leaving behind a somewhat cryptic note in Peter's somewhat unreadable handwriting.

"There's more to it than that." Alice lowered herself onto the chair next to Cassie and took a sip of her tea, her brooding expression remaining fixed regardless of her other movements. "I hate what he's done to you. This isn't fair."

"I'm sure he didn't intend for his hotel to turn him away. Would you have had him sleep on the streets?"

"No, but I do wish he'd behaved himself like a gentleman from the first moment he met you."

Cassie pressed her lips together. "He treated me as well as he knew how to." Perhaps that was overgenerous, but Patrick had always been kind to her. He'd cared to hear her thoughts and feelings, taken time to listen to her concerns, and offered counsel when she needed it most. He just wasn't in a place to have a serious relationship with a woman—and perhaps never would be, though she hoped God would change that.

At least, she hoped—for Patrick's own good and for the good of the woman herself—that he wouldn't marry Blanche Linden. It would be so unfair to both of them—and Cassie just had an unshakeable feeling about it: almost a desire to call him to herself, where she ideally could keep him on the straight and narrow.

But that was no way to live a life. In fact, it was the opposite of her duties and the expectations surrounding her.

The front door opened and closed, and she stiffened at the sound of his voice. He was chatting with Peter about something, his voice as light as ever—quieter, perhaps, but still cheerful.

Then the two men entered the dining room, and Patrick's and Cassie's eyes met.

She rose. "Patrick Hilton. I didn't know you'd be in Cincinnati!" An obvious remark, but she was grateful that words had come to her, even if they were nonsensical ones.

It was better than looking into his eyes and realizing that there was a spark there after all. It was better than acknowledging that the beseeching look on his face must mean something. It was better than admitting to herself that her own heart was not unaffected by his presence.

He smiled at her. She wasn't sure *why* he smiled at her, and she disliked its effect with a passion, but at least he was happy to see her. Though did she want him to be happy to see her? "I didn't know myself until a week ago, and I didn't think we'd see each other. Yet now that we have, I want to talk. After breakfast, I have time, if you're available." He cocked his head. "I just think we'd better eat before the food gets cold. I'm sorry for dragging your husband off, Mrs. Strauss. I promise it was for a good reason, but I know we must've made you wait."

"Actually, it was my idea." Peter slipped onto his seat. "Anyway, I didn't think you would wait. I left a note."

Alice raised her eyebrows. "We determined that either you were going for a walk or that you were journeying to the center of the earth. Your handwriting allowed for either interpretation."

The conversation was light and surface-level after that. Peter protested that his handwriting was not that bad, and the note was passed from Cassie to Patrick and back again so both could give their opinions. They discussed how it was a relatively cool summer in Cincinnati. The subject of how pleasant Patrick's journey had been was broached. He talked about his sisters, his dog and her litter of puppies, and a boat trip he'd been on with a few friends lately.

Cassie ate quickly and quietly. She had nothing to say, not about those subjects. Too much curiosity within her prohibited much speech.

He wanted to talk with her. Had something changed?

For an unguarded moment, a thousand emotions had flashed across his face when he'd seen her for the first time. Even if he didn't want to admit it himself, which she was not yet sure of, he certainly had wanted to see her.

What did that mean for them?

She had missed him. Missed seeing him smile at her, missed hearing him talk and laugh. He seemed more at ease now than he had been on the boat—than any of his letters had spoken of. Was he changing? Did it matter if he was?

Once again, she found herself wondering if she was being an utter fool to allow him in her life at all. He was not strong. He was not brave. He did not love her more than he loved his parents' approval, if he loved her at all.

She wondered if she had fallen for a real man or one made of gilded glass.

Surely he could not love her. Men who loved women did not ignore them. Men who loved women put them first. Men who loved women sought them out and chose them, even if there were outside factors standing in the way. Even if the relationship were impractical, improbable.

Patrick was not ready to be in that kind of relationship. Even if he had been, Miss Linden existed.

At last, Cassie could stand it no longer. She needed a few quiet moments with God. Sitting here wasn't helping, so she rose, set her plate on the counter, and turned to the table.

All three pairs of eyes were on her. Of course.

"I'm going out into the garden."

And she went, without another word, before anyone could react.

She tipped her head upward to the clear, blue sky, to the fluffy, white clouds drifting aimlessly across its expanse. Her eyes closed, but she couldn't pray. So she stood still in the middle of the garden and waited for God to find her.

"Cassie?"

She opened her eyes to find Patrick had followed her. Of course he had. She hadn't explained the need for time alone.

He approached but stopped himself in the very act of reaching for her. Why did it have to be that way?

"I'm fine. I just wanted a moment." She said the words mildly, not betraying her frustration. She'd rather not fight with him, as that might lead to tears. "You should finish your breakfast."

He started to turn, then hesitated. "Are you angry with me?"

"Yes." There was no use trying to hide that. "You made me hope, and that's such a dangerous thing. Yet I've known for a long time that nothing could come of it. I simply haven't admitted it to myself. I can be more careful; I will be more careful."

He pressed his lips together. "I ... I fully intend to—"

"But intentions aren't enough, are they, Patrick?" She wrapped her arms around herself, but other than a slight trembling, she was surprised at her own sense of calm. "It's not enough. Your letters made me dream of a different life, but I don't want that life if I have to fight for it. That sounds silly, perhaps, to an American. You all have this asinine dream of being 'self-made,' but you're not self-made. You are your parents' man, molded into the image they thought would be most stylish this year. And if I have to fight and fight to break that mold, to make you into something you are not ... Patrick, why don't I start out with someone who is what I want in a man in the first place? Tell me that. Why would I wait for you?"

He stood, his hands in tight fists by his side, and said nothing. She wondered if she had made him angry or if he was simply pouting. It was like him to pout, wasn't it?

She would not, could not, marry a man who pouted. It was a most unattractive quality, and more than that, she wanted to do far more in life than watch a man suffer. She wanted a man who overcame.

"Perhaps it's because you are young," she offered, by way of a condolence. "But I am younger than you, and my life holds more risk. I was not afraid to anger my parents; now I have no future, but I have God on my side. I don't understand how you can pretend to be a Christian—"

"I don't pretend." His stormy, gray eyes pinned her to the spot. "I told you that I—"

"Have been praying, I know. But you haven't done anything. Have you? Truly?"

"I have people who are reliant on me, Cassie. I have my sisters. I have a responsibility to them. Before I can break things off with Blanche, I must make sure they will be all right."

"They are your parents' daughters, too! While you stand with your parents, you are doing them no good. Whether you are here or not, their lots will be the same."

"But I need to be present for them." He looked about to stamp his foot, like a child forced to give up a toy he wanted. "Once I marry, I want them to go with me, but that cannot happen unless my parents agree, and my parents will not agree unless—"

"Unless you are the heir. That's really what's at the root of this, Patrick. You're unwilling to give up the family fortune, the business, the connections. But if your situation is as miserable as you tell me, if they would force you to marry a woman you cannot be married to, and if their control over you is really so loathsome, you would simply leave. You are twenty-one, aren't you?"

"I am."

"Then what holds you to your parents? Why do you stay? Why don't you just leave?" Her tone rose, then, to match the fury inside her. "Don't you bring up your sisters again. This is not about them. You have no control over their lives, Patrick. Admit it to yourself, please, if you can admit nothing else. You cannot save them. They are your parents' daughters, as surely as you are their son. You would do far better to give them a safe, separate place, whether or not you had any money or power, than to stay with your parents, where they must then remain, too."

"I would have my ... my own household ..."

"Patrick, you would not. You would have an extension of your parents' household." Didn't he see that? Couldn't he understand that his parents would not allow him to live his own life unless he broke ties with the fortune, with the company?

Then he said nothing. For a long time, they stood in silence.

At last, Cassie sighed. "Patrick, I'm sorry this couldn't go anywhere. I'm sorry you won't let this go anywhere. But I can't wait for you to find some solution to make your parents happy *and* allow you to be with me. I can't marry you and your parents. That wouldn't be good for either of us. The Bible says, 'Therefore shall a man leave his father and his mother, and shall cleave unto his wife: and they shall be one flesh,' and you are not going to leave. You never are, no matter what you tell me. I don't want to spend the rest of my life married to the Hilton Shipping Company."

He nodded and had the nerve to smile. "That's more than fair."

"Good. I'm glad I'm being fair." She wanted to go on, to tell him that he had not been fair to her and was not being very fair to himself either, but that would do no good. She also didn't want to spend the rest of her life badgering a man into submission. That sounded miserable.

"Can I talk now? That's something else that seems fair." He shrugged in an exaggerated manner. "What do you think?"

"Fine." She bit out the word, but at least she said it.

"I'm not asking you to wait for me in the first place. The only reason I wanted to talk is to let you know what I'm doing. Cassie, if I thought it would do me any good, I'd throw myself at your feet now and offer you everything I have. Yet we have established that that would be unfair. My plan is to officially end things with Miss Linden when I return to Boston. What effects that will have on my circumstances are underdetermined. However, I have an idea that I will then be without a home or ... I'll be without anything, simply put. That seems to be where God is leading me, and I have made a few sensible precautions with that in mind. That said, I would not be able to offer you much of a life."

She waited, lips pressed together and arms wrapped around herself, for him to continue. She had no response to give him, yet words came readily to her mind, silent prayers for the Lord to guide her on this matter, too.

"The truth is, I do want you to wait for me. I want that more than anything in the world. I know I can't ask for that yet—but will you let me write to you?"

She closed her eyes. Everything within her was screaming to accept this offer, the implication of a courtship and a relationship with this man. Yet she ignored the shouting within her and searched out the still, small Voice, and in that, she found her answer.

"Patrick, I can't."

Her eyes flew open and met his. He looked somber but not angry; he had that to his credit.

"Very well." His voice was shaky, but he said the words. "You realize you've had a profound impact on me, don't you? I'm so sorry God didn't bring you into my life when I was a better man, but I don't think I would be on the path I am without you. Thank you."

What could she say to that? Nothing came to mind, so she waited until he smiled at her again and turned and left.

She could not offer him hope when there was none within her anymore.

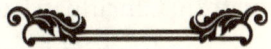

CHAPTER TWENTY-ONE

Boston, Massachusetts

"I THINK MOTHER IS trying to throw me at Herbert Jackson." Lorelei slid her arm through Patrick's as they walked up the steps to the Jacksons' home. "Please tell me you'll scare him off."

"I don't think you'll have to worry about that." Patrick glanced down at his sister, taking note of her hair, swept up again in that oddly grown-up style, her skirts long and flowing now. When had she become a woman? "No man with a bit of sense in his head would agree to spend the rest of his life with you."

She sent him a glare that would've been withering if he hadn't seen her in diapers. "Fine. But you'll be the one supporting me in my old-maidhood."

"Nonsense." He reached into his jacket pocket and withdrew their invitations; the butler took them, and a footman scurried forward to relieve them of their coats. "I'll put you in a home."

"Thank you, darling. You always were so caring."

He chuckled to himself as he led Lore into the familiar ballroom. Not so many years ago, he'd played a game of football on a rainy February day in this room. Behind him, his parents bickered under their breath even as they smiled at the guests who greeted them. Playing nice to the public while their children hunched their backs under their barely veiled jabs. He wouldn't put a child of his in the same situation. Never.

His resolve strengthened further at this thought. He knew a relationship with Blanche would be nothing short of torturous. He hadn't seen her since arriving back in Boston from Cincinnati late last night, but he should meet with her and let her know that he'd be speaking with his parents tomorrow.

He'd have to catch her tonight and tell her.

"Hilton!" Herbert appeared out of the crowd and shook Patrick's hand, then greeted Lorelei and their parents. "Mr. and Mrs. Hilton, Miss Hilton, I'm glad you were able to make it. Could I steal Patrick for a moment?"

Permission was granted, and Patrick was pulled to the side.

"What is it?"

"Blanche will be here?"

"Yes."

"She said … she said she told you." Guilt-filled eyes rose to Patrick's face. "What do you think?"

"I think I will not hold her to a relationship that she has no interest in." Patrick pressed his lips together for a moment, debating what to say. "I wish you had told me when it began, though, Jackson. I could've been humiliated. How did either of you know I didn't want to marry her? You couldn't have. Even if you had, at least you could've let me know that there was a relationship between you two. I was completely taken by surprise." It had been a happy surprise in a way, as it had given him the final push he needed to sort out a way to break his understanding with Blanche and finally seek the life he believed God wanted for him. Not that he knew how he would go about that—yet. "It could have been embarrassing."

"Honestly, it wasn't supposed to be public knowledge, ever. Not that it is now. I had wondered if I'd ever convince her to marry me in the first place." Herbert Jackson couldn't resist a smile then. "But now she has agreed to, once you publicly break with her. I am to swoop in and make believe I'm comforting her shattered heart."

Patrick resisted scoffing. What Herbert Jackson saw in Blanche was beyond him, but if Herbert was glad to take Blanche off Patrick's hands, he would accept it without question—even though a part of him hurt seeing his old friend so manipulated, forced to do what Blanche wanted when she wanted it.

Much like Patrick would've done all his life if this hadn't happened.

There was a great deal to be thankful for, he supposed.

All he said aloud to Herbert was, "I don't begrudge you that."

He went back to Lorelei and led her about, introducing her to people and making sure she knew who was there. It was important that his sister was well-connected.

That would be even more important if he wasn't always there to take care of her. Not that he intended to let anything or anyone get in the way of his ability to take care of Lore and Winnie.

Lorelei was in rare form that evening, her eyes bright and happy. He saw her contentment in her interactions with her friends, despite the fact that he would rather her engage with his father's partners. He wanted Lorelei to establish herself as the intelligent, savvy woman she was—the woman he'd entrusted all the secrets and tricks of Hilton Shipping Company to. He wanted Father to look to her as Patrick's natural replacement if he was forced to leave.

He wanted Father to break the will as written for her. He wanted others in Boston, and throughout their business empire, to accept this decision when Father inevitably made it.

He wanted Father to need Lorelei too much to toss her away into just any marriage that provided a decent deal.

Yet Patrick could no more make that happen than he could fly.

Father would pull the strings, and Lore and Winnie would have to decide how much they fought the inevitable jerking. Lore already seemed convinced an expedient marriage was the best way out of her current difficulties. Perhaps she was right. Patrick had once thought so.

He lingered close to her despite the fact that she clearly wished him gone so her conversation with her friends could be a bit freer, but despite his stumblings and his need to tease her at every point, he would die before he let any ill fortune come to her.

He felt like he was abandoning her.

I have her in My arms.

Was it a thought in his head or a still, small Voice in his soul? Either way, Patrick shuddered, earning another glare from his irritated sibling.

I will protect her as you never could. I have her best interests in mind without any ulterior motives. I love her, treasure her. The same is offered to Winnie.

Patrick knew it was true. He knew it. So why was he delaying his action a moment longer?

Let go of them. Let go now and obey.

Obey.

Obey.

Just obey *Me.*

Patrick left Lorelei, went to Blanche, and drew her aside.

"I am going to tell my parents tonight, when we go home, that I will not marry you. Stand by Jackson; tell him what I've told you. He will offer for you, and your parents will accept. It will make little difference to them, and even if it doesn't, his parents will take you both in and love you. They are good people."

Blanche turned her pale face up to his, her eyes dancing between the other residents of the parlor and him. The others were beyond the hearing of their brief conversation, but still, she feared. Much as Patrick always had done.

He would not live with that fear any longer.

"But …" Yet she said nothing more. She had no objection. She had not been raised to protest when men told her how she was to behave; Patrick knew this. And there was no real reason for her to protest.

It would be good for Blanche Linden to ride out a storm, no matter how mild.

"I'll take you to him; tell him what you will. Make plans," he whispered, and he led her to Herbert Jackson and left her with him.

He then went to Lorelei. "Can you play sick and get us out of here?"

"Um." She raised her eyebrows. "That's really more Winnie's sort of thing, isn't it? I'm not sure that's something I can do."

He smirked. "You can't go to our mother and say, 'I have a headache; can we go home?' Please tell me you can do this little thing for me."

"If I can do it, so can you," she hissed.

"Me?" He frowned. "Why can't you just do it?"

"Look, I don't care if it's not manly or whatever it is that's stopping you; if you have a reason to go home, then go tell your mama you have a headache and need her to take you home." She made a shooing motion. "Go on. I have friends here, and contrary to popular belief, you are not the only person in the world."

"I'm not sure if it's possible for me to ..." Then he stopped himself and closed his eyes. "All right. Fine. But you'll have to go home with us."

She sighed. "Whatever."

He turned away and went to his father, who was standing with his friends. "Father, could I talk to you for a moment?"

The look Father gave him indicated that he very much did not want to be interrupted, but he made his apologies and distanced himself from his conversation partner. "What is it, son?"

"I know this may be an imposition, but would it be all right if we left early? There are some things I would like to discuss with you."

He gave Patrick a somewhat indiscernible look. "What could that possibly be?"

"It's a personal issue I need to raise with you and Mother."

"And it can't wait?"

"It is urgent."

"Then you convince your mother. I'll get our carriage around."

Father disappeared, and Patrick took a deep breath and went to seek out his mother.

She was more difficult than Father. Mother was always a thousand times more stubborn, even though in some ways she had a milder personality. However, at last, perhaps prompted by her own curiosity about what he wanted to tell her, he convinced her.

Back at the Hilton home half an hour later, Father sent a reluctant Lorelei up to bed, and Patrick followed his parents into Father's study.

"What is it that you have to tell us, Patrick?" Father asked. He clearly wasn't taking this seriously, whereas Mother's eyes were bright with the light of intrigue.

"Mother, Father." *Lord, don't let this be a mistake.* "I am going to be breaking my understanding with Blanche Linden tomorrow. I don't intend to marry her."

For a moment, all the air seemed to leave the room, and they all stood there, struggling for breath and staring wide-eyed at each other.

"Patrick Clarence Hilton, have you lost your mind?" His mother took a step toward him, then stopped, her mouth half agape. "You must marry Blanche. You are promised to her!"

"I understand that. But—"

"No." Father's hand slammed onto his desk. "Sit down. You will explain yourself immediately. You have been promised to Blanche Linden since your infancy. She has always been your intended, and her father and I have arranged extensive business deals with the assumption that our families would someday be joined. No, that they are as good as joined." Red-faced, he practically growled at Patrick. "What do you mean?"

"I mean what I said. I will not marry her. I am going to go to her and her parents tomorrow and make it clear that I never will marry her. I don't care about her any more than as a friend and a woman who deserves respect, and I don't feel that God is leading me to that relationship." He knew that his parents would not accept this easily. He would have to stand here, with their anger focused on him, until they cast him out of the office.

He braced himself and again prayed silently as his parents looked at each other, then him, in utter shock.

Of course they were surprised. He had never stood up to them before. But now it was time. It was long past time.

"You must marry her. In fact, I order you to marry her!" His father's voice rose, and even his mother moved away from him, as if afraid of his fury.

But Father couldn't touch him now. "You do not have the right to order me to do anything. I am twenty-one years old. Honestly, Father, I have long felt I was unfairly treated in this family. You trail me along, forcing me to work at the company without pay. Granted, my needs are provided for, and I appreciate that, but in the future, I will need to establish my own household and support myself. How can I expect to marry at all if I can't stand on my own two feet?"

"I will not allow it!" His father paced back and forth like a caged bear in a zoo; he was practically foaming at the mouth. "You cannot be a part of this family and reject all that we have provided for you. Young man, if you do not marry Blanche Linden, you should not expect to live in this house, work for my company, or receive any kind of inheritance. That is your choice, plain and simple."

Mother was pale, her gray eyes standing out like harsh, clear lights on her white face. "Clarence, I hardly think—"

"No! It is your spirit of rebellion that has prompted this, Lynnie. You've turned them all against me, and look where that has led."

"What?" The mix of betrayal and anger in her voice reminded Patrick once again that his mother didn't want her position any more than he did. But she had made her choice years ago. Patrick still had room to make his own. "You know I don't want this. But, Clarence, to throw out my son, my only son! What will you do without him?"

"We'll discuss the logistics if Patrick makes such a drastic decision, but I feel confident that he will not, faced with simple logic. Patrick, you choose this day who you will serve. Will you choose a life of chaos and poverty—separated from your family, from your mother and sisters—forever, or will you choose the right path? Will you stand by our family, by your name and birthright, and receive what you have always been meant to receive?" Father narrowed his eyes. "Make this decision now, and choose wisely."

Patrick stared at his father in some sort of shock. Yes, he had expected to be disinherited eventually. He'd thought there would be fussing and threats for a time, and that if he continued in disobedience, he might be thrown out or at least forced to move.

But so quickly? Within a few words, his father was willing to toss him out? As his mother said, he was Clarence Hilton's only son and heir. Granted, the girls would receive a third share when their father died, but it was always understood that they would marry men who would become partners or that Patrick would buy their shares away from them.

He had never anticipated the possibility that his father would give him an ultimatum.

Yet at the same time, he couldn't be truly surprised. He had seen this writing on the wall for years. His father did not love him. He was nothing more than a pawn in a game fueled by wealth and influence. Hilton Shipping Company was his father's first and only love. He would do nothing that was not in its best interest.

Apparently, that included disinheriting his only son over a slight disruption to a business association.

Yet as Patrick stood there, hearing his father's threats even in the face of his mother's clear dismay, the choice was obvious.

He could not remain here. He could not live his life like this. He could not serve two masters.

The choice was between the Hilton legacy and God, and Patrick knew which he would have to choose. His father was right; he had no choice. He must follow God no matter what his parents, especially his father, thought was best for him.

"Very well then." Patrick forced himself to relax his posture, to affect a cheerful air—for the last time, he hoped. "I will take from your household what belongs to me by right. I consider my allowance to be wages paid for my work at the company; it has always been administered by the payroll staff, so I believe you will have no legal precedence to claim otherwise. That money has been used to buy my clothing and other personal effects; I will be packing them and taking them with me. I will not spend another night under your roof."

"Patrick." His mother's eyes, stricken with panic, rose to his face. He wondered then if she loved him, if she had ever really loved him. Perhaps she had. But it didn't matter now. "*Patrick.*"

"I'm sorry, Mother, but you can see he's left me no choice."

His father stood, trembling with rage, and Patrick met his gaze evenly. "I'm sorry it's come to this, but I will not marry Miss Linden. And I will not work for a company that abuses me. I cannot allow myself to be so treated. I'd rather die in a gutter than live in a way that was not aligned with God's will."

"Does it not align with God's will to honor your father and mother?" his father asked through clenched teeth.

"Not when I am asked to do something opposite of what God has ordained in my life." Patrick turned to his mother, nodded to her, and left the study behind.

It was going to be a long night.

CHAPTER TWENTY-TWO

THERE WAS NOTHING MORE comforting than a happy, wiggling puppy that had at last settled down and fallen asleep on his lap. Patrick stroked Venus's ears and stared at the hearth of the kitchen fireplace at the Jackson residence.

"What will you do next?" Across from him, with Vulcan sleeping at an odd angle with his legs dangling from the crook of his arm, Herbert looked Patrick over with a mix of pity and curiosity. "My parents don't mind you staying here, but you understand that it may get awkward. Blanche and I have every intention of announcing an engagement soon. I'll probably approach her father in a day or two."

Patrick nodded. "I have no idea of staying for more than a few days." Less, if he could manage it. "Thank you for this. I can't imagine it's easy to welcome a homeless man and seven dogs into your home, but your parents have been such good sports."

In the last twelve hours, Patrick had visited his father's business, confirmed his legal separation from the company, and then called on the Lindens.

They were furious. Blanche had been weepy—endless crocodile tears. The entire experience was a miserable one, but he knew she would be all right in the long run. Her parents would blame him, especially given his fall from grace within his own family.

So now he had to decide what to do with his own life.

"Tomorrow, I'm going to arrange a visit with my sisters." He had to say good-bye—he had to. Even if he was leaving them to God's providence, he couldn't do so without so much as a farewell. "I'll leave Mars with them."

"I bet you can get my parents to keep this one." Herbert smiled. "That gets you down to four."

"I think James was willing, and I already have someone taking Mercury and Venus—and maybe Diana. That more or less solves my problems." The dog-related ones, that was. "Bell and I will stick together, of course, and I'm going to keep Juno until I find someone special to give her to."

"Not your sisters?" Herbert said with a half-incredulous laugh.

"No, I'd rather them have Mars." Patrick couldn't explain the logic. "Anyway, I'll deliver Mercury and Venus and maybe Diana this afternoon, along with Mars. It'll be easier then, especially if you're keeping Vulcan."

Herbert nodded. "Thanks. I like the little things, but they do create a bit of a smell, all together."

"They do at that." He pushed himself up to a standing position and placed Venus in the large wooden crate they'd found to store the puppies in. Thankfully, it had high enough sides to keep them from escaping. Yet.

His next step, after delivering some puppies to their new owners and making sure all was settled in Boston, was going to see Cassie again. He didn't know what he was going to say, but he wanted to see her one last time—and perhaps beg her to let him find a future that could include her.

Of course, it was a lot to ask. She didn't owe him anything, and she'd made it rather clear that she didn't want to board his sinking ship. No, Cassie was far too clever for that. Yet he still felt so drawn to her. Wouldn't it make him even more of a coward if he didn't do all he possibly could to win her?

"What did you do last night?"

He straightened, focusing his attention back on the present and his friend who hadn't seen him until six in the morning. "I walked the streets most of the night, praying, until I decided a next step and went to collect the pups and bring them to you. They're all I have now, you know—I'm fortunate to have three buyers set at fifty dollars a pup, but the rest will have to be given away."

Herbert nodded, rubbing his chin thoughtfully. "Anything else?"

"I've a few hundred dollars in a bank account, and of course my two suitcases, which are full of clothes, papers, and one or two items of sentimentality. That said, I left most of my things at my parents' house, even what I could've taken. It isn't safe to go back there, and I know it. I won't give my father any further opportunity to exercise his wrath on me."

Herbert nodded. "That's fair enough. I wish you'd given yourself a bit more time to gather your assets, Hilton. You realize you don't have much of a place to go, and the fewer assets you have, the harder time you will have establishing yourself."

"I don't mind it, really." Patrick grinned, giving a carefree wave of his hand. As if he could ever be carefree again. "I'll miss my boat, but it was never really mine to begin with. The same goes for my horse." He drummed his fingers against his leg. "Anyway, I suppose the biggest question is, what do I do now? Obviously I have a lot of experience in administration at a shipping company, but I won't claim that qualifies me for anything else." He shook his head. "Unfortunately, my work has been quite limited."

"I don't think that is entirely true. You have a lot of experience; it's just of the type that might be hard to use to get an actual job. At least, I assume so. You have a number of skills. If you were to get a lower-level position, you could undoubtedly go far. After all, isn't that the whole American ideal? Working from the bottom and reaching the top?"

"Perhaps." He forced his shoulders not to slouch despite the overwhelming desire to do so, to give up. "Really, I ought to go to Philadelphia and beg the Strausses for help. I have a friend in Cincinnati, staying with their son and his wife, but I think I'd be better off approaching either the former Miss Caroline Strauss and her husband or her parents."

"That's not a half-bad idea."

He chuckled. "Further, Delaware Bay is home to my father's greatest shipping rivals, Baldwin & Sons. I'm sure they wouldn't want to see me anywhere near their docks, but there are other jobs not involving the sea." Almost as he said these words, though, an idea popped to the front of his mind. "Or perhaps they would."

Herbert raised his eyebrows. "What do you mean?"

"I'm not sure if they would credit me as having really done it, but I could always go to Baldwin & Sons and offer my services. If they would believe that I have truly broken things off with my father, they might ... they might just hire me." Suddenly, Patrick rose, and his hat fell from his knee to the floor, rolling about like it had a life of its own. "That would be interesting."

"You could tell them all you know about how to make connections, where there is opportunity at present." For the first time in a while, something other than boredom filled Herbert's voice. "Of course, you wouldn't want to do anything unethical, but you could do a lot for them using your general knowledge."

"Right, right." Patrick ran his hands through his hair despite knowing that would cause it to stand on end. "I could at least try, and if nothing else comes of it, I could throw myself at the mercy of Mr. Christopher Strauss. I think the Strausses know about everyone in Philadelphia on some level, and I'd take just about any job an unskilled worker can do."

"That seems like a perfectly reasonable plan. You will try that?"

"There is little for me in Boston now. I suppose all I need to do is find a home for another puppy and bid good-bye to my sisters. I ..." He paused then and pressed his lips together. "Perhaps as they come of age, they can at least travel to see me. I'm not sure. It's beyond my control."

"Oh, they'll be fine." Herbert tossed away all Patrick's varying concerns with a wave of his hand.

Patrick could not be so easygoing about this. He hated the idea of being separated from them at all, let alone with the understanding that his parents' full attention must now be turned on them.

But it couldn't be helped.

He'd have to say good-bye to Lorelei and Winnie and trust them to the Lord, much as he had trusted his own future to Him.

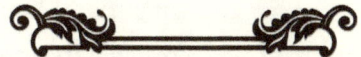

He was fortunate that Lorelei had chosen to wander into the garden mid-afternoon and, further, that he happened to catch her and urge her to bring Winnie. This would allow them a hushed, brief conversation in the stables before he caught a train to Philadelphia that evening.

Winnie immediately wrapped her arms around him, sobbing and insisting that he could not leave, but somehow, that only firmed his conviction. He wasn't Winnie's father, and he could not be expected to provide the comfort and support of a parent.

It was time both of his sisters grew up and learned to fend for themselves. Lorelei was already more than capable of doing so, and Winnie would follow her soon enough into womanhood.

If anything else, his remaining would hold them back.

"I'll write when I can, but I can't promise Mother and Father will let you receive those letters." Gently prying Winnie from his waist, he placed a hand on both of his sisters' shoulders. "Be good. Follow God. All right? For me?"

"Of course." Lorelei shrugged. "I'm better at that than you are."

Patrick clucked his tongue like an old woman determined to give sage advice to a young whippersnapper. "And so much humbler, too."

She rolled her eyes. "I'm smarter than you are half the time, and you know it. Where are you going?"

"Philadelphia, I think. Don't let this get out, but I'm going to try my luck with Baldwin & Sons. I think I have half a chance with them, and if not, I know the Strausses. Caroline Strauss Webster and I are acquaintances, and I like her husband, so maybe they'll help me find something to do. The Strauss family has stakes in a lumberyard. Might as well grow some muscles sometime, if they'll take me."

Winnie giggled. "I can't imagine that."

"Hush." He reached over and ruffled her hair; she swerved away but not before he'd mussed a few of her auburn curls. "I'll manage."

"Oh, and I almost forgot." Lorelei reached into the pocket of her dress. "Here." A small, black box was withdrawn. "You'll need this."

His brow wrinkled, but he accepted the box. "What for?"

"It's a ring."

"I know what a ring box looks like."

"I wondered, because I never saw Blanche with one."

Winnie giggled, and Lorelei smirked, and Patrick was tempted to find something annoying to do in retribution. Instead, he settled for ignoring them and opening the box. As promised, a ring sat inside, an intricate gold band with five diamonds clustered around a center emerald. Two more emeralds graced the band. It was old-fashioned but very pretty, as far as rings went.

"What do you expect me to do? Sell a family heirloom? This was Grand-mother's. I know we never met her, but I think we owe the woman some respect. After all, I was named for her husband, wasn't I? Patrick McCul-lough? And Mother certainly thinks Grandmother was a saint."

"Don't sell it! See, I told you he doesn't know what to do with a ring." Lorelei cast another grin at Winnie. "No, you idiot. It's for Cassie."

He snapped the box closed. "I don't know if I'll ever see her again."

"But you hope to! You want to. Even now, you can't pretend a part of you isn't going to Philadelphia in hopes of seeing her again, or at least hearing word of her." Lorelei folded her arms in front of her chest. "Don't lie to me, Patrick Clarence Hilton. You never have been able to, and that won't start now."

He stared at the box in his hand, so small yet packed with meaning both to his family and to himself. "I only take it because it is yours, and I think Mother fully intended you to take it into your marriage. I consider it a great gift, though, Lore."

She shrugged. "I won't marry a man who won't provide me with my own ring, and a nicer one than that, so it's no sacrifice. And you need one. I've always thought our fingers were about the same size, too."

His eyebrows rose. "Oh, have you?" When had she even had time to make that observation? Would he be surprised if somehow she'd managed to measure Cassie's ring finger without her knowing?

"Yes, and if not, any decent jeweler will be able to resize it."

"I'm glad someone made a plan for this." He placed the box in his jacket pocket. "I'll try to make use of it, but I can't promise."

"I wouldn't blame her if she turned you down, but you must ask her, Trick." Lorelei placed a hand on his arm. "Please don't ruin this any more than you already have. We adore her, and frankly, I can't imagine anyone better for you."

He sighed. "Look. I said I'd try. That's really the best I can offer."

"Good." Lorelei hesitated, then briefly wrapped her arms around him in a somewhat awkward but sincere hug. "Please be careful. Don't die in a gutter somewhere."

"I won't." At least, he hoped following God's will would lead him away from that situation. "As for you, know that Father is going to have to redraft wills and make new decisions regarding the company. What I've always understood is—"

"I'm sure we'll figure it out." Lorelei smiled and stepped back. "You'd better go. Don't miss your train and don't worry about Winnie and me."

"I'm working on the 'not worrying' part, but it takes a while to dismiss years of anxiety. Plus, you are both so concerning." He smiled as best he could. An uncomfortable lump grew in his throat. It might've been easier not to see his sisters, but he couldn't have avoided it. Not without breaking their hearts, though they doubtless would've come to understand his reasoning. "But here's what you need to know. Lorelei, Father will either look to you, if he determines that you are capable of taking on more than you currently do with the business, or decide that you need a husband before you're of any use to him. Likely both, with the understanding that you will hand all power to your husband and all the inheritance to your future son, if you have one—I don't know what he'd do if you had only daughters. Regardless, if this is the case, he could rearrange the will to have your inheritance be contingent on your marriage to someone of his choosing, someone who he can easily manipulate. Further, for Winnie, this would mean—"

"Either she'll be used to bring in another company or she'll be cast off, as if she's of little importance. Meanwhile, my husband will likely be an easily malleable second son. That means Herbert Jackson will no longer do. They'll be looking to someone like James Pent's younger brother—William. I expected that. Mother and Father will cause an awful fuss and I'll have little say, but it hardly matters. Billy Pent isn't such a bad boy. To our parents' credit, they're sure to choose someone young who can grow up with the company, and that doesn't concern me. If I can marry Billy, or someone like him, and give him a son, then you won't have to worry about Winnie ... and you shouldn't worry about me. I'm tougher than I look; I'm not like you. I can thrive here. You know that."

He swallowed. To have her put it so plainly hurt, but she was right that they were of different breeds, despite being siblings. Lorelei wasn't as tenderhearted as Patrick, nor as cooperative. Where Patrick did nothing but fail, she might succeed

It was possible she could navigate being a Hilton without any dangerous side effects.

So he kissed Lore and Winnie and whispered that he loved them and went on his way, unsure when he would see them again and hating that fact.

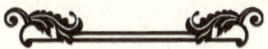

CHAPTER TWENTY-THREE

Late June 1883
Cincinnati, Ohio

CASSIE HAD NOTED TEARS in Maddie's eyes that morning when she came down from her room. Riley's expression was strained, and as there seemed nothing amiss between them, Cassie suspected the situation had more to do with Polly and Susie.

This was confirmed when a somewhat sullen Polly scuffed her way into the kitchen, hair slightly-less-perfectly combed than normal, red around the nose and eyes in a similar way to her mother.

Susie was the same as always, but she was the type of one-year-old that walked early and fast and got into everything.

Cassie began to question which person in this neighborhood needed her most today, and it didn't look like that was Alice. She stepped away for a moment and spoke with her friend, who immediately offered to take the girls for the morning.

"You know how I feel about our esteemed Mrs. Farjon," Alice said, a trace of wryness in her tone. "I'm exhausted with her, truly, but I don't actively want her to suffer."

Cassie grinned. "An improvement. And I'm sure she will be grateful."

Maddie *was* grateful, to the point of more tears, and Alice and Cassie gathered a basket of blocks and two dolls from the nursery and herded the little girls over to Alice's garden, where they laid out a large quilt and set Susie up to play with blocks. Meanwhile, Polly examined every flower in the garden and shared her thoughts on them. She was thorough and dedicated and never failed to find a way to compliment even the flowers she didn't particularly care for. Cassie knew this because, in an undertone, Polly would murmur, "It's not your fault you're not bwootiful," in her soft, little voice.

Cassie focused her attention on Susie, who needed a lot of guidance to manage even the simplest of block creations, and Alice played with Polly.

Noon came around, and Cassie and Alice prepared a lunch of bread, cheese, and fruit for a picnic. Polly chattered cheerfully about this and that, clearly high on energy but not an ill-natured child.

After eating, she seemed to fade a bit, leaning against Alice as Cassie and she talked quietly. Susie, of course, had passed out in a patch of sun and was now being guarded by the enigmatic Ophelia, Peter's cat, who had taken an instant liking to the fiery-haired child.

Polly grabbed Alice's arm. "Auntie Alice?"

"Yes, Miss Dolly?" The affectionate nickname rolled off Alice's tongue naturally. There wasn't a person in the neighborhood who wasn't in love with Polly.

"I'm sorry you don't have your baby."

Alice stiffened, and Cassie's eyes flew to her face. How would Alice react to that? Yet she took a deep breath and relaxed her posture before she responded. "I'm sorry, too."

"Daddy says not everyone gets to ... to keep their babies." A chubby fist rubbed at her drooping eyelids. "He said someday maybe you can have another one."

"Yes. Maybe someday." Alice's controlled voice gave Cassie hope she wouldn't have dared to have unless she'd heard it herself. "In the meantime, don't you worry. I'll be just fine. All right?"

"All right."

Moments later, Polly drifted off, and Alice picked her up and tucked her in on the sofa in the living room, while Cassie laid Susie opposite her.

"I don't know that she still naps, but she obviously needed it," Alice remarked after Cassie and she had tiptoed into the kitchen. "She's a sweet thing."

Cassie nodded. "She is. And you ... you're all right? Being with her and Susie? I didn't think until today that Susie is about the same age ..."

"Mm. June to August. It's not exact. But the time does draw near, doesn't it?" Alice cocked her head. "What is it about anniversaries? We celebrate them—for birthdays, for weddings. And in our hearts, we keep the death days, too. I think next month, it'll be hard to manage myself, but Peter will get me through it, as he always does, and I'll be there when he needs me. Let's not talk about it now; let it be enough that I feel all right today. We leave for Philadelphia next week—are you ready?"

Cassie offered a smile, which she hoped was as gentle as she meant it. "Yes. I'll be glad to see Peter's family again, and hopefully to meet his latest niece or nephew whenever the little one comes along. There's nothing for me in Cincinnati save you, and I know you'll want your privacy back."

Alice shrugged. "I love having you here, but I admit that Peter and I need to establish ourselves alone now. It'll be interesting to see how things go. But returning you to Philadelphia and seeing you off will be a happy ending to this adventure, I hope. What will you do in England?"

"Oh, I don't know." Cassie would likely be banished back to Ireland, but whatever the case, she would do her best to serve God.

The thought of Patrick always crossed through her mind when she thought of the future. However, there couldn't be anything to that. She must learn to not think of him—to move on in joy and courage and begin to think of their relationship as what it really was.

Two ships passing in the night.

Philadelphia, Pennsylvania

The large brick building, a hundred years old or more based on its architecture, rose above the street, and for once in his life, Patrick was afraid of a large brick building.

It wasn't so much that the actual building itself intimidated him. His father's company's headquarters was housed in a similar structure, though nearer to the docks. The Baldwin & Sons business did more inland trade than the Hiltons did; therefore, it was not such a necessity they be so near the sea or, in this case, the bay.

Patrick swallowed at the thought, his fingers reflexively tightening and loosening on the briefcase he held. He knew little of trains or coaches, and his knowledge of riverboat travel was rudimentary at best.

However, he was basing everything on the assumption that of late, the Baldwins had been more interested in international trade than they ever had before. He suspected it was the eldest son of the family who was pushing for that change, while the father continued focusing on domestic.

Which was, of course, why Mr. Hilton was so threatened by the Baldwins. In another world, Father would've considered an alliance with them, but he felt the Baldwins were stepping into a space they had no right to be in.

That was nonsense, but no one ever said Father was purely logical. He tried, but his anger got the best of him more times than not.

Much as, often, Patrick's fear got the best of him.

This would not be one of those times.

"Sit, girl," he mumbled to Bell, and she obediently found a spot for herself near the door. "I'll be out soon." With one last pat to the top of her silky, black head, he entered the building.

He was greeted by a young man about Lorelei's age sitting behind a reception desk.

"Welcome to Baldwin & Sons." The young man smiled, dimples appearing on his ruddy cheeks. He was slightly pudgy but neatly dressed with one of those modern bow ties that must've been done by a woman. Probably his mother—he was of that age. However, his dark hair stuck up at a spot or two. "How may I help you today, sir?"

"Good morning. My name is Patrick Hilton, and I'm here to meet with someone in administration." Patrick put forth his best grin. "I know none of the Baldwins are likely to be here today, and I understand that anyone who might be willing to hear my proposal may be unavailable, but perhaps I could arrange an appointment?" There. The words were said, and in a surprisingly more confident tone than he'd feared.

The boy's eyes widened. "You're not ... you're not *the* Patrick Hilton? Only son of Mr. Clarence Hilton?"

Patrick's eyebrows rose before he could help it. This desk clerk knew of the Hiltons? Particularly, that there was a *Patrick* Hilton? "Yes, that's me. But I'm not here on behalf of my father. Actually, it's quite the opposite. I'm here in spite of my father." He might as well avoid beating around the bush.

For a moment, the clerk stood in silence, regarding Patrick as if he were some circus oddity on display. Then he circled the desk and came forward, extending his hand. "I'm Rupert Baldwin. John Baldwin's second son. It's nice to meet you ... I suppose."

Oh. So John Baldwin had his son seated at the front of operations? Strange. They certainly could afford to hire a secretary, if need be. Why have his own son take on such a mediocre task? Yet Patrick couldn't let his surprise stop him from this first impression. He shook Rupert Baldwin's hand. "Nice to meet you, too." He ignored the "I suppose" and thought about how he would've likely felt if one of the Baldwin boys showed up at his father's offices. Granted, they never would've met Patrick, but all the same, it would've been an interesting story when Patrick heard of it days or weeks later, whenever his father decided to fill him in on the details.

"My father and brother are here, but I suppose I shouldn't have told you that." A flush overcame the already-present healthy red in his cheeks, causing them to turn into two ripe tomatoes. "Father put me out here today because he said my ability to use my tongue for my own good was lacking. I like to work with my hands not my head, but he's determined I ought to make something of myself. Is your father determined you ought to make something of yourself?"

Patrick considered the rambling fellow for a moment before he nodded. "Yes. Usually. But at present, I have broken with my father. Which is why I'm here. Perhaps I could explain this to *your* father."

Rupert turned even redder, if that were possible. "I'll see what I can do."

So Patrick was left standing alone in the empty foyer. He'd expected more activity first thing on a Monday, but to be fair, he was intentionally there at the beginning of business hours.

So he fidgeted in the room for perhaps fifteen minutes until Rupert reappeared, followed by two other men.

One of the men must be John Baldwin's other son, John Jr. He was several years older than Patrick, with the same round cheeks and black hair as his brother, but he was slimmer and obviously had a little more control of his faculties. He had the look of a man who knew what he was about without appearing particularly unkind.

John Baldwin Sr. was shorter and lighter in eye- and hair-color than either of his sons, round as a pumpkin, and possessing a smile as wide as the United States of America.

That was reportedly how far his railroads went, after all, so it made sense.

"Good morning." Despite his cheery features, it was clear Mr. John Baldwin Sr. lacked no brains. His blue eyes surveyed Patrick keenly. The family resemblance was there, but if Patrick had not been looking for it, he wouldn't have seen it. Mrs. Baldwin must have dark hair and eyes, like her sons, and perhaps be slimmer, like John Jr.

However, that was neither here nor there. For now, Patrick met the eldest man's eyes evenly and forced another smile. "Good morning, sir. I presume you are Mr. John Baldwin?"

A slight nod. "I am. And you are Patrick Hilton? No less, Patrick Clarence Hilton, if I've heard correctly, of the Hilton Shipping Co."

"Yes, sir. I am." Patrick cleared his throat. "I came here to—"

Mr. Baldwin held up his hand. "Now is not the time to talk. I'll have you and both my sons with me in my office. Rupert, please get Anders to cover the desk for now."

"Thank God," Rupert mumbled before turning and half jogging through the door behind the desk.

Mr. Baldwin gestured after him. "Follow me, please, Mr. Hilton."

In a few moments, they were seated in a large office that equaled Father's in size if not in grandeur. A portrait of a woman in an old-fashioned style—obviously painted many years ago, given the build of her clothing and the style of her hair—confirmed Patrick's suspicions that Mrs. Baldwin was a slim, dark beauty—or had been thirty-odd years ago.

"Well, son." With a heavy sigh, Mr. Baldwin settled on a throne-like chair behind the desk that must've been built specifically for him. "I've a feeling you have a story to tell me. But before you begin, know that I'm weighing every word you say not just with my own knowledge, but with the help of my sons—whose youth allows them to have quicker, keener minds than I ever will at my age—and with God's provision. If my sons and I cannot discern a lie or a half-truth, know that God can—and He always finds you out, my lad." A smile graced his face once more. "So speak as if the Lord were in the room. Your appearance has certainly sent us praying, hoping we haven't let a fox in the den—and knowing that if we did, in good faith, the Lord will care for us regardless."

Patrick nodded. "I respect that, sir. I would not tell a lie before God, but you can hear me out and decide what you think. Simply put, I come here seeking a job. I will plainly say that the only work I have ever done is for my father's company. He raised me to be his heir, and if you know nothing else of Clarence Hilton, I will tell you he is an involved owner." Father trusted no one, and as such, he worked much, to the neglect of his family. "He expected me to be the same. He required I understand every aspect of the company, that I do every kind of work. Now that we have parted ways, I am without funds. I'm a hard worker, and though I have benefited greatly from the wealth and security of my family, I am not above any type of employment. I have great reason to do what is required to establish myself in this world based solely on my own merit."

Mr. Baldwin folded his hands on the desk in front of him, keeping his eyes trained on Patrick as he spoke. "Indeed. What break have you had with your father, my lad?"

Patrick pressed his lips together. Honesty truly was the best course here. "My father chose a woman for me to wed when I was a child. It was always expected that I would marry her. You know of the Linden Railroads, surely?"

"Ah." Mr. Baldwin nodded. "Their daughter would be your age."

"Yes. She is. But she is not ... We are not ..." Patrick paused and shook his head. "Sir, you are a God-fearing man, aren't you?"

Mr. Baldwin nodded. "I pray so."

"Then if I were to say that I wasn't able to marry her because I received a direct order to do otherwise, and because I feel that to marry any woman, I must have some separation from the control of my family, you would not doubt me, would you? I feel strongly that God called me away from marrying Miss Linden and toward ... That's neither here nor there." He didn't want to muddy the waters with Cassie. Even without her, the command to leave Blanche and his father and strike out on his own had been clear.

"Oh, there's a girl!" Mr. Baldwin leaned back on his seat and chuckled, placing his hands, still folded, across his chest. "Johnny could tell you a thing or two about that. Whenever there's a girl, I almost stop asking questions about young men's strange actions. Not to say I will stop, Mr. Hilton, but I'm rather inclined to. I suddenly see a bit more reasoning."

John Jr. cleared his throat. "I wouldn't call my behavior surrounding Henrietta strange. Just—"

"Terribly odd," Rupert inserted with a grin.

Mr. Baldwin cast a look of combined amusement and "shushing" at his sons before returning his attention to Patrick. "Continue."

"As you suspected, there was a girl—in fact, there is a woman I'd like to marry if I had a way to support her, and if she were to accept me despite it all. But much as that played into my decision-making process, the reason I am no longer an employee of my father is because when I came to him and told him I would not be marrying Miss Linden—and that I required in future to receive fair wages for my work and establish a separate household for myself—he gave me a choice between his path for me and complete separation and disinheritance. I chose the latter and walked out of his house that night. I have no intention of returning, even if it means dying in a gutter. However, I do not believe it will come to that. I'm confident God will provide a path forward. I'm just not sure what way that is."

Mr. Baldwin glanced at John Jr. briefly. "We could confirm this story easily. Especially the disinheritance."

Patrick nodded. "Yes. In fact, I have no doubt it'll sneak its way into the papers soon enough. I'm surprised it hasn't already—my parents must be keeping it hushed up until they decide what to do next. I assume the company must be inherited by my sisters, or by their husbands, when the time comes. However, they are too young for that at present. My father may decide to train the elder of my sisters to take my place, but I know that would be an unpopular decision with anyone he worked with."

Mr. Baldwin nodded. "Indeed. I suppose you did leave your father in the lurch."

"I know." Patrick paused, then continued. "But, sir, all my life, my father has treated me as nothing but a cog in his giant machine. He does not care about my welfare, and tossing me out over something that should be insignificant in the long run proves that. I could tell you any number of things about my treatment, which would readily indicate to you that any situation but that of a dependent of my father is preferable. I will not go into detail, but I have been more his servant than his son. I took my time to consider this decision, and I am certain that I want nothing further from my father unless he changes. Perhaps if my father were to become a devoted Christian, then I could return to him, but I do not see that happening for a long time."

Mr. Baldwin rubbed his chin. "God is a God of miracles."

"He is, but He's also not a God Who expects us to live our lives dependent on our parents forever. His Word has made that clear."

"Indeed." Mr. Baldwin shifted on his seat. "And you came to us first?"

"I did. After you, I don't know where I will turn. No one in Boston, no one associated with my father, will ever work with me. My best hope is to rely on friends in Philadelphia to help me find suitable employment."

"Is your lady still in Boston?"

"No. She is in Cincinnati at present but may be in Philadelphia at some point in the next few months." At least, Patrick prayed so. He longed for a chance meeting, and he would certainly do his best to ascertain when she might be returning to England, so he could speak with her beforehand.

"Ah. All the more reason to come here." Mr. Baldwin leaned forward and practically rolled to his feet. "Mr. Hilton, you have given us much to think about. I think I will leave my son John to speak to you further about your experience and qualifications. I find I need time to consider the implications of having you join us ... and perhaps to do some research on where you might be suited. Leave any contact information with Johnny, and we will be in touch."

"Thank you, sir." Patrick, too, rose and shook Mr. Baldwin's hand. The older man left the room, and Patrick settled in to speak with the sons.

He found them both to be intelligent. As he'd originally guessed, Rupert had less of a business mind but was still valued as part of the organization. Both sons evidently adored their father and, further, seemed happy with their work.

Patrick was able to discern that John Jr. was married to Henrietta, though recently, and of course had his own household, whereas Rupert was still a bit too young for that and apparently attended college nearby when not at work at Baldwin & Sons.

The name of the company itself spoke of its history of working with its family in a healthy way; it was truly an enterprise meant to be run by father and sons. It ran back several generations, like Hilton Shipping Co., only gaining real traction in recent years as the world advanced and needed to get places faster.

Yet Baldwin & Sons' reputation, though perhaps not as gilded as that of the Hiltons, was certainly a better one, in Patrick's mind. He would not have said that a month ago, or even a week ago, but now he saw things a little differently. There was a great deal more to be valued in a business that treated all members with respect.

After John Jr. and Rupert ran out of questions, they invited Patrick to take a brief, somewhat guarded tour of their headquarters, and Patrick met a few employees. They all seemed fiercely loyal to their employer, and Patrick liked that.

He wasn't at all sure that, behind his back, his father's employees would be similarly loyal. This was confirmed when Rupert mentioned the wages of a few employees for no reason other than to hear himself talk, and though John Jr. quickly shushed him, Patrick knew very well that every one of those employees, given their duties, received a higher rate of pay than his father's did.

Especially a higher rate of pay than Patrick ever had. Even factoring in his father's claim that his room, board, and access to their charge accounts were included in his allowance. Even factoring in a perhaps necessary pay cut as a junior employee.

There was no way in which Baldwin & Sons was not the better employer, unless Patrick was missing something big—which, as familiar with how these things worked as he was, he doubted.

Oh, Lord, please. This would be such an ideal position, even if they had me minding the front desk like Rupert. Whatever situation they place me in, I am confident this would be the best possible job for me. Help me, Lord. Help me earn this position. Help them see that I will be loyal, I will work hard, and I will help them in any way I can.

He gave the address of the hotel he could afford to live at through the end of the week to John Jr. and went to report his progress at the Strauss home—though, truly, only one person's opinion mattered to him.

Mr. Baldwin was right. There was a girl.

The next morning, Patrick was summoned back to the Baldwin & Sons headquarters. Rupert escorted him straight to his father's office with a broad grin that gave Patrick hope.

But Cassie was right. Hope was a dangerous thing.

He bit his lip at the thought as he lowered himself onto the chair across from Mr. Baldwin and his sons. Yes, hope was a dangerous thing—but Patrick served a greater God, and he had faith that, one way or another, the Lord would carry him through this. Whatever happened would be the result of God's love for him.

"Well, son." Mr. Baldwin folded his arms across his chest. "I've given some serious consideration—and some serious prayer—to your request to work with us. You've certainly proven you have the experience, and both Johnny and Rupert feel you are a decent fellow. My wife respects the opinion of Mrs. Strauss, too, and I, in turn, trust my wife, but that was not a deciding factor in the end. The truth is, you have impressed me, and I've decided to give you a chance."

Patrick released a deep breath and leaned forward. "Thank you, Mr. Baldwin. I won't let you regret it."

"I don't expect to." Mr. Baldwin's serious expression was replaced by a cheerful smile. "Even if you were to prove a liar or simply a poor worker, I would know that I have done my best to both give you the benefit of the doubt while remaining wisely cautious. I trust God to do the rest."

"I certainly appreciate that perspective." It was enough to be given a chance, but to be given a chance by a company that so clearly based their foundations on God's will was more ideal than Patrick ever could have imagined.

"Further, this will be a relatively entry-level position. I didn't consider you suited for basic clerk work, much less to work at a shipping yard—not after all you've done—but you will be working closely with my elder son, under his supervision. I can't promise that it'll be anything but a lot of assistant work, but I'd suspect you'd be accustomed to that by now."

Patrick nodded. After being his father's right-hand man for years, it would be far easier working directly under someone like John Baldwin Jr. "As I believe I said before, sir, any position would be appreciated—and this seems to suit my skills far better than others might have."

"Indeed." Mr. Baldwin folded his hands over his chest. "But, son, of course in time, I hope that if you are diligent and prove yourself through your work, your position and your pay will reflect that. That said, at first, you will likely be working on day-to-day details with Johnny—and that involves managing the men at the docks, plenty of paperwork, and perhaps an occasional trip up or down the coast to broker deals." He rose and reached out his hand.

Patrick shook it. "Thank you, sir. I cannot express enough how much I appreciate this."

"No need. Just do your best." Mr. Baldwin turned to John Jr. with a nod. "Why don't you take him into your office and discuss the finer details? He'll want to know about pay rate—and what he'll actually be doing—which you could tell him better than I could."

Awash with gratitude toward God for His providence, Patrick followed John Jr. and Rupert out of Mr. Baldwin's office to learn more about his new job.

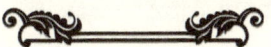

CHAPTER TWENTY-FOUR

Early July 1883

CAROLINE WENT INTO LABOR two days after Cassie, Alice, and Peter arrived in Philadelphia. The baby ran a few weeks behind, as babies are wont to do, but Peter and Alice both wanted to meet Caroline's second child so badly that Cassie couldn't help but feel supreme relief when Barnaby Webster stopped by the Strauss home and told them it was time.

Alice accompanied Lilli to the Webster home. Both Peter and Cassie questioned the wisdom of this, but Alice would not be stopped. She wanted to see the baby safely delivered.

Sometimes Alice forced herself to do things that weren't particularly healthy, and Cassie knew this as well as Peter did. Yet Alice had seemed calm as she had gathered a few things and followed Lilli out the door.

Even if they had considered stopping her, Alice was going where neither Peter nor Cassie could follow. A home where a child was being brought into the world was strictly off-limits for men—or most men, anyway—and unmarried women, and they both knew it.

The day was a long one. Barnie Webster, a cherub of a fellow with a shy, concerned look on his chubby face, was brought over, and Cassie played with him while Mr. Strauss limped from window to window, as if he could see across the street, several houses over, and through walls to check on his daughter.

Peter walked over halfway through the day to make sure all was well. When he returned, he first reported on how Caroline was doing, then murmured a few words about Alice to Cassie.

"She's fine. Fetching water and cloths. She seems so cheerful." He sat next to her, watching Barnie build a large tower with brightly painted blocks. "I don't know how she can be so calm about it. I know I couldn't be, and I ... Obviously my experience with that sort of thing is the waiting and the worrying. Alice actually ... Alice knows what is happening, and it was horrible. Horrible, Cassie. I just ..."

The tower crashed to the ground.

"You don't know how she can handle it." Cassie began picking up the blocks, smiling at Barnie, whose squeals of delight could not be stemmed. How young boys loved destruction. What would she do if she had one of her own someday? Other than loving him unconditionally, she foresaw a great need for growth in herself should she ever be so blessed. Of course, that might never happen. "I know how. She has a great God. As do you."

Peter grunted, rose, and walked to the window. He spoke with his father softly, and Cassie watched him, mildly concerned.

Peter plainly didn't want to talk about God just now. That was a sentence that should never have been thought, not about him.

Peter's youngest sister, Dahlia, entered the room and knelt beside Cassie. "Is Peter being odd?"

"Yes!" Finally, someone else had said it. "Dreadfully so."

"Hmm." Dahlia attempted to pull Barnie onto her lap, but he squawked, and she released him. "I'm worried about him."

"I am, too."

"He was sad when he came back to England." She cocked her head. "I thought he would be better by now, though. Alice certainly is."

"They're both still grieving. Alice is just handling it better right now." Cassie's eyes returned to Peter; his father had gone to sit down and pretend to read, but Peter still stood by the window, hands gripping the sill.

"Granted, I imagine he must be terrified. His wife almost died in childbirth, and they lost their son. Caroline is the first person close to him who has had a baby since then. We can't expect him to be happy."

Dahlia frowned. "I suppose not. Though I hope he will be happy someday. I love Peter and Alice, and I can't bear the idea of them being sad forever."

Cassie sighed. "They won't be. God is going to change them. He's a God of miracles, after all, isn't he?" He certainly had worked miracles in Cassie's life, even if they seemed like small, insignificant things in the moment. Every part of her life was controlled by God; how could she fear for herself or for those around her?

Dahlia stood up and crossed the room; she placed a hand on Peter's back. "Peter, I think I'm going to go see Caroline. She said I could be there this time, if I wanted. Maybe then I could come back every so often and tell you what is happening."

He shifted to face his sister, his eyes slightly glazed over. "Oh, Dally, you shouldn't have to ... have to ... No. It's all right. You should stay here."

Dahlia smiled. "I'm not scared, and Mama says I ought to see a few children born before I get married and have my own."

"That's a long way away, though." He put an arm around her shoulders and kissed her forehead. "I don't want you to think about such things until you're ready."

Dahlia sighed. "I'm sixteen, Peter. And you know there are boys who have expressed—"

"It doesn't matter. You should wait." He pulled away from her and walked out of the room. Cassie heard his heavy, slow tread up the stairs to the bedroom Alice and he were staying in.

"Let him overcome this fear on his own, Dally." Mr. Strauss reached for his daughter, and she slipped into his arms. "It won't be long now, and when he sees his new little niece or nephew, I'm sure he'll feel better. All of us will."

"Perhaps." Dahlia wiggled away from her father and paced across the room. "But Peter just told me I should wait to be married, and he was the only person I've convinced that I ought to be allowed to have a beau—"

"You cannot have a beau," Mr. Strauss said in a monotone without turning from the window.

"Exactly what I mean. I needed him." Dahlia scowled. "But I also think he can't be happy. Not if he's not listening to God. When has Peter not listened to God? Someone in this family needs to keep us all grounded."

"Peter is not responsible for—"

But Dahlia plainly wasn't in the mood to listen to her father or anyone. "I want to go over to see how Caroline is doing. I *don't* want to see her having the baby, though. That sounds like a messy experience, from what I've heard."

Mr. Strauss turned, hands shoved in his pockets. "And that is why we can't let you seriously entertain suitors, Dally."

"The two things have nothing in common." Dahlia pointed at Cassie. "She's had suitors, and she's never seen a baby born. Have you?" Her hazel eyes, full of both enthusiasm and curiosity, turned sharply to Cassie.

"Never. But then, I've never had the opportunity."

"Also, Cassie is older than you and has shown her maturity in other areas."

"Fine. If I were to help Caro with the baby, would you let me have a beau?"

"No."

Dahlia mumbled in frustration and left the room. Her footsteps were heard stomping up the stairs.

Mr. Strauss smirked, went to sit on the chair, and took up a newspaper. Then he hesitated, lowered it and watched Cassie thoughtfully. "I'll take Barnie and play with him for a while, if you don't want to be here."

"I've enjoyed spending time with him, but I was thinking about going to check on Alice." She would stay out of the way, of course, but poking her head in couldn't hurt anything.

Mr. Strauss nodded, set the paper aside, and stood. "Why don't you go now?"

Fifteen minutes later, she slipped into the front door of Barnaby and

Caroline Webster's house. It was small but neat and charmingly pretty, much as she'd expected from Caroline. Somehow, the whole place smelled of flowers and was moderately cool despite the hot temperature out of doors.

"Miss Cassie." Barnaby Webster greeted her; his hair stood up in even more places than normal, and he had a slightly frightened look in his eyes, yet his manner was still polite and gentle, as per always. "Alice was down about ten minutes ago; she said it wasn't going to be much longer. I'm sorry you missed her. I could go ask if she—"

"No. That's all right, Mr. Webster." Though she wasn't quite comfortable with Caroline's husband yet, she did think he was a kind man who clearly adored his wife and son. Anxiety practically oozed out of every pore now; his hands shook whenever they didn't grip the arms of the chair he now jumped from, as if too restless to stay still. "You should sit. I just thought I'd come over and see if there was anything I can do."

He lowered himself back onto the chair, and a nervous smile flitted over his lips. "There's nothing to be done. I keep being told that. I'm not even qualified to boil water at this point. Apparently, if I spill it on myself and end up needing a doctor, that would cause more problems than the distraction solved. So I sit."

Cassie took a seat on another chair opposite Barnaby and folded her hands on her lap. "How long has it been?"

"It's been ..." He pulled a watch out of his pocket. "It's 3:34 now. She woke up around 5:30 in the morning. Or woke me up, rather."

Cassie nodded sympathetically. "But it's the right time, isn't it? And the doctor thinks everything is all right, doesn't he?"

"Yes. Yes, of course." Barnaby ran his hands through his hair, and Cassie realized how he'd managed to get so frazzled-looking. "I just ... I worry. She should be fine. She *ought* to be fine."

"Of course she will be." Cassie prayed so, but such things were both foreign to her and impossible to predict. Perhaps she ought to qualify the statement. "God is in control, and He loves you both. What better guarantee have you?"

"Right, right." His hands gripped the arms of his chair once more. "I think we're all a bit shaken. After ... after Alice."

"Naturally." She scrambled for something with which to distract him, a virtual stranger. "Are you hoping for another boy, or would you like to have a daughter?"

"Either is fine. Caro wants a girl," he mumbled.

He was definitely deeply consumed by his worries. That seemed to be a trend amongst the men in this area. "What is Barnie like?"

That did send him into a small speech about his son, whom he clearly adored, and Cassie asked enough questions about him, about the rest of his family, about their church, and about his work that Barnaby was kept busy until his sentence trailed off in shock, for a baby cried out in the bedroom upstairs.

He rose without a word, and Cassie sat alone and waited for news.

Alice came down about fifteen minutes later and lowered herself onto the chair that Barnaby had vacated. "It's a girl. She's doing fine, as is Caroline."

"Good."

"Barnaby is delighted, of course, and Caroline hasn't stopped crying—joy, I presume. She's not very coherent. She did want a girl badly, though."

"Right. And how are you?"

Alice raised tired eyes. "I'm fine. Surprisingly, I'm just fine. Grateful I was there. Surprised at myself, a little. I've never been in the room before."

"She is your sister." Cassie knew Alice wouldn't bother with the "in-law." Peter certainly didn't with any of Alice's siblings.

"Yes." Alice smiled. "Yes, she is."

The next few hours passed swiftly. Cassie helped with laundry, with preparing a meal for Caroline, and with keeping various members of the family from bothering Caroline, Barnaby, and their new little girl. Eventually, Barnie was brought over, screamed at the baby, and was put to bed after a scolding. Alice said that Caroline simply laughed; Barnaby was the one who was offended on his daughter's behalf.

Toward the end of the night, Cassie went into the bedroom for the first time to deliver Caroline a glass of water and meet the baby, who was red-faced and wrinkled and absolutely adorable.

"Do you want to hold her?" Caroline asked, nodding toward the bassinet where her daughter slept. "She won't wake up. The first night, they act like angels, then they gain their strength and make you miserable. Enjoy her while she's not howling."

So Cassie lifted the tiny thing out of the bassinet and cradled her close, cooing soft things and marveling at her tiny hands and nose and mouth.

Alice came in, approached, and brushed a hand over her niece's head. "So precious. Do you know what you'll name her, Caroline?"

"Yes. We'd already decided on Maud, so we'll definitely call her 'Maudie.' But after today, Barnaby and I decided her full name will be Maud Alice."

Alice stilled; her eyes remained glued to the child. "Oh, Caroline. You shouldn't."

"I'm going to. It's decided."

Alice turned, walked to the bedside, and embraced Caroline wordlessly.

Sometime later, Alice and Cassie returned to the Strausses' home. Peter met them at the doorway.

"You could have come over," Alice noted.

Peter smiled and shook his head. "I needed the day alone, and I knew they would both be tired enough not to miss me. I heard it's a girl and that they are naming her for you."

Alice slipped into his arms and dropped her head against his shoulder. "Yes. In a manner of speaking. I ... I was deeply touched." At last, there was the catch in her voice that Cassie had been expecting all day.

"Of course." He wrapped his arms around her and pressed a kiss to the top of her head. "You deserve it. Caroline told me the other day that she was thinking of it but unsure if it was the right choice. I think you confirmed it today when you stood by her so faithfully."

"And how are you?"

His eyes darkened. "We'll have to talk about it. Tomorrow, though."

Alice drew back from him, watched him for a moment, then nodded.

"All right. Let's go to bed now. Good night, Cassie."

"Good night, Alice. Good night, Peter."

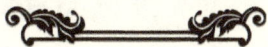

CHAPTER TWENTY-FIVE

J OHN JR. HANDED A bundle of papers to Patrick and bid good-bye to the dock manager, then the two walked back down the street toward the main offices.

"I think the situation will resolve itself," John Jr. commented, shoving his hands in his pockets. "The men are fairly treated, and they would not find better work anywhere. But it's hot and tiresome, and once the cooler days come and the work gets more plentiful, it'll get easier."

Patrick knew that, yet there was always a tricky act of pleasing employees and not running the company into the ground to do so. In theory, it would be nice to continually raise wages and allow the men to do whatever they wanted rather than the work that had been laid out for them. However, that was no way to run even the fairest company. The Baldwins treated their employees well, and that included wages and time off. They certainly valued God's command to rest and enabled their employees to do so if they wanted; however, it was not possible to keep workers who didn't work hard.

"Are you coming to dinner tonight? I believe Henrietta is expecting you."

"Yes, I can come. Though this must stop and I must learn to fend for myself soon. My salary is generous enough; I can't be living and eating on the company's dime." Despite his best efforts to remove himself from the younger John Baldwin's hospitality, somehow Patrick had ended up staying in a spare room while he searched for a more permanent residence.

John Jr. shrugged. "It is a little thing for us. We enjoy the company, and you earn your keep."

Patrick had been teaching himself to do tasks such as painting, fixing broken doors, and cleaning to try to make up for the burden he must be—but even he knew the few hours he put in every evening couldn't account for a free room and meals. "I hardly do anything."

"You do a lot for the company. Besides, Henrietta said you learned to do laundry over the weekend. Especially just now, I would rather her not do anything too strenuous."

Patrick nodded sympathetically. He'd been informed about a week ago that Henrietta had suffered a miscarriage last month, and John Jr. was incredibly protective—and seemed to think it was his fault for letting her "do too much." Based on what little Patrick knew of Henrietta, she would be a difficult woman to make to do anything—and he knew that there was never any blame to be assigned in such cases. It was another tragedy that failed to find explanation or reason in human minds. Yet as a man who wanted children desperately someday, he could sympathize with the devastation and the tendency to blame oneself.

"Actually." John shoved his hands deep in his pockets. "She wanted me to ask if you would come to our church on Sunday. I know you've been attending Christ Church, but you know my father wants to see every aspect of you develop, and that includes establishing a community. Henrietta thinks you can do that better at our church than off by yourself. It's just a friendly, cheerful Baptist church."

Patrick nodded. That was fair enough. "The theology is a bit different than mine, but honestly, the community is probably equally as vital."

"Oh, and I remember you said you were friends with the Strausses. Henrietta is close friends with their eldest daughter, Mrs. Caroline Webster, and the whole Strauss family attends. It might be a good opportunity for you to reacquaint yourself."

"Oh, I didn't realize it was the same church." Frankly, he hadn't given it much of a mind, having been so busy day and night lately. "I would like to see them all again. Mr. and Mrs. Webster, and their son, are friends of mine."

John Jr. nodded. "Barnie is a sweet fellow. And they've just had a daughter, too. Not a week ago. You'll not see them for another week, I think, but Caroline's parents will be there. Oh, and I think Peter Strauss and his wife are in town."

Patrick's hands unwittingly clenched. "Oh?"

"Yes. With a guest, too. I think they came to see her off. She's from England or Ireland—I confess I didn't catch the whole story, and you remember Henrietta and I went home early last Sunday on account of ... To get some quiet. Away from things."

Patrick wanted to be sympathetic to their plight, which he believed was the obvious emotion when confronted with a close friend receiving what you most wanted but couldn't have. Yet his mind reeled.

Cassie was here, but she might not be for long.

This was his last chance.

Cassie was out in the Strausses' garden, resting under the shade tree that eliminated some of the summer heat, when a movement behind her caught her attention.

It was Patrick.

Heart racing, she stood still and stared at him, her mind trying to grasp a coherent sentence, but what was she supposed to say?

"Patrick." She straightened and glanced around, almost expecting someone from the Strauss family to emerge and offer an explanation.

None came.

"Cassie. I ... I'm in Philadelphia." He paused and cleared his throat. "Obviously. I ... I broke off with my parents."

"So I've heard." It'd been in the papers a few days ago, and Alice and she had discussed it at great length. The papers had not, however, said where he'd gone.

Why here?

"Baldwin & Sons." He supplied the answer to the question she didn't ask. "They agreed to hire me, so I've been working with them for the last two weeks. It's going well—and as you might know, the Baldwins attend the Strausses' church."

She hadn't known, but then, she'd stayed with Caroline on Sundays since they'd arrived. Cassie delighted in spending time cuddling Maudie and, by doing simple chores around the house and watching Barnie, enabling Caroline to rest.

"I heard from the Baldwins' elder son that you were in Philadelphia, and when I realized you must be returning to England, I couldn't wait. I ran all the way here—and Mrs. Strauss pointed me in the right direction." He stepped toward her hesitantly. "I had to see you, even if this is the last time, Cassie. I had to.

"This position with Baldwin & Sons has given me hope," he continued. "Granted, it's just a beginning-level position, but it pays well enough that I can rent something in Philadelphia and make a living wage. Enough to ... enough to support a family. In a small way, but in some kind of way, which is more than I could do before. I can move up in the company. Mr. Baldwin seems to have taken a liking to me. He said he would make sure I always have enough to get by if need be. And, Cassie ... Cassie, I don't know if you feel anything for me." His words slowed and softened, and he reached for her hands. She let him take them, press them. "But I want you in my life. I want you to be my family. Have I any hope?"

For a moment, she didn't respond. She just stood, squeezing his hands for all she was worth, and staring into his joy-filled face. The urge to close the distance between them was strong, but before she was that stupid, her common sense rose.

Fear flooded her like a tidal wave that she could not dismiss.

"I ... I'd need to pray about it," she murmured.

The light in his eyes faded but was not extinguished, and his hands squeezed hers gently, not nearly as tightly as they had moments before. "Of course. Of course you do. And I ... I've been praying for days now, whereas I suppose you ..." His voice trailed off, and he glanced to the side. "Should I leave you?"

"Yes." The word came quickly. "Will you come back to see me this evening?" She wasn't sure if that was enough time, and she couldn't rush God, but she wanted to give Patrick some sort of timeline. It didn't seem fair to leave him without an answer for too long.

"I will." He leaned back, and his grip on her hands loosened, then he paused and brought both her hands to his lips. "Remember, I know I need much improvement, Cassie. But that's all got to come from God, and I can't imagine a better partner for pursuing Him than you."

She nodded. "I know that. I ... I promise I'll keep it in consideration."

"Thank you." Then he was gone as suddenly as he had arrived.

She deflated against the tree and pressed her eyes tightly closed. Her pulse pounded through her head, but she forced the prayers through, confused and muddled at first and eventually clear and full of all her heartache and agony.

What should she do?

She wanted him. However, simply wanting a man was not a good reason for marrying. Though Cassie believed that Patrick had turned his life around, a small part of her doubted that he had really surrendered himself completely to God.

Had he chosen the path he was on or been forced onto it?

Lord, what do I do? How do I know if Patrick is the right choice for me? How do I know if Your will is in this marriage or if it's just my own desires clouding my judgment?

Why did she want him?

The thought popped into her mind, and she stood still for a moment and began to mull the question over.

She had to admit that she found him attractive, but so were a great many men. Granted, she never had experienced much of a temptation to touch any of those other men, but she wasn't overly concerned with that fact. It had arisen from her admiration of other aspects of Patrick. It was important but not a key factor in her longing for him.

The truth was, she had fallen for him because of his character. Despite the fact that he'd obviously spent several years ignoring God and kowtowing to his father, his behavior toward his sisters, toward her, and even to random strangers spoke a great deal about the type of man he was.

He was honest. Loyal. Strong. He loved his sisters devotedly, and she had some evidence that he would love his wife that way, too. In their letters, they had discussed some aspects of their hopes and dreams, and she found hers much aligned with his. Their beliefs were certainly identical on all the essentials and similar on the small points.

She liked his humor. His grace under pressure. His ability to reach into her and figure out what she was thinking without her needing to express anything—especially in the moments when she felt frozen and wordless. His control of himself, even if at times that same control could lead to his stepping back when he ought to step forward. Yet she also believed that those days were over. Something inside him had snapped with his father's rejection. He seemed more confident now, more sure of himself. He was Patrick still, of course, but stronger and better.

That seemed to be the case at least.

As she stood there in the heat, sweat beginning to trickle down her neck and back as the sun grew higher in the sky, she prayed.

The fears were soothed then, the flood waters retreating back from whence they had come. Peace came before the answer. She had no reason to fear, not really. Not when she had a great God Who certainly loved her and cared about these important moments in her life—though, of course, God cared about the details, too. It was just that these types of decisions were so vital that she dared not move without His guidance.

At last, she went inside and met Mrs. Strauss in the kitchen.

"Patrick Hilton came by," Cassie said, "which apparently you know."

"Oh?" Mrs. Strauss gestured for Cassie to take a seat at the kitchen table, and set about pouring them glasses of lemonade. She always seemed to both know when Cassie needed to talk and have refreshments at the ready, which she very much appreciated. "What did he have to say for himself?"

"He got a job at Baldwin & Sons." Cassie took a deep breath and spoke the next words in a rush. "He asked me to marry him."

Mrs. Strauss set the cool glass in front of Cassie. "You turned him down?"

"I asked for time to think and pray. Especially to pray. He'll come back this evening to discuss it further."

Mrs. Strauss lowered herself onto the seat across from her, and her eyes—so like her son's that Cassie never failed to be surprised by them—regarded her with a gentle, inquisitive kindness. "I wondered why you stood out in the hot sun for so long after he left, but I decided it was best not to bother you."

"I prayed and prayed, and all I know is that God loves me and will help me whatever happens. I also believe ..." She paused, then pressed on. "I believe my reasons for caring for him as much as I have come to are valid. I believe he is a good man and is on the way to becoming a better one. But he has wounded me. If I were a sane woman, perhaps I would not even consider a proposal from him."

"None of us are quite sane when we are in love."

Cassie inclined her head and took a sip of the lemonade.

"I have been praying for you both, as you know. I've been impressed with Patrick's behavior based on hearsay—I know Mrs. Baldwin quite well—but honestly, I have always liked him and yet never known him well enough to truly understand his character." Mrs. Strauss shrugged and sloshed her lemonade back and forth in her glass. "I don't have any words of wisdom, nor are you my child to advise."

"If I were, what would you say?" Cassie asked. "I don't happen to be in possession of a loving mother. I know that if I told my own of my current situation, she would banish me to a nunnery rather than have me marry an American. She intended me to marry a titled Englishman, or at least a very wealthy one, and she would not be happy with Patrick, especially as he is now separated from his parents and has no fortune to speak of. My father would react similarly. But you ... I know you only see us as two of God's children, stumbling about and trying to decide what is best. So what do you say?"

"I say be cautious but not too cautious." Mrs. Strauss shook her head and laughed. "That's not helpful. Marriage is a very difficult endeavor for any young couple, and being dreadfully in love can make it even harder ... in some ways. There's always a certain degree of disillusionment, I suppose. I faced that throughout the early days of my marriage. Yet it's also worth it, and I don't believe anyone truly marries the wrong person—or almost never. I believe that God helps us be happy in the marriage we are given, and I also believe He gives us the strength to run if we must due to cruelty. That said, in a normal situation, there is no reason any young couple living their life according to God's will shouldn't be able to have a perfectly happy marriage."

"That's true. But I also don't want to make it any more difficult than it needs to be. Everyone says marriage is hard, and I suppose I'm just trying to ..."

"Find the relationship that will be the easiest version of hard. I understand that. I think, if I were to marry logically, which I did not and never will, I would do the same." Mrs. Strauss cocked her head. "I married thoughtlessly, while blissfully in love and stupidly young, and it has been a great blessing. There is not even a small part of me that regrets marrying Chris. I love him with all my heart. I always have and always will. Honestly, there was never any regret within me even in the hard years. Regret over certain actions, yes, but not that he was my husband. Yet I don't think I am at all usual. I'm a bit of a romantic ... I am *very much* a romantic ... and I think I'm incapable of being sensible about Chris. Which I suppose is all right. But I never know what to say to people who are able to keep their heads on straight. Peter is the only child like me. He has never been sensible about Alice."

Cassie nodded. "And we love him for it."

"Of course we do! And my husband loves me for loving him ... Oh, and he has other reasons, I suppose. Yet it is comforting to know that I won't stop loving him even if sometimes I get the desire to strangle the idiot." She took a determined sip of her lemonade. "Did I mention that marriage is frustrating?"

Cassie laughed. "You did."

"You can love someone with all your heart and, if you're as young and as stupid as I was when I got married, still be furious at them for simply doing something you didn't particularly want them to do, no matter how petty. Though that happens less with the years."

"That's good to hear."

"Yes, and I'm still being unhelpful, aren't I? None of this applies to your situation. You love him?"

"Yes, I do."

"And you have no indication that God does not approve of your relationship?"

"None."

"Yet you fear."

Cassie hesitated. "Yes. I do fear."

"Much as Patrick feared moving forward toward being with you?"

Cassie didn't think it was at all the same thing, but still, she nodded, for of course it must be. Fear was fear, wasn't it?

Yet hers felt so much more grounded in logic.

"You may be right. I am quite fearful. Yet ..." However, she wasn't sure how to finish that sentence. She rose and reached for the glasses. "Thank you for the lemonade."

"Of course." Mrs. Strauss gestured her away. "Let me clean those. You just keep praying. I will, too."

Cassie turned, intending to go upstairs and do as she was told, but something bound her there. "How does one know the difference between fear and necessary caution? I want to be wise. I know I must be—about this more than anything else. But God keeps bringing Patrick back into my life."

"I don't think anyone really knows the difference without spiritual discernment." Mrs. Strauss set the first of the two glasses to dry on the counter and picked up the second one. "It gets easier as your relationship with the Lord deepens. However, we are finite creatures, and sometimes we are asked to take a step in faith without knowing anything but that God will use whatever happens for the good. I know I would give Chris another chance—but this decision is your own. Also, you don't have to agree to marry him. Nothing so drastic as that." She set the second glass down, picked up a towel, and turned to Cassie. "You realize most couples court for a while before they fully commit to marriage."

That was true. Yet even that seemed unfair. "I don't want to give him false hope."

"Romance is nice that way, because it's all about giving hope—and it grows you whether your hope is rewarded or not." Mrs. Strauss laughed. "Though I don't want anyone to get a broken heart, a childhood infatuation going awry has trained more souls than many a larger tragedy. This is not to say you should allow his advances if you know he has no chance, but perhaps it's good for both of you to put out a fleece, if you will. Allow God to show you both how best to serve Him—and if that be together or separately."

"Of course." Perhaps it was enough to walk forward and see where God guided her steps. "So you would not disapprove if I were to court him?"

"Cassie, I would not disapprove if you were to chase that man down now and tell him all that I said."

That seemed more than fair to Cassie, so she left the kitchen behind, found her hat, and hurried out of the house. She went in the direction of the river. She knew that he'd be there, as it was the nearest body of water. When, twenty minutes later, she found him pacing along the banks of the wide, somewhat dirty river and mumbling to himself, she was unsurprised.

"Patrick?"

He stilled, then turned to face her. "Cassie."

She walked to meet him, though he stood still, seemingly frozen in place. "You should have hope."

"Cassie?" he repeated, softer but more of a question than a statement now.

"I prayed and prayed." She drew near and placed a gentle hand on his arm. "And I realized that if God wants me to step out in faith in this way, I have no choice but to follow Him—and it seems that path is leading me toward you."

A smile spread across his face. He pulled her toward him, and his breathless voice whispered into her ear, "Do you mean it? Will you marry me, my love, my angel, my heart? There's nothing certain about me anymore. I've nothing to offer you of any worth now, and God will determine what I will have in the future. But I don't think I'd mind having nothing if I had you."

"There's a great deal about you that's certain." She withdrew slightly and reached up to cup his face in her hands, forcing his eyes to meet hers. "You are certainly a man of God, and I certainly love you. That's enough for me. More than enough."

He leaned forward, resting his forehead against hers. "All right then." His voice was shaky, half with laughter and half with what she assumed was a variety of emotions. "I love you, you know. I think I've loved you since you scolded Caleb Knight on the stairs. Only, you didn't scold him. You just stood there calmly and managed him, and I was mad enough to suddenly wish you'd manage me, too."

She pressed closer, wanting to ingrain this moment upon her very spirit and keep it there forever. "You do need a lot of managing."

"I do, at that." She felt his shoulders rise in a slight shrug. "But then, so do you."

"Not nearly as much, I don't think. Yet I suppose that's the principal duty of a wife, to be managed."

"No, to be loved." Then he suddenly drew away, leaving her gasping at his absence. "Now, look here, you never said yes, and here you are, presuming upon my husbandly duties."

She raised her eyebrows. "Don't you think it's a bit soon for that?"

"I don't."

"I do." She cocked her head. "I am not as venturesome as you, I suppose.

I need more time. We can court—but we need to be slow about it. I won't jump into anything. I can't."

"I understand that. It's enough that God would grant me any time with you. Just promise me you'll give me a chance."

"Oh, Patrick, of course."

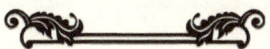

Chapter Twenty-Six

September 1883
Charleston, South Carolina

Dear Patrick,

We need to talk about these two-week trips. I know you said they would be frequent, unless you had an excuse to stay home. (Oh, is that what I am now? An excuse? At least my position has been determined.) However, despite knowing that until we wed, there is no reason why you shouldn't take these trips, I dislike them. It is criminal not to see you at church and every evening, and I deeply miss our Sunday afternoon walks.

I'll get this out of the way as I know you are eager to hear it: Bell is doing fine. She and Dahlia have become fast friends, and I am trying to walk Bell every day. I suspect she resents me slightly, but it is never easy to be replaced, so I have great pity for her.

Mrs. Strauss and I went to your apartment a few times and straightened things up. I hope you don't mind, but you shouldn't have entrusted me with the key if you did not desire my presence. Please don't judge me too harshly—I have added curtains. I apologize, but you needed them, and it's only the one window.

That action did bring up some questions from both the Strausses about where our relationship rests. I understand why—that type of decision seems like the type an engaged woman would make, doesn't it? In truth, it is hard knowing that I am the one holding us back and yet have the selfishly human desire to insert myself in your life.

I shouldn't get your hopes up. You know how I feel about you, yet I want to enter this decision with a great deal of foresight and prayer. I like that we pray together and talk about things and take those walks. I like that I can see a future forming with you. I like that we have given it more than a passing thought.

Why shouldn't we take things slowly, Patrick? "Fools rush in" and all that. I cannot risk this. It is too vital to my future.

Yet I believe God will help us both. You, in patience, and me, in impatience. I hope He makes me impatient—I hope He gives me some sort of sign.

I hope that I will know my answer when you ask me again.

P ATRICK HOPED SO, TOO.

The letter continued on for some time, describing Cassie's day-to-day life and offering some thoughts in response to his latest series of questions. At the end, there were her own questions. Personal ones, queries about dreams and goals for the future, and more. Cassie was good at coming up with questions, and lately, Patrick had enough on his mind that he was almost able to match her.

At last, the letter was concluded, and he folded it and put it away. He could not respond until the evening, especially since at that moment, John Jr. entered the room.

"Ah, I see you've finished the letter from your sweetheart." Grinning, John Jr. resumed his seat across from Patrick. "I suppose you'll be distracted all day, as per normal. Honestly, Hilton, I don't think I've ever seen a sane man go downhill so fast. Not that I don't approve wholeheartedly, but it is certainly amusing to watch."

Patrick just smiled. He had no problem with everyone on earth knowing he was smitten with Cassie. Not now, when he finally had permission to do whatever he wanted. He would use that freedom to serve God and love that woman.

He just had to figure out how to win her.

That was the gist of the issue. Though Cassie spoke to him with affection, though she dreamed of the future, though she spoke with longing of a time when they might be wed ...

She did not seem interested in hearing another proposal or in setting dates to her dreams at all. That concerned Patrick. Words without actions were nothing; he had learned that lesson the hard way. He knew why she was exercising restraint, much as he understood why they couldn't go further than a few kisses in the brief moments when they found themselves alone.

Yet some of this made no sense to him. She wanted him, and God seemed to be allowing the relationship. Patrick certainly felt sure of *her*. And though he would give Cassie all the time she needed, he couldn't help but wonder how much time would be enough.

Or if any time could be enough. If it would ever come to a head, or if she'd string him along forever.

Oh, he deserved it. No doubt about that. Yet it was a hard thing to expect a man to wait when he felt about her the way she did.

"John, how do you know when the time is right to propose?"

John Jr. looked up from the contract papers he had already begun sorting through again and smiled. "Considering it already?"

"I'm not just considering it. I did ask her to marry me. I'd do so again every day if I thought it would do any good, but I know that would be foolhardy." Patrick shrugged. "She says she's not ready."

"Then you wait until she is."

Patrick frowned. In theory, he accepted that answer. In practice, it was not easy. "I have no idea how to know when she will be ready."

John Jr. smirked. "I think, of all women in the world, she'd be likely to tell you."

"Honestly ..." Patrick wasn't sure of that. Yet perhaps John was right.

Patrick was willing to wait if that was all there was to it—waiting for Cassie to give him the right sign, to invite his asking. "What if she never does tell me?"

"Would you want to marry a woman who wasn't sure of you?"

Patrick shook his head. "No, but I don't think it's a matter of whether she's truly unsure. I fear I've embedded doubts in Cassie from the start of our relationship. I don't know if she can ever trust me. Or, at least, be willing to throw her lot with mine unrestrainedly. I don't know how to show her that that old self is gone. Christ cast me into the refining fire; I am changed."

"Then, should she be as godly as you say, she will see that. God will show her." John Jr. caught up a pen and dipped it in the inkwell. "You have to have faith."

Easy for a man who was already wed to the love of his life to say. "You're right, of course, but I just wish I was sure of her feelings."

John Jr. shrugged without looking up from his writing. "Maybe it's good for you to doubt a little."

Patrick sighed. It probably was. Yet that didn't make him any more patient for her answer.

Dear Cassie,

We are settled back in Cincinnati now. Peter finished a draft of his latest novel at last. I feared he would not be able to, but he pushed through, and I am very proud of him. I helped where I could, but of course there is only so much I can do, much as I try.

Maddie's girls are doing well. Dolly comes over almost every day, and Rosey often begs to follow her. They're such sweet girls that I can never resist inviting them over and filling them with biscuits. Riley appreciates this; Maddie doesn't. I'm trying to be more considerate, but I confess I have some growing to do in that area. Maddie is so certain we are dear friends—I am quite sure we never will be.

This will be a short letter as I've much to do today, but please do write more details about how things have been going with Patrick Hilton. I'm dying to know how the relationship is progressing. Is there a proposal imminent? I mean, a successful one. I don't care if he proposes; what will your answer be?

Honestly, I can't help but urge you to make a decision. Whatever it be, Cass, just make it! You so often get stuck in one spot. I know sometimes one is called to wait, but is that truly what is happening this time? Or is it something else entirely? You would know better than me, but I pray every day, as does Peter, that God will give you peace.

Oh, but don't worry too much, darling. God will give you "rest for your soul." He has given me so much rest lately. There have been some dark days, but Peter has coaxed me through them. Last month was as hard as I thought it would be, but facing it with Peter was the right choice. I think we grew more through that than anything. Of course, I miss my sons dreadfully, but I always will. There can't be any helping that.

Enough of that. I'd best get on with my day and send this off. A longer letter shall follow soon, but please do not wait for it to send your own reply. Truly, I must know more about this entire affair, or I shall explode!

Your friend,
Alice Strauss

Cassie set the letter down with a sigh. Alice echoed the words repeated to Cassie again and again by Mrs. Strauss, Caroline, and even Dahlia. Cassie couldn't hold Patrick off much longer. Not if she wanted to continue their relationship as it was now. It had to progress or regress. There was no in-between option.

Yet she didn't know how she'd answer him.

It was fear, truly. She'd come so far in her relationship with Aubrey

Montgomery before realizing what a mistake it would be to marry him. She'd fallen hard for Patrick before testing his true mettle. Now it seemed foolishness to rush forward.

Yet everyone treated them as if they were engaged. Perhaps they were, or as good as. However, Cassie couldn't help but see flaws in their relationship, flaws that made her hesitate.

Oh, every relationship had its flaws. Cassie knew that as well as anyone. Yet despite the fact that she was trying to trust God with this, it seemed that there was a part of her, perhaps deeply rooted in her old sins, that couldn't let go of this one thing.

She put the letter away amongst the many others like it and picked up a different sheet of paper, also covered in Alice's carefully-refined script. Alice had written the list just before returning to Cincinnati, hoping to give Cassie some directions on what to do while she made up her mind—and what might help make up her mind.

For the hundredth time, Cassie perused the list. She had laughed when Alice had given it to her, but now she cherished the advice.

1. Go to church every Sunday (make Patrick join you, too) and find out how to serve there. Involve Patrick as much as you can as an unmarried couple, but also find ways you can serve while he works. Make it your community.

2. Make even better friends with my mother-in-law, and with her friends. Older women are wonderful at giving lots of advice. Just sort through it with discernment.

3. Spend time with Caroline and her children; offer to watch them and learn how to tend babies. She likes you, and it will be an invaluable skill in the future. Even if you have no children of your own, you'll want to know how to take care of them.

4. Talk to Dahlia Strauss. Encourage her to confide in you about her various boy-related concerns especially. (I can't always be there, and she currently detests her mother and sister.) Offer to read the Bible with her. I'd appreciate it.

5. Write to your Irish friends and make sure they are settled. You don't want to forget about them in your own worries, and it'll take your mind off things.

6. Ask Patrick if there's any way you can be in contact with his sisters. It's unlikely, yes, but explore every option and pray about whether it isn't worthwhile to have some secretive correspondence. Weigh this carefully, as you don't want to encourage them to rebel against their parents, even if they are being unfair.

7. Learn how to manage Bell. It's not so bad. Dogs are nice, Cassie. They're man's best friend, after all. Remember, I have Juno now, and she's a dear.

8. Continue praying with Patrick every evening before he leaves you and reading the Bible together at every opportunity. Encourage his private studying; find ways to check in on his spiritual state regularly.

9. Write me with any questions, though don't expect me to have answers.

10. Remember that there are people who love you regardless of how this continues.

Cassie sighed as she tucked the list away. She'd been trying to pay heed to every single one of those points. So why was the decision not becoming clearer?

It was always lovely to have Cassie back in his arms, no matter how briefly, and her lips on his for even a fraction of a second.

Of course, they must pull back immediately—decorum and sense called for it—but she was smiling at him, blushing, glad to see him.

"I missed you," Patrick said, and she nodded but didn't vocalize the thought. She seldom did anymore.

They walked into the Strausses' home. Mr. and Mrs. Strauss always acted delighted to see him, and Bell certainly was, but he wondered if the three of them weren't wearing out their hospitality—Bell more so, of course, but having two human beings count on you as surrogate parents couldn't be easy.

Yet Mrs. Strauss seemed giddily excited at the sight of him, like a girl at her first dance, and Patrick assumed she liked being involved enough that she would host dozens in her household if she could be a part of their stories.

Mr. Strauss was another matter, but it seemed he humored a great deal of his wife's desires regardless of their practicality. Patrick could understand the impulse.

The visit progressed as well as could be expected. Unsaid things remained between Cassie and him and, therefore, between everyone else. The missing timeline made everything a little awkward for everyone, he supposed. A few times, he caught Mrs. Strauss starting to say something but stopping herself.

Eventually, he coaxed Cassie out onto the back porch where there was a swing, and they sat, with Bell as chaperone and likely one or two Strausses keeping an eye on them from the window.

Cassie talked about what she'd been doing—largely, a lot of work at the church, which he deeply admired. She was nothing if not motivated. And Patrick told her what he'd done on the trip, which was boring and overcomplicated all at once, as per usual.

"What's odd is that even though you should hate the work, you seem cheerful about it." Cassie smiled at him, head slightly cocked in that amusing way of hers, like a collie with a problem it wanted badly to solve. "Why is that?"

"I do like the work." He shrugged. "I always have. I never pretended that. It's interesting to me, in its own way, even as it has its frustrating elements. It's figuring out how to make different companies work together in a way that equally benefits both. I get to watch trade goods ship all over the world."

"I confess, you manage to make it sound more romantic than it is."

Patrick grinned. "I'll admit, there are fewer high seas adventures than I'd like."

"Oh? No pirating?"

"None whatsoever, though we always act as if it's a concern. Honestly, the biggest problems come from clerical errors."

She laughed softly. "Fascinatingly dangerous."

"Indeed. One misplaced decimal can mean days of work. But most companies hire clerks to sort out that kind of thing."

"Yet you have?"

"I've done a little of everything. I still do." Being just where he was needed most was of vital importance, in his opinion.

"I'm sure you're a good hand to have around."

"So I've been told."

They sat in silence for a time, rocking the swing slightly and looking out at the autumn-tinted garden, slowly relinquishing its summer hues and letting the reds and golds of a new season take hold.

"You haven't said anything about whether I might ask you a question sometime soon," he said softly, when he felt enough time had passed. "I'd like to know that, you know."

A tight smile lined her pink lips. "I know."

"Cass, if I'm just bothering you, I really do want to let you go. You don't have to ..." He hesitated, catching a deep breath despite the pain in his chest. "You don't have to keep me around. I'd be all right. You wouldn't need to worry about me or my heart or anything of the sort. God would sustain me. That's never been your job."

A nod. "I know."

Patrick refused to let himself sigh or press her further. He glanced out over the garden again. The shadows were deepening to the point of taking over the world, and he knew he'd better get home. It'd be a full day of work in the morning. "Let's pray, and then I'll leave you until tomorrow."

"All right."

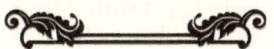

Chapter Twenty-Seven

"**T**HESE ARE COPIES OF the papers for the southern merger." Patrick set the folder on Mr. Baldwin's desk. "I filed the originals, but I thought you might want to glance at them and perhaps keep these in your office until everything is finalized."

"Thank you, Patrick." Mr. Baldwin immediately opened the folder and began flipping through its contents. "Other than secretarial work that I didn't ask you to do, what is on your mighty list today?" A slight smile appearing behind the papers indicated that he wasn't entirely serious, but Patrick took everything as seriously as he could these days while still maintaining a sense of humor.

"Rupert and I are going to work on researching our options on Canadian railroad lines, which will be beneficial to both of us. Then we've a meeting at lunch with Mr. Jensen—coal, you know. We've got to renegotiate it, and you said Rupert should do it by himself, but I thought—"

"Yes, yes, go with the boy. He can't go wrong with Mr. Jensen. We're old friends. However, it won't hurt to give Rupert a boost of confidence. He trusts you."

Patrick shrugged. "I do my best to help him where I can, but he knows more than I do about—"

"About areas of this business you had no reason to know about." Mr. Baldwin grinned. "Despite your best efforts, we've found out. You're competent. Don't deny it. After lunch, what?"

Patrick always reeled a little from those types of compliments, but he shook himself to stay on track. Mr. Baldwin didn't like excessive thank-yous. "John Jr. and I will be at the docks the rest of the day. We're still working on making our loading and unloading systems more efficient."

"John said you had come far there. How much longer until you'll have it up to your standards?"

Patrick couldn't help but flush at that. "It's ... Sir, it's not that the systems weren't fine to begin with. I'm simply hoping that these changes will—"

"Heavens, Patrick, settle down." Mr. Baldwin chuckled, his eyes twinkling as he, at last, set the folder that he had been perusing most of this time aside. "That wasn't what I meant at all. We appreciate your help. I've been deeply impressed by your knowledge. Actually, why don't you take a seat?" He gestured at the chair across the desk from him. "I want to ask you something."

"Oh." Patrick forced himself to sit and placed his hands on his knees to prevent any fidgeting. "What is it, sir?" He knew it wouldn't be a reprimand, but he was so accustomed to being berated rather than praised for his work that these types of conversations always seemed a little daunting.

"How is your girl?"

Patrick cocked his head. That seemed unrelated to their topics in general. "She is well."

"Happy?"

"I hope so, sir."

"I notice you work long hours here. Sometimes dawn to dusk. Does she mind? And do you?"

Patrick blinked. He'd never known that either of them had an option to "mind." It was a necessity, after all. Patrick needed to have a career, for their future and for their children, if she ever accepted that future herself. There was no "minding" that. "I don't think so, sir. I'm happy with my work here, and she knows that I must ... that I must work so once things are settled, I can support her."

"Indeed. How does she entertain herself in this strange city that she knows few people in?"

"I understand she spends much of her time with friends or at church-related functions." Cassie always had exciting adventures to tell him about at the end of each day. They weren't particularly exciting in and of themselves—tales of watching babies, knitting circles, and Bible studies—but Patrick found them interesting because they gave him more insight into what Cassie liked. Every word she said was to be tucked away and treasured, something to think about while the logical side of his brain pored over legal paperwork and mathematical figures. "We are both fully committed to my work for Baldwin & Sons. She desires that I should work hard, and though someday I hope I may be able to spend time with her—with our family, if we are able to start one—I think we both went into this knowing that the first several years would not be easy."

"Hmm. Very well then." Mr. Baldwin tented his fingers and scanned Patrick's face in a way that made Patrick feel he was being weighed in the balance. "In that case, I have a proposition for you."

Patrick straightened further on his seat. "Sir?"

"You know that I am sending John to San Francisco to settle that deal with the Phillips Company. He'll be gone for at least two months, if not more. If you want, you could go with him."

Patrick froze, his mind whirling with the pros and cons. He couldn't think fast enough to come up with a coherent answer, but thankfully, Mr. Baldwin continued speaking.

"It would, of course, come with a promotion and a raise. Patrick, we like you here. We hope you'll be with us for a long time. Honestly, your work could become invaluable to us very quickly. I know my sons see you as one of the family. This would be an opportunity for us to further establish you as a member of our company and proudly state you are affiliated with Baldwin & Sons." Mr. Baldwin paused. "But this is optional. It's a fast route to the top at a grand cost, and this may not be the time in your life, and particularly in your relationship, for such a long trip. I am more than happy with what you are doing here, but I want to give you an opportunity—and you should know, I will continue giving you opportunities. This is no solitary test of your mettle that will never come around again. I will not think less of you for taking either option. Stay or go. But pray about it, talk to your intended, and make that decision together."

Patrick nodded. "Of course."

"In fact, I do not want to hear an attempt at an answer until a week has passed. That ought to give you both time to think about it. We still have three weeks until the trip is planned, and there is much preparation to be done in the meanwhile. And while John is there, you could still do much here. I want you to consider all the details—and pray for God's will."

"Yes. I can ... We can do that."

"Good. Let me lay out for you what you'd be doing so you're in possession of all the facts."

By the end of their conversation, Patrick realized the full scope of the opportunity Mr. Baldwin was offering him. He was sending him out in a position of trust equal to that of his elder son, placing the reputation of the company equally on both of their shoulders. The advancement in the company would be much speedier if Patrick took the trip, and it was clear the financial impacts would be immense. If they secured this merger, Patrick could theoretically become a manager of the new branch along with John Jr., which would mean, in the future, he would also be prepared to reach out to new ports around the world on the Baldwins' behalf.

But then there was Cassie. Mr. Baldwin never failed to remind him of that—Cassie, patiently waiting in Philadelphia, supportive in all things, sweet and kind and probably too permissive with him. And, more than that, alone in a strange land with no real reason to stay there except him.

He spent the rest of the day brooding. How would he ever begin to tell her?

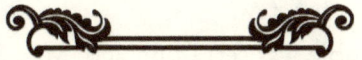

From about noon onward, Cassie spent her days anticipating Patrick's return in the evening.

Granted, she kept herself busy. She was never short of an occupation, for God had presented her many fulfilling ways to give of herself to others while she stayed with the Strausses. There was always something to do, and Cassie loved doing it. Of course, she didn't fill all her time. She'd discovered a library, and many an afternoon was spent buried between the pages of a book, barely tearing herself away in time to make her way back and help Mrs. Strauss with "supper."

Thank goodness, again, for Mrs. Strauss and her loving guidance.

Yet despite all of that, and the beautiful fulfillment Cassie felt in doing all those things to God's glory, she waited for Patrick—eager to see him, to talk to him, to savor his embrace and kisses, to hear his laughter. He laughed more now than she had known him to do during their previous acquaintance, and though she longed to take credit, she acknowledged that the joy of the Lord dwelt within his chest, where before there had been none.

Even now, she busied herself learning to knit a sock, a book balanced against a vase of yellow September roses in the middle of the Strausses' kitchen table, and tried not to glance at her watch. The more she checked the time, the longer the minutes seemed to stretch. If she kept looking, Patrick would seem to take twice as long to arrive.

Yet she was only a woman, and she did glance once or twice, not too swept up into the adventures of the mischievous lad Tom Sawyer to resist.

Then the time was near, too near for any kind of focus. She put the mangled sock and the book aside and joined Mrs. Strauss in her cooking. The kitchen was hot, and the boiling stew was not improving the situation. Patrick called it an "Indian summer," which meant the warm days were stretching into autumn's territory, but as far as Cassie was concerned, the calendar indicated time for stew.

The dining room table was set. Long ago, Mrs. Strauss had begun insisting that Patrick come to dinner every night when he was in town, and Cassie couldn't find any cause to object.

"How much longer until you'll be eating dinner in your own home, Cassie?" There was a hint of teasing in Mrs. Strauss's voice. "Not that I want you gone, but I'd like to watch another wedding."

"I wish I knew that." He'd been hinting about officially proposing lately, and she wasn't sure of her answer. "Honestly, Aunt Lilli, I'm afraid I'll never have an answer."

Mrs. Strauss turned to her with a soft smile. "I know, Cassie. I know. Yet I feel like the decision is almost made. None of us are really sure if it is the right time to make a leap of faith—and yet we do, again and again, when we live under God's will. You have an hour until he comes—we're so early today. Why don't you use it to pray?"

It was sound advice, so Cassie disappeared up to her bedroom to spend some time with God.

Cassie paced up and down the floor for a time, half mumbling her prayers, then went to her trunk and withdrew her letter box, hoping to find something physical around which to direct her cries to God. From within, she pulled out a range of notes and letters from Patrick and his sisters.

She sat on the floor with them scattered about her and read, searching for answers to the impossible question.

It wasn't perhaps the right choice, because all it did was remind her how much she genuinely did like Patrick. His cheerful descriptions of everything and anything. His adoration for his sisters. His consideration of her, his concern about her every thought, about the small details of her life. The quiet wisdom hiding beneath his own pretenses, behind his jokes and the half-truths he fed himself.

As she read, she saw the marks of his parents, especially of his father. She saw how his words were measured against the standard of Hilton Shipping Co. She saw how he trembled under the pressure, how he had always existed in a world surrounded by the looming presence of his parents' will.

Further, she saw how God had been there still, shining through Patrick in spite of the muck his parents had covered him in. Somehow, God had claimed Patrick's heart for His own, despite the seemingly impossible odds. Raised without a backbone of faith, how had Patrick managed to be the man he was today?

How had God brought Patrick to where he was now?

It was nothing short of a miracle.

Cassie had always had Alice and the Knights. Patrick undoubtedly had some small influences in his life that had led him to grow into the man he had become and was still becoming, but it was clear the Holy Spirit had been his primary Influence.

Then she knew. She should accept his proposal. This thought filled her with joy, and she sat still on the floor, praising God for this simple confirmation.

How did she know? How could she *possibly* know? Yet she did somehow, and it made her feel lighter than she had in days, months, years.

If she could give him any encouragement this evening—or even simply tell him that she would be favorable to the request—she would do so.

The next half hour dragged longer than the entire day before it. Mrs. Strauss instantly knew she'd arrived at a decision, and though they didn't talk about it, the idea had made her giddy. She decided to make a pie to celebrate, though she worded it as an impulse, and disappeared into the kitchen once more, leaving Cassie painfully alone.

At last, Patrick arrived. He greeted Cassie and the Strausses as he always did, but his face was drawn and pale. "Can you talk to me before dinner?"

Was it to be that easy, then? She glanced at Mrs. Strauss, who nodded. Patrick and Cassie walked out to the back porch and sat on the swing.

He turned to her slightly. "I have something to tell you. I'm not sure how you'll take it, but I have almost come to a decision about it, and I hope you will feel similarly."

Cassie nodded and folded her hands on her lap. "What is it?"

He sucked in a deep breath. "I was offered a new opportunity by Mr.

Baldwin. It would mean furthering my position in the company, a pay raise, and opportunities of many types."

She blinked. "Patrick! That's incredible! You've only just begun working there, and already they have those types of opportunities open to you? I ... I can scarcely believe it!"

"Yes, it falls within my area of expertise." He flushed. "Mr. Baldwin did say he was impressed with me."

"Of course he did!" Cassie's chest felt ready to burst with pride. "You have incredible skills and talents. Anyone outside of your father couldn't fail to see that. How wonderful!"

"It comes with a catch, of course."

Cassie nodded. "All right, lay out the details. See if I can't help."

He seemed to struggle with his next words, brow furrowed and eyes avoiding hers. Odd. "That's just it. We would ... we would have to bear a considerable amount of separation. The assignment is in San Francisco, opening a new branch of the company there with John Jr. I would be away for months. I know it's not ideal right now, while nothing is certain, but, Cass, it's an incredible opportunity. I ... I could do so much."

She was frozen on her seat, her tongue stuck to the roof of her mouth. What would she say to that? He sat there, trembling for fear that she would snuff this dream of his, this desire to be independent and do great things, as so many others before him had done.

And all she could think of was watching the door every night, and his not coming home.

"I'll be honest," he said, perhaps feeling obligated to say something in the face of her lack of response. "I want to go. It will be torture to be separated from you. Don't mistake me—I love you, Cassie, and I will hate every moment. But this opportunity will not come around again for some time. It will allow me to make connections, extend goodwill, establish myself as almost a partner to the Baldwins. Perhaps it is not wise for us to be separated. I have been fighting this all day, but God kept telling me to put it in your hands, so I am."

"I ... see." She dropped her hands on her lap and looked away from him.

"It would be hard to be without you. Very hard." Her voice sounded so small, so pitiful, not at all like the brave woman she wanted to be.

He moved, rocking the swing slightly, and suddenly his hands were cupped over hers as he knelt before her. He brought her clasped hands to his lips. "I trust you ... and further, I trust God. We have time to make this decision. We'll pray about it, and God will guide us. All right? I will stay if I need to, but perhaps you can come with me. Oh, Cassie, I don't know if you're ready, but I would love for you to be my bride. It'd be a rocky start to a marriage, but we could make it work. There may be things that keep you here should I need to travel in the future—no, when I do need to travel in the future. Children, a home, other responsibilities. But if you were to marry me now, and if you want to come with me to San Francisco, I believe the Baldwins would allow it. I know Henrietta used to journey with John Jr."

Cassie frowned. "I would be in the way."

"No, you wouldn't. You'd be a marvelous help. Cassie, do you have any idea what a comfort you are to me? I know we'll have a shaken-up life for some time. But I wouldn't want to live that shaken-up life with anyone but you. Not now, not ever. I love you."

She raised her eyes slowly to his. "I love you, too."

"Does that mean you'll marry me? It couldn't be much of a wedding, but I know we've said we didn't want that anyway." He leaned closer, reaching up to cup her face with his hand. "Darling, come with me. Be my wife."

She closed her eyes for a moment, searching for any lingering doubts, but none remained. So she opened her eyes and reached for him. "I read your letters this afternoon and watched God bleed through them despite you and your parents doing everything you could to stop Him. He was there anyway. He's not leaving you anytime soon, even if you wanted Him to. And, Patrick, I want to be a part of that. I'd follow you to the ends of the earth and the bottom of the sea if that's where God sent you."

He immediately surged forward and pressed his lips to hers. She returned the kiss, slipping a hand up to run her fingers through the short hair at the back of his head.

"Cassie. Patrick."

She withdrew at the sound of Mrs. Strauss's voice and turned, somewhat bashful but too happy to be truly guilty.

"So it's decided, I hope?"

Cassie looked back into Patrick's eyes and nodded. "Yes. Yes, it is."

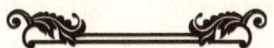

CHAPTER TWENTY-EIGHT

I T WAS HER WEDDING day.

Cassie ought to be frightened, but she wasn't. The fear she had once experienced was gone now, and all she could think of was the future.

It might not be a glorious future. Certainly, even now her wedding would not be what she had expected. It would be a simple ceremony, with only a few of her friends in attendance and none of Patrick's. She was dressed in a pretty enough gown, a light-blue one with lace trim that she'd bought for Ivy's wedding, but it would've shocked her mother with its lack of stylishness.

Everything about today would shock her mother.

Of course, her mother was furious as ever, but far away in London, she couldn't touch Cassie. Not quickly enough. Cassie had telegraphed shortly after her engagement three weeks ago and received an astonishingly quick reply, insisting that she give up "that American boy" and return to England at once.

She had known from the start that her parents would not be happy, but that could not be helped. Their demands were expected but also ineffectual given that by the time said demands arrived, the date had been set. Cassie and Patrick were both determined to wed quickly.

She didn't see any other way of doing it. Haste was a necessity. After all, what if something else came up to keep them apart?

Now she stood before the mirror in the small bedroom she was staying in at the Strausses'—a room that had belonged to Peter's brother, Andrew, a room that still bore the marks of a happy, young boy who apparently liked model sailing ships. Behind her, Alice was sorting through a small box of jewelry. She'd taken a train back to Philadelphia with Peter after Cassie sent a telegram to them.

"Here." Alice withdrew a pearl necklace with a gold clasp. "This—and these earrings. They're not much, but they will look pretty."

"Thank you." Cassie drew back her hair, still loose about her shoulders as she hadn't any idea what she would do with it, and Alice fastened the necklace for her and placed the earrings in her hand.

"I'm going to ask Caroline to do your hair. She's better than I am." Alice squeezed Cassie's shoulder. "I'm more used to being served than serving. Whenever I need something more elaborate, it takes me longer than I like to admit."

"There are adjustments to be made, certainly." Thankfully, Alice had walked the path before her. She already had offered Cassie many words of encouragement.

Cassie clipped the earrings on, adjusting them not once but twice, while Alice rustled around in a trunk behind her. She'd dragged it into the room that morning with Mrs. Strauss's help and had been withdrawing various odds and ends from it since then. "What are you looking for?"

"My veil."

Cassie blinked. "Oh, Alice, I can't—"

Alice held up her hand. "You can. It was far too long to wear with that dress, but I at least want you to wear a shorter one. We'll trim it."

"*Alice*. We cannot do that. What if ... what if you have ..." Cassie didn't want to say it. She didn't, but she forced herself to, to recollect Alice to reality, a hopeful reality. "What if you have a daughter?"

Alice didn't speak for such a length of time that Cassie wondered if she should have said anything. Alice turned from the trunk, walked up behind Cassie, and placed a hand on her arm. "You know that cannot happen this year and likely will not happen in the next. If it ever does, if I ever have a daughter at all—and I have told you that if I am to have a child, I pray it is a boy—even so, I would have at least two decades to wait until I would see her wed. And, Cassie, in that time, fashions will have changed. We may not even wear veils for weddings by then—God only knows. My mother could tell you how fickle all things related to dressing women are." She drew back then and returned to the trunk. "Meanwhile, I am not the type to attach sentimental value to a piece of clothing. My mother isn't either, and if she had been, Ivy would have been the better recipient of such gifts."

"Yet, Alice, to cut up your veil, the one you wore on your wedding day—"

"If it makes you feel any better, I wasn't going to keep it anyway. But it is in my other trunk, so I'll leave you here to decide that you're going to give in to me." Alice turned to the door. "That is, unless you really don't want it?"

Cassie pressed her lips together, for a moment unsure, then nodded. "I want it. I think that'll complete the outfit."

"My thoughts exactly." With that, Alice disappeared, and Cassie was left to contemplate her reflection in the mirror and wait.

The few hours left in the morning flew swiftly after that. Patrick and Cassie were to be married at ten, and it suddenly felt too early.

A part of her had yet to acknowledge that it was her wedding day. She wanted to believe she was prepared. Yet there must still be things they missed. Surely people had long engagements for a reason.

God didn't make mistakes, however. Peter had reminded her of that last evening when her hands shook after Patrick had bidden her farewell for the last time before she would become his bride. If God's will was in favor of their relationship, there was much hope. Further, neither Cassie nor Patrick believed humankind had the ability to operate outside of God's will; therefore, regardless of where they started, if they sought Him, their relationship could not fail.

Not that Cassie truly believed failure was an option. But as she had often heard, it was possible to make the process easier with the right man—and much more difficult with the wrong one.

She'd asked Peter to walk her down the aisle. She was marrying without her parents' consent, and as such, perhaps the very idea of being walked down the aisle and given away at all was ridiculous. However, she still wanted something of a wedding. Some memory to cling to, to make the moment of her joining to Patrick special.

Perhaps it was the fact that she was marrying him that ought to make it special, but she was feminine enough to place some value on the traditions that had, more or less, been adhered to for generations before her and likely would be for generations after.

Before she knew it, she was walking down that aisle to some simple piano music that Alice had chosen, something classical and not too grandiose. And Patrick stood there at the altar with the elderly pastor she'd only properly met a few months ago. Patrick's eyes fastened on her face, and he smiled.

It would be all right. She'd keep looking into his eyes, and it would be all right.

The vows were said, and he placed a ring she'd never seen before on her finger. It looked expensive but in an old money way.

She raised her eyes swiftly from her hand to meet his gaze. "Where—?"

He shook his head with a trace of a smile around his lips and solemnly whispered, "With this ring, I thee wed."

The pastor was speaking again, but Cassie didn't hear a word he said. She just clung to Patrick's hand and watched his face and tried not to tremble.

It was done.

The next few minutes were a blur. She knew he kissed her, but barely registered it somehow, and then suddenly, before she quite knew what had happened, she was down the aisle.

There wasn't a great crowd of people, and only a few would accompany them to a brief meal at the Strausses' house. Patrick's new employers wouldn't be among them, though they had attended the ceremony and met Cassie at the church on Sunday a time or two. They seemed like nice people—a lovely middle-aged woman, her round husband, her two fine sons, and a daughter-in-law, all of whom smiled and shook Patrick's hand and congratulated them both.

But Cassie was focused on Patrick. She wanted to be alone with him, wanted to tell him what she was thinking and feeling and confirm that she wasn't insane. That those simple moments at the altar before God and man had forever changed something, and she was right to shake from the depth of it.

Because, like it or not, she had dived in deep, out too far past where the land ended and miles of endless water began, and there would be no return.

Heaven help her if she ever wanted to return to port.

It took far too long for them to have a moment alone.

He supposed that was the nature of weddings. They were designed to keep a couple unselfish for an hour or two longer than suited them. Yet the first weeks of marriage were meant to be selfish in the most utterly selfless way selfishness could be performed, and Patrick wanted to be selfishly selfless with her. Alone. For at least two years.

The ceremony had been brief, and they didn't linger at the Strausses' home long afterward, but still, he slouched with relief as soon as they got into the carriage that was to take them to their apartment.

Their apartment. *Theirs.*

Granted, it was quite small. Further, they'd only be staying there for a week before they left for San Francisco. But it was all theirs, and that felt precious in this moment.

Her fingers were twisted in his as the hired hack trotted its way from the Strausses' beautiful house on Franklin Street toward the more industrial district where he'd found this moderately suitable apartment. The Baldwins had advanced him his raised paycheck so he could obtain housing before their wedding, and though it was nothing more than a scattering of crates and boxes, hardly a honeymoon suite, they could be alone.

There was a bed.

He shivered, and she pressed into his side, a subtle movement but reassuring. He looked down to meet her deep-blue eyes and couldn't resist stealing another kiss from her full lips.

It was her turn to shudder, to draw away too soon as he'd been forcing himself to do all week. "If we'd had a longer engagement, I would've had to do something about you."

He laughed. He couldn't help it. He was full of joy, and everything seemed worth laughing about. "You mean you would have had to keep me off of you?"

"Hmm. The fault is mine. You've always had enviable self-restraint. But yes, I couldn't have kept kissing you for long, not while maintaining any kind of sense." She shrugged, as if those were simple words, not laced with all the longing he'd ever felt in his life. "I'm not used to feeling this way. I've been kissed—you know that. But this is different. I never understood before, never believed anyone could lose control over something so seemingly insignificant."

Did she have any idea what it did to a man to hear those kinds of words? He wasn't quite sure where Cassie's wisdom ended and her innocence began. There was only so much an unmarried couple could say to each other on that score.

Yet they weren't unmarried. His grip on her hand tightened. "It's been much the same for me. But, Cassie, we are in love. It's different—everything has to be different. God-designed, holy, uniting. What affects the soul affects the body. You know this."

She smiled and again pressed slightly into his side. "Tell me about my ring. We need to be logical until the time is right, or we'll both regret it. Everything is new enough without hurrying."

She was right, of course.

"I hope you won't mind that the ring wasn't chosen for you." He lifted her hand and examined the gold band with intricate clusters of diamonds and emeralds, almost flower shaped. "It was my grandmother's, on my father's side. Upon her death, it was gifted to Lorelei. But Lore had dozens of beautiful rings, and when I said good-bye to my sisters in Boston, she gave it to me. I think she had a very specific plan as to whom the thing should be bestowed upon. I'm reminded that emeralds are the jewels of new life."

"Oh?"

"Yes." He turned her hand over and brought the palm of it to his lips. "And every time you look at it, I would have you remember that you are my new life. The woman who pushed me toward a deeper relationship with my Savior. The woman who gave me a new purpose."

He saw the start of tears on her eyelashes and leaned back slightly, unwilling to say such things to the point that he got her blubbering. Not now. Not today. Not unless, for whatever reason, it couldn't be helped.

Yet when she did speak, her voice was steady and strong. "Don't emeralds also symbolize strength through adversity?"

He was the one struggling with a lump in his throat now, as gratitude rose and most—but not all—of his somewhat less pure thoughts stepped back. "Thank God for you," he whispered. "That's all I can say, my darling. Thank God for you."

Epilogue

November 1883
San Francisco, California

B ELOW THEIR HOTEL ROOM, a busy street kept Cassie entertained with its jostling multitudes. Cassie had assumed San Francisco would be a little less like a city and a little more like the location of a western adventure, but apparently, it seemed perfectly civilized. Patrick insisted it was not, but she couldn't see any proof of this.

"What are you looking at?" Patrick's amused voice caused her to turn.

He sat at a small desk he'd installed in their room, scratching away at some contract he'd become determined to finish from home to elongate his lunch break and, therefore, his time with her. However, apparently it was not fascinating enough to keep his eyes off her for long.

"Oh, just people-watching. Wondering about their lives and their stories and what they're going through." She leaned away from the window. "Are you almost done?"

"Yes, and sadly, I'd better go join John Jr., and you can get back to your book without me bothering you all the time." He smiled. "Then it's home to Philadelphia—back to our church, to the Strausses, and hopefully to the beginning of a new life."

"It has all felt rather like a honeymoon, hasn't it?" Her eyes returned to the throng below. "Of course, it had to end someday."

"In material ways, yes; however, I don't think a change of location is going to change *everything*. Not yet, at least." She could tell from his half-absent voice that he had gone back to the papers in front of him. "We have a year, don't we?"

"A year?" She had to laugh at that. Until what? Until their marriage expired?

"Yes, as in Deuteronomy. 'He shall be free at home one year, and shall cheer up his wife which he hath taken.' It was about war, but sometimes a business deal is like a war." She felt and heard his look, his smile, rather than seeing them. "We have a year, and in that year, I am to cheer you up. Granted, I can't stop working, but I think Mr. Baldwin understands that if I do leave Philadelphia, you must come with me."

"Hmm." That might have to change, given the news she had to tell him this evening. "I've an idea he's the reason why his son has given us so much space."

"Probably so. We could take a trip or two together, if you like. It's been fun, I think."

"Oh. Actually ..." She turned to him on an impulse. "That'd be impossible. I need us to take the rest of the year."

"You need us to take the rest of the year." He set his pen in the inkwell and faced her. "Why?"

"Because I don't want us to be separated." And she smiled, as if it weren't the most obvious thing. "Come sit with me for a moment."

He rose, eyebrows slightly quirked and lips trying to smile but failing in his confusion. "You mean you didn't enjoy this trip? You do realize that I'll often be traveling in my line of work. We'd discussed it at length, I thought—and of course, I understand if I need to limit the trips. Yet I can't do so all the time, and I hate to think we're condemned to a life of separations, no matter how brief."

"I enjoyed it greatly and would be happy to do so—later. Come sit." She patted the window seat beside her, and at last, he obeyed. "It's not that I don't want to be with you; I just know that until our year is ended, it would be unwise for me to join you. This is going to be my last trip for a while."

His expression wavered between confusion, disappointment, and amusement. He looked absolutely flustered by her pronouncement. "I had ... I had certainly hoped you would join me. I can't imagine going anywhere without you, and this seems like the best time in the world for you to be near me. Yet if you feel it's right ..." He paused. "Actually, Cass, I don't understand at all. I feel a little abandoned. Perhaps you could explain your logic a bit?"

She reached up and cupped his face with her hand. "I need you to stay home with me, and I think you'll be glad of the reason. You're going to be a father, Patrick."

He stilled for a moment, then pulled her into his arms and buried his face in her hair.

She laughed at his exuberance. "There, don't be crushing me. He'll be coming along in June, and I expect I shall begin feeling the effects of it more strongly soon. I'd barely have known it if I hadn't been so tired lately. I spoke to a doctor, who told me these things might worsen in the next few weeks. I don't anticipate the trip, but I *do* anticipate finding a home where I can settle."

He shuddered, though whether it was with laughter or tears, she couldn't determine, and he didn't let her go.

"You're happy?"

"I am ... I am tremendously happy." His shaky voice betrayed him; he was weeping. "I hoped ... But of course, I didn't think it could ... happen so ... fast."

She leaned back and put her hands on his shoulders. "That's often how it works. I'm told it only takes once, and that's about all it took us, if you count the dates." She scrambled for her small, lacy handkerchief and pressed it into his hand. "We were dedicated to the task."

He caught her hands in his and examined her face earnestly. "You want this?"

"Yes. Oh, Patrick, of course, yes." She leaned in for a kiss, which was enthusiastically given. When she withdrew, she made sure to add, "Nothing could please me more than to be the mother of your child."

He nodded but said nothing else; she could tell how deeply affected he was, and it filled her with delight.

So it was back to Philadelphia—back home. "Of course, there will be time for adventure later, when our little one is old enough to travel. After all, I did promise to follow you to the ends of the earth and the bottom of the sea."

He drew her closer and dropped his face into her hair once more. "That's excellent news. I wouldn't want to go to the ends of the earth or the bottom of the sea if you weren't going to be there, too."

A Note to the Reader

Dear Reader,

Thank you for embarking with on this this journey! I'm so grateful that you were willing to read my novel—and I deeply hope you enjoyed it.

Like a Ship on the Sea was one of the most difficult books I have ever written.

I'm honestly not sure why this novel was so hard to write. It seemed like a simple enough premise when I first began, but I soon realized that there was more to the story than met the eye. More to the characters than met the eye, in truth—a veritable host of issues just waiting to be addressed popped up before my eyes, and before I knew it, I was in over my head.

Patrick was refusing to cooperate. Cassie took off on her adventure far sooner than she was supposed to. I wasn't sure if the side plots were weaving together in a way that made sense. Some of my original research wasn't making sense, and my characters were demanding a different ending than the one I originally planned on.

And here I was, the poor innocent author, stuck in the middle of all this mess!

I'm a steadfast "outliner," which means I carefully plot out my books before writing them. To have the book go this far off the rails into creative nonsense was unusual for me—or had been for many years.

So, tired and busy and dealing with some pretty big things in my personal life, I pushed back dates with my editors and sat down to figure out how to make this story work. A lot of prayer and hard work went into this story ... and after several months of messing with the plot, I finally finished a draft that I actually liked.

This isn't a usual romance. I know that. Yet I must trust that the Lord has plans for this story even despite the often unlikable hero, the heroine who takes a few risks too many, and the plot that spirals more than it rises and falls. I hope you'll see it more as women's fiction than a true romance novel ... and yet I also accept that it's not everyone's cup of tea! Which is how it should be.

If you'd like to follow along and read Lorelei's story (or maybe even backtrack and read Alice's stories!), make sure to keep in touch! You can do so by following my newsletter at:

https://kellynrothauthor.com/newsletter/

Or you can just head to my website, which is that URL without the /newsletter/ to more information about my published works ... and my blog where I post random, fun stuff!

May the Lord bless and keep you all.

TTFN!
Kellyn Roth

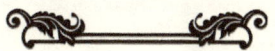

A Free Novella for You

Interested in a free novella, available only for subscribers to my mailing list?

January 1944

June Halsted moved her son to Hearthstone Cottage to escape the memories of her failed marriage and estranged family. A struggling artist in the midst of one of the coldest winters in Yorkshire, she finds herself seeking solace at church ... only to meet Mark Hayes, a kindly farmer with a limp and a knack for cheering up her son.

Inspired by The Tenant of Wildfell Hall, *this novella is a sweet romance with Christian themes.*

Go to *kellynrothauthor.com/newsletter* and subscribe to my email list to receive your free story!

Also by the Author

The Chronicles of Alice & Ivy

The Dressmaker's Secret
Ivy Introspective
The Knights of Pearlbelle Park (novella)
Becoming Miss Knight (novella)
At Her Fingertips
Beyond Her Calling
A Prayer Unanswered
After Our Castle

The Hilton Legacy

Like a Ship on the Sea
Like the Air After Rain
Like a Storm Against the Cliffs

Kees & Colliers

Souls Astray
Goldfish Secrets (short story)
The Lady of the Vineyard
Flowers in Her Heart

Standalone Short Stories

Esther Ashton's New Dress
Kind: a Christmas short story of post-WWII Munich
Eddy & the Tidepools

Anthologies

Springtime in Surrey
Novelists in November
Fingerprints in Frost
Voices of the Future: Stories of Courage & Compassion